Phoenix Rising

Fire and Claw 1

Jennifer Allis Provost

Bellatrix Press

CONTENTS

TRIGGER WARNINGS

N ot gonna lie, a lot happens in these pages—however, most of the gory stuff is described, but not directly depicted. Does that make it better? Who knows! Having said that, if you have any questions about this list, please don't hesitate to reach out to me. The easiest way is via the contact form at https://authorjennierallisprovost.com. Happy reading!

- Childbirth (traumatic)

- Separation of parents from newborn

- Death of parents/siblings (past events)

- Parental abuse

- War

- Death on a massive scale (due to war)

- Captivity

- Extreme punishment

- On page sexual situations

PROLOGUE

I n the beginning, all creatures inhabited the Otherworld.

For many an age, the creatures lived and worked together according to their natural hierarchy. Stronger creatures, such as gryphons and minotaurs, kept order, while the smaller, gentler beings minded the land. Selkies and merpeople managed the waterways, and fairies and wood sprites looked after the forests. Life was simple, and good.

One day, new creatures appeared. Some said they were sea monsters, but they had legs and moved about on land. Some called them living nightmares, but all those who had truly seen them either died by the mysterious creatures' fangs and claws, or soon afterward. No one knew what the new creatures were, and they were afraid.

And the monsters appeared to be multiplying.

As they always did in times of strife, the creatures looked to the strongest among them: the dragons. To combat this new threat, the dragons met in their most secret cave, spoke for thirty days, and emerged with a plan. The dragons would use their fire to tear a hole from the Otherworld to the Mundane realm and thus lead an escape while leaving the nightmares behind. Any who wished to accompany them were welcome, but no one was forced to leave their home.

And so, a year and a day after the nightmares appeared, the largest and oldest dragon burned a hole between worlds. The ensuing movement was thereafter known as the Great Migration, and it was the event that brought both creatures and magic to the lands of humans. In time, creatures and humans mated, and shifters were created from their mixed blood. Soon, the shifters organized among themselves, and the kingdom of Alessia was created.

The dragon clan was offered kingship, but they declined, instead preferring to make their home among the mountains and raise their broods in peace. Even so, the dragons watched over the lands and were always prepared to defend their neighbors and their nests with fire and claw. Some say you can still see dragons flying among the clouds, keeping watch over their children. Others know that the dragons are all but extinct, and only one remains in the Mundane realm. He needs to find a bride and produce an heir before his kind is nothing but a memory.

CHAPTER ONE

THE ARRANGEMENT

"Rosalie," Lord Osman Irontooth barked as her chamber door banged open. "Caterina has shamed me for the last time!"

Rosalie looked up from her book and wondered what her sister's latest transgression was. With Caterina, it could be anything. "I'm sure it's not so bad, Father," Rosalie soothed as her father paced; whenever Caterina irritated their father, Rosalie was always there to calm him down. "And her wedding is tomorrow. After that, she'll not be your problem any longer."

"She will remain my problem for years to come." Osman stopped in front of his younger daughter and wiped his hand down his face. "Last night, Caterina fled the castle along with her guard."

Rosalie carefully schooled her face into a neutral expression. She and the rest of the Keep knew about Caterina and Curran's months-long affair. But by silent agreement, not a single person had said a word about it to Osman. No one wanted him to assume they were complicit in Caterina's schemes because Osman's punishments were as legendary as they were cruel.

"That's awful," she said; while her voice was even, her heart was breaking. Rosalie adored her older sister, who was one of her very few allies in her father's house. Now that Caterina has run off with Curran, she was worried she'd never see her again. "Has a party been sent after her?"

"No. When I offered Caterina to Lord Blackmoor, I assured him of her chastity. After yesterday's events, he'll never accept her." Osman lowered his hand. "You must marry the duke in her stead."

"What?" Rosalie demanded, as she leaped to her feet. "I can't marry someone called the Black Duke," she said, referencing the duke's common name.

"Why not?" Osman demanded.

"For one thing, you promised me that I would retire to the convent on my next birthday!"

"Things have changed. You need to do your duty for your family, not hide behind a tower filled with monks."

Rosalie was so mad her hands shook. It had taken her years to convince her father to let her move into the convent and away from his life of political schemes. Now, thanks to Caterina's inability to understand the consequences of her actions, Rosalie's own plans were dashed. "I can't marry him," she insisted, as she balled her trembling hands into fists. "I've never even met him!"

"Nor had Caterina," Osman said. "But the contracts have already been drawn up, and this alliance is very important to me."

"Why?" Rosalie demanded, surprising both herself and Osman. "What is so important about this one man that you need an alliance with him so badly?" She'd never been one to question her father's orders, but this was different. This was more important than Osman banning leeks from the kitchens because some got stuck in his teeth and embarrassed him in front of the prince's envoy, or him forbidding dancing because he once tripped in front of the entire court.

This was important.

"It's simple," Osman said. "The duke's region, Dragon Ridge, is the wealthiest and most powerful in Alessia. I desire both."

At Osman's straightforward explanation, Rosalie felt her resolve wither away to almost nothing. Osman's only true love was gold, and whatever influence he could buy with it. He'd even purchased his title, though it galled him that he wasn't actual nobility. But if he pawned his remaining daughter off to a duke, he could claim nobility by association.

That was all Rosalie had ever been to him. A pawn.

"Will he accept me?" Rosalie asked. She didn't mention that unlike Caterina, whose mother had been true nobility, her own mother was one of Osman's mistresses. That meant Rosalie wasn't Osman's official heir, and had very little standing in her home court, or anywhere else. Of that, they were both aware.

"He will," Osman said. "The contract states that the duke will take the hand of my daughter. Which daughter is not specified." When Rosalie remained silent, he continued in a softer tone, "Rosalie, my child, will you do this for me?"

She fought the urge to laugh in his face; Osman Irontooth never asked people to do things. He only issued orders and expected immediate and total compliance. While she could refuse to marry the duke, it would cause her father to hold a grudge—and he was a vindictive man.

But should she refuse? Rosalie had never been happy in Osman's home. Her father was little more than a tyrant, feared by his staff, his serfs, and most of his family. Caterina, being the eldest child and the only real nobility in the house since her mother's death, was the sole person who dared to openly defy him. Rosalie worried that Caterina's latest act of defiance would cost them dearly, her most of all.

However, Caterina had read the wedding contract, and she'd explained it to Rosalie. It had stated that Osman's daughter would remain with the duke as his spouse for one year. Once that time was up, Rosalie could dissolve the marriage if she so desired. A year wasn't so much time in the grand scheme of things, and no matter what life would be like in Dragon Ridge, she would finally be free of her family's schemes. Hopefully, for good.

"I'm sure being the duke's wife won't be so bad." Rosalie's hands were trembling again, so she shoved them underneath her arms, though she could do nothing about the tremor in her voice. "When will I meet him?"

"The ceremony will be held in the chapel tomorrow at midday," Osman replied, as he turned to leave her rooms. "You'll meet him then."

"What should I do in the meantime?" Rosalie asked.

"I suggest you begin packing. The duke wishes to return to his home at Dragon Ridge as soon as the marriage is consummated."

After Osman left to scream at the staff about tomorrow's wedding, Rosalie went to her sister's rooms. Caterina had a large apartment in the eastern tower befitting her station, complete with an atrium where her guard, Curran, slept. Rosalie shook her head, since everyone now knew where Curran had actually been sleeping. According to Melly, Caterina's maid, the two had been caught half-dressed in each other's arms. Curran was then hauled off to the dungeon, and Caterina was locked in her bedroom. Afterward, Osman threatened Melly and the guards into silence so the wedding could proceed as planned.

Caterina's escape had only foiled Osman's plans temporarily, and now Rosalie was the bride-to-be.

She passed by the dressing table and saw her reflection in the mirror, and considered how alike yet different she and her sister were. Caterina was beautiful, tall, and well-proportioned; with pale blonde hair that reflected silver in the sunlight and blue eyes that always sparkled. Her sister had looked like the princess she was, and she would have made a good match for the duke.

Rosalie resembled her sister—they shared a father, after all—but she didn't share Caterina's jaw-dropping beauty. Rosalie was a head shorter, and while her hair was blonde, it was a much darker shade. Her cheeks were round, and she blushed easily in both embarrassment and anger. The most striking aspect of Rosalie's appearance was her dark green eyes; a feature passed down from her own mother. She leaned toward the mirror and made a face, wondering what her mother would say about this upcoming marriage.

She would probably scream in Father's face. Scream and throw something at him.

Rosalie sighed. Her mother was gone, as was her sister—which meant there was no one left to help her fight her battles. When a tear threatened to escape her lashes, Rosalie dashed her hand against her eyes and sat in front of the dressing table. She had many fond memories of sitting in that very spot while Caterina brushed and braided her hair, or let her try on her gowns and jewels. Most of Caterina's jewelry had been passed down from her mother and was set with green stones marked with a rampaging basilisk, Alessia's official seal. Now, the jewelry box was empty, and most other sentimental items were gone save for a tin of tea. The main ingredient in that tea was dried orange peel, and it was Caterina's favorite blend. Rosalie opened the box and smelled the bright citrus aroma. She then noticed two letters lying underneath the tin. One was addressed to her and the other to Lord Blackmoor.

She tucked the letter addressed to the duke in her pocket, then she opened the one made out to her. When she read her sister's words, she clapped a hand over her mouth to stifle her sobs.

Dearest Rosie,

I'm so, so sorry to run off without saying goodbye to you. Please know that this isn't how I wanted things to go, but I cannot marry the duke. I just can't! I refuse to spend even one year of my life trapped in marriage to a man I do not love, especially when I've already found love. What sort of fool would I be to throw away what I have with Curran when it's only just begun?

By the time you read this letter, I expect we'll be far away from Father and all his mad schemes. Even as I write this, I already miss you, my dearest sister. When it's safe to do so, I will come find you at the convent. Then, once we're together again, I'll tell you everything.

With all my love,

Cat

Rosalie wiped her eyes, then she refolded the letter and slipped it into her pocket beside the other envelope. She didn't begrudge Caterina's happiness with Curran, and hoped they would have a good life together. She only wished she could be part of it.

With a sigh, Rosalie stood and surveyed the rest of Caterina's room. Knowing their father, he would have the entire apartment emptied and scrubbed as soon as possible. Rosalie had never been sentimental about her possessions, but Caterina had been. And Rosalie knew just what she would've wanted to preserve.

She got down on the floor, reached under the bed, and pulled out a wooden trunk. Inside the trunk were various cosmetics like perfumes and creams, but it was also where Caterina kept her mother's letters. Even though Danae had passed while her daughter was still young, she had written almost a hundred letters to Caterina, with subjects ranging from entering womanhood to how one should carry oneself at the king's court. After Rosalie's own mother had passed, Caterina shared the letters with her, and thus both sisters benefited from Danae's kindness.

Rosalie hoisted the trunk of letters, set the tin of tea on its lid, and gave her sister's room one final look. It was long after noon, and Rosalie had much to do before nightfall. After her wedding to the duke, her new life would begin.

CHAPTER TWO

The Wedding

The next day at noon, Rosalie stood shivering outside the chapel doors as she clutched a bouquet of lilies. She was wearing a pale green dress edged in gold brocade, and pink and white roses were woven into her blonde hair. She was also barefoot, which was why she was so cold. There was a custom about the bride walking unrestrained from her father's house to her husband's, and somehow shoes would interfere with that walk, but Rosalie had never paid any attention to the particulars of the adage. Once her father had agreed to send her to a convent, she hadn't thought much about marriage at all.

In fact, unlike most marriageable women, she didn't even have any wedding finery. Wearing Caterina's abandoned wedding dress was also out of the question, since Osman had burned it in a fit of rage after last evening's dinner. Other girls kept a special chest filled with lengths of silk and lace, but Rosalie filled her chests with books and dried flowers, interesting rocks, and whatever art supplies she could find. She wondered if the Black Duke liked to read, or paint. She wondered if he liked anything at all.

Most of all, she wondered why he was called the Black Duke.

It wasn't that she hadn't asked, because she had. She'd asked every single person she'd encountered since she'd been told about her pending matrimony about how the Black Duke had gotten his ominous moniker. Most, like her brothers, had laughed in her face at the term "ominous moniker." Cretins. But a few, like Melly and some of the scribes, had heard of Dragon Ridge and its mysterious lord. None of them knew exactly how he'd earned his name, but they all agreed that something devastating had happened in Dragon Ridge, and that the region still bore the scars today.

One scribe, newly employed by Osman, claimed the duke had left a trail of bodies in his wake, and wore black as part of his penance. Rosalie hoped that was nothing but a rumor.

Rosalie shook her head and sat on the edge of the fountain in the chapel's courtyard. The water was dedicated to the Fates, and that morning it flowed clear and cool. Rosalie took that as a good omen and hoped that happiness would flow between herself and her new husband.

"This is the path that has been set before me," Rosalie murmured as she dipped her fingers in the holy font and dabbed the sacred water onto her forehead and breast. "The Fates have deemed me worthy to walk it with my husband, and walk it I will. I will see this through."

At last, the chapel doors opened. Rosalie held up her bouquet, tossed her hair back, and proceeded toward the altar. Waiting for her at the far end of the aisle was Lord Blackmoor, and she got her first glimpse of the man she was about to marry.

True to his name, the duke was clad in a black velvet jacket and black trousers tucked into tall black boots. The only flash of color was his ivory shirt, which was visible at his collar and cuffs. Even his hair was black, and Rosalie noted that it was an even jet hue without a hint of gray. She'd assumed the duke was a bent, bitter old man like her father and was glad to be wrong. Hopefully, his personality was the opposite of her father's as well. The musicians changed their tune to announce her arrival, and the duke turned to watch Rosalie approach.

She gasped.

He was the most handsome man she had ever seen.

The Black Duke was tall and broad shouldered, his features fine and even. His eyes were an icy shade of blue, though the way he looked at Rosalie chased the lingering chill from her bones. A well-trimmed beard darkened his jaw, and she saw a glint of gold at his throat. Most importantly, he appeared to be close to her own age, and she dared to hope the two of them would have something in common.

Rosalie realized she was staring at him, and focused on his hands instead of his face. The duke kept up his scrutiny of her, and she was amazed she didn't stumble up the aisle. Then she noticed the sword belted at his hip, and briefly imagined him leading a charge across the mountains. She raised her bouquet to hide her smile; when she dared look at the duke's face, she saw the corner of his mouth curled up. He'd caught her.

He's tall, and handsome, and he has a sense of humor. Fates, please don't let him be an idiot too.

When Rosalie reached the altar, she smiled at her almost-husband. Now that she was standing next to the Black Duke, marrying him didn't seem so bad. He was just a man, and Rosalie could handle a lone man. Then, the duke opened his mouth. Rosalie assumed he'd introduce himself, or say hello, or tell her how happy he was for their wedding.

Instead, he turned away from her and stared straight ahead at the cleric. Rosalie swallowed her humiliation and faced forward. She hadn't expected love at first sight, but she hadn't expected outright rejection, either.

The cleric opened his book of rites to begin the ceremony and droned on about love and duty and service to the Fates. He spoke so slowly that Rosalie worried she would faint from hunger and thus fail to complete the marriage. Finally, the cleric reached the crux of the matter.

"Lochlyn Blackmoor, do you claim this woman as your wife?" the cleric asked.

"I do," the duke replied.

"Do you, Rosalie Greenwood, accept this man as your husband?"

"I do."

"I now pronounce you man and wife," the cleric intoned. "You may kiss your bride."

They faced each other, and Rosalie realized her very full bouquet was in the way of them kissing. "I don't know where to put this," she began, when the duke took her hand.

"It's very pretty," he said, kissing her knuckles. "You like flowers?"

"Yes, I picked these myself," she said before the duke lowered their hands. They walked down the aisle and left the chapel, and as the courtiers and well-wishers tossed petals and rice at her and her new husband, all Rosalie thought about was how she hadn't even gotten to kiss him.

The wedding party was ushered directly from the chapel to the feasting hall. To Rosalie's dismay, most of her brothers were already drunk. Or perhaps they were still drunk from the night before. Either way, she was well and truly mortified.

"This way," the duke said, placing his hand on the small of her back. "I requested a small table just for the two of us."

"Thank you," she murmured, and they wended their way through the crowd. "You must think us barbarians."

"Not at all." The duke held out her chair. "A wedding is a joyous occasion. Your family is happy for us."

Rosalie smiled at him and didn't mention that this level of debauchery was a normal occurrence in her father's hall. "I suppose they are. Do you have a large family, as well?"

"I did, once." A shadow moved across his face. Rosalie recalled the rumors of a tragedy happening at Dragon Ridge and wondered if that event had included his family. "Although, I only had three brothers."

"Most don't have as many siblings as I do." That was because most men didn't take as many mistresses as her father did. "I'm told you live in the mountains?"

"Yes," he replied, and Rosalie saw a glint of happiness in his eyes. "Dragon Ridge is on the highest peak, so high we can reach out and touch the clouds. I do hope you'll like it there."

"I'm sure I will," she said, then she remembered the small parcel she had for him. "I realize this is an odd time to broach the subject, but Caterina wrote you a letter." Rosalie set the letter on the table in front of him. The duke picked it up, then he slipped it inside his breast pocket.

"Thank you," he said, a bit stiffly. "Do you miss your sister?"

"Yes." Rosalie swallowed her latest sobs. "I do."

"Blackmoor!" Osman yelled across the hall. "Come speak with me, so we may conclude our business. You can spare him for a few moments, can't you, Rosalie?"

The duke grimaced. "I'll be but a moment," he said, and Rosalie watched as her father drew the duke toward the far end of the hall. While Rosalie struggled to discern what they were discussing, her only full-blooded brother, Devlin, sat in the duke's empty seat.

"What's that all about?" Devlin asked, jerking his chin toward their father and the duke. "Father making enemies already?"

"Most likely." Rosalie noted the duke's stiff shoulders, and how he was facing away from Osman as he spoke. "Have you heard anything about Caterina?"

"Not a word. After you leave tomorrow, we won't have any women left in the house." Devlin leaned back and held out his goblet for the serving girl to fill. "Save for these lovely wenches, of course."

"Devlin!" Rosalie hissed. "Could you please control yourself, at least until my wedding's over with?"

"All right." He drained his goblet and set it on the table. "You always were my favorite sister. When can I come live with you?"

"Never," Rosalie said, but she didn't mean it. Aside from Caterina, Devlin was the only sibling she got along with. Even though he was at an age where he desperately wanted to impress their older brothers, she still remembered when he was a small, sweet boy, who looked to her for everything after their mother passed away. "At least, not for some time. I can't arrive at Dragon Ridge with my family in tow! What would the duke think?"

"Distract him well enough tonight, and he'll let you get away with anything," Devlin said with a wink. Rosalie moved to swat his arm, but he evaded her. "Here comes your happy husband now."

Rosalie looked up, and saw the duke stalking toward their table, his eyes as dark as thunderclouds. "Fates, what did Father say to him?"

"No idea," Devlin said as he stood and grabbed his goblet. When the duke reached the table, he said, "Just keeping my sister company until you returned. May the Fates smile upon your union."

"Thank you," the duke said as he reclaimed his seat. Devlin flashed an apologetic smile at Rosalie and went off to find more wine.

"I saw you speaking with my father," Rosalie said. "Was he... disagreeable?"

"Not at all." The duke smiled tightly. "We were discussing our departure tomorrow morning. Have you already packed?"

"Yes." Rosalie gazed around the hall, expecting to feel sad, or at least a bit melancholy. Instead, she was ready to leave Irontooth Keep in the past and begin the rest of her life. "I'm as prepared as I can be."

The wedding feast went on through the afternoon and straight into the evening. About an hour after sunset, when three of her brothers were passed out drunk on the floor and two others were in a brawl with the miller's son, Lochlyn announced that they would retire to their room. Initially, Rosalie had been glad to escape the crowded hall, but as soon as she entered their chamber, relief gave way to trepidation.

Now she was to face the duke, *in bed*.

At least Melly was there, though she couldn't resist offering Rosalie some unsolicited advice. "Don't be nervous, pet," she said as she helped Rosalie out of her wedding dress. "We all go through this at one time or another. It's just our lot as women."

Rosalie smiled at Melly since she was only trying to be helpful. But the duke wouldn't be Rosalie's first bedmate. And, while she wasn't as adventurous as some, she knew her way around a man. "I suppose that's true."

"There's a girl." Melly eased Rosalie's nightgown over her head, then she slipped out of the room. With a sigh, Rosalie stepped out from behind the screen. Her husband was sitting on the bed, already clad in nightclothes similar to her own. He stood when he saw her.

"Um. Hello," Rosalie said.

"I'm sorry we didn't have more of an opportunity to speak earlier," he said. The celebration had been quite chaotic and, thanks to the loud musicians and even louder guests, she could hardly hear the duke over the din.

"It's alright," she said. "We can always talk now." Rosalie took a step toward him but was startled when a servant bustled into the room.

"I'm afraid people will be in and out all night," the duke said after the servant had left. "Since we're departing so early tomorrow, the preparations need to happen overnight." He extended his hand to her. "You look tired. Would you like to lie down?"

She accepted his hand, and they got onto the bed. The blankets had already been drawn back, and Rosalie wished someone had warmed the bed as she slid her feet against the cool sheets. The duke moved to speak, but another servant approached them.

"We'll just close you in nice and snug," the servant said as she snapped the bed curtains closed. "Not that we don't all know what you'll be up to in here! Bed him well, my lady."

Rosalie's face heated as she swallowed her shame. She wasn't a particularly modest person, but the concept of everyone in the castle knowing she was in bed with the duke tied her guts up in knots. Lochlyn frowned, then he slashed his hand so quickly Rosalie never saw the weapon.

"Why did you do that?" she asked, as his blood dripped onto the bed.

"Anyone who sees the sheets will assume our marriage is official," he said. "Now, no matter what happens tonight, no one will question us. "I don't enjoy being intimate with servants rushing around my bed," he added.

"Neither do I, but you didn't have to cut yourself. Also, it's a myth that women bleed when they first lie with a man." Rosalie took his hand and pressed her fingers over the wound to halt the blood. "Does it hurt very much?"

"I'll be fine." With his other hand, he stroked her hair. "You're very kind."

"As are you." She glanced up at him, and his smile calmed her nerves. "Would you like to talk for a bit?"

"I'd like that very much." He sat up against the headboard. Rosalie sat next to him and pulled the blankets up to their waists. "Your surname is Greenwood?"

Of course, he would start with that. "My mother was only a mistress," Rosalie replied. "Therefore, I have her surname. Although, I suppose I'm a Blackmoor now."

"Rosalie Blackmoor, the Lady of Dragon Ridge," he said. "You don't have to change your name if you don't want to. Many keep their mothers' names to honor their family."

"I wish my mother was here now," Rosalie said, a tear slipping down her cheek. "She's been gone for so long, and I miss her terribly. But no, I won't keep her name. I'll be a Blackmoor like I'm supposed to be."

The duke set his hand on top of hers. "Whatever you wish. I'll have the paperwork drawn up once we're home."

Home. When the duke said that simple word, the gravity of what Rosalie had done came crashing down around her. She married a man she didn't know, and in a few short hours she would leave the only home she ever knew, never to return. Her mother was gone, as was her sister, and she wouldn't even have

Melly with her either. Rosalie looked up at her handsome, patient husband, and burst into tears.

"What's wrong?" he demanded. "I don't know what you've heard about me, but I won't—"

"It's not you," she said, turning away. "So much has happened, and... and..." Rosalie hid her face against the pillow, wishing her heart would harden and her tears would dry up. She felt her husband's hand on her shoulder, and when she didn't object, he drew her back against his chest.

"I'm so sorry," she began.

"Don't be sorry," he said. "Be overwhelmed, or sad, or whatever you need to be, but know this: you never need to be afraid of me. We have each other now, and I will always take care of you."

Rosalie moved onto her back and gazed at him. Of all the things she'd expected, she hadn't dared hope that her husband would be kind. "Do you wish Caterina was here with you instead of me?"

"No." He used his thumb to wipe away her tears. "I'm very glad I'm here with you."

CHAPTER THREE

DRAGON RIDGE

Lochlyn awoke with his new wife nestled in his arms. Last night, he held her as she cried, and once her tears slowed, they talked a bit more. Rosalie told him stories about her mother, and her siblings, and how she'd personally gathered the lilies for her wedding bouquet from the Keep's gardens. All the while Lochlyn watched her and wondered how he'd gotten so lucky.

He'd been amused when his original betrothed had escaped with her lover, and even a bit relieved. Amusement became annoyance when Osman insisted that Lochlyn marry his younger daughter, Rosalie, instead. Lochlyn would have preferred to return to Dragon Ridge alone, leaving all thoughts of matrimony behind. But Osman advised that his daughter had already agreed to the union, and Lochlyn prepared to wed a woman he knew almost nothing about.

The next morning, when he'd taken his place in front of the altar, he briefly considered leaving—Osman and his contracts be damned. But while he didn't appreciate being dragged into Osman's family drama, he was loath to renege on his word and sully the Blackmoor name. Fates knew, it had already been sullied enough.

The guests filled up the pews in twos and threes while the musicians played a somber tune, and the cleric began reciting his benedictions. When the cleric called for the guests to stand, he knew his bride had arrived. Lochlyn turned around as Rosalie stepped onto the aisle and nearly lost his breath.

She was beautiful.

Rosalie's hair was the color of spun gold, and it tumbled over her shoulders and back in loose, shiny curls. Pink and white roses were woven into her hair, and her skin was eggshell smooth, and her pale green gown showed off her lovely form. As per custom, her feet were bare, and even her toes were perfect.

When Rosalie reached the altar, Lochlyn discovered that her eyes were a darker shade of green than her gown, and her lips were two, perfect, pink rose petals. He opened his mouth to speak, to greet her, to say anything at all—but not a sound issued forth. Ashamed, Lochlyn faced the cleric, and he didn't look at his bride again until the vows were done and it was time for him to kiss her...

And he didn't. He couldn't. What if Rosalie recoiled from his touch and shrank back from him as Carys once had? Lochlyn doubted he would survive another rejection, certainly not a public one. He kissed his new wife's hand instead of her mouth and saw the first glint of disappointment in her eyes. No matter, he resolved to make it up to her as soon as they were someplace private.

Now, they were alone in bed, and in contrast to the night before, Lochlyn couldn't hear a single other person in the room with them. It was the perfect time to whisper a few endearments in her ear, to prove how well he would care for her... But they were due to leave at dawn, and Lochlyn did not want to rush their time together. That didn't mean he couldn't do something special for his bride.

"Rosalie," he whispered. "Beloved."

Her eyes fluttered open, and she smiled. "Good morning," she murmured, then her eyes widened when she realized how close they were. "Forgive me," she began, but he hushed her.

"Stay," Lochlyn said as he stroked her cheek. "Unless you're not comfortable?"

"I am. Very much so." Rosalie relaxed against him. He moved his hand to her neck and felt a patch of slick skin over her spine.

"You have a scar?" he asked. The scar was large enough to fit three coppers, and Lochlyn felt a surge of anger at whoever had dared to hurt his bride.

"It happened when I was a baby. Apparently, I was burned." She walked her fingers up Lochlyn's chest. "No one's ever called me beloved before."

"Good. I like having a name for you no one else uses." A man should have such names for his wife, pet names that made her feel safe and loved. He would do anything to ensure she never felt fear ever again, except perhaps of him. That couldn't be helped. "What I don't like is that it's time to get up."

"Do we have to?" she asked with a pout. "Can't we just stay in bed forever?"

"Once we're home, we can stay in bed for days at a time," he said, almost sighing aloud at the thought of an entire day in bed with Rosalie. "Weeks, even. But we do need to get there first."

"Very well." She caressed his jaw. "I take it that everything else is awaiting our arrival at Dragon Ridge?"

"If it's all right with you, I'd like to get to know you a bit more," he said. "I want to tell you about my family, and to show you around the Ridge. The mountains are beautiful and I hope you'll love them as I do."

"That sounds wonderful." Rosalie sat up and stretched. "Very well, my lord husband. Give me a few moments to dress, and we'll be off."

Lochlyn kissed her cheek. "As you say, my lady wife."

Rosalie blushed when he called her his wife, then she opened the curtains and spoke to the maid who had been sitting quietly next to the hearth. After they left Rosalie's chamber, Lochlyn dressed quickly and went to where the carriages were waiting for their departure. Unsurprisingly, Osman had not deigned to see his daughter off.

"Despicable, old fool," Lochlyn muttered as he checked his and Rosalie's luggage. "The man's been blessed with a dozen children, yet he treats them all like possessions."

"What's that, my lord?" the driver, Borneas, asked.

"Nothing of consequence," Lochlyn replied. "As a surprise for my wife, I'm going to go ahead and make Dragon Ridge ready for her arrival. Please let her know my intentions," he added, pressing a gold coin into the driver's hand. "A dozen of my guard will ride with you, but I'm trusting my wife's safety to you in particular. Take good care of her, and there will be a permanent position for you in my court if you so desire it."

"Thank you, my lord," Borneas said. "I'll look after her as if she were my own daughter."

Lochlyn dipped his chin toward the driver, then he made ready to depart for his home in the mountains. Alone, he could travel much faster, and with the extra time, he intended to do everything in his power to make Rosalie feel like Dragon Ridge was her home too.

Lochlyn arrived at Dragon Ridge a few hours later. He immediately sought out his staff, sharing with them his plans for welcoming his new wife. Silas, the steward who oversaw the day-to-day affairs of the castle, was sent to the village for baskets of lilies like the ones from their wedding; while the housekeeper, Madchen, filled Rosalie's chambers with cakes and other sweet treats. As for Lochlyn, he went to the wine cellar and retrieved a few bottles of the claret he'd watched her enjoy at the celebration. Satisfied that he had made Rosalie's rooms comfortable, he waited.

And waited.

Close to sundown, a messenger arrived. Rosalie's carriage had thrown a wheel, and they had thus been delayed. Lochlyn wanted to go to her, but the messenger assured him that repairs had already been made, and his wife was on her way to him. Lochlyn remained where he was, watching the road, eager to show Rosalie his home.

In the cold hour just after dawn, Rosalie's carriage finally rolled past the gates. Lochlyn ran down the castle steps to greet her, bouquet in hand as he waited for the door to open. When it did, and Rosalie appeared in the carriage's small doorway, he smiled.

She sneezed. Twice.

"You're sick?" he demanded, instead of offering her a proper greeting, or telling her how he'd missed her, or asking how her journey had been.

"Being confined to this drafty, cold carriage for a full day and night has given me a chill." She stumbled when she attempted to step out of the carriage. "I believe my feet went numb some time ago too."

"Here, take my arm," Lochlyn said, but she waved him away.

"Really, I'm fine," Rosalie said, then she stumbled again. Lochlyn caught her and lifted her in his arms.

"I'll carry you to your rooms," he said.

"You don't—"

"There are many stairs, and I don't want you to risk a fall. I'm sorry your journey wasn't good. I heard about the broken wheel," he added.

"Really, my lord, none of that was your doing," she said as she wound her arms around his neck. "Why are there flowers on the ground near the carriage?"

"I brought you a bouquet. When you faltered, I dropped it in order to catch you."

"Oh. Thank you."

"There are more flowers in your rooms." He gave her a sheepish grin. "I may have gone a bit overboard."

"Well, then. Thank you again." Rosalie craned her neck to take in the surroundings as they crossed the atrium. The rising sun was at the perfect angle, and the light shining through the stained-glass windows illuminated the space like a cathedral. "Your home is beautiful."

"*Our* home," he amended. "Dragon Ridge is yours now too. Here we are."

Lochlyn swept into the bedchamber with Rosalie in his arms and settled her on the closest chair. "I need a hot foot bath for my lady, as well as some hot tea," he requested from an attendant, then asking Rosalie, "Is tea what you prefer? We can make anything you like here."

"Tea is fine," she said, with a grimace. "Really, I just want to warm up and enjoy not being in a carriage. It was my first time in one, and I hope it will be the last."

"First time? Do you usually travel by horseback?"

"I've never left home before."

Lochlyn bowed his head. He hadn't meant for her to endure her first journey alone. "I'm sorry I went on without you," he began.

"It's fine," she said. "I just need to get these cold boots off and sit near something warm."

"Let me help you," he said, then he knelt and started unlacing her boots.

"My lord!"

Lochlyn looked up, and for the first time he noticed the dark circles under her lovely jade eyes, and the way her shoulders slumped. Rosalie didn't want help with her boots. She wanted to be left alone.

"Forgive me," he said, releasing her foot and standing. "I wanted you to feel welcome here, but it appears that I've failed on all accounts."

"You haven't failed at all," she said. "I appreciate the lengths you've gone to for me, but I'm also exhausted. I fully intend to drink that hot cup of tea you sent for, and then I'll sleep for a day. Perhaps two days."

Lochlyn took her hand and pressed a kiss to her knuckles. "I wish you a good rest. When may I call on you?"

"Whenever you'd like," she replied, and Lochlyn left his new bride alone.

"How is our new lady?" Madchen asked when Lochlyn stepped into the corridor. She was carrying a tray laden with tea and, because Madchen loved feeding people, a plate of biscuits.

"Tired," Lochlyn replied. "She said she wants to drink a cup of tea and sleep for a day."

"Then I'd best get in there," Madchen said. "Will you be joining her? I brought two cups."

"Not this time," Lochlyn said. "Rosalie said she desires rest, and I mean to honor her wishes."

"Honorable you are, but don't stay away too long," Madchen said. "Husbands and wives need each other."

"Is that what you say to Silas when he stays up too late working?"

"Oh, you," Madchen admonished. "Go on. I'll make sure our lady is settled in."

"Thank you, Madchen," Lochlyn said with a shallow bow. Lochlyn watched as the old housekeeper entered his wife's room and smiled. Rosalie's arrival hadn't gone according to plan, but she was here. Everything else would work itself out. He was certain of it.

Desiring rest as well, Lochlyn retreated to his rooms at the peak of the southern tower. He'd debated moving Rosalie directly into his rooms, but he wanted her to have her own space in the castle and not feel smothered by his presence. Many mistakes were made when Carys came to Dragon Ridge, and Lochlyn was determined not to repeat any of them.

He sat on his bed and pulled off his boots, his own exhaustion finally creeping in. Lochlyn had remained awake all day and night waiting for Rosalie, and he needed sleep almost as much as she did. As he set his coat aside, he spied the letter Rosalie had given him during their wedding feast. It was written by his intended bride, Caterina. He unfolded it, wondering what she could have wanted to say to the man she was abandoning.

Lord Blackmoor,

I'm sorry, but I cannot marry you. Please understand that the fault is entirely mine. I beg you, do not hold my actions against my family.

May the Fates guide you well,

Caterina de Serpens

Lochlyn laughed softly before stowing the letter with the rest of his correspondence. He couldn't fault Caterina for wanting to be with the man she loved instead of a stranger and wished her well. What's more, he was positively smitten with Rosalie. His wedding hadn't worked out the way he expected, but those much wiser than he claimed the Fates would change the path of those They favored. Lochlyn took this as a good omen for his union with Rosalie.

Smiling, Lochlyn shed the rest of his clothes and took a bath, then he slept for a few hours. By midafternoon, he had relocated to his study. He'd just opened his ledgers when Madchen entered the room.

"My lord, we have a problem," she said, without preamble.

"I doubt there's a problem in this world or the next that you can't fix," he replied, but she shook her head.

"My lord, it's your wife."

"What's wrong?" Lochlyn demanded as he stood. "Is she unhappy?"

"She's quite ill," Madchen replied. "Silas has already sent for the doctor."

"How did she become ill?" he asked, striding past Madchen and heading toward Rosalie's rooms. "Was it something she ate?"

"I believe she caught a chill," Madchen replied, struggling to match Lochlyn's long strides. "She could barely finish her tea. And once she got into bed, she was taken over by coughs. Since then, she's been consumed by a fever."

With his heart in his throat, Lochlyn entered Rosalie's rooms and went straight to her bed. He found his wife tossing and turning, her skin covered in a thin sheen of sweat.

"Rosalie," he murmured as he dropped to his knees at her bedside. "The doctor will be here soon. What do you need from me, beloved?"

"There's that name again," she mumbled. "I'll be fine. I just need a bit of rest."

"Rest you shall have." He kissed her forehead. "Anything you need in order to recover is yours. Anything at all."

Hours later, Lochlyn was pacing across the corridor in front of Rosalie's door while Silas looked on. The doctor and Madchen had been alone with Rosalie for a small eternity, and Lochlyn's whirling thoughts put together one awful scenario after the next. What if it were a serious illness? What if Rosalie loses the ability to walk, or speak? Fates forbid, what if she never recovered?

"She's going to be fine," Silas reassured him. "Rosalie is a healthy young woman. Before you know it, she'll be out of that bed and exploring the Ridge with you."

Lochlyn rubbed his eyes. "May the Fates make it so," he murmured; just then, the door opened and the doctor emerged.

"How is she?" Lochlyn demanded. "Can I see her?"

"Lady Blackmoor has a touch of fever, from which she will certainly recuperate," the doctor said. "I've given her something to help her sleep."

"Thank you, Doctor." Lochlyn grasped the doctor's hands in his, then he rushed inside Rosalie's chamber. Behind him, he heard the others speaking.

"He loves his wife quite dearly, doesn't he?" the doctor asked.

"Indeed," Silas replied. "I've never seen him so taken with another."

Lochlyn approached Rosalie's bed as Madchen gathered up some used linens. "She's sleeping?" he asked.

"She is," Madchen replied. "The doctor said that sleep is what she needs, and I believe him. Don't worry, my lord, she'll be up and well and at your side soon enough. We only need to be patient."

Madchen patted his forearm as she left the room. Lochlyn sat next to the bed and watched Rosalie sleep. Her hair was damp and her cheeks flushed bright pink, but she looked peaceful. Lochlyn hoped that meant she would be recovered by morning.

"What are you dreaming about, I wonder?" he murmured as he stroked her hair back from her forehead. "I'm told you need rest, so rest you shall have. As soon as you're well enough, we'll have dinner, just the two of us, and we'll decide, well... everything." He kissed her brow. "I can't wait to start our life together." Rosalie shifted and smiled in her sleep.

"Soon."

CHAPTER FOUR

VILE SOUP

Rosalie set down her brush and scowled at her reflection. Her skin was sallow, and there were dark shadows underneath her eyes. Nevertheless, she felt better than she had in days. Physically, at least.

She succumbed to a chill and took to bed after arriving at Dragon Ridge. The subsequent week had been filled with fever dreams and the occasional unfamiliar face checking on her. One person she hadn't seen was her husband, the Black Duke.

Madchen, Dragon Ridge's eminently capable housekeeper, became Rosalie's constant companion during her illness. She worked tirelessly, seeing to Rosalie's needs and managing the near endless flow of doctors and servants going in and out of her rooms. The only thing Madchen did not do was bring the duke to her bedside. Rosalie wasn't sure if she was more irritated with Madchen for not bringing her husband to see her, or Lochlyn for not coming up with the idea himself.

Despite her husband's absence, Rosalie's fever broke two days ago. Now, she finally felt up to venturing out of her rooms and seeing more of her new home. Then, Madchen delivered a note written in her husband's hand, which made her want to crawl back beneath the covers.

Rosalie,

I am glad to hear you're recovered. Join me for dinner?

Lochlyn

She read and re-read the note, then she crumpled it up and threw it into the fire. How dare he write her a note? Rosalie had been bedridden for a week, and her supposed husband—the man who called her beloved, and who tricked her into thinking he cared for her—hadn't visited her once since the beginning of her illness. And now he expected her to eat dinner with him?

"How dare he," she muttered, then she dashed her hand across her eyes.

"I've aired out all of your gowns," Madchen said as she emerged from the dressing area. "Is there one in particular you'd like to wear to dinner tonight?" Madchen spied the half-burnt note lying in the hearth, and Rosalie felt like a fool. If her time in Osman's home had taught her anything, it was to never show weakness, especially not in a new environment where you had no allies.

"I thought adding it to the fire was for the best," Rosalie said. "We always burned such missives at home." Madchen pursed her lips, signaling that she didn't believe Rosalie's explanation for a moment.

"I can always bring you something to eat here instead of you attending the formal dinner," Madchen said. "We can make excuses until you're ready to face the duke."

"Oh, I am going to eat with him," Rosalie said. She had many questions for her husband, and for his sake he'd better have answers. "Madchen, which dress do you think I should wear? I do want to look especially beautiful for my husband. After all, he hasn't seen me for a week."

"Very well," Madchen said. "Blue is his favorite color, so let's pick one in that hue."

"I brought with me a gown the color of forget-me-nots," Rosalie said. "It was my mother's, but I believe it will fit me well."

"Even if it doesn't, I'm sure we can make a few alterations." Madchen held out her hand and beckoned Rosalie toward the dressing area. "Don't worry, my lady. You will be so beautiful tonight the duke will never forget the sight of you walking into the dining room."

When Rosalie entered the dining room—exactly thirty minutes late—dressed in her stunning blue gown, which was more appropriate for a ball than a simple meal, she found the duke standing next to his seat. "Were you waiting for me?" she asked. When he didn't reply, she prompted, "My lord?"

"Yes," he said as he met her eyes. Then, his gaze traveled down the length of her body. Her gown was made of heavy blue silk, edged with lace at the sleeves and pearls across the top of her bodice. The gown was a bit tighter than Rosalie thought it would be. If she hadn't been living off broth and tea the last week, it might not have fit at all. As it was, the bodice was lower and more fitted than Rosalie intended, but Madchen dismissed her concerns and assured her that the dress was perfect for her reunion with her husband.

And now her husband was staring at her as if she were the meal.

"You are a vision," the duke said at last, and Rosalie felt her face warm. As much as it irritated her to have such an instant reaction to his compliments, she did appreciate them.

"Thank you." When they only stared at each other, she said, "You didn't answer. Were you waiting for me?"

"I was." He held out the chair to his right, and Rosalie sat in it. "I didn't want to start without you."

"Apologies for my late arrival," she murmured.

"Since dinner cannot begin without the lady of the house, you are exactly on time." The duke pushed her chair in, then he took his place at the head of the table and signaled for the food to be served. "You really do look lovely."

"Thank you again, my lord." While Rosalie would never admit to it if anyone asked, she greatly enjoyed showing the duke exactly what he'd missed out on this past week. "Are more people joining us?" Rosalie asked when she saw the large number of platters being brought in by the servants.

"Ah, no. I wasn't sure what you would like to eat after your sickness, so I ordered quite a few dishes." He frowned, then asked, "You are feeling better, aren't you?"

"Yes, the endless parade of doctors and nurses you sent to my rooms ensured that I am quite recovered," she replied. "I assume you had some pressing matters to handle this past week?" she asked, hoping he'd been called away, or otherwise occupied. Really, she would have accepted almost any explanation for his absence from her rooms. "Were you forced to deal with a particularly difficult situation elsewhere?"

"Not at all," he replied, filling her wineglass. "I've been home the entire time."

"And you didn't think to poke your head into my room even once, if only to see if I were still alive?" she bit off. Her husband's eyes widened, and she realized he didn't think he'd done anything wrong. Perhaps it was common for men in this mountain clime to ignore their wives' illnesses. "Forgive me, my lord, being ill has made me forget my manners."

"I'm sorry," he said. "The doctors said you needed rest and that visitors weren't a good idea. I didn't want to disturb you."

"You left me to be cared for by strangers," she said, her voice catching at the end. She opened her mouth to say more, but saw the servants nervously glancing between the two of them. In her brief time at Dragon Ridge, Rosalie learned that the duke's staff adored him. Being that Rosalie was the newcomer in the house, the last thing she needed was to start a fight with him at their first shared dinner. "But now, as you say, I am recovered. We can move on."

He leaned toward her. "You're certain?"

"I am," Rosalie said, folding her hands together in her lap. Despite her outward capitulation, she fully intended to take up this discussion with him at a later time. "Thank you, my lord, for your compassion and generosity."

His brows knit together, but he didn't question her further. Rosalie's nails dug into her palms as she fought to keep her composure; damn it all, she wanted to fight with him and she didn't understand why. Perhaps she wanted to punish him for ignoring her, or force him to admit how he felt. Then again, he probably felt hardly anything at all for her. They'd only known each other for a few days. They hadn't even kissed.

Rosalie's eyes burned with unshed tears, but she refused to cry at the table. She had endured dozens of terrible dinners in her father's hall. She would endure this too. Then, a bowl of fragrant broth was set in front of her, which she was sure was some mountain delicacy. To her, it smelled like hot grease. Rosalie shifted in her chair, trying to get comfortable within the confines of her tightly laced dress, and felt her stomach lurch.

"I have to go," she said as she shoved back from the table. "Apologies, my lord!"

"Rosalie," the duke called out as she was walking toward the door. Rosalie opened her mouth to respond and almost lost her lunch. With her hand clamped over her face, she fled.

Soon after Rosalie ran from dinner, Madchen found her in her rooms, curled up on the couch in front of the fireplace, crying so hard she'd lost her breath. "There, there," Madchen said, patting Rosalie's back. "Dinner didn't go as planned?"

"I was so mad at him," Rosalie said between sobs. "I wanted an explanation—not an excuse but a real explanation—of why he ignored me for an entire week... Then he looked at me with his sad eyes, and I realized he hadn't thought he'd done a single thing wrong—and that made me even more mad." Rosalie wiped her face with her sleeve and faced Madchen. "But I didn't want to fight with him. If he thought he'd behaved appropriately, that was enough for me, at least for now. We could always talk again later... I'd just resolved to make the best of dinner, then the soup was set out..." Rosalie shuddered. "It was all I could do to not vomit on the table."

"I'll ask Cook to refrain from making oxtail soup for now," Madchen said. "Let's get you cleaned up, my dear."

Rosalie looked down at herself. "My dress is ruined."

"We can wash it. Or we can have a new one made," Madchen said as she helped Rosalie to her feet. "Have you met our seamstress yet? She is truly gifted with a needle and thread. I can have her visit you tomorrow."

Rosalie gazed at the floor. "I don't want anyone going out of their way for me."

"My lady," Madchen said. "I don't know what sort of position you occupied at your father's home, but you are Lady Blackmoor now. Everyone in Dragon Ridge is here to serve you."

"I don't want servants," Rosalie grumbled. "What I need are friends." She glanced at Madchen. "I sound like a spoiled brat, don't I?"

"Not at all," Madchen soothed. "You sound like a young woman who's been uprooted from her life and thrust into the unknown, one who's trying to find her footing. The way I understand it, you weren't supposed to marry the duke?"

"The arrangement was between him and my sister," she replied. "But my sister felt the need to do something dramatic and ran off with her lover two days before the wedding. My father then got the idea to have me marry the duke instead, and here we are." Rosalie paused as Madchen helped her out of her soiled gown and into a robe. "Why is Lochlyn called the Black Duke?"

"Is that what people call him?" Madchen asked, trying and failing to act as if she'd never heard the name before.

"Is that name new to you?" Rosalie asked. After Madchen murmured that it wasn't, Rosalie continued, "Everyone whispers Lochlyn's name behind their hands as if he's some kind of monster, but he's not, is he? The few times he's talked to me, he's been nothing but kind and patient." She faced Madchen. "You've known him for a long time, haven't you?"

"Oh, yes," she replied. "I remember when he was born, and his three brothers before him. They were all good men, though I've always had a soft spot for the duke, what with him being the little one."

"Did something happen to him?" Rosalie pressed. "Is that how he got this name? It surely can't be because he favors black clothing, or that he has black hair."

Madchen sighed. "Yes, something did happen, but it's the sort of thing that he should tell you directly. I can tell you that we of the Ridge stand by him, and that he was the one wronged."

Rosalie nodded. "That's all I need to know for now." She understood that some memories were painful and difficult to speak of. "However, I can't spend my days sitting in my rooms and waiting for Lochlyn to have time for me. I'll need to set up my own routines if I'm to be happy here."

"An excellent idea," Madchen said. Rosalie sat at her dressing table, and Madchen began brushing out her hair. "I did notice the case of painting supplies among your things. Are you an artist?"

"I don't know if I could call myself an artist." Especially since her father had often derided her love of painting as common, and a waste of time and money. "But I do enjoy painting flowers and landscapes."

"There is an art shop in the village," Madchen said. "Let me know what you need, and we can set up a studio for you. Perhaps near the windows in your sitting room, overlooking the garden?"

"That sounds wonderful, Madchen." Rosalie moved to say more but was interrupted by a pounding at her door.

"Rosalie," the duke called through the door. "Please, Rosalie. I need to talk to you."

"So, he does remember where my rooms are," Rosalie muttered, then she glanced at Madchen. "Sorry. Being sick at dinner was quite upsetting."

"Please, my dear, you never need to apologize to me," Madchen said. "However, you are going to have to face him," she added, nodding toward the door.

"Could you please tell him that I was ill?" Rosalie said. "I was mad at him, that much is true, but I left the table because of the soup, not him. I'll talk to him tomorrow."

"Very well," Madchen said. "Get yourself in bed, and I will speak to our lord. Afterward, would you like some tea?"

"Yes, please. Thank you, Madchen. I feel like you're my only companion here."

"We will have to work on that," Madchen said. "A young lady needs more people in her circle than old housekeepers. Go on, now. I'll be back in a bit."

Rosalie smiled and retreated to her bed while Madchen dealt with the Black Duke. While she'd temporarily won over Madchen, Rosalie understood her precarious position at Dragon Ridge. She'd occupied a similar position at home and had only managed as well as she did by befriending the servants. She resolved that she would employ the same tactic here. That way, even if the duke couldn't be bothered with her, at least she would have people to talk to.

CHAPTER FIVE

RECONCILIATION AND THEFT

The next day, when Lochlyn came down from his rooms, he found Rosalie standing in the atrium, watching the world through the front windows. She was wearing one of her dresses from home, complete with a wide neckline that exposed her neck and the tops of her shoulders; such dresses wouldn't do here in the mountains, where even the summers were cool. However, even though her clothes were poorly suited for the climate, Lochlyn had to admit that his wife looked beautiful in them.

He paused on the stairs and wondered if he should approach Rosalie. Everything he'd tried to do for her had gone wrong, from the debacle of her traveling alone in a carriage, to him listening to the doctors and not checking on her during her illness, to last night's dinner—he was half convinced he should leave her be, and he'd just decided to return to his rooms, when Rosalie spoke.

"I can see your reflection," Rosalie said, thus undoing his planned retreat. "Afraid I'll flee at the sight of you?"

Lochlyn bit back his short reply. It wasn't Rosalie's fault she'd been put in this situation. "Are you feeling better today? Madchen told me that the soup bothered you."

"That soup was vile," she said. "As soon as I smelled it, my options were either leave immediately or vomit on your lap."

"In that case, I applaud your quick thinking." They stood together, admiring the view. "But you are feeling better now?"

"I am." She smiled at him, her green eyes clear and sparkling. "Thank you, for asking."

"Of course," he murmured, then he gestured toward the scenery. "Do you like the mountains?"

"They're beautiful, and so different from where I grew up. People say you can still spot the occasional dragon flying among the clouds, but I haven't seen one yet. Except for this handsome fellow," she added, indicating the sculpture of a black dragon that curled above the windows.

"Ah. This fine dragon is my ancestor, the first Blackmoor."

Rosalie smiled again, a simple twitch of her mouth that warmed his heart. "You really are descended from dragons? My father once claimed the Irontooths were descended from giants."

"Are you?" he asked, curious about his wife's ancestry. Times past, all nobility were descended from Otherworldly creatures, but few families still carried the blood as strongly as the Blackmoors did.

"No," Rosalie replied. "Father bought his title, and we have no idea what we're descended from. Irontooth is naught but an old pirate name."

"A giant wouldn't fare well against a dragon, nor would a pirate," Lochlyn continued, just to watch Rosalie's smile widen. "Especially my ancestor. He settled these mountains and defended the village below from all manner of evils."

"Are there many evils in the mountains?"

"There's evil everywhere. It's our job to remain vigilant." Lochlyn stepped closer to her. "What you said last night, about me not checking on you."

"It's all right," Rosalie said as she turned back to the window. "I shouldn't have behaved as I did."

"The doctors told me you needed your rest, and that visitors would impede your recovery," he continued, undeterred. "I really thought that by staying away, I was helping you get better. I'm sorry I left you alone."

"I understand," she said. "And I was a mess. You were probably better off staying away."

"Perhaps. I missed you a great deal, though."

Rosalie glanced at him, and admitted, "I missed you, too." He held out his hand. Rosalie accepted it, then she stepped closer and let him gather her against his chest. "Just wait until you're ill, and I leave you alone in your sickbed for weeks."

Lochlyn laughed. "I suppose I deserve that. Do you mind me holding you like this?"

"No. I like being in your arms."

He kissed the top of her head. "I'll hold you more often, then."

"You're so warm," Rosalie murmured as she nestled herself against him. "Does the castle seamstress make all your clothes?" she asked, stroking his vest. "Perhaps I'll ask her for a few dresses in this same velvet."

"Are your rooms too cold for you?" he asked.

"They're very nice, but being in your arms warms me in an entirely different way."

Lochlyn closed his eyes as he tightened his arms around his wife, hardly believing she'd said that. That she wanted him still, even after he'd made a mess of their first weeks together. But Rosalie's words gave him hope.

"I still need to show you around our home," he said, his lips against her hair. "We can start with the southern tower, where my rooms are. Would you like to go there now?"

Rosalie leaned back and gazed at him through her lashes. "Why would I want to go to your rooms?" she asked, then she laughed. "All right, if you insist."

Lochlyn grinned. "I don't recall insisting anything," he began, then he noticed a commotion in the courtyard. Rosalie twisted around in his arms, and they saw several members of the castle guard running across the area.

"What's all that about?" she asked.

"I'm not sure," he said, before the captain of the guard burst into the atrium.

"My lord," the captain said, halting when he saw Rosalie. "If we could step away for a moment, I must tell you something."

"Anything you can say to me, you can say in front of my wife," Lochlyn said. Rosalie glanced up at him, her brow furrowed. "You are my equal. Never forget that."

Rosalie nodded. "Then we'd better find out what's happening."

Lochlyn caressed her cheek, then he stood next to her and faced the captain. "Please, tell us what's happened."

"Very well," the captain said. "There's been a theft in the stables. The perpetrator appears to be the driver that brought Lady Blackmoor to the estate."

"Borneas stole something?" Rosalie asked. "That's so unlike him. He's worked for my father for years and has never done anything untoward."

"Sometimes people surprise us, and not always in good ways," Lochlyn murmured, then he turned back to the captain. "Any idea what he took?"

"He was seen loading a large chest into a cart," the captain replied. "This just happened, my lord. We should give chase."

"Agreed," Lochlyn said. The captain bowed and withdrew. Lochlyn then held Rosalie's face in his hands. "Stay in the house. Don't let Silas or Madchen admit anyone they don't know."

"Do you think Borneas may seek to rob you again or... or something worse?"

"I don't know, but I need you to be safe." Lochlyn searched her face, saw the fear in her eyes, and pressed his lips to hers. Fates, but kissing her was like coming home. "Don't worry. You are my most precious wife, and I will destroy anything that attempts to harm you."

Rosalie nodded. "Go. Defend our home. I'll be right here."

Lochlyn kissed her again, then he left in pursuit of the thief. He felt Rosalie's gaze on him as he descended the stairs and crossed the courtyard. When he turned a corner and was out of her sight, he unbuttoned his coat. He shed it as he walked toward the stable, then he loosened his shirt from his belt. By the time he caught up to his captain, he was bare to the waist.

"Does the lady know?" the captain asked, nodding toward Lochlyn's scales.

"Not yet," Lochlyn replied, then black wings sprang from his back and he leaped into the sky.

CHAPTER SIX

ENJOY YOUR BATH

R osalie spent the rest of the day setting up her new easel and paints in the corner of her sitting room near the windows overlooking the garden, just as Madchen had suggested. Once that was done, she rearranged the furniture, twice, and spent an inordinate amount of time standing in front of her windows as she sought the best light. Despite the hours of focused activity, it did little to ease her mind. She was worried about Lochlyn. Even though he had dozens of men in his guard to protect him, anything could happen out there in the mountains.

Fates, but the thought of Lochlyn being hurt tied up her stomach worse than that awful soup had done.

By midafternoon, Rosalie had given up all pretext of painting and watched for her husband's return. Close to dusk, Rosalie saw him walking across the courtyard. Everything in his manner was weary—from his slow cadence, to how he carried his coat balled up in his hands, to his disheveled hair. Rosalie left her rooms and ran across the castle to meet him. She reached the atrium as he was about to ascend the stairs.

"My lord," she called, and he halted. "Did you catch him?"

"No," he grumbled, then he stood up straighter. "Forgive me. I don't mean to take my frustration out on you."

"It's all right. You were saying he got away?"

"Yes," he replied, his weariness evident in his voice. "Amazingly, a lone man in a slow, lumbering cart evaded us all."

"I'm sorry," she said, taking a tentative step toward him. "Do you know what he took?"

"Oddly enough, it seems to have been a chest of maps."

"Maps? Of this area?"

"I'm not sure. Silas is completing an inventory now. We'll know soon enough." He paused, and said, "My spies have learned something else."

"You have spies?" Rosalie had thought spies and espionage were the domain of kings and other powerful men. She had no idea her husband was one of those powers. "Whatever for?"

"The Ridge has its share of enemies." He frowned, and continued, "Your father has put out a bounty on Caterina and the knight she ran off with."

"I can't say that surprises me," Rosalie said. "The only thing my father loves more than gold are grudges. I daresay they're all that keep him warm at night."

The duke grunted. "That sounds like a lonely life."

"It is," Rosalie agreed. "Hopefully, he never finds Caterina. I shudder to think how he'll punish her this time."

"Has Osman ever hurt you?" he demanded. Rosalie blinked. For a moment the duke's eyes were glazed in red, then black.

"What happened to your eyes?" she asked.

"My eyes are fine. Answer me."

Rosalie pursed her lips and looked away. The last thing she wanted to do was tell her husband about the many humiliations she'd experienced at her father's hand. "It doesn't matter, not any longer. Is there anything I can do for you?"

The duke frowned at her evasion. But what did he expect? Rosalie had no intention of reliving her worst days at Irontooth Keep now that she was finally away from that horrid place. "I just want to go to my rooms, have a bath, and forget this day," he said.

"I'll help you," she said, but when she reached to take his coat, he caught her hand.

"I... I am not comfortable being undressed around others," he said.

"Others?" she repeated. "Is that all I am? An other?"

"I..." He bowed his head. "Forgive me. I'm not at my best."

"No, you certainly aren't." Rosalie stalked away from him. Then she turned around and said, "Earlier, you called me your most precious wife. Now I'm just some person bothering you. Which is it?"

The duke regarded her, his brow pinched. Rosalie glanced at her reflection in the window; there were bright spots of color on her cheeks, and her hands were clenched into fists. She looked as furious as she felt.

"I didn't mean to make you mad," he began.

"I am not mad," she bit off. "I am hurt, and confused, and, and... Fates, Lochlyn, why did you bother arranging a marriage if you didn't want a wife? What did you get out of the agreement you made with my father?"

"What did you get?" he countered. "Don't stand there pretending you wanted me as a husband. You saw this as an opportunity to improve your station, nothing more."

"I married you because I was *ordered* to!" Rosalie yelled; her heart felt like a boulder on her chest. She hadn't expected her husband to love her, but she'd wanted him to, even before she saw him waiting for her in the chapel. "My options were either marry you or deal with the consequences."

Lochlyn's eyes flashed black again. "Osman has hurt you!"

"I told you, it doesn't matter," Rosalie said, throwing up her hands in frustration. "My life in the past isn't the problem! It's my life now that I'm trying to salvage. Don't you at least want to try to make this work?"

The duke bowed his head. "I know you don't want to be married to me, and that you don't want to be here," he began.

"You seem to be an expert on what I want, which is rich seeing as you've never once asked me," Rosalie snapped.

"I want you to be happy," the duke said. "You don't have to stay here for a year as the contract says. I won't hold you to me."

Rosalie took a step back from him. "You want me to go?"

"No," he replied. "I want you here, with me." He met her gaze. "Ever since the first moment I saw you, you've held my heart in your hands."

Rosalie gasped, then she shook her head. "No. I don't believe you."

"I would never lie to you," Lochlyn began.

"You tell me what I want to hear, and then you go off and do something entirely different," she said. "Act like you want me here—or I'll take you up on your offer and leave before a year's up."

Lochlyn's jaw dropped. "More than anything, I want to be with you."

"Then make an effort," Rosalie said. Then she turned on her heel and stalked back to her rooms.

"Rosalie!" the duke called.

"Enjoy your bath," she said over her shoulder, before entering her room and shutting the door behind her.

"I am not going to him anymore," she muttered to herself as a hot tear rolled down her cheek. "From now on, he can come to me." She slid down the door to the floor and wrapped her arms around her knees. "Fates, I hope he comes to me."

CHAPTER SEVEN

A Visitor and Dinner

"**M**y lady," Madchen said as she stepped into Rosalie's chamber. "A woman has just arrived, and she's asking to come inside."

"Who is she?" Rosalie asked, looking up from her easel. As the lady of the house, she could have sent someone else to investigate this woman, but the two months since she'd been given in marriage to the Black Duke had been the most boring months of her life. At least this mystery person's presence broke up the monotony of her days.

"That's the thing of it," Madchen replied. "She won't give her name, but she claims she must speak to a Blackmoor. We've got her waiting out in the courtyard."

"Well, let's have a look at this traveler." Rosalie exited her apartment and walked toward the front of the castle. For all that her days were boring, her home was not. The castle was an imposing fortress of black marble streaked with iridescent white bands that sparkled like opal when they caught the light. Many rooms had high ceilings topped by ornate glass roofs, and Rosalie never wanted for light during the day. What she did want was companionship. Ever since the duke had chased down the thief and subsequently refused to let Rosalie near him while he bathed, he'd kept to his own side of the castle while she'd remained in her rooms. Now, she only saw her husband at dinner, where he was courteous and kind and maddeningly calm—she may as well have married an etiquette pamphlet.

Rosalie reached the entrance to the balcony overlooking the front courtyard. Arching above the doorway was a sleek dragon, carved from a single piece of black marble. The dragon was fierce, with razor sharp teeth and wicked talons, but he didn't scare Rosalie. She felt safe with the dragon watching over her and the rest of her home. She grazed her fingertips across the dragon's tail as she stepped out onto the balcony. When she saw the woman waiting below, she gasped.

It was her sister, Caterina, astride Curran's stallion.

"Rosalie?" Caterina asked, clearly shocked that her sister was Lady Blackmoor. "Please, Rosie, may I beg your help?"

"Of course," Rosalie said, then she turned to Madchen. "Admit her at once and have her brought to my chamber."

"Then you are acquainted with her," Madchen said, after issuing a few instructions to the footmen.

"Yes," Rosalie replied as she watched her sister disappear beneath the balcony floor and enter her home. "I am indeed."

"Should we alert our lord?"

Rosalie bit her lip. "I suppose we must."

Madchen curtsied and went off to find the duke. Rosalie sighed, and wondered what her calm, distant husband would think about Caterina's sudden reappearance in their lives. She never thought she would see her sister ever again. While she was happy to be reunited with Caterina, she wasn't so naïve as to assume this would be a joyful event. If Caterina had sought her out alone, things between her and Curran must have taken a turn for the worse. Just how much worse remained to be seen.

And there was the fact that Caterina was supposed to marry the Black Duke, not her.

Rosalie reentered her chamber and asked that a bath and a luncheon be prepared. She imagined her sister could do with both. The servants had just left to carry out her requests when Caterina was ushered into the room.

"I'm so happy to see you," Rosalie said as she embraced her sister. "I missed you so much."

"I missed you too, Rosie," Caterina said. "I had no idea you'd be here!"

"Then what made you ride all the way to Dragon Ridge?" Rosalie asked, since the journey across the mountains wasn't an easy one.

"Curran told me to come here and nowhere else if I needed help," she replied. "I thought it strange, but he insisted. Did Father force you to marry the duke?"

Rosalie nodded. "He did."

"Oh, Rosie, I'm so sorry," Caterina said, and Rosalie nodded. "And yet you still took me in."

"No matter what's happened, you're still my sister. I'm always here for you." Rosalie stepped back, then she spied Caterina's swollen belly. "Curran got you with child?" When Caterina nodded, she continued, "Is this why you ran off instead of going through with the marriage?"

"Partly," she replied. "I couldn't very well marry a man when I was already pregnant by another, now could I?"

"I suppose not," Rosalie murmured as she stared at Caterina's rounded midsection. Her sister and Curran must have become close sooner than she'd realized, for her to be showing that much. "And the other part?"

Caterina cast her gaze downward. "If I married the duke, that would have been the end for Curran and me. I wasn't ready to let him go."

"But you came here alone," Rosalie said. "Have you been living with Curran? And where is he now?"

"We've been staying at a hunting lodge. Then, a week ago, he went to get supplies for us and never returned. I don't know what happened to him..." Caterina dashed her hand across her eyes and faced her sister. "Something must have happened to him. He would never leave me, not intentionally."

Rosalie took Caterina's hands. "I'm sure he wouldn't have. I remember how he doted on you. But when he left for these supplies, he didn't mention where he would obtain these goods?"

"All he left me was a map of these mountains," she replied. "I'm sorry to just turn up like this. I had nowhere else to go."

"It's all right." Rosalie indicated two chairs set before the hearth. "I'm sure you need some rest. You can tell me everything that's happened since you two disappeared."

"There's not much to tell." Caterina removed her cloak, and Rosalie saw her sister's mended bodice.

"You're wearing the same dress you left in?" Rosalie asked.

"It's the only one I have. You remember what I was wearing?"

"I remember that the bodice was torn. The story was that you flashed your tits to one of the guards and he let you and Curran abscond with one of Father's horses."

"That is not what happened, and we only took Curran's own horse," she said. "But my dress was ripped thanks to Father's brutish guards. That much is true." Caterina moved to say more, but Rosalie raised her hand. A moment later, a bevy of servants led by Madchen reentered the room and began laying out platters of food and pitchers of drink.

"Thank you," Rosalie said when they were done. "When will the bath be ready?"

"Soon, my lady," Madchen replied. "The water is heating now. Will you be partaking?"

"Not I, but Nina will," Rosalie replied, gesturing toward her sister. "Madchen, Nina was one of my ladies at home. She has asked to enter my service here, and I have accepted. For now, we would like some privacy as we reacquaint ourselves."

"As you say, my lady," Madchen said. "Wonderful to meet you, Nina." Madchen curtsied, then left the room and closed the doors behind her.

"I'm your lady?" Caterina asked. "Nina?"

"Father has put out a reward for your and Curran's capture," Rosalie whispered. "The duke's people are loyal, but they all have mouths. The last thing we need is someone mentioning that my sister came to visit, have the wrong person overhear it, and have Father crashing down on us."

"Thank you," Caterina said, her voice wavering.

"You can thank me by eating." Rosalie poured two cups of tea. "The duke's staff is excellent, including the cook."

"You refer to your husband by his title?" Caterina asked. When Rosalie only shrugged, she asked, "Is being married to him that bad?"

"It's hardly anything." Rosalie sipped her tea and thought about the past weeks she spent painting alone in her room, and the infrequent dinners with her husband. Ever since she'd challenged him to make an effort in their relationship, he'd been avoiding her. It hurt Rosalie that they weren't as close as she'd wanted them to be, but what did she expect? After all, it was an arranged marriage, not a love match.

Every night, while Rosalie was laying in bed, she remembered how handsome he looked at the chapel as he waited for her, and his barely restrained passion when he kissed her in the atrium. Perhaps they were a love match, but Rosalie had no idea how to breach the chasm that had grown between them.

"Our marriage has turned out to be rather boring," Rosalie continued, instead of telling her sister how she was the loneliest married woman in the realm. "We hardly know what to say to each other."

"Surely, it's not that bad," Caterina said. "You two must have something in common."

"A mutual distaste for relationships, perhaps," Rosalie said. "But it's fine. As you know, I was never supposed to marry at all."

A knock sounded, and none other than the Black Duke himself opened Rosalie's door. It was the first time he'd set foot in her chamber since the day Rosalie arrived at Dragon Ridge.

"My lady," the duke greeted. "I was told we have a visitor."

"My lord," Rosalie said in return. "One of my ladies from home has come to seek employment with us. We were just having some refreshment."

"One of your ladies came all this way," he began, then he rounded the table and paused when he recognized Rosalie's visitor. "Caterina?"

"You know her?" Rosalie demanded as she shot to her feet. Not only had she lied to her husband, but she had been immediately caught as well.

Shrugging off her doubts, she continued, "I was told you two had never met!"

"We spoke—briefly—when Curran and I fled the keep," Caterina said. "And when the Black Duke arrived, Father pointed me out to him."

"People still call me that?" he countered. When neither woman responded, he continued, "Yes, Osman indicated us to one another, and the next I'd heard of my betrothed was her running off with another man." The duke rubbed his chin. "Is the knight here?"

"He's not," Caterina said, then she dropped her gaze to her hands.

"Curran's whereabouts are unknown," Rosalie said. "After he got my sister with child, he went out for supplies and disappeared."

The duke's gaze flicked to Caterina's belly, then he stepped closer to Rosalie. "I understand you were only trying to protect your sister, but you don't ever need to lie to me," he said quietly.

"Forgive me," she said. She bowed her head, leaving off that, had she known Lochlyn would have immediately recognized Caterina, she wouldn't have attempted the falsehood. "I wasn't sure how you would react to her being here."

He tilted up her chin. "No apologies are necessary. Sometimes, we act irrationally for those we love." The duke smiled at his wife, then he turned to Caterina. "We will, of course, offer you sanctuary. Does anyone know you're here?" When Caterina shook her head, he pressed, "Did anyone follow you?"

"No," she replied. "Curran and I were alone for weeks, and I didn't see another soul." She met the duke's eyes. "Before Curran left, he told me how to find Dragon Ridge. He told me to come here if I needed help."

"I wonder why that is," the duke murmured.

"I've told the servants her name is Nina," Rosalie said. "In light of Father's bounty, I thought that it was for the best, at least for now."

"Agreed," the duke said as he dipped his chin toward his wife's sister. "Please, Caterina, rest and refresh yourself. Our home is yours."

"Thank you," Caterina said. "And what about my baby?"

He glanced at Rosalie, and replied, "Let us leave that discussion for a later time."

Rosalie stood outside the dining room, debating whether or not she should join the duke for dinner. Ever since she'd challenged him to come to her, she'd taken to eating alone in her chamber unless he specifically asked her to join him for a meal, and those invitations were few and far between. However, things had changed since her sister arrived at Dragon Ridge, and she needed to have a private conversation with her husband.

Mustering all of her resolve, Rosalie strode into the room. When the duke saw her, he stopped eating and stood.

"My lady! I wasn't expecting you," he blurted out. "But I am glad you're here." He pulled out the chair on his right. "Please. Join me?"

"Thank you," Rosalie said as she accepted the seat. A servant filled her wine-glass as the duke began filling her plate. Rosalie marveled at the vast amount of food laid out both on the table and on the duke's plate. Every time she had taken dinner with him, the cooks had brought out enough food to feed half the village, and her husband consumed almost all of it. Despite the abundance of choices, it was soon obvious that he had no idea what Rosalie liked to eat.

"What would you prefer?" he asked. "We have some mutton, as well as roasted fowl... here are some stewed vegetables... I believe this is some sort of pie..."

"Whatever you're having will be fine with me," Rosalie said. "The pears look nice." He ended up choosing a joint of mutton, a slice of fowl, and a few poached pears for her dinner.

"This is perfect. Thank you," she said when he set her plate in front of her. "And thank you for readily agreeing to help earlier."

The duke nodded, then he looked toward the servants. "You may retire for the evening," he said. The servants filed out and closed the doors behind them.

"This is the first time we've been alone in weeks," Rosalie murmured. Even on their wedding night, they slept in a room filled with servants since they were due to leave for Dragon Ridge at first light. "And it's to discuss my sister."

"I've been trying not to intrude upon you," the duke said. "Forgive me if I've appeared standoffish."

"I just assumed you didn't like me any longer," she mumbled into her pears.

The duke's hand hovered over hers. "May I?" he asked. When she nodded, he placed his hand on hers. "I assure you, that is not the case."

Rosalie nodded again, equally caught off guard by his admission and the heat from his hand which spread through her. "I do appreciate you so readily agreeing to help Caterina," she said, sliding her hand out from underneath his.

"No thanks are needed," he said as he watched her cut up her pears. "You are my wife. Your burdens are mine, as are your troubles. We will bear them together."

"Is that what it's to be between us? Burdens and troubles?" she asked, struggling to keep her voice even. Even though she'd all but given up on having a loving marriage, she'd hoped her husband would be her friend. His words made their union sound even more like the business transaction it was.

"It will be whatever we make of it," he said.

They ate in silence for a time. "How is Caterina?" he asked.

"Resting. In fact, she fell asleep almost as soon as she was done with her bath."

"Rest is good. I've sent for a midwife to assist her with the baby. She should arrive early tomorrow."

Rosalie hadn't even thought about a midwife, but her sister was with child. "I wonder how close she is to giving birth."

"I was wondering that too." The duke pushed back his plate. "You didn't know about the baby before she ran off?"

"I didn't," Rosalie replied. "I only found out when she arrived earlier today."

"Has she mentioned anything about the baby? Or anything more about Curran's whereabouts?"

"Only that she's despondent without him." When the duke grunted, she asked, "What is it? You seem to know something about Curran."

"The reason your father specifically hired Curran to protect his daughter's virtue is because he's from the Order of the Sun. Their knights are legendary, their honor without reproach," the duke began, then he paused as he regarded her. "You never received such a guard?"

"Since my mother wasn't his wife, Father didn't care what I did," she replied. "I was never supposed to marry. In fact, after your marriage to Caterina was complete, I was going to retire to a convent."

The duke bowed his head. "And I brought you here instead. Are you quite religious?"

"No, not really. But the convent I'd chosen had quite an extensive library, and an attached school. I could have continued my studies, perhaps even become a teacher. I did want to work with children," she added. "However, the library was what really drew me to the location."

He cocked his head to the side. "Books are what please you most?"

"Why, yes. It's one of the reasons why I never had official suitors or went to balls and other court events. I mostly stayed in my rooms, reading every night."

The duke stood and offered his hand. "If you wouldn't mind interrupting your meal, there is something I'd like to show you."

"All right," she said, accepting his hand. Again, the warmth of him spread through her, and she followed him out of the dining hall and to the eastern tower. They ascended the spiral stairs, and he brought her to a door on the second landing.

"A moment," he said as he grabbed a long match from a niche in the wall and ignited it, then he lit an oil lamp. He took a moment to adjust the flame before he opened the door.

And revealed a library.

"Oh," Rosalie said as she stepped further into the room. The lamp illuminated a small portion of the library, but she could see staircases in the distance, and rows and rows of tall shelves. "This has always been here?"

"This library is one of the jewels of Dragon Ridge," he replied. "I'm descended from a long line of avid readers. My family has always valued knowledge. We have about ten thousand volumes in our collection, give or take." He bowed his head, adding, "It doesn't come with cloisters, or a school, but it's all I have in the way of books."

"It's amazing," Rosalie breathed, hardly believing the library was real. She didn't know so many books existed in the entire world, let alone in her home. "And I may come here to read? Whenever I'd like?"

"Of course you can." The duke stepped in front of Rosalie and tilted her chin upward. "When I said we will now share everything, I didn't mean only burdens and troubles. All I have is yours, this library included. I'm only sorry I neglected to tell you about it until now."

"Don't be sorry," she said as she placed her hand on top of his. "I know about it now, and no harm was done for the waiting. After all, it's not like I ever asked if there was a library in the castle."

The duke smiled. "Your kindness humbles me yet again."

"I must say, this feels like the greatest gift I've ever received," she said in a rush, trying to tamp down the butterflies fluttering up from her stomach; the more the duke touched her, the less rational she became. "I truly don't know how I'll ever thank you for this."

He stroked his thumb across her jaw. "There is one thing you could do that I would accept with the utmost gratitude."

Rosalie swallowed. "What is that, my lord?"

"You almost never call me by my name."

"You hardly ever refer to me by my name."

"You're right. I hardly do." He stepped closer, so close their shoes were touching. "We weren't meant to be together, that much is true. But together we are, and I fear that in my quest to not intrude upon you, I've been somewhat cold. I'd like to remedy that if you're agreeable to it."

"And that remedy is for me to say your name, Lochlyn?"

His smile deepened. "I believe it will be a good start, my Rosalie."

CHAPTER EIGHT

MADE FOR EACH OTHER

"Are you sure you don't want to bring back any more?" Lochlyn asked. After they'd spent some time exploring the stacks in Dragon Ridge's enormous library, Rosalie had selected a dozen books on as many subjects to bring to her rooms. Lochlyn, of course, tasked himself with carrying them.

"These will do for tonight," she replied. "Are they too heavy? I can carry half of them."

"You absolutely will not," Lochlyn said. He was certain the books in his hands weighed nearly as much as Rosalie and he didn't want her to struggle. "It's a man's duty to carry books for his wife."

"And what is the wife's duty?" she asked.

"Reading them."

Rosalie laughed, and Lochlyn felt his own heart lighten. "Must I read them all by morning?" she asked.

Lochlyn's gaze slid toward his smiling, happy wife. "I'll give you two days."

She laughed again, then they turned a corner and were at the door to her rooms. Rosalie opened her door, and she surprised Lochlyn by leaning up and kissing him. Her unexpected endearment startled him, and he almost missed his moment to return the kiss. It had been weeks since they last kissed. Lochlyn feared it would never happen again, save in his memories, but Rosalie had surprised him yet again.

"Thank you, Lochlyn," she said, claiming the stack of books from his hands. "Sleep well, my husband."

"Good night, my wife," he said, as the books and Rosalie slipped away from him.

Lochlyn closed the door to her chamber, his heart thundering in his chest as he paused to rest his head against the heavy oak. Rosalie had been overjoyed to learn of the castle's library—and hearing her laugh and seeing her smile only reinforced Lochlyn's belief that she was meant to be here at Dragon Ridge. Now she was inside her chamber, and he was alone in the corridor, wishing he could come up with an excuse to stay.

But he'd already wished her a good night, and she was excited to start on her new books. If only he'd realized her love of reading sooner, perhaps they could have spent many lazy afternoons together in the library, reading passages out loud and reciting bad poetry, laughing and getting to know one another. Like almost everything else in their marriage, Lochlyn had mishandled things, and no one suffered from it more than him.

No, that wasn't true. His sweet Rosalie had suffered most of all. That reason alone was why he'd offered to release her before the marriage contract's expiry in a year. But now that he'd finally made some inroads into his relationship with Rosalie, he knew that dissolving the contract early was a poor notion. The way she smiled at him in the library, and the way she laughed when she skipped down the aisles of bookshelves... Rosalie was happy, and he was the one who made her happy. After weeks of wondering how he could make her smile, he finally did, and a singular thought formed in his mind.

He could never let her go.

"I can't force her to want to be here," Lochlyn muttered as he crossed the atrium toward his study. "If she wants to leave, I'll not stand in her way." He looked up, and saw his steward, Silas, standing at the bottom of the central staircase.

"You heard that, didn't you?" Lochlyn asked, trying to hide his annoyance. It wasn't Silas's fault he overheard him muttering like a fool.

"I did," he replied. "And you've left out one very important question."

"And what is that?"

"You're prepared for Rosalie leaving you, but what if she wants to stay?" Silas asked. "That's still a possibility, isn't it?"

"I suppose." Lochlyn leaned against the balustrade and regarded the old steward. He has been looking after the estate since the time of Lochlyn's grandfather. In fact, since Lochlyn's father passed away, Silas has been filling the role of parent too. "Earlier, I showed her the library. She loved it."

"Of course she did. I've been curating that collection for most of my life." Silas descended the last step and faced Lochlyn. "Now that she knows about the library, you two can spend some time there together. If you don't mind my saying so, with you only seeing her at the occasional dinner, you'll never get to know her."

"You're right about that," Lochlyn muttered. It distressed him that he couldn't manage to spend more time with Rosalie. She was always tucked away in her rooms, which were well-appointed and had everything she needed. What Lochlyn needed was a reason to coax her out of her rooms and into the rest of the castle.

"What if I invite her to breakfast?" Lochlyn asked. "Then we can see each other twice a day and... and perhaps more."

Silas bowed his head. "An excellent idea. I'll let Cook know your plans." Silas turned to leave, saying over his shoulder, "Is there anything in particular you'd like to eat?"

"I'm sure whatever Cook's planning will be fine," Lochlyn replied. "I'll go invite Rosalie now so she's prepared to join me tomorrow morning." Lochlyn hurried back to Rosalie's door, pleased that Silas had helped him come up with such a simple solution to seeing his wife again that evening, and more often in his day-to-day life.

Lochlyn reached Rosalie's door and raised his hand to knock, then he paused; part of him was loath to disturb her. He almost walked away... but he couldn't. Wouldn't. These past few weeks, when he'd existed on one side of the castle while his wife was sequestered on the other, had been hard on him. He needed Rosalie, and more importantly, he needed to repair the rift that had grown between them.

Finally, Lochlyn knocked. He heard Rosalie moving inside her rooms and breathed a sigh of relief since he hadn't woken her. He imagined her smiling when he asked her to eat with him in the morning, perhaps taking his hand again. Then Rosalie opened the door, and his mind went blank.

"I didn't think you'd be undressed," Lochlyn blurted out. Instead of the deep red gown she was wearing earlier, Rosalie was clad in an ivory chemise that clung to her curves. His gaze traveled from the lacy neckline down to the curve of her hip as his temperature rose and his mouth went dry. Lochlyn deliberately dragged his gaze back to Rosalie's jade green eyes and asked, "Is this a bad time?"

"It's not, and you've seen me in my nightgown before," Rosalie reminded him.

"I have," he murmured, remembering how beautiful she looked on their wedding night with her golden hair spread out like a halo against her pillow. "I came to ask you something."

"Well, come inside and ask me." Rosalie took his hand and drew him inside her chamber. Lochlyn stroked his thumb across her knuckles, reveling in her soft skin. "There's no reason for you to stand out in the cold corridor."

Lochlyn looked around her chamber, with the fire blazing in the hearth and the candles burning in their sconces. Her rooms were as warm and welcoming as her smile. "Is that your latest work?" he asked, nodding toward the easel. She'd moved it away from the windows and closer to the fire, and he wondered if she'd planned on spending the evening painting.

"It is. I didn't think you knew about my paintings."

"I knew. The botanical studies are my favorites."

"Oh." Rosalie blushed and ducked her head. "I suppose I now know what Madchen's been doing with my finished pieces. She said she was putting them in storage."

"She did." Lochlyn took a breath as he centered himself; he hadn't come here to talk about paintings or nightgowns, and he refused to let himself be distracted. He looked at their entwined hands and steeled himself.

"Will you have breakfast with me tomorrow morning?" he asked. "And all the mornings afterward?" When she didn't respond, he added, heart in his throat, "I need to see you more often."

Rosalie tightened her fingers around his. "Lochlyn," she began. They were interrupted by the door creaking wide open.

"Good evening, my lady," Madchen announced as she pushed a cart through the door Lochlyn had forgotten to close. "Silas told me how you'd discovered the library, and since I knew you'd be up late reading, I thought I'd bring a few treats to help you pass the time. Oh, hello, my lord."

"Hello, Madchen," Lochlyn said as his mouth curved up in a wry smile. Based on how quickly Madchen had arrived with her cart of treats, she and Silas had engineered this late-night meeting between him and his wife long before that conversation in the atrium.

Rosalie glanced between him and the housekeeper, and said, "Madchen, our lord has asked me to have breakfast with him tomorrow. Do you think we can make room for him?"

"You two eat breakfast together?" Lochlyn asked.

"Oh yes," Madchen replied. "In fact, we've been having our meals in the kitchens, at the same table that you and I used to eat at when you were small. Back then, we all called him Lochie," she added with a knowing smile.

"Lochie?" Rosalie asked, her brows halfway up her head. "Madchen, you have been holding out on me."

"I'll issue you a challenge," Madchen said. "For every breakfast the three of us share, I'll share a story of Lochie as a boy. Do you agree to those terms, my lord?"

"I suppose I have no choice," Lochlyn said. "Thank you for letting me join your table, Madchen."

"No, I should be thanking you. I've missed our breakfasts." Madchen set her hand on Lochlyn's cheek. "Never doubt that you've grown into a good man. Isn't that right, my lady?"

"Agreed, Madchen," Rosalie said, and Lochlyn felt his heart warming.

"See that, my lord," Madchen said with a wink. "I'll leave you to it. Good night, my charges."

Madchen withdrew from Rosalie's chamber and shut the door behind her. Lochlyn faced his wife, saying, "It looks like we're having a second dinner."

"It does, doesn't it?" Rosalie said. Lochlyn watched as she investigated the cart. "Madchen has brought us some tea, hot chocolate, and a platter of biscuits and such to nibble on. What would you like?"

"I'll take whatever you give me, beloved."

Rosalie glanced up at him, her cheeks having gone bright pink. "You haven't called me that since I was ill." Rosalie set down the delicate porcelain teapot. She continued, "Every time you show me the least bit of affection, you turn around and push me away. Is that what's happening now? Will we play the happy couple tonight, then act like strangers again in the morning?"

"Rosalie," he began, but words failed him once again. Frustrated with his lack of courage, he turned away, but Rosalie stepped in front of him.

"Oh, no you don't," she said. "You are not avoiding me. Not anymore, not until you talk to me."

Lochlyn cupped the back of her head with his hand. "I want to talk to you. Truly, I do. But sometimes, the words won't come." He blew out a breath and rested his forehead against hers. "That's not a very good explanation."

"It's a start." Rosalie placed her hand on his chest. "I know something happened to you. Even without you speaking of it directly, I can feel the weight of it on your heart. You said we'll share our burdens. Won't you let me share this burden with you?"

"It's not fair to you," he began.

"It's not about fairness," she said. "It's about us being partners." When Lochlyn only nodded, she asked, "Why did you marry me?"

"You remember. Caterina was unavailable, and Osman insisted I marry you instead."

"Let me ask again. Why do you want a wife?"

Lochlyn didn't respond right away. "I do need an heir," he said. "I'm the last Blackmoor. I don't want my family to end with me."

"Then you want a legacy," Rosalie said, sliding her hands behind his neck. "So, your family won't be lost to time."

"Yes, but even more than that, I want a partner," he said, stroking her hair behind her ear. "Not just in looking after Dragon Ridge. I want someone I can laugh with, and cry with, and everything in between. I want someone I can grow old with, and with whom to watch our children and grandchildren grow up and start their own lives. I want a family, and I want to care for them as best I can."

"Then you do want children?"

"I do. When I was younger, and there were more servants in the house, they had their families here with them. The halls teemed with children running and playing and laughing," Lochlyn closed his eyes, remembering the games he'd play with the other children. "Those were some of my happiest days."

"I've always wanted children, too," Rosalie admitted.

"I thought you wanted to go to a convent," he said. "Why didn't you plan to marry instead?"

"I only chose the convent because Father made it plain he didn't want me to marry, not unless it benefited him politically. I gave up on having children some time ago."

Lochlyn pulled her closer, and said, "Please, beloved, don't think you can't have every happiness life offers. Osman may have hurt you in the past, but you're here now. Remember what I told you when we were first married?"

Rosalie's fingers glided across his neck, and it was all Lochlyn could do to keep from purring. "That you'll always take care of me."

"And I will," he promised. "No matter what." Lochlyn caressed her cheek. "Words sometimes fail me, that much is true, but please believe me when I say that the happiest moment of my life was waking up with you in my arms."

Rosalie sank her fingers into his hair. "What if I told you that my happiest moment was the first time you called me beloved?"

Lochlyn dipped his head and kissed her. Her lips were soft, and warm, and that gentle touch healed one of the cracks in his heart. "Fates, I need to kiss you more often. I'm not very good at being a husband, am I?"

"If it's any consolation, you're the best husband I've ever had." They smiled at each other, and Lochlyn decided to stop being so cautious with his wife. Rosalie was tired of declarations of affection, so he needed to show her how deeply he felt about her—and he liked surprising his wife.

With a grin, he swept Rosalie into his arms, spun around, and settled them on the couch with her on his lap. Rosalie yelped as she clutched his shoulders. "Lochlyn! What if you'd dropped me!"

"I would never drop you." Lochlyn closed his eyes and breathed in the sweet lavender scent of her hair. "I would carry you to the ends of the earth, my beloved."

Rosalie's cheeks darkened. "I had an idea, about Caterina," she began as she traced the edge of his collar with her fingertip. "It would wholly depend on your opinion, though."

"Tell me," he said, even though discussing Rosalie's sister was the last thing he wanted to do.

"If you're agreeable to it, we could give my dowry to Caterina, to help her with the baby."

"That's very generous," he began, and almost left it at that. However, the truth was always better than a lie, even one of omission. "Rosalie, you didn't have a dowry."

"Yes, I did," Rosalie insisted. "I remember Father going on about it."

"Caterina had a dowry, but you did not," Lochlyn clarified. "Osman made that apparent, though he wouldn't explain why."

"Oh." Rosalie covered her mouth with her hand. "And you married me without one?"

"He didn't tell me until afterward. At the feast." Lochlyn took her hand and kissed her knuckles. "I told him he could keep his money, since I've plenty of my own. You were already my wife. I wouldn't turn you out over such a petty reason."

"There's something you should know," Rosalie said. "Caterina's mother was nobility. My mother..." She closed her eyes and took a deep breath. "My mother worked in a brothel. That's why Father wouldn't arrange a marriage for me, at least not until Caterina ran off, and why I planned on entering the convent instead of marrying."

Rosalie trembled, and Lochlyn wasn't sure if she were angry at her father's last insult, or afraid of his reaction. "Thank you for telling me about her," Lochlyn said as he tightened his arms around her. "Why are you shaking?"

"Sometimes, it's hard to talk about her," Rosalie replied. "I miss her so much."

"I'm sure you do." Lochlyn's parents and brothers had passed many years ago, and he still thought of them every day. "After you were born, did Osman move your mother into the Keep?"

"For a little while," Rosalie said. "After my brother was born, he tired of her and sent her away. He wouldn't even give her a stipend to live on, so she had to go back to work." A tear rolled down her cheek, and she dashed it away. "I used to bring her money and other little things whenever I could."

"Of course you did," Lochlyn murmured; his wife was sweet and soft hearted despite having been sired by an Irontooth. "What happened to her?"

"She got sick with fever about ten years ago," she replied. "It was an odd fever, and none of the doctors could help. Her skin was so hot... After she died, she was buried in their common yard."

"Do you want her moved here?" he asked. "So, she can be closer to you?"

"No," she said, shaking her head. "The expense alone—"

"Is one I would gladly bear, for you," he said over her.

"Thank you, but my answer is still no," she said. "The courtyard where she rests is quite lovely, and peaceful. She's happy there." Rosalie glanced at him, then, away. "When you told me you would release me from our contract, I assumed you knew about her."

"How she lived her life doesn't matter. At least, not to me." When Rosalie wouldn't meet his eyes, he continued, "When we argued in the atrium and I accused you of only marrying me to improve your station, I never would have said such a thing had I known. I would never use your mother against you."

"Then why did you say it?"

"Most beautiful young women wouldn't choose a life in the cold mountains with a man they'd never met," he replied. "I'm still astonished that you did, and very, very grateful."

Rosalie laid her head on his shoulder. "Lochlyn. Husband. It baffles me that you want a lowborn woman like me as your wife, and I am so very glad you do."

Lochlyn kissed her forehead. "It appears we were made for each other."

She laughed softly. "Yes, it appears we were." She traced the line of his arm with her fingertip. "Thank you, for coming back and talking to me tonight."

He kissed her forehead again. "Thank you, for being patient with me," he said, his lips against her skin.

"What are we going to do about Caterina?"

"Let's leave that for after the midwife arrives in the morning. Tonight, I only want to think about you."

CHAPTER NINE

BREAKFAST AND BIRTHDAYS

When Rosalie awoke the next morning, she took a moment to snuggle into her pillow. It wasn't like she had any early morning tasks to attend to, and the Fates could grant her a few more moments of comfort. She realized her pillow was firmer than usual, and warmer, and covered in black velvet...

Rosalie moved onto her back, and learned her pillow was Lochlyn's lap. They were still on her couch in front of the hearth, where they'd sat late into the night talking. He'd even removed his coat and laid it across her in lieu of a blanket.

Since Lochlyn was still sleeping, she took a moment to gaze at her husband. He looked younger, his features having been softened by sleep, and peaceful, with his lashes a dark fringe against his cheeks. She reached up to feel the gold chain at his throat, but he woke at her touch.

"Good morning," Rosalie said as he blinked sleep from his eyes. "I see you spent the night."

"I thought you might need me," he said, drawing her hair back from her forehead. "Madchen told me that husbands and wives need each other."

"Do you get all of your advice from Madchen?"

"Absolutely not. Most of it comes from Silas."

They laughed, then Rosalie sat up. "We have to tell them who Caterina is," Rosalie said as Lochlyn put his arm around her. "I don't like lying to Madchen."

"We do need to tell them the truth," Lochlyn agreed. "They can help us keep Caterina and her baby safe. We can tell Madchen when we meet her for breakfast. Why don't you invite Caterina to come with us? I'm sure she'll be hungry."

"Will it be safe to speak of such things in the kitchens?"

"Absolutely. No one enters Madchen's kitchens without her approval."

Rosalie glanced at the clock and stood. "I'll wake her and we'll get ready. Will you meet us there?"

"No," Lochlyn said as he rose to his full height. Rosalie often felt small next to her husband, but never scared. In fact, she felt as if Lochlyn would stand between her and all the evils of the world. "I will wait right here, and we will go together," he continued, bringing her hand to his mouth and kissing her knuckles. "If you'd like me to, that is."

"I would," Rosalie said, her cheeks warming. "I'll be but a moment."

With that, Rosalie went to the bedchamber at the back of her apartment to wake her sister. The room was meant for a lady's maid, but it had suited her sister's needs quite well. "Up, now," she said as she gently shook Caterina's shoulder. "We've been invited to breakfast in the kitchens."

"Have we?" Caterina asked as she pushed herself upright. "You're taking up with the servants, just like you did at home."

"Not just the servants," Rosalie said; if it hadn't been for the groundskeepers letting her help in the gardens and teaching her about plants or the kitchen staff sneaking her leftover food, she would have run away from Irontooth Keep years ago. "Lochlyn will be there too."

"The duke eats in the kitchens?" Caterina asked. "I'd imagined him dining off golden plates."

"We use regular plates. But they're very nice." Rosalie rummaged through her wardrobe and handed Caterina a dress. "Here. This should fit you. We can send for the seamstress later so she can take your measurements and get started on a few things for you to wear."

"I didn't come here for handouts," Caterina said as she stared at the dress in her hands.

"I realize that," Rosalie said. "However, you can't go around in the same dress day in and day out. It will be good for you to have a few things of your own."

Caterina's shoulders slumped. She clutched her borrowed garment to her breast. "Thank you. I'm sorry for snapping at you."

"It's all right," Rosalie said. "But please hurry and put that on. Lochlyn's waiting for us in the front room."

"Is he?" Caterina went to the door and opened it a crack. "He doesn't look impatient. I thought you two didn't get on well."

"We haven't really had a chance to get to know each other," Rosalie said as she finished buttoning her own dress. It was pale lilac, perfect for the morning. "But we stayed up talking last night. I feel we may get along after all."

"That's wonderful. Now sit, and I'll do your hair."

Rosalie complied, and Caterina set about brushing and braiding her hair. "Cat."

"Hmm?"

"I saved your mother's letters," Rosalie replied. "The entire trunk is under my bed."

Caterina leaned forward and embraced Rosalie. "Thank you," she said, squeezing Rosalie's shoulders. "They're all I really wanted to take with me, but the trunk was too heavy for me to carry. Saving them is the best thing you could have done for me."

"Of course. Danae's letters helped me, too." Rosalie hardly remembered Caterina's mother, but her kindness was evident in the many letters she wrote to her daughter so long ago. "Are you going to write letters to your child?"

"Perhaps," Caterina said as she straightened and resumed braiding Rosalie's hair. "I can explain how to escape from a locked tower and evade armed guards. Won't that be helpful?"

Soon enough, Caterina had twisted Rosalie's long blonde curls into a coronet. When the sisters joined Lochlyn in the sitting room, he immediately took Rosalie's hand.

"You look wonderful," he said as he ran his hand over her hair. "I've never seen your hair up before."

"Caterina did it," Rosalie said. "Do you like it?"

"I do." Lochlyn cleared his throat and offered Caterina a shallow bow. "Lady Caterina. I trust you slept well?"

"Yes, thank you, my lord," she replied. "I'm told we're off to breakfast?"

Lochlyn offered Rosalie his arm, and the three of them crossed the castle to the warm, bustling kitchens. Madchen had a table set in a window niche that was far enough away for them to enjoy their meal in peace, but close enough for her to keep an eye on everything. When they arrived, Rosalie went to Madchen and took her hands.

"Madchen, I lied to you, and I'm so sorry," she said.

"There, there," Madchen said. "I'm sure that whatever happened, you acted with the best of intentions."

"I did," Rosalie said, then she drew Caterina beside her. "This is my sister, Caterina."

"Well met, my lady," Madchen said as she curtsied. When she straightened, she glanced between Lochlyn and Caterina, but that was her only acknowledgment of the awkward situation. "Will you be joining us for breakfast?" she asked, motioning for a fourth chair and table setting to be brought over.

"Yes, thank you. And please don't be cross with Rosie," Caterina added. "This is quite possibly the first lie she's ever told."

"Unlike you, who always had a story to back up whatever nonsense you were getting into," Rosalie said.

"I never got caught, did I?" Caterina asked, then she frowned as she set her hand on her belly. "Well, not until the end."

"And what a capture it was," Rosalie said as they took their places around the table and Madchen retrieved their meal.

"My lord and ladies, I do hope you'll enjoy what we've prepared today," Madchen said, bringing over a covered platter.

"Madchen, everything you've ever served me has been wonderful," Lochlyn said. "But I was hoping for griddle cakes."

"You're in luck," Madchen said as she removed the cloche and revealed a stack of the warm, syrupy cakes. Lochlyn served everyone himself, and even Caterina admitted how good the cakes were.

"Lady Caterina," Madchen began, refilling everyone's teacup, "I recall that your mother was the king's niece, is that right?"

"That's true," Caterina said. "She was the Princess Danae."

"Caterina was the only real nobility in the house," Rosalie added. "It vexed our father that even with all his money, he couldn't buy himself a lineage. How he ever convinced Danae to marry him is a mystery."

"That was a double failure on his part," Caterina said.

"How so?" Madchen prompted.

"He's always tried taking up with women who were descended from either nobility or directly from the Otherworldly creatures, thinking it would make him royalty by association," Caterina explained. "However, even though the king is descended from basilisks, and is a shifter himself, that blood is only ever inherited by men. My mother didn't have a drop of it, and neither do I."

"Thank the Fates for that," Rosalie muttered. "Basilisks are so unnerving."

Lochlyn stilled, his fork halfway to his mouth. Seeing his discomfort, Madchen asked Rosalie, "Do you not care for scaled creatures?"

"Oh, it has nothing to do with them being scaly or serpentine," Rosalie explained. "It's their round, watery eyes that can mesmerize you into doing all sorts of awful things." She shuddered, adding, "In the matter of scaled beasts, I prefer dragons. Like the one in our atrium."

"Do you?" Lochlyn asked as he resumed eating. "I recall you once said he was handsome."

"He is," Rosalie replied with a coy glance.

"Rosie, what did you do for your birthday this year?" Caterina asked loudly, interrupting their flirting and silencing Rosalie.

Lochlyn looked up at Madchen, who shook her head slightly. "When was your birthday?" he asked.

"A few weeks ago," Rosalie replied. "And to answer your question, Cat, I spent the day painting."

"Really?" Caterina asked. "At home, you always made such a spectacle of your birthday. Out of all our siblings, your birthday was the only one known by the entire household."

"Yes, well," Rosalie said, pushing her food around her plate. "It was nice having a quiet day this year."

"Lady Caterina, the midwife should be arriving soon," Madchen said as she checked her pocket watch. "Is there anything I can assist you with beforehand?"

"I'm not sure," Caterina said as she placed her hand on her belly. "I think I've had enough. The cakes were wonderful, Madchen. I'll just go rest for a bit."

"Please, let me assist you," Madchen said, and the two got up and left the table.

"I should go with them," Rosalie said, pushing back from the table and following her sister and Madchen. When she got to the corridor, she felt Lochlyn's hand on her arm.

"Why didn't you say anything about your birthday?" he asked after she halted. "Caterina made it seem like it's important to you."

"It is, but..." Rosalie exhaled and crossed her arms over her stomach. "It was shortly after we fought, and I challenged you to make an effort. I didn't want you to think I was expecting a certain type of celebration, or that you honoring my birthday was some kind of a test. One of Father's mistresses frequently dropped hints about her expectations, and he flailed around like a fool trying to make her happy. It was exhausting watching her lead him around by his..." Rosalie glanced at Lochlyn. "Nose."

"And you don't want to lead me by my... nose?"

"I don't," she replied. "And the fact remains that when you married me, I was twenty-one, and now I am twenty-two."

Lochlyn set his hand on her nape, his thumb stroking the corner of her jaw. "Twenty-two? I thought you were almost ten years younger than me."

Rosalie raised her brows. "You thought I was twelve?"

"No, no! More like eighteen, maybe a bit older. I'm twenty-six," he added. "I don't think I ever told you that."

"You didn't." Rosalie fingered the top button on his vest. "Is your birthday soon?"

"It's in autumn." His hand trailed from her jaw to her neck. "I like that we're close in age."

"Is that why you're so careful with me?" she asked. "Because you thought I was little more than a child?"

He nodded. "I don't want to hurt you. Not in any way."

Rosalie tentatively set her hands on his chest. "I don't think you'd ever hurt me."

"Never," he said as he gathered her against him. "You're the safest woman in the realm, my rose petal. And next year we'll have a double celebration for your birthday."

"We will?" she asked, her voice wavering. Until that moment, she hadn't been sure she'd still be at Dragon Ridge in a year's time. But now Lochlyn was planning something for her birthday, and she could hardly believe it. "Can we have cakes? And I still need a story about young Lochie."

"Is that so, Rosie?" he asked, then he held her face in his hands. "We will have whatever you want."

CHAPTER TEN

MIDWIVES AND MESSENGERS

Lochlyn stood in front of the windows in Rosalie's front room, his back straight as an arrow and his hands clasped behind him as he contemplated the world outside. Rosalie watched her husband for a time, admiring his dark hair and broad shoulders, and wondered if he was scanning the horizon for danger. Ever since he'd told Rosalie about Dragon Ridge's network of spies, she'd been curious as to why exactly Lochlyn needed them. Perhaps the rumors she'd been told the day before her wedding were true, and there was immense wealth hidden in the mountains in the form of ancient dragon hoards. Then again, Lochlyn might not have been thinking about spies and subterfuge at all; perhaps he was only watching the clouds scurry across the sky.

With a sigh, Rosalie selected a book from the stack she'd brought back from the library. She smiled as she recalled how Lochlyn showed her around the shelves, meticulously explaining how the books were organized, and the lengths to which Silas had gone in order to add to the collection. Lochlyn was proud of his home, and treated his staff with kindness and respect, which in turn made Dragon Ridge a calm, comfortable place. Her new home was the opposite of the harsh environment she'd grown up in, where her father would publicly berate the staff for the slightest misdeed. Rosalie appreciated every difference between the two.

After a final glance toward Lochlyn, Rosalie sat on the couch and opened her book. It was one of the botany texts she'd found, and it had an entire section on ornamental vines that she was eager to start on. She'd only thumbed through a few pages when Lochlyn abandoned his vigil and sat beside her.

"Do you like that book?" Lochlyn asked.

"Forgive me," she said, fearing he'd thought her rude for paying more attention to the book than to him.

"No, no," he said as he set his hand on top of hers. "Please, keep reading. I like seeing you happy. I'm glad you're enjoying the books."

"The ones on botany are most helpful." Lochlyn's thumb stroked her little finger, and Rosalie felt the sensation all the way to the roots of her hair. "The illustrations give me ideas for my paintings."

Lochlyn leaned forward to the low table and selected the other botany text Rosalie had picked out. He flipped through the pages until he found a section on roses. "As I recall, this is the breed of rose you wore in your hair at our wedding," he said, turning the pages toward her.

"I can't believe you remember that," she said. "Or that you knew where to find that entry."

"You forget, beloved, I grew up here. I've read many of our books. And," he added, "I remember everything about that day."

Rosalie's cheeks warmed, then she glanced toward the closed bedchamber door. When she and Lochlyn had returned to her rooms, they found that Caterina and the midwife were already sequestered, and they had decided against disturbing them. "They've been in there quite a while."

"I imagine there is much to discuss." Lochlyn set down the botany text and picked up one of the other books he'd carried back to Rosalie's chamber. It was a thick volume about Otherworldly creatures and the lore associated with them.

"What do you know about the Order of the Sun?" he asked.

"What everyone else does, I suppose. I know that they're the best trained knights in the realm, and that Curran is a member. I don't know much more than that." She eyed her husband. "Something tells me you're quite familiar with them."

"They're called the Order of the Sun because the knights themselves are sunbirds. Phoenixes," Lochlyn amended. "Each and every one of them."

"You mean to tell me that Curran carries the blood of phoenixes?" she asked. "How could you possibly know that?"

"I am certain because to be admitted to the Order you need to not only carry the blood, but it must also be strong enough for the bearer to shift forms," he said. "When your father said he would set your brothers after Curran as punishment, it wasn't a death sentence. After the fight's conclusion, he would have burned Curran's body and caused him to be reborn."

Rosalie's brow pinched. "If what you say is true, what does that mean for the child? Will he carry the blood, too?" She grasped Lochlyn's hand. "What if the Order comes for the baby, or for Cat?"

"If they do, I will protect them." Lochlyn moved closer to her and caressed her cheek. "I won't let anything happen to your sister or the baby. Not if I can help it."

"How can you protect them against a host of phoenixes?" Rosalie asked, her voice rising as she imagined a swarm of fiery birds descending upon their home. "Lochlyn, they could destroy us."

"They won't." Lochlyn pulled her into his arms and tucked her head beneath his chin. "Dragon Ridge is strong, beloved, and I don't let my people suffer. We're all safe here." Rosalie nodded, because she believed in Lochlyn. She heard the bedroom door open, just then the midwife joined them.

"My lord, my lady," she said as she curtsied. "Our mother is healthy, if a bit undernourished. The boy has been taking everything from her."

"Boy?" Rosalie repeated.

"Aye, it's a boy," the midwife replied. "I've a bit of the sight, and I've never been wrong when it comes to seeing a babe's entry into the world."

Rosalie was impressed; she'd heard of midwives who could see a pregnancy's outcome, but their services were so valued they were usually employed by kings. "A son, then," Rosalie murmured. "Caterina must be pleased with the news."

"She was," the midwife said. "She's already considering a few names."

"Have you any idea when this boy will join us?" Lochlyn asked.

"Soon," she replied. "Inside of a week, perhaps even later today."

"That's impossible," Rosalie said. "Cat only met the father a few months ago. There is no way she could be so close to her lying in."

"Normally, I would agree with you, but a phoenix's heat makes the babe grow faster," the midwife replied. "The fledglings usually come in four months, sometimes much less."

Rosalie stared at the midwife. "Phoenix? Exactly what made you use that word?"

"Oh yes, the boy is assuredly a phoenix. All the signs are there."

A knock sounded at Rosalie's door. "Not now," she yelled, then she faced Lochlyn. "What are we going to do?"

"Whatever we need to," he said. Rosalie's door opened then, and Silas entered the room.

"My lord, the king's messenger has just arrived," Silas announced.

"Why did the king send a messenger here?" Rosalie demanded. "Today of all days, why is this happening?"

"It's not that unusual," Lochlyn soothed. "Olivar corresponds with me regularly."

"My lord, the messenger is waiting for your reply," Silas said.

"That is unusual," Lochlyn murmured. "Beloved, I must deal with this. Talk to the midwife and be with your sister." When Rosalie remained silent, he asked, "Will you be all right without me for a short time?"

"Yes, of course," she said. "Go. Handle what needs to be done."

Lochlyn held her face close to his and kissed her. "We will get past this," he promised before leaving with Silas. Rosalie turned toward the midwife, who had been watching their conversation with interest.

"Are you quite familiar with phoenix births?" Rosalie asked. "Are they dangerous?"

"I have attended a few, and, yes, they can be," the midwife replied. "As for the degree of danger, it all depends on how strong the blood is within the child. If he's a phoenix in legacy only, it will be a regular birth."

"And if he's strong in the blood?" Rosalie pressed. "What then?"

"I cannot say, exactly," she replied. "Some say the mother will run hot, both in her body and in her temper, but the strongest phoenixes are born in fire."

"Fire?" Rosalie squeaked. "Is my sister going to burn to death?"

The midwife spread her palms. "That, I cannot say. But what we can do, my lady, is prepare."

"Yes," Rosalie said, nodding frantically. She'd been preparing for disasters her whole life, beginning with when her father sent her mother back to the brothel and Rosalie was terrified she'd be sent there next, to her sister's impending marriage and therefore the day Caterina would leave her, to Rosalie's own unexpected wedding. She would listen to the midwife's advice and prepare for Caterina's baby so well that both mother and child would emerge unscathed. "Tell me what we need, and I'll make sure we have it ready."

Lochlyn closed the door to Rosalie's chamber and paused to take a breath. He regretted leaving his beloved wife when she so clearly needed him, but he had to deal with the messenger as soon as possible and send him on his way. The last thing Lochlyn needed was for word to get back to the king of Caterina's presence at Dragon Ridge.

"Did the messenger disclose anything to you?" he asked Silas as they began walking toward the castle's receiving room.

"He's hardly said a word since he arrived," Silas replied. "He's got the sealed message on his person and claims he'll hand it to no one but you."

"How efficient of him. Did he arrive with a guard?"

"Yes, he came with two men. Madchen's serving them refreshments in the kitchens."

Lochlyn smiled; his housekeeper excelled at distracting unwanted guests. "After they've gone, I'll need you to do a bit of research for me. It may involve you acquiring some new stock for the library. Or gaining knowledge through other means."

"Oh?" Silas enjoyed research, almost as much as he enjoyed deploying the Ridge's vast network of spies. "What will I be researching? New breeds of roses for Lady Blackmoor's garden?"

"Of course." Lochlyn entered the receiving chamber and regarded the messenger. He was dressed for battle, clad in chain mail with a tabard depicting a basilisk and his sword worn across his back.

"Lord Blackmoor," the messenger greeted as he bowed. "I bring word from King Olivar."

"So I've been told. Let's have it, then." He accepted the letter from the messenger and lightly touched the wax seal. It was emerald green, and bore the imprint of a basilisk that matched the messenger's insignia. Lochlyn cracked the seal through the center of the creature and began reading.

Lord Blackmoor,

It saddens me that I cannot address you as nephew, being that your marriage to my niece did not occur. Osman, her despicable sire, tells me that Caterina ran off with a phoenix knight. Is this true? And have you tried to locate her?

I understand that you married Caterina's half-sister once my niece became unavailable to you. While I appreciate you making the best of the situation, I would much prefer it if you were linked to my dynasty, especially after the disappointment that was Carys. Once Caterina is found, assuming she is unharmed and of sound mind, I expect you to dissolve your current union and wed my niece as intended. In the meantime, please keep me apprised of your efforts to find her, and to bring the rogue knight that kidnapped my niece to justice.

May the Fates guide us well,

Olivar the Majestic

Lochlyn lowered the parchment and took a slow, steadying breath. If the messenger hadn't been in the same room as Lochlyn, he would have crumpled up the paper and thrown it into the fire. How dare Olivar command him to dissolve his marriage to Rosalie! King's edict or no, there was no way Lochlyn would give Rosalie up for anything short of death; even then, he wouldn't hesitate to cross the veil in order to reunite with her. Rosalie was his perfect mate, of that Lochlyn was certain, and he would do anything to keep her with him.

However, these were opinions best kept to himself. At least, until the messenger had departed. "I trust you have a parchment and quill?" Lochlyn asked.

"Of course, my lord." The messenger set a sheet of parchment and a quill and inkpot on the table and stepped aside. It was Olivar's practice to have those writing to him do so in the presence of his man, to ensure the letters hadn't been compromised. Lochlyn dipped his quill in the ink and began writing his reply.

My most gracious king,

Thank you for your recent missive. What you have heard is correct, and Caterina did indeed run away with her guard before we could be married. It was most disappointing, but there is a bright spot amid the tragedy. My marriage to Caterina's sister, Rosalie, has brought me great joy. We are quite compatible with one another, and I foresee spending many happy years with her. Truly, when the Fates end one path, They guide us toward another.

Regarding my wife, I sent paperwork to the royal scribe to have her formally named Lady Blackmoor some time ago. I realize that the search for Caterina is ongoing, yet having Rosalie officially added to my house will ensure the legitimacy of our children. As you know, heirs are quite important to the Blackmoor line.

As for Caterina, I can assure you that the search will continue. Please know that no one wishes for her safety more than Rosalie and myself, and I will do everything in my power to ensure her wellbeing. I have no notion of where the phoenix, a knight that goes by Curran, could be sequestered, but I have my guard searching for him. I will keep you apprised of the results.

May the Fates keep us in the palms of Their hands,
Lochlyn Blackmoor

Lochlyn fanned the paper to dry the ink, then he fetched a bit of wax from the supplies Silas kept in the chamber to seal the letter.

"I have a brass spoon for melting the wax," the messenger offered.

"No need." Lochlyn folded the letter shut and set the wax on the seam. He exhaled a fiery breath onto the wax; once it had melted, he withdrew his pendant and pressed it onto the molten liquid. Thus sealed, he handed the letter to the messenger.

"Please give my regards to our most gracious king," Lochlyn said. He noted how the messenger's hand trembled, and he smiled. It pleased him that Olivar's lackeys feared him and what he could do. "Would you and your men care to remain for supper?"

"No thank you, my lord," he replied, stowing his quill and ink in a leather pouch. "We have instructions to return to the palace immediately."

The messenger bowed. He was then escorted from the chamber by Silas. Lochlyn resumed his seat at the writing desk and withdrew a fresh sheet of paper. He opened his inkpot, dipped the pen, and began making a list. By the time Silas returned, Lochlyn had already filled half of the sheet.

"Working on your correspondence?" Silas asked.

"Have Olivar's men left?" Lochlyn asked.

Silas went to the window overlooking the front courtyard. "Yes. I see them on the road."

"Good. Olivar is quite interested in the fate of his niece, understandably so. I, however, am more interested in phoenixes as a whole. I need you to procure whatever information you can about all aspects of their life, from birth onward. If anyone questions you, explain that we are acting at the behest of the king." He offered the sheet of paper to Silas. "Here. I've made a list of what I need to know."

"Very well. Our spymaster has a contact within the Order. Shall I reach out to them first?"

"Yes. Do." Lochlyn rubbed his eyes. "Olivar also said that when Caterina is found, I'm to end my marriage to Rosalie and take Caterina as my wife."

"It seems like no one would want that, except Olivar," Silas said. "And won't Caterina prefer to return to her child's father?"

"One would assume." Lochlyn drummed his fingers on the desk. "While the king didn't say as much, I believe he's held up the paperwork that will formally name Rosalie a Blackmoor."

"That he cannot do," Silas said. "The lineages are held within the temple and guarded by priestesses. The only person who could contest Rosalie's name changing is her father, and we know Osman won't do so."

"True. Does Madchen's cousin still work within the temple?"

"She does. I'll have Madchen reach out to her today." Silas folded the list Lochlyn had given him and placed it in his coat pocket. "As for the midwife, she's compiling a list of supplies we'll need for the princess's lying in. We've seen many things here at Dragon Ridge, but this will be the first phoenix birth we'll have."

"Hopefully, it's the last," Lochlyn murmured. "Spare no expense for the lying in. If anyone questions why such supplies are needed, say they're for my wife." Lochlyn withdrew his pocket watch and checked the time. "I should return to her now."

"Actually, my lord, the masons will be here shortly," Silas said. "They're due to present the plans for the bridge."

Lochlyn snapped his watch shut and stowed it in his pocket. "Very well. I'll deal with them before returning to Rosalie. If she asks for me, please let her know I'll be in my study."

"As you wish," Silas said, then he departed. Instead of immediately retreating to his study, Lochlyn approached the front windows and gazed toward the village nestled in the valley below.

He understood quite well why Olivar wanted his family line attached to the Blackmoors: power. Olivar believed in making shows of power, and he regularly reinforced his ranks with phoenix knights. However, Lochlyn had proven more than once that he was stronger than a company of phoenixes, and he was much stronger than Olivar—who was unable to fully shift—would ever be. Lochlyn wasn't afraid of the king, and he had no intention of dissolving his marriage. Instead, he would use every ounce of his strength to keep Rosalie by his side. If his actions displease the king, so be it.

CHAPTER ELEVEN

MANY FAULTS

After the midwife left for the village to secure supplies for the impending lying in, Caterina and Rosalie remained in the sitting room. Much to Rosalie's surprise, Caterina was unbothered by the possibility of her son entering the world in a blazing fire.

"I'm still shocked that Curran is a phoenix," Rosalie said. "He's the only person I've ever met with enough of the old blood for them to manifest as a creature. He never mentioned anything about that, or his Order?" She poured a glass of claret and offered it to her sister.

"No, thank you," Caterina said as she waved the glass away. "The bigger I get, the more wine tastes like vinegar. And to answer your question, Curran spoke very little about himself. He was proud of being a knight though. The Order meant a great deal to him."

"Perhaps he returned to them," Rosalie said. She almost asked Caterina, again, if she were scared about the baby being born in fire—but she held her tongue. Caterina had an uncanny ability to ignore the consequences of her actions until it was too late. Rosalie knew very little about phoenixes and births in general, so she decided to leave such matters to the more experienced midwife.

"Have you decided when you'd like to write to your uncle?" she asked instead. When Madchen came to check on the sisters, she advised that the king had written to Lochlyn, asking for news of his niece. Thankfully, Lochlyn hadn't revealed the truth in his response.

"Oh, you mean our gracious king?" Caterina grimaced. She shifted her position. "Yes, I suppose he'll be interested in this turn of events."

"I'd say so," Rosalie murmured. "Your child has a claim to the throne."

"A very small claim," Caterina said.

"Still," Rosalie said. "If he's anything like Father, he'll want to keep a close eye on all of his heirs." Rosalie paused, then said, "And you were supposed to marry into the Blackmoor line. I wonder if the king had a hand in arranging that."

"Personally, I don't think the king is overly concerned about where I end up," Caterina said. "He's corresponded with me exactly once since my mother died, and that was only to remind me that I am far, far down the line of succession. However, I can confirm that Father has wanted an heir in Dragon Ridge's bloodline for years. It looks like that's up to you now."

"I don't know when that will happen," Rosalie muttered. "Lochlyn seems intent on treating me as if I'm made of glass. And did you know that Father told Lochlyn I'm ten years younger than him! Can you believe that?"

"Father probably thought the duke was an old lech like him, that he'd prefer a younger wife," Caterina said. "He went out of his way to show me off like a prized calf to whomever he wanted to ally with. It's why he went through the trouble of hiring Curran to guard my chastity." She laughed shortly. "And we know how that worked out."

"But offering you up as a virgin was a more attractive option," Rosalie murmured. "Though I wonder why Father wanted to be associated with Dragon Ridge so badly. If he only wanted to marry you off to a noble, or even to someone with shifter's blood, there were simpler options."

"Look around; Lochlyn has what father loves most: wealth." Caterina gestured toward the carved marble columns, the fine artwork on the walls, and the delicate crystal Rosalie was drinking from. "Lochlyn has more wealth than he knows what to do with. Father's convinced there's a hoard of gold inside one of these mountains, and he wanted me to find the key. Though, I suppose, finding the treasure's also up to you now."

"I wouldn't know where to look," Rosalie said as she refilled her glass. "Lochlyn and I only really started spending time together yesterday. Did you know that he barely looked at me when we got married? Then he left me to ride alone in a freezing cold carriage all the way here. And when I finally arrived, I was in bed with a fever for more than a week. He never even checked on me."

"Most men can't handle sickness; theirs or someone else's. After you recovered, how long did it take him to get in your bed?"

"He hasn't even tried. He's always polite and formal, and even affectionate. But he's very controlled." Rosalie twirled the stem of her wineglass in her fingers. "I can count on my fingers the number of times he's kissed me."

"Interesting. Is he a eunuch?" Caterina asked.

Rosalie almost choked. She set down her wineglass and asked, "Do you think he might be?"

"I can think of no other reason why he would keep to himself. His prowess on the battlefield is legendary, and everyone knows that warriors tend to be just as lusty in the bedroom," she added with a knowing glance.

Rosalie imagined Lochlyn in the heat of battle, shirtless and sweaty and wielding a sword. "He's a warrior of some renown?"

"Oh, yes," Caterina said. "Stories have been told about his many conquests, both on and off the battlefield, which is why I find it all the stranger that he's left you be. Honestly, Rosie, you've got to pay more attention to what goes on in the world."

"I don't like the world," she replied. The world was hard and cold and cruel—which was why she'd made herself a warm, soft sanctuary in her rooms. "Perhaps we should discuss your baby."

"My baby is fine where he is. But you must see how poorly your habit of hiding from the world has served you," Caterina said.

Rosalie arched a single golden brow. "Are you truly lecturing me about my choices?"

"Someone has to," Caterina replied. "Do you like being married to Lochlyn?"

"Yes," Rosalie replied without hesitation. "When we do spend time with each other, we get on quite well."

"Then I don't understand what's keeping you two apart," Caterina said. "Does Lochlyn keep a lover?"

"What?" Rosalie demanded. "First you think he's lost his manhood, now you think he has a mistress?"

"I wasn't serious about Lochlyn being cockless," Caterina admitted. "However, he probably does have a lover, or two. Most lords do."

"He does not," Rosalie insisted, though her voice wavered. "There's no one here but us and the servants!"

"Then one of the servants is likely warming his bed. Unless he makes sure his lovers stay down in the village."

"No." Rosalie shook her head, hardly able to consider that Lochlyn had been sharing his bed with someone else, but it would explain where he'd been all these nights. "Lochlyn's not like that."

"How are you so certain? By your own admission, you barely know him."

Rosalie clutched her wineglass so tightly that the stem snapped. She yelped as the jagged glass sliced into her skin. She watched the blood drip through her fingers.

"Are you all right?" Caterina demanded.

"I'm fine," Rosalie muttered. As she pressed a napkin against her palm, she prayed that her sister was wrong about Lochlyn.

Caterina went to lie down while Rosalie remained before the hearth, everything they'd discussed swirling inside her head. She got herself a new glass and poured herself some more claret. She stared into the flames as she thought about her unusual relationship with her husband.

She knew Lochlyn held some form of affection for her. He said so often enough. From his favored pet name for her, beloved, to when he claimed she held his heart in her hands. But that didn't explain why, in the months since coming to Dragon Ridge, she hadn't once seen his rooms, or why he'd never attempted to take her to bed. Even when she sat on his lap wearing nothing but her nightgown, he hadn't done more than kiss her. No man would ignore their wife for so long, unless that man was having his needs met elsewhere.

Rosalie's heart fell as she realized that Caterina was right. Lochlyn *was* keeping a lover, and she was a fool. She looked down at the cut on her palm, then clenched her fist.

She was mad, and she needed answers. Now.

Rosalie stalked out of her apartment and toward the main staircase, intending to let Lochlyn know exactly how she felt about him taking a mistress while she wasted away in her rooms. When she got to the atrium, she stopped short. Lochlyn had never given her that promised tour of the castle, and she had no idea where her husband could be. As she contemplated where she should begin her search, Silas entered the atrium from the main doors.

"Lady Blackmoor," Silas said as he approached her. Rosalie had never known her own grandfather, but she imagined he was like the steward: a kindly old man filled with knowledge, and a head of wild gray hair that had a mind of its own. "Is there something I can help you with?"

"I want to speak with my husband," she replied. "Do you know where he is?"

"Why yes. He's in his study. If you'd like, I can escort you there."

"That would be wonderful, Silas," she said, rather harshly, but Silas didn't deserve her anger. "Thank you," she added in a softer tone.

"Think nothing of it," Silas said as he swept his arm toward the stairs. "His study is on the second floor. I'll just bring you to the door."

Rosalie climbed the stairs in front of Silas, pretending she knew the way. What sort of woman couldn't navigate her own home? A fool who'd been ignoring what was happening right under her nose, that's who.

"Here we are," Silas announced when they reached the study's door. "Now, I'll be in my own study, which is at the end of this hallway," he said, pointing the way. "Please, feel free to call on me if you need anything at all."

"Thank you again, Silas," Rosalie said, then she knocked on the door.

"Yes?" Lochlyn called. Rosalie opened the door and closed it behind her; she didn't need the staff to hear what she was about to discuss with her husband. When she turned around, she saw Lochlyn sitting behind his desk with many ledgers and other stacks of paperwork spread across the surface.

"Rosalie," he said, smiling. "What can I do for you?"

"What's wrong with me?" she demanded.

"Nothing," he replied, though he was visibly taken aback. "You're perfect."

"Then why won't you touch me?" she demanded. "Why did you marry me if you didn't want to sleep with me?"

"I do want you." He rose and came around the desk. "What brought this on?"

"I was talking to Caterina. She wanted to know what our life was like, and all I did was tell her about what we hadn't done. Damn it, Lochlyn, it's been months and you've all but ignored me."

He stopped short as his brow furrowed. "I didn't want to force myself on you."

"Well, you've accomplished that." Lochlyn reached for her hands, so Rosalie crossed her arms over her breast to evade him. "Do you have a lover?"

He stepped closer to her as his eyes darkened. "I would never dishonor you by taking a lover."

"Then who are you fucking?" she demanded.

Lochlyn blinked. She'd shocked him. Good. "No one!"

"You expect me to believe the Black Duke of Dragon Ridge is celibate?"

"Don't call me that," he said, his eyes flashing red, then black. "And you can believe it because it's the truth."

Rosalie wanted to believe him, but she didn't know if she should. Instead of continuing that line of questioning, she asked her second, more scandalous question. "Are you a eunuch?"

Lochlyn snatched her hand from under her arm and set it on his crotch. "No."

Rosalie gasped, before realizing that he was trying to shock her as she'd done to him. Deciding to call his bluff, she grasped his cock and squeezed.

"Trying to make me a eunuch?" he asked. "Going to take more than your pretty fingers."

"Oh, so my fingers are pretty?" she asked. His body hardened as she tightened her grip. "Is that all you like about me?"

Lochlyn hooked his fingers in the front of her dress and pulled her against him with such force she bumped against his chest. Rosalie gasped as she set her hand on top of his, concerned he would tear her dress open. While she'd intended to confront Lochlyn, things were rapidly getting out of hand.

"You know I think you're stunning," he said, his voice a growl that prickled her skin.

"Then why do you stay so far away from me?" she demanded. "You stuck me in those remote rooms on the other side of the castle, and you hardly ever see me. Don't you know how humiliating that is? You've been treating me more like a sister than—"

Lochlyn's eyes went fully black, then he crushed his mouth to hers. Rosalie yelped, the sound softening to a moan as his hands roamed across her body. Without breaking the kiss, he slid his hands down to her bottom, picked her up and set her on the edge of the desk. Once they were more of a height, one of Lochlyn's hands moved to her nape while the other grasped her hip. Rosalie's lips parted for him, and she shivered when his tongue stroked hers.

Rosalie had been kissed before. Many times. But she had never been kissed like that.

She sunk one of her hands into his dark hair, while the other clutched the front of his shirt. When she moaned into his mouth, Lochlyn's hand slipped under her skirts. He grasped her calf and pulled her to him, so close her breasts were pressed against his chest. She flattened her palm between them and felt his heart beating under her hand.

"I don't think of you as a sister," Lochlyn rasped when they parted. "Have I made my point, or do I need to spread you over the desk?" he asked, his thumb stroking the bare skin of her knee. Rosalie swallowed hard; just then the door opened behind them.

"My lord, the masons here," Silas said as he poked his head into the study.

"Come no further," Lochlyn ordered.

"Apologies," Silas said. Rosalie wondered if the steward had ever caught his master in such an awkward situation before. "I'll tell them you're indisposed."

"My wife and I were just having a discussion," Lochlyn said without breaking Rosalie's gaze. "Please ask them to wait for me."

"As you wish," Silas said. As soon as the door clicked shut, Rosalie ducked her head.

"I should go," she mumbled, embarrassment hot on her cheeks.

"You should stay," he began, then he saw the cut on her palm. "You're hurt? When did this happen?"

"Earlier, I broke a wineglass. It will heal."

"Stay put," Lochlyn said, before going to the wall behind his desk. It was covered with several wooden drawers with brass pulls. The lower drawers were wide and shallow, perhaps to store maps, while the upper drawers ranged in sizes; from being large enough to store writing implements, to so small they could only hold a single finger ring.

"Lochlyn, you really don't need to go out of your way for me," Rosalie said as she watched him search through the drawers. "It's just a cut."

"You're hurt, which means I need to care for you." Lochlyn found what he was searching for and returned to Rosalie with a glass vial and a length of linen.

"What's that?" Rosalie asked.

"It's an antiseptic, to keep infection from setting in. This may sting a bit," he added as he poured some of the liquid onto the linen and dabbed at the wound. Rosalie bore the pain silently and watched as he bandaged her hand.

"Thank you," she murmured. Between the sting of the antiseptic and the gentle warmth of Lochlyn's hands, her thoughts were once again swimming inside her head.

"Of course," he said as he set the vial and linen aside. "Let's finish our talk."

"I don't want to keep you from your work," she said. "Go, deal with your visitors." Lochlyn put his hands on her hips and kept her in place.

"You're more important than any visitors," he said. "And you're right. I haven't been a good partner to you. I was so focused on not pushing you to do anything you weren't ready for that I ended up pushing you away. I'm so sorry, beloved."

"And I am guilty of not pushing back on you when I should have," she said as she draped her arms around his neck. "I hid in my rooms when I should have gone out to find you. I'm sorry for that. And for squeezing your cock," she added.

"Oh, you don't need to apologize for that. Your hand on my cock has been the best part of my day."

Rosalie laughed, hiding her face against his chest. The top buttons of his shirt had come undone, and his gold chain glinted against his throat. "You always wear this," she said as she stroked the links.

"It was my father's seal." Lochlyn withdrew the chain and showed Rosalie the shield-shaped pendant. "This is our coat of arms."

"There's a tiny dragon," Rosalie marveled as she traced the raised design and the ruby beneath it. "It's lovely."

"I'm glad you think so. And, actually." Lochlyn went back to the many drawers behind his desk and withdrew yet another item. In his hand was a more delicate version of his own necklace. "This one was my mother's. I want you to have it."

"Oh, no, Lochlyn." Rosalie shook her head. "I couldn't."

"It's meant to be worn by Lady Blackmoor," he said, fastening the chain behind her neck. "No one has more of a right to wear it than you, beloved."

"Thank you," Rosalie said as she examined her own pendant. Unlike Lochlyn's, hers was set with a sparkling blue stone. "Is this a sapphire?"

"It is. These stones were taken from the Blackmoors' first hoard." Lochlyn smoothed back her hair. "I don't have a lover here in the castle, down in the village, or anywhere else. I have many faults, but unfaithfulness isn't one of them."

"I believe you. I was just talking to Caterina earlier, and she was saying how you're a warrior, and how warriors are lusty in bed... And I got mad because you haven't been in my bed." Rosalie offered him a smile. "I shouldn't have barged in here and started a fight with you."

"Yes, you should have," Lochlyn insisted. "It's your right to know where I'm sleeping."

"Does that mean you'll sleep with me tonight?" she asked, when Silas knocked again.

"My lord, how long should I keep them waiting?" Silas asked, then he saw how close Lochlyn and Rosalie were. "I can tell them to return at another time."

"We'll be along in a moment," Lochlyn said. "Thank you, Silas."

The steward bowed and withdrew. Lochlyn grasped Rosalie's hips, then he lifted her off the desk and set her on her feet. "Ready to meet the masons?"

"You want me to go with you?" Rosalie was surprised and pleased by his request.

"Of course. We're partners. The Lord and Lady of Dragon Ridge." Lochlyn took Rosalie's hand and kissed her knuckles, then he kissed her lips. "You are so beautiful," he said when they parted. "And, yes, I'll gladly sleep with you tonight."

"We'll have to stay in your room," she said. "As you know, Caterina is sharing mine."

"Very well." Lochlyn kissed her once more before stepping back and offering her his arm. "Ready, Lady Blackmoor?"

"Ready, Lord Blackmoor."

CHAPTER TWELVE

MEETING THE MASONS

R osalie felt like she was walking on air.

With her head held high, she grasped Lochlyn's arm as they descended from his study toward the atrium. Finally, she felt as if she was Lochlyn's wife in more than name only. She was his partner, Lady Blackmoor, and they were handling the affairs of Dragon Ridge together.

When they stepped onto the lower portion of the staircase, Rosalie saw the group of masons who'd come from the village. Standing next to Silas were three men clad in clean but well-worn working attire. The central man, who Rosalie assumed was their leader, carried a leather case slung over his arm. When the men saw Rosalie and Lochlyn, they bowed, but she saw them whisper among themselves once they rose.

"Pay their conversation no mind," Lochlyn murmured when she stiffened beside him. "They're merely surprised that my wife is such a vision."

"Do you know why the masons have come today?" Rosalie asked as her cheeks warmed. "Do they have an appointment?"

"Yes, they do. They've been tasked with reinforcing and repairing the main bridge into the village. They've brought the plans for my approval. Our approval," he amended. They reached the atrium floor, and Lochlyn addressed the masons.

"We apologize for keeping you waiting," he began, placing his hand on Rosalie's shoulder. "Allow me to introduce my wife, Lady Blackmoor."

Rosalie covered Lochlyn's hand with her own and squeezed. Her husband was going out of his way to include her, and she appreciated it. "Hello."

"Well met, my lady," the head mason said as he dipped his chin. "Congratulations on your marriage, my lord. I'm sorry to have missed it."

"Thank you, Zephyn. We were wed at my bride's father's estate," Lochlyn replied. "I'm told you have a few plans for us to review?"

"Let us move to the receiving room, so we can examine the plans in detail," Silas suggested, ushering the five of them into the adjacent chamber. In a lower voice, he said to Rosalie, "In the village, they celebrate all of the past year's marriages at midsummer. If you'd like, I can make the arrangements for you and Lochlyn to be included."

"That's an excellent idea," Rosalie said. Out of the corner of her eye, she saw Lochlyn smile. "Please let me know how I can help."

"Of course," Silas said, then he approached the masons and indicated where they could display their plans for the bridge.

"You never told me about these celebrations," Rosalie whispered to Lochlyn.

"I'd forgotten all about them," Lochlyn whispered back. "I haven't attended one in years."

"Oh, we don't have to," she began, but he placed his fingers on her lips. Rosalie's pulse leaped, and as much as she enjoyed Lochlyn's gentle touches, she wished he'd keep his hands to himself when others were around.

"If you want to go, we will go. Now, let's have a look at these plans."

The head mason, Zephyn, unrolled his blueprints and spread them across the wide wooden table. Rosalie, who had always been interested in artwork of any sort, leaned closer. The drawings depicted a wide bridge set high above a chasm, with sculptures of dragons guarding either end. Pine forests blanketed both sides of the mountain, and the village was nestled in the valley below.

"This chasm appears to be amazingly deep," Rosalie said; there was a key in the lower corner, and, assuming everything had been drawn accurately to scale, crossing the chasm beneath this bridge was not for the faint of heart. "How can you complete the work safely?"

"We have a system of ropes and pulleys," Zephyn replied. "It's quite secure, and I haven't lost a worker yet. I also avoid hiring those with a fear of heights."

"Yes, that would be a detriment," Rosalie murmured, then she turned toward the windows to get a glimpse of the bridge in question. Her carriage had arrived via the main road, and Rosalie had never seen the bridge or the chasm. She thought of those down in the village, and wondered if such features made them feel safe, or isolated.

Rosalie placed her fingers against the window. Like many of the rooms in Dragon Ridge, an entire wall was made of glass from floor to ceiling. All that glass was lovely, but thanks to the fog she couldn't see a bridge or anything of note. Behind her, she heard Lochlyn questioning the masons about what materials would be used for the work, and when they expected the repairs to be complete.

"Everything appears to be in order," Lochlyn said after everything had been explained and agreed upon. "My lady, is there anything you would like to add?"

Rosalie pursed her lips. She wanted to make the crossing safer for all involved, but she needed a way to do that. "Can we see this bridge from here?" she asked.

"Absolutely." Lochlyn stood next to her and pointed toward the place where the bridge was located. "Well, usually we can. The valley is fogged over right now, which happens often this time of year. But the bridge is straight ahead, and through those trees."

"The fog must make crossing the bridge even more treacherous," Rosalie said, just then she thought of the perfect addition to the bridge. She faced the masons and asked, "These dragon statues. How big are they?"

"About half the size of a natural dragon," Zephyn replied.

Rosalie's brows peaked. Since she'd never seen a real dragon, that comparison meant nothing to her. Before she could ask exactly how big dragons tended to be, Lochlyn said, "Each statue is about two times my height."

"Why don't we have lanterns added to the dragons' mouths?" Rosalie suggested. "That way, it will make traveling much easier on foggy days. And it will mimic how real dragons breathe fire," she added.

"An excellent idea, my lady," Zephyn said, then he looked to Lochlyn for approval. "My lord?"

"You don't need my say so to move forward on these lanterns, or anything else," Lochlyn said. "An order from Lady Blackmoor is no different from an order issued directly from me. We give you leave to move forward with your repairs, and to add the lanterns."

"As you say, my lord and lady," Zephyn replied as he bowed. "Lady Blackmoor, our lord said you were wed at your father's estate. Is he Lord Irontooth?"

"Why, yes," Rosalie replied. "Have we met before?"

"I cannot say I've had the pleasure," Zephyn replied, "but I have done work at Irontooth Keep. It is a beautiful property."

"Thank you," Rosalie said, though she'd never found it beautiful. Oppressive and suffocating, yes. Perhaps the mason had noticed a bit of fine stonework she'd overlooked. "When I next speak with my father, I'll tell him you said so. Perhaps he'll have more work that needs to be seen to if you'd be interested."

"Much appreciated, my lady. My lord," Zephyn said, then he and his assistants bowed and withdrew. Lochlyn stood behind Rosalie and wrapped his arm around her shoulders.

"We have a problem," he murmured against her hair.

"Oh?" She twisted around and faced him. "What's that?"

"Since we had our talk upstairs, all I can think about is kissing you," he said, dipping his head and pressing his lips to hers. "How am I to ever get anything done?"

"We could do these things together," she said as she threaded her fingers into his dark, thick hair. "Although, I do need to check on Caterina. Will you be all right without me for a short time? Or," she asked, as she tugged at his vest, "do we have a few moments now?"

"We do," Lochlyn said. His brow then furrowed. "I haven't yet told you about my message from the king."

"What did it say?" Rosalie asked.

The mason returned to the doorway and cleared his throat. "Yes, Zephyn?" Lochlyn asked.

"Forgive me for intruding, but should these lanterns hang beneath the dragons' maws, or be placed inside?" he inquired.

"I defer to your expertise, my lord mason," Rosalie replied. "I'm certain whatever you create will be both functional and attractive."

"My lady honors me," Zephyn said, then he withdrew, and Rosalie's attention returned to her husband.

"We do get interrupted quite often," she said.

"I'll order everyone to leave the castle right away," Lochlyn said. "We'll have to cook our own meals and handle our own washing, but we'll be alone."

"If we're alone we won't need to do the washing," she said. "We can do away with our clothing and run around as bare as eggs. Although, I remember how you don't like being undressed around others," she added.

"You're never going to let me forget that, are you?" he asked as Rosalie laughed against his chest. "In all seriousness, beloved, we need to talk about that letter from the king."

"Was it bad?" she asked.

"Not bad, not yet." He caressed her cheek. "You're aware that he asked for news of Caterina?"

"Yes." Madchen had told her as much when she came to collect the list of supplies the midwife had put together. "He doesn't think she's here, does he?"

"I don't think so. However, he was quite plain that once Caterina is found, he expects me to end our marriage, and take her as my wife."

"Oh." Rosalie's breath hitched as her heart fell to the floor. "I suppose Caterina is a better match for you. She's a princess, after all, and I—"

"And you are my wife," Lochlyn said, tilting her chin upward. "Nothing will change that, not ever."

"Then why did you tell me about this?" she asked as her hands trembled.

"Because we are now as one, which means you should know what the king's thoughts are on the matter," he replied. "Olivar is a complex man, and his schemes have many layers to them. More importantly, I didn't want you to find out some other way and worry I agreed with him."

Rosalie's fingers walked up his chest and stroked the bare skin at the base of his throat. "Does this mean you'll defy the king's wishes for me?"

"Yes," he declared. "Now and forever, yes. If Olivar doesn't like who I'm married to, he can stuff his disapproval up his arse." Lochlyn held her gaze and added, "Nothing could make me give you up, not even the Fates Themselves."

She watched his face for a moment, but his earnest expression, coupled with his serious blue eyes, held only honesty. Satisfied with her husband's words, Rosalie slid her arms around his waist and laid her cheek against his chest. "Did I ever tell you that I prayed to the Fates the morning we were married?"

"No." Lochlyn's arms came around her shoulders, and he kissed the top of her head. "What did you pray for?"

"I thanked them for setting me on this path with you, and promised to see it through to the end," she said. "Who cares what a stupid king thinks anyway?"

Lochlyn laughed against her hair. "We Blackmoors certainly don't, do we?" He drew back and stroked her forehead with his thumb. "I only care what my intelligent, compassionate, beautiful wife thinks."

"And I only care for my strong, handsome husband's opinions," she said. "What are we going to do?"

"While Olivar is most concerned with Caterina, he also wants Curran found. I do agree with that," Lochlyn replied. "I've tasked Silas with sending word to our spies. Hopefully, we'll have news of him before the baby comes. I've also asked Silas to compile everything he can about phoenixes, so we're as best prepared for this birth as we can be."

"Madchen and the midwife have already been sent to the village for supplies," Rosalie said. "Perhaps we should fetch a doctor as well?"

"Perhaps," he replied. "How is Caterina doing?"

"She's her usual self. Cat pretends that everything is as she wants it to be, even when the world is crumbling around her." She paused. "When Cat ran off, I was devastated. I don't want to lose her again."

"Then we will do everything we can to keep her here," Lochlyn replied. "Why don't you go to her now, while I attend to the search for Curran? Unless you'd rather work with Silas and me."

"I wouldn't know the first thing to say to a spymaster," Rosalie said. "I'll go to Cat, as you suggested. And, perhaps tonight we could have dinner together. Just the two of us."

"An excellent idea, Lady Blackmoor." Lochlyn brought her hand to his mouth and kissed her knuckles. "I'll count the moments until we're together again."

CHAPTER THIRTEEN

Waylaid, Again

Lochlyn waited for Rosalie in the dining room, wearing the same black velvet coat and breeches, and the ivory shirt he wore when they were married. Earlier he received a note written in his bride's own hand requesting he wear those exact clothes. He wasn't sure why she'd made such a request, but he honored it regardless. Then, Rosalie entered the room, and she took his breath away.

She was wearing the jade green dress from their wedding. The gold thread on the edging sparkled in the candlelight. Her hair was pinned up at the nape of her neck, and several pink and cream roses were woven into a crown that rested on her golden hair. As they were on their wedding day, Rosalie's feet were bare, and Lochlyn had to restrain himself from falling to his knees to caress them.

"You are so lovely," he said, his voice raspy. "Are we having another wedding?"

"I thought we might complete our original wedding," she replied. "Our feast was filled with my father's and brothers' posturing, then our wedding night was something of a disaster."

He remembered lying in bed next to Rosalie, comforting her as she wept, and servants bustling in and out of their room all night... but it was also the day he'd met and married his rose petal, which made it perfect. "It was one of the best days of my life," he said, and he meant it. "You didn't like it?"

"I did," she said as she took a step toward him. "I was so excited to meet you and start our new life together. We got a bit off course, but perhaps our life can start tonight."

"Tonight," Lochlyn repeated, then he remembered all the things he hadn't yet told Rosalie. Things she needed to know before she fully committed herself to him, not afterward. "Beloved, may I bring you to my chambers?"

She glanced at the table. As ever, it was laden with enough food to sustain an army. "You're not hungry?"

"I'll eat later. Unless you—"

"I'll eat later too," she said, taking the final step toward him. "I would very much like to go to your chamber, Lochlyn."

Lochlyn held her face as he kissed her. "In the old days, the men of my clan would throw their women over their shoulders and haul them off to bed."

"And how did the women react to such treatment?"

"Those eunuchs you mentioned earlier? We ended up with a few of those." They laughed together. "So how are we going? Over the shoulder or walking?"

"Walking will do just fine."

Lochlyn kissed her again, then he took her hand and led her out of the dining room. As they crossed the marble floors of the atrium, he recalled her bare toes.

"Are the floors too cold for your feet?"

"Stop trying to toss me over your shoulder."

"Never, beloved," he said; then they entered the southern tower. His chambers were on the topmost floor, and he'd made sure the lamps were lit. When Rosalie entered his rooms, she gasped in delight.

"These rooms are gorgeous," she said as she stepped farther inside. The walls were clad in dark wood paneling, while thick, jewel-toned carpets covered the floor. When she saw the ceiling, she exclaimed, "You have a glass roof, just like the library!"

"Watch this," he said, and he went to the crank that opened the roof.

"You can practically be one with the stars," Rosalie said as the roof opened to the sky. "Show me the rest?"

"Of course." Lochlyn took her through the front room, and through his dressing area. When they reached his bedchamber, she noticed some familiar paintings on his walls.

"These are my paintings." Rosalie gently touched a canvas filled with morning glories. "Why have you got them in here?"

"Because they remind me of you." Lochlyn stood behind her and wrapped his arms around her. "Those weeks when we avoided each other were hard. I missed you so much, but I didn't know how to reach out to you."

"You could have just said hello," Rosalie pointed out. "But I missed you too. I could have done the same."

"We've both learned from our mistakes." He kissed the side of her neck. "When I saw Madchen putting some of your paintings in storage, I claimed the ones you see here." He kissed her again, this time resting his lips on the soft spot behind her ear. "This way, I could have a part of you with me, even when I was too stupid to fix what went wrong with us."

"You were never stupid," Rosalie said as she folded her arms over his. "But I'm glad you found comfort in my work." She turned to face him. "Show me where you sleep?"

Lochlyn took her hand and led her to the far corner of the room. His bed was set on a high platform, close to the glass ceiling. It was also three times the size of a regular bed.

"Your bed is very big," Rosalie observed. Lochlyn sighed, taking Rosalie's hand.

"Sit with me?" She obliged. They sat on the bench at the foot of the massive bed. "Before we go any further, there are many things I need to tell you. I haven't been intentionally vague, but there's a lot you don't know about me, or my family."

"That's all right," Rosalie said. "You can always tell me now."

"I was married before." Lochlyn rubbed his thumb across Rosalie's knuckles. "Her name was Carys."

"Oh." Rosalie gazed at their hands. "Did you love her?"

"I did. At least, I tried to." Lochlyn cleared his throat, and he continued, "Carys was also related to the king. She was his cousin on his mother's side."

"Then the king has always wanted you in his family," Rosalie deduced. "What was your marriage to her like?"

"It was a similar situation to ours. The marriage was arranged by her father, and I traveled to her home for the wedding." Lochlyn cleared his throat again. He hadn't spoken of Carys in such a long time that he'd forgotten how painful the memories were. "Carys and I spent two months getting to know each other before I brought her here."

"What happened when you arrived? Did Carys fall ill?"

"She hated it here. She hated my home, the village, the mountains... Most of all, she hated me. The more I shared with her, the more she withdrew from me." He closed his eyes, recalling the singular time he shared her bed, and how she recoiled from him in fear and disgust. "Less than a month after we arrived, I gave Carys a carriage with a horse and driver, and she left."

"This is why you insisted we leave Father's home right after we were married? To find out if I would leave you, too?"

Lochlyn bowed his head. "Yes."

Rosalie set her hand on Lochlyn's cheek, ducking her head so she could see his eyes. "You know I don't hate you," she said. "I never have, not for a moment. And I don't hate Dragon Ridge, not at all. Our home is beautiful, and I'm happy here." She rubbed her thumb against his jaw. "Do you still love her?"

"No. Not after..." He squeezed his eyes shut, remembering the curses she'd screamed at him on their wedding night. "We were never together," he added, nodding toward the bed. "That meant our marriage wasn't valid. Therefore, letting her go was the best solution."

"Lochlyn. Husband," Rosalie said. "Look at me." He opened his eyes and met Rosalie's pale green gaze. "Carys wasn't meant for you. I'm sorry she hurt you, but if I may be selfish, I'm glad she left. Her being gone means that we can be together."

"Do you really mean that?" he asked. "I know these past few months have been hard on you."

"Actually, they haven't. Living in my father's house was awful. He was always embroiled in political scandals and intrigues, Caterina was causing trouble any way she could, and my brothers were vying for attention in the most depraved ways possible. Add in my father's endless parade of mistresses, each of them worse than the last, and it was like living in a circus."

"No wonder you chose life in a convent." Lochlyn drew the roses from her hair and watched her curls tumble onto her shoulders. "Thank you for giving up your quiet life to be my wife. I know we're still quite new to each other, but I truly cannot imagine living without you."

"Nor I, my husband." Rosalie took the flowers from Lochlyn's hands and set them aside, then she stood and gave him her back. "Help me remove this dress?"

Lochlyn paused. "I have much more to tell you."

"Can you tell me in bed?" she asked as she peeked over her shoulder. "Or perhaps in the morning?"

"Yes, beloved." Lochlyn stood and moved her hair over her shoulder, then he kissed the nape of her neck. "The morning will be a wonderful time to talk." He plucked the laces free from the grommets, then he helped her withdraw her arms from her sleeves and step out of the gown. Rosalie gathered it up and tossed it onto the bench. She stood before him clad only in her chemise. It was so thin Lochlyn could see her navel, and other things.

"Rosalie," he rasped, his hand trembling as he caressed her hip. "Beloved."

"I'll take care of this for you," she said as she unbuttoned his coat and pushed it off his shoulders, her fingers resting on his belt. "We can do away with this now too. If you'd like."

Unable to breathe or speak or even wait a moment longer, Lochlyn kissed her. When Rosalie wrapped her arms around his neck, he lifted her and sat with her legs on either side of his waist. He kissed a path from her jaw to her neck as his hands moved underneath her chemise and stroked her soft skin.

"Rosalie," he murmured against her throat. "You're certain you want this?"

She moved her hips against his erection, sending waves of sweet agony across his skin. "I've never been more certain of anything in my life."

They were moving too fast, there were many things he still needed to tell her, and he was a moment away from losing his last shred of control. "Be warned, my kind mates for life."

"Life," Rosalie breathed. "Our life, together."

He unfastened his breeches as he stood, the hot, heavy weight of him pressed against her thigh, then he turned and set Rosalie on his bed. Lochlyn had just tugged her chemise down to her elbows when a knock sounded at his main door.

"Ignore it," Lochlyn said, his lips pressed against her breast.

When the pounding continued, Rosalie asked, "What if it's important?"

"Nothing means more to me than you," Lochlyn said, but his bride was right. His people needed him as much as she did. Reluctantly, he rose and fixed his clothing. "Stay here. I will handle this."

He stalked toward the door and flung it wide. Madchen was standing in the doorway, wringing her hands. "I assume there is a true emergency for which I am needed desperately?" he demanded.

"Apologies, my lord, but it's Caterina," Madchen replied. "Her labors have started, and she's asking for Rosalie to attend her."

"Wouldn't the midwife be more of a help?" Lochlyn asked.

"We've already fetched the midwife, but she doesn't think she can help Caterina or the baby. You see, her water broke, and it was hot!"

"Hot?" Rosalie demanded, standing beside Lochlyn. She'd put his coat on over her chemise, and her mass of gold curls were bright against the black velvet. Lochlyn adored the rumpled look of her because he was the cause of it. "Exactly how hot?"

"It scalded everyone who came in contact with it, though your sister got the brunt of it," Madchen replied. "Poor thing's legs are all red and raw."

"The baby must be heating her from the inside out, like the midwife warned," Rosalie said. "Lochlyn, can we help her?"

"We will," he said as they left his chambers to go to the laboring Caterina. Lochlyn knew precious little about childbirth, and only a bit more about phoenixes. Fates, he hoped it would be enough to keep Rosalie's sister alive.

CHAPTER FOURTEEN

BORN IN FIRE

Rosalie and Lochlyn hurried across the castle to be with Caterina. When they entered the room that had been set up for Caterina's lying in, they found her asleep on a couch. Her skirt was pushed up past her knees, and wet linen was packed around her legs.

"Why is she wrapped up like that?" Rosalie asked.

"It's for the burns," the midwife explained. "After her skin cools down a bit more, I'll apply an ointment to her legs and feet."

Rosalie glanced at the midwife's hand and saw the bandages wrapped around her fingers. "Are you all right? Was her water very hot?"

"I'll be fine," she demurred, "but it was near boiling, I'd say."

"Have you ever dealt with such a birth before?" Rosalie pressed. She'd heard many stories of childbirth going badly, but she'd never heard of a birth actually burning someone. "Are there precautions we can take so no one else gets hurt? What can we do for Cat?"

"Truth be told, any precautions would have needed to be taken months ago," the midwife replied. "I'm told that no one ascertained the father's true nature as a firebird beforehand?"

"Curran never mentioned anything about hot births or boiling waters," the now-awake Caterina wailed. "And he was a man, not a bloody bird! Surely, you don't think I'm so stupid that I wouldn't know the difference between a man and a bird!"

"No one thinks you're stupid," Rosalie soothed. Lochlyn stood to the side, frowning. Caterina opened her mouth to speak, then she squeezed her eyes shut and hissed as she grabbed her belly.

"Can anything be done for her pain?" Lochlyn asked.

"The cure is for this boy to make his way into the world," the midwife replied. "But if we had a proper lying in room—proper for a phoenix, that is—that would help a great deal toward easing both mother and child."

"All right," Lochlyn said. "Tell us what we need to do."

Madchen and her legion of servants assembled the supplies they'd procured from the village earlier that day, and they set about arranging things per the midwife's orders. While Lochlyn assisted them, Rosalie remained by Caterina's side as she labored throughout the night. By noontime the next day, Caterina had grown so hot steam was rising from her skin.

Rosalie had never been so scared in her life.

"Let's move everything to the tower's roof," Lochlyn suggested after Caterina's newfound heat had fogged up all the windows. As the others were relocating some of the supplies to the roof, Rosalie caught Lochlyn's arm.

"Do you really think her being on the roof will help?" she asked.

"I think she'll be more comfortable out in the cool air," he replied. "And the roof's made of stone. It won't burn."

Rosalie nodded, unable to comprehend that her sister may go up in flames. Her hands wouldn't stop shaking, so she thrust them into the fold of her skirts, but not before Lochlyn noticed.

"Beloved," he said as he took her hands. Unlike Caterina, her fingers were icy cold. "We will do everything we can."

"I know," Rosalie said, wiping her cheek and squaring her shoulders. "We should fashion a stretcher for Cat."

"I'll take her," Lochlyn said, then he approached Caterina. "If it's all right, I'll carry you up."

"It's fine," Caterina replied, but there was a note of fear in her voice. Lochlyn lifted her and brought her up to the roof with Rosalie following close behind. Caterina peeked over Lochlyn's shoulder and met her sister's gaze.

"It's going to be all right, Rosie," Caterina said. "Dozens of babies are born every day. Hundreds, even."

Rosalie nodded. "I hope you're right."

"Aren't I always?" Caterina asked, then she grimaced as another contraction took her. Finally, they were on the roof, and Lochlyn set her on her feet.

Under the midwife's direction, a bed of clean straw had been prepared on the tower's roof. To Rosalie, it resembled a sheep pen. Only Rosalie and Lochlyn had accompanied Caterina to the roof. The rest remained inside the castle, and would join them when necessary.

"He was not a bird," Caterina muttered when she saw the hay scattered across the roof. "I keep telling you people he was just a man, yet you've gone and built me a nest. Do I look like I'm about to lay an egg?"

"The midwife said this would be best for you and the baby," Rosalie said.

"That woman's daft; as is your husband for listening to her," Caterina said bitterly. "When it's time for your lying in, will you let him treat you this way?"

"I won't need a lying in for some time." Rosalie glanced at Lochlyn, then she leaned closer to her sister. "We still haven't been together."

"Then you're not really married," Caterina said. Louder, she added, "Lochlyn, my unwed sister and I will be leaving now."

He dipped his chin. "As you wish, madam."

Rosalie smiled at her husband. He was kind enough to do everything in his power to help Caterina, even though she humiliated him by running off with Curran the day before they were to be married, and wise enough not to argue with a woman in labor. Caterina, however, was not amused.

"Does nothing irritate you?" Caterina screamed at Lochlyn. "Why are you always so calm?"

"It's maddening, isn't it?" Rosalie asked as she guided Caterina to the tower's perimeter. The midwife had explained that, as Caterina's labor intensified, the baby's natural heat would affect her temper, and walking would calm and cool her. "Walk with me now."

"You think I'm maddening?" Lochlyn asked when they passed him.

Rosalie's cheeks warmed, then Caterina snapped, "Maybe, if you finally fuck my sister, she'll have a better opinion of you."

Lochlyn erupted in laughter as Rosalie looked for a hole to crawl into. "Cat, have a care how you speak to him," Rosalie began.

"I challenge you to have a care when you have a baby's head splitting your hips apart," Caterina snapped, then she went to her knees as she clutched her belly. Her body shuddered as curls of smoke rose from beneath her.

"What's happening?" Rosalie demanded. "Should we get the midwife?"

"Curran," Caterina screamed at the sky. "You promised you would always find me! Find me now!"

Smoke thickened around Caterina's knees, then she doubled over and screamed. Rosalie reached for her sister, but Lochlyn dragged her away.

"She needs me," Rosalie protested.

"We can't help her now," Lochlyn said, then he yelled toward the stairs, "Midwife! Get the midwife!"

"Let me go to her," Rosalie said as she struggled against Lochlyn.

"Stay with me." Lochlyn wrapped his arms around Rosalie, keeping her back pressed against his chest as they watched Caterina. The smoke grew so dense that they could barely see Caterina, then bright orange flames surrounded her.

"Cat!" Rosalie shrieked as she lunged toward her, but Lochlyn's arms were like steel bands. Helplessly, she watched as flames licked up Caterina's legs and engulfed her belly. "She's dying!"

"Look," Lochlyn said, pointing toward the clouds. Rosalie shaded her eyes as she looked toward the sun... but no, that wasn't the sun. A bird larger than any eagle or gryphon was descending toward the tower, leaving a flaming trail in its wake.

"It's a phoenix," Rosalie breathed, then she reached toward her sister. "Cat," she yelled as Lochlyn held her in place. "Cat, look up!"

Caterina raised her head as the phoenix reached the tower's roof. Its massive talons grasped Caterina's shoulders as the bird's feathers ignited into a shower of sparks. The flames exploded into a blinding light and the phoenix and Caterina were gone.

Rosalie's body went limp as she stared at the circle of ash left in the phoenix's wake. Lochlyn kept his arms around her and lowered both of them to their knees.

"Cat," Rosalie wailed as tears flowed down her cheeks. "Fates, what just happened?" She turned into Lochlyn's arms. "Was that phoenix Curran? Did he save Caterina and the baby, or are they all dead?"

"I don't know," Lochlyn said, stroking Rosalie's hair. "If that were indeed Curran, I imagine he came to take them wherever phoenixes belong. Otherwise..." Lochlyn kissed her forehead. "I'm so sorry, my love."

"I can't believe she's gone," Rosalie choked out around her sobs. Her cries were so violent her ribs ached, and for a moment she worried she'd retch onto Lochlyn's chest—then she heard a cry from the ashes.

A baby's cry.

"Her son!" Rosalie cried as she wrested herself free of Lochlyn's arms. "They left behind their son!"

Rosalie began sifting through the hot piles of ash that were slippery like soap flakes. The hay and cushions had been incinerated by the firebird, which meant that a lone infant's survival was impossible. Or was it?

The baby cried out again, and Rosalie found him. He'd been fully buried in the ash. His skin was streaked with gray, but his eyes were bright, and the inside of his mouth was pink and healthy.

"Phoenixes are born in fire," Rosalie whispered as she raised the boy from the ashes. "Lochlyn, I need a blanket for him."

"Here." Lochlyn removed his coat, then he knelt in front of Rosalie as she wrapped up the baby. "He's strong, isn't he?" he said as the baby grasped his finger.

"What are we going to do?" Rosalie whispered as she stared at the filthy, squalling infant in her arms. "We need to find someone to take care of him."

"We can take care of him." Lochlyn put his hand on Rosalie's cheek. "He can be our baby."

"We can't just keep someone else's baby," Rosalie said, her gaze never leaving the boy. "It's not right."

"It isn't, but we can't tell people he's Cat's child either," Lochlyn said. "We can keep him safe while we search for your sister and Curran. When we find them, we'll return him to his parents."

"But no one will believe he's ours," Rosalie protested, albeit weakly. "We've only been married a few months."

"Won't they? What would be more unusual, a childless couple, or one who had their first son arrive sooner than anticipated?" When Rosalie didn't answer, he continued, "He will need parents who can protect him, who understand what he is and how to help him if and when the time comes."

"Help him?" Rosalie asked, panicked. "Will he also burst into flames?"

"We don't know yet," Lochlyn replied. "Mortality breeds truer than magic regardless of the creature. Most likely, he's just a human baby."

"A human baby." Rosalie looked at the infant in her arms. He'd quieted down and was watching her with his big, dark eyes. She'd always wanted children, as had Lochlyn, and she couldn't let Caterina's son go to an orphanage to be raised by strangers. And the boy might be all that was left of her sister.

Rosalie wiped her cheek, then she adjusted Lochlyn's coat around the boy's small body. She stroked his forehead and the downy hair that, underneath the ash, was blond like Caterina's. Rosalie was blonde, too. "What if he's not only human?"

"Then, when the time comes, we will handle it."

"So, it is to always be burdens and troubles with us," Rosalie said, then she blew out a breath. "Burdens, troubles, and now a baby. Fates, Lochlyn, I don't know how much more I can take."

"Let the burdens rest on my shoulders," he said. "I'll shelter you in any way I can."

"Thank you, but no," Rosalie said as she set her hand on his cheek. "We will bear these burdens together; including the search for Cat and... parenthood."

Lochlyn drew her face close to his. "Is that a yes, my Rosalie? You'll raise this baby with me?"

"Yes," Rosalie replied, then she leaned her forehead against his. "Lochlyn, we have a family."

CHAPTER FIFTEEN

ASHES AND AFTERMATH

L ochlyn knelt in the circle of ash, his arm around Rosalie as he shielded her and the baby from the wind. He was fascinated by the tiny, curious person in his wife's arms. But more than fascination he felt, something had settled into place in his heart. He and Rosalie had a son.

He considered the coming search for Caterina and swallowed the lump in his throat. Once they found either her or Curran, the boy would go to them, which was only right. Even so, a protective urge deep within him didn't want that to happen. Lochlyn recalled stories his mother told him of dragon sires guarding their nests with fire and claw, and he understood his ancestors a bit more. He would never stand between the boy being returned to his rightful parents, but until that day comes to pass, he would defend his foster son with every power and tool at his disposal.

Perhaps this version of his family was only temporary, but he loved it all the same.

"Beloved," Lochlyn murmured, his lips against her temple. "We should bring him inside."

Rosalie nodded. "Do you really think Curran took Caterina away?" she asked as she watched the ash blow away in the wind.

"I think he must have," Lochlyn replied. "Why else would he come here, if not to save her?"

"But they left the baby," Rosalie said. "Why would they do that?"

"Perhaps wherever they're going isn't safe for a baby. Or perhaps they knew he would be safe with us." Lochlyn stood and helped Rosalie to her feet. "Can you walk? I can carry you."

"I can manage." She took a step toward the entrance, then rounded on Lochlyn. "Thank you," she said, her eyes shining with tears. "I don't know what I would do without you, Lochlyn."

"You'll never have to know," Lochlyn said as he embraced her. "I'll always take care of you. Both of you." He closed his eyes and laid his forehead against her hair. His love for Rosalie was so strong he would challenge the Fates Themselves for her, and for the baby. "Come, now. Let's get inside, where it's warmer."

They navigated the narrow staircase inside the tower and reentered the chamber below. The midwife and Madchen stood when they saw them and gasped at their ash-streaked appearance.

"What happened?" Madchen asked.

"We have a baby," Rosalie replied, then she smiled at the bundle in her arms. "A fine, strong boy."

"And Caterina?" Madchen prompted.

"No." Rosalie shook her head. "She's... she's gone."

"We'll go up and get her," Madchen began.

"There's nothing to get," Rosalie said as a fresh tear coursed down her cheek. Lochlyn put his arm around her, and she turned into his chest.

"Nothing but ash remains," Lochlyn said. He thought it best not to mention the phoenix's appearance over his home. The fewer people that know what happened atop his tower, the better.

The midwife looked like she was about to faint, but Madchen squared her shoulders. "I'm so sorry, my lady," she said. "Let's see about getting you and your boy cleaned up." Madchen put her hand on Rosalie's arm and drew her away from Lochlyn.

"Silas has some information to share with you, my lord," Madchen continued, but Lochlyn hardly heard her. All he knew was that his wife was being led away when she needed him most. Rosalie looked at him over her shoulder, and her wide eyes told him she didn't want to leave him either.

"Rosalie," he said as he closed the distance between them. "Do you want me to stay with you? Anything Silas needs to tell me can wait. What do you need?"

"It's all right," Rosalie said, though he didn't miss how her shoulders relaxed. "Madchen will take good care of us. Go. Handle what needs to be done."

Lochlyn caressed her cheek, then he dipped his head and kissed her. "I will be back as soon as I can," he promised, then he left Rosalie and the boy to be cared for.

He crossed the castle quickly and went straight to his chamber. Lochlyn paused, his hand on the doorframe. The last time he had been in this room, he'd been in bed with Rosalie. Now, less than a day later, his entire life had changed. While the tragedy of losing Caterina weighed heavily on his heart, he and Rosalie had become closer than ever...

And, now, there was a baby. Their baby.

Lochlyn washed up and changed into clean clothes before meeting Silas in the steward's smaller study. Long ago, they had agreed to keep the information gathered by their spies in Silas's office, in case the king ever demanded to see Lochlyn's ledgers and his other paperwork. It wasn't the strongest precaution, but as far as Lochlyn knew, King Olivar didn't know about Dragon Ridge's intricate spy network. For now, his people were safe from the king's mad schemes.

"Please, tell me you have good news," Lochlyn said when he joined Silas.

"It's news," Silas replied. "Time will tell how good it is." He set a sheaf of letters on the desk. "These are copies of all the correspondence we've managed to intercept from the Order of the Sun since your return from Irontooth Keep. There's no mention of Curran or a missing knight, and nothing at all about Caterina."

"Good." Lochlyn scanned a few of the pages. "Curran may have made an appearance earlier today in his phoenix form. Do you know if anyone saw him?"

"No one's reported anything as of yet, but I'll take a trip to the pub this evening," Silas replied. "If anyone saw a phoenix, they'll be talking about it there." He paused, then added, "There's something else."

Lochlyn set down the papers and gave Silas his full attention. "Please. Tell me."

"I've read through scores of these missives," Silas began. "The Order has strict rules regarding offspring that may carry the blood. They're either raised within the Order, or, if the parents refuse, the entire family is eliminated."

"Barbaric," Lochlyn muttered, though he now understood why Curran took Caterina but left their baby behind. "Put an extra guard at each gate, and two on the bridge. I want to know immediately if anyone new comes into the village."

"Understood. What about people leaving?"

Lochlyn hesitated. He trusted his people, but people could be bought. "Our people are not to be restricted in any way," he replied. "However, unusual activity should be noted. As to what constitutes unusual, that's anyone's guess." He rubbed his eyes, trying to purge the bright image of the phoenix from his mind. "Have you spoken with Madchen about what happened earlier?"

"Only briefly," he replied. "She told me that Caterina has left us, one way or another, and that you and Rosalie now have a son. Congratulations," he added.

"Thank you," Lochlyn said, surprised at the swell of pride in his breast. No matter that this boy had been unexpected or wasn't related to Lochlyn by blood. The baby was his and Rosalie's responsibility, and they would raise him with all the love and care the child deserved.

Lochlyn glanced at the sheaf of letters. Based on what Silas had told him, as long as the baby presented as a mortal human, he would be safe from the Order.

And, if the baby grew to be a true phoenix, well, Lochlyn had his own ways of defending his people.

"Alert me of any new correspondence from the Order at once," Lochlyn said as he prepared to return to Rosalie. "They aren't to receive higher priority than other matters, but I do want to keep abreast of their dealings."

"Understood, my lord," Silas said. "Forgive me for being so direct, but about your wife."

"What about her?" Lochlyn demanded. "Has she somehow offended you?"

"No, my lord, not in the slightest," he replied, unperturbed by Lochlyn's ire. "But I was wondering if you've told her everything."

Lochlyn's shoulders slumped. "I've barely begun. Do you think she'll hate me for it?"

"I've seen the way she looks at you, and it is not with hate," Silas replied gently. "But I don't think she'll be pleased to have been kept in the dark for so long."

"No, she won't." He thought about Rosalie's wide jade eyes, and the relief that shone in them when he asked what she needed from him. "How did my mother react when Father told her about his lineage?"

"Ah." Silas smiled, no doubt recalling when Lochlyn's parents were young. "Their situation wasn't quite the same as she knew him before they were married. Also, your father did not carry the blood as strongly as you do."

"And Rosalie and I have been wed for months and now have a child, yet she knows nothing of my true nature." Lochlyn wiped his hand down his face. "She'll be furious when I tell her, rightly so. I know I must talk to her, but I don't want to drive her away."

"A word of advice, my lord?"

"Please."

"Things between the two of you have changed drastically over a handful of days. Perhaps now is the best time to reveal the truth—but even if it isn't, this isn't the sort of information that gets better the longer you wait. Tell her now because if she learns on her own, she might never forgive you."

"You're right. I'll go to her now. Thank you, old friend."

Lochlyn departed from Silas's study and went directly to Rosalie's rooms. He found his wife directing half the household staff as they rearranged one side of her apartment into a nursery. When Rosalie saw him, she rushed into his arms.

"Is everything all right?" he asked, fearful something had happened to her or the baby.

"Yes. I missed you." She leaned back and smiled at him. Her hair was still damp from her bath and had curled into ringlets at her temples.

"I missed you too," he said as he stroked her hair. "I couldn't stop thinking about you."

Rosalie blushed, delighting him. "Did you handle what needed to be done?"

"Yes." He set his hands on her shoulders. "How do you feel, after everything that happened?"

"I..." Rosalie looked away and cleared her throat, then she began again. "I've chosen to believe that Curran spirited Caterina away, and that I'll see her again someday. I know it's naïve of me, but we don't really know what did occur, and... And for now, it's what I need to believe, so we can move forward."

"Then that's what we'll do." Lochlyn took her hands, intending to take her some place quiet where they could talk a bit more about Caterina's fate, as well as his own lineage. That was when one of the maids presented the baby to Rosalie.

"Look who had a bath," Rosalie cooed, holding him close. "Has he eaten yet?"

"I thought you might want to feed him," the maid said as she handed Rosalie a bottle of warmed milk. Rosalie accepted the bottle, then she turned to Lochlyn.

"Hold him for a moment?" she asked as she thrust the baby into his arms. He barely had a moment to think before he was confronted with the boy, who had been bathed and swaddled, and was now wriggling and gurgling at Lochlyn.

"He's so curious," Lochlyn began, then he saw Rosalie unfastening her bodice. "Why are you undressing?"

"I'm not," she said as she bared the skin beneath her collarbones. "The midwife said I should hold him against my skin while he feeds. It's supposed to help us bond." Rosalie reclaimed the baby and gave him the bottle. "You should open your shirt, too."

"Me?"

"You're his father. He needs to bond with you too." Rosalie glanced up at him through her lashes, and in that moment, Lochlyn would have torn the moon down from the sky for her. He unbuttoned his shirt, then stepped closer to his wife and son.

Son.

"You're right. This is wonderful," Lochlyn said as he pushed Rosalie's hair behind her shoulder. She smiled at him, then something caught her eye.

"Is this a bruise?" she asked as she touched a mark near his neck.

"It's not." He knew exactly what she had seen. "More of a birthmark."

"It doesn't give you any pain?"

"No. Never has." He took her hand from his skin and kissed her knuckles, then he scooped her into his arms.

"What are you doing?" she asked.

"This." He sat on the cushioned bench at the foot of Rosalie's bed with her nestled in his arms and the baby between them. "Now we're all bonding, together."

Rosalie laid her head on his shoulder, and, for the first time in a long time, Lochlyn felt like he had a family. "Together."

CHAPTER SIXTEEN

REVELATIONS

The baby drank about half of his milk before falling asleep in Rosalie's arms. "He must be so tired," she murmured as she held him against her shoulder and patted his back. She'd held many newborns, but never before had a tiny life depended on her. It was amazing, and humbling, and Rosalie hoped she would do right by him.

"It's only his first day and, already, so much has happened," she continued.

"I wonder if he'll ever know," Lochlyn began, then Rosalie stifled a yawn. "Beloved, you must be exhausted. You haven't slept in two days."

"Neither have you," she said. "But you're right. I should put him down and rest while he's sleeping." Rosalie looked around the room. "Oh, they left the cradle in the front room."

"I'll bring it in here," Lochlyn said as he went to retrieve the item.

"I think it might be heavy," Rosalie called.

"It's fine," Lochlyn said, returning with the solid oak cradle held aloft in his arms. He was only wearing a linen shirt without his usual vest and coat, and Rosalie noticed the muscles working in his arms and shoulders.

"You're quite strong," Rosalie observed as he set the cradle down next to her bed as if it weighed nothing. "Do you train with your guard?"

"Sometimes, I do. Why?" He flashed her a grin. "Do you think I need to train more often?" When she narrowed her eyes at him, he continued, "I've always been strong. My father was strong too, as were my brothers."

"That must have been a sight," Rosalie said. "Four Blackmoor boys running amok in the mountains."

Lochlyn smiled, but she noticed a tightness around his eyes. "It was. Is this a good spot for the cradle? I know you don't want him too far from you."

"It's perfect." Rosalie set the baby down to sleep. She arranged, then rearranged, his blanket. "Lochlyn, we have a son. I know he's only ours until Caterina returns but, Fates, isn't he wonderful?"

"He is." Lochlyn stood beside Rosalie, his arm wrapped around her shoulders as they admired the baby. She pressed herself against him, so filled with love for her husband and the baby she thought she might burst.

"When I spoke to Silas earlier, I learned something unsettling about the Order," Lochlyn continued. "They don't take kindly to their offspring being raised outside their clan."

The happy warmth drained from Rosalie in an instant. "Is the baby in danger?"

"He won't be if no one knows about him," Lochlyn replied. "Hardly anyone knows that Caterina was here, so we have that in our favor. However, I think we should refer to him as our natural son, at least until we find your sister."

"I agree," Rosalie said, relieved there was no immediate threat to her tiny family. "It's better to put forth an untruth than to risk his safety."

"I'm glad you agree." Lochlyn kissed her forehead. Rosalie yawned against his throat. "And you, my beloved, need to sleep."

Rosalie didn't protest as Lochlyn led her to the bed. "Do you need anything before you lie down?" he asked. "Something to drink, maybe?"

"Stay," she said as she caught his hand. "I need you close to me."

"As you wish." Lochlyn pulled off his boots and removed his belt, then he got into bed with Rosalie. She burrowed into his arms, her cheek pressed against his chest so she could hear his heart beating.

"Sleep well, my love."

Rosalie blinked herself awake and moved closer to her sleeping husband. She glided her fingertips across his warm skin, reveling in touching him so intimately. She'd just reached his breastbone when the events of the past day came crashing back to her.

Fire.

The phoenix.

Cat...

Rosalie rolled onto her back and covered her mouth, stifling her sobs so she wouldn't wake her husband or the baby. Her sister had been the one constant good thing in her life, the one person who'd always been kind and caring and didn't try to use Rosalie against her father. And after Rosalie's mother had passed, Caterina was the only one who looked after her.

Now, the baby sleeping next to Rosalie's bed might be all that was left of Caterina.

Once her tears slowed, she rolled onto her side and looked into the cradle. The boy was asleep in his blankets, his tiny fist curled up next to his cheek. Rosalie would care for him as if he were her own child, and if she found Caterina, they would continue raising him together.

No. Not if. *When.* Because Rosalie fully intended to find her sister.

Rosalie tucked the blanket around his small body, and she recalled how the Order didn't want baby phoenixes to be raised by outsiders. As she considered ways to keep the baby safe, she nestled against Lochlyn. His shirt was open. She tentatively put her hand against his chest. He was so warm that Rosalie worried he had a fever, so she pressed the back of her hand against his forehead.

"What are you doing?" Lochlyn murmured.

"You're very warm," she explained, feeling foolish. "I was checking you for fever."

He took her hand from his forehead and kissed her fingertips. "You take very good care of me. He's still sleeping?"

"He is."

"You take good care of both of us." Lochlyn released Rosalie's hand and gathered her against his chest. "What would you like to call him?"

"I'm not sure," she replied, "but I've been thinking about what you told me about this Order of the Sun, and their views on children. I have an idea about keeping the baby safe."

"Do you?" Lochlyn stroked her hair off her cheek. "Tell me."

"If someone came here looking for a baby phoenix and found only our foster son, he would be a target," Rosalie began. "But if we had several children, all around the same age, they would all blend together and, perhaps be overlooked."

"True. Where would we obtain these additional children?"

"We could adopt them from the village. Surely there's an orphanage?"

"There is." He tugged her closer to him, his blue eyes locked on hers. "We can go there as soon as tomorrow. That is, if you'd like me to accompany you?"

"You'll do this?" she asked, shocked at his easy acceptance of her plan.

"Of course. We have plenty of room, and it will be good to have many children in the castle again."

"I'm so glad you agree," she said, relief flooding her voice. "And... and maybe, in time, a few of these children could be ours. As in, not adopted."

Lochlyn grinned. "Beloved, nothing would make me happier."

"Me, too," she began, though her words were lost as he kissed her. Rosalie slid her fingers along his neck and into his hair, and wondered just how much time they had before the baby was due to wake. When they parted, she noticed another dark mark on the side of his neck.

"Are you sure these marks aren't bruises?" she asked as she lightly touched the area. Lochlyn caught her hand and rested his forehead against hers.

"They're not, and I must tell you something." He sighed as he released her, then he sat up and swung his legs onto the floor. "Come out to the balcony with me?"

"Why the balcony?" Rosalie asked. "Why can't you tell me here?"

"I fear you may want to shout at me, and I don't want to wake him." Lochlyn stroked the baby's cheek, then he extended his hand to Rosalie. "Will you indulge me?"

Rosalie bit her lip, wondering what he could possibly want to tell her. She briefly considered insisting they remain in the room so she could potentially use the baby as an excuse to end their conversation—then she recalled one of her father's mistresses who'd often done just that. Rosalie hadn't been fond of that woman, and she refused to hide behind a newborn, no matter the situation.

That, and Lochlyn's wide blue eyes and beseeching face held nothing but honesty.

"I don't see why not." Rosalie accepted his hand. And, after giving the maid who'd been waiting in the front room a few instructions about the baby, they stepped onto the balcony.

"Well?" Rosalie asked. "What is it? If you don't like the idea of more children—"

"I like it." He took her hands. "I like it very much."

"Then what is this all about?"

"This is about the many things I should have already told you, but my cowardice won out every time," he replied. "I've been guilty of this cowardice since we met. The first time I saw you, when we stood in front of the altar together, I couldn't stop staring at your lips. I thought they looked like two perfect rose petals, and I wondered if that was how you got your name. When I tried to talk to you, my voice dried up in my throat."

"I got my name from a rosebush outside my mother's window." She stepped closer to him. "Surely you didn't take me out here to talk about my mouth."

Lochlyn bowed his head. "You know how Curran was—is—a phoenix. And you've noticed the marks on me."

"Has one of them attacked you?" Rosalie demanded.

"No, no. I haven't been attacked."

"Then... you're a phoenix, too?"

"Also, no." He dropped her hands and pulled off his shirt, revealing dozens of greenish black scales that glinted just beneath his skin. Rosalie's heart pounded as she resisted the urge to run. Her mind knew that Lochlyn would never hurt her, but her body registered him as a predator.

"Why... why are you green?" she asked, her voice barely a whisper. "Are these... scales?"

"They are." Lochlyn's brows peaked She wondered why he was worried when she was the one stuck on the balcony with a snake man. "Rosalie, I'm a dragon."

Rosalie nodded and stepped closer to Lochlyn. The scales ran in orderly rows down his well-muscled arms, fading away just above his wrists, and along the sides of his torso. She tentatively put her hand against his chest and saw that the scales beneath his throat and atop his heart were ivory, and nearly invisible against his skin. The ivory scales disappeared below his collarbone, and Rosalie realized that her husband's modest clothing completely covered his scales.

She remembered when he wouldn't let her help him bathe, and understood. He wasn't modest. He was hiding.

"These are scales, then. Dragon scales," she murmured as she reached toward his shoulders. "Why don't they cover your entire body?"

"I don't know," he replied. "My hands and face have always been regular skin. My feet and some other areas, too."

She nodded, too entranced by the colors swirling under his skin to meet his gaze. "May I touch them?"

"Yes." Lochlyn tossed his shirt aside, standing with his back rigid and his arms straight at his sides. "Touch me wherever you want."

Starting at this shoulder, Rosalie traced her fingertips down Lochlyn's arm. Despite the scaly pattern, his skin was smooth, as if the design were painted on. Satisfied with her examination of his arm, she moved around to his back. The scales were wider over his spine and shoulder blades, and the color brighter.

"Do you have a tail?" she asked as her fingers lingered near his waist.

"Only when I am in dragon form," he said over his shoulder.

"You can change form?" She'd known Lochlyn's family was descended from dragons, but she had no idea his blood was strong enough to shift forms. That made him stronger than the king, who'd been trapped in a half form for years.

He bowed his head. "Yes."

"What about wings?" she demanded, her head spinning. Her husband was a dragon and occasionally *had a tail*. "Do you have those too?"

"Sometimes. Yes."

Rosalie glanced inside her rooms, noted the servants bustling about. "Does your staff know?"

"Yes. Many have been in my family's employ for generations."

"Then, everyone knew but me." She clenched her fists and turned away from Lochlyn, her face hot. "Everyone knew about your true nature except your poor, stupid wife!"

"Rosalie." Lochlyn stood behind her and wrapped his arms around her waist. She leaned back into the warmth of him, letting it comfort her even through her anger. "I never wanted to tell you, not at first. My plan was to be married to you for a year, then it would be annulled, and I would send you wherever you wanted to go. Your convent, perhaps."

"You would rather I was in a convent than here with you?"

He replied, his words rough, "I would rather you be happy than burdened with me."

The pain in his voice cut through her anger, and Rosalie finally understood her husband's many odd behaviors; how he wouldn't disrobe in her presence, his reticence to be intimate with her, how he rarely talked about himself. He worried that his being a dragon meant he wasn't good enough for her.

He was wrong. Because Rosalie thought he was perfect.

Rosalie twisted around in his arms. "You are not a burden. You are infuriating and maddening and, sometimes, insufferable. But never a burden." She held his face between her hands. "You are my husband, the one and only man I'll ever marry, and I adore you."

"And you are my much-loved wife." He tucked a stray tendril of hair behind her ear. "Soon after you arrived here, it was plain that my plan to annul our marriage would never work."

"Why is that?"

"Because I can't imagine living without you," he replied. "Rosalie, I will never let you go."

"You'll never have to," Rosalie said. "I'm yours. Now and always." She trailed her fingers across his shoulder. "Do you always have these scales?"

"Yes. They never quite go away after I resume my human form."

"May I see your dragon?"

"There isn't enough room for my dragon out here on the balcony."

"Oh," she said, her eyes widening. "Do you get very big? Big enough to ride?"

"No one has ever ridden me," Lochlyn said. "But you may ride me, my Rosalie, whenever you'd like."

Rosalie didn't know if the heat spreading within her was from her proximity to Lochlyn, his smoldering eyes, or something else entirely. Either way, she liked it. "Where may I see this dragon of yours that's big enough for me to ride?"

He smiled devilishly, then he turned her around in his arms and pointed to a nearby mountain. There was a stone citadel on the peak, and Rosalie remembered the fort's name: Dragon's Den. "There," he said. "The citadel has plenty of room for whatever you'd like. We can go now."

"How long will it take us to get there?" she asked, mindful that the baby would wake soon, and that the citadel was clear across the valley.

"Not long. I can fly us there."

"I thought you said there isn't enough room out here for you to change."

"There is an in-between form I can take. Some call it a warrior form."

Fates, how many forms can one man take? "Very well. I would like to see this warrior form."

He gave her a crooked smile. "I, ah, need a bit of room."

"As you wish." Rosalie stepped back and watched as black sparks swirled around Lochlyn's form. Before her eyes, leathery wings erupted from his shoulder blades, and long, curved talons grew from his fingertips. His wings—which weren't scaled, but rather an even expanse of black—arched over his shoulders, but Rosalie was more interested in Lochlyn's hands.

"This is how you cut your hand on our wedding night," Rosalie said as she stroked Lochlyn's wickedly sharp talons. She'd never understood how he'd cut himself, being that there were no knives in the room. "You could kill me with these."

"Beloved, I would never," he began, but she hushed him.

"I know. I was just making an observation." Rosalie released his hands and reached over his shoulder to investigate his wings. "No feathers?" Rosalie teased as she stroked the inner curve where they attached to his back.

"Stop," Lochlyn said, his eyes flashing. "My wings are sensitive."

"You said I could touch you anywhere."

A low growl emanated deep in his chest. "When you stroke my wings, there's a reaction."

"Is there?" she teased as she linked her hands behind his neck. "Tell me about this reaction."

"Not here." He put his hands on her waist and gripped her hips. "Ready to fly, beloved?"

"Not yet." Rosalie tugged his head lower until they were nose to nose. "I understand why you kept your true nature from me. Truly, I do. However, I need your word that you will never keep anything this important from me ever again."

"Never again," he said. "I swear it. What I know, you know."

"All right," Rosalie said, then she screamed as Lochlyn leaped straight up into the sky.

CHAPTER SEVENTEEN

The Dragon's Den

The ground sped away as Lochlyn flew higher. He swooped and rolled across the sky. Throughout it all, Lochlyn's grip on Rosalie's waist never faltered even as she screamed for the Fates to protect them. Soon enough, Rosalie felt the cold stone of the citadel beneath her feet as they landed.

"You may have ruptured my eardrum," Lochlyn said as he released her.

"We were so high up," Rosalie said, unashamed of her screams.

"Did you worry I would drop you?"

"No. I loved every moment." Rosalie stood on her toes and kissed him. "Whenever you want to fly, I'll be your companion." She stepped back before he could respond, looking around the citadel. They were standing on a wide, flat shelf carved directly into the living rock. It was easily as big as a ballroom, and

Rosalie felt a frisson of anticipation as she wondered just how big her dragon could get.

"This is enough room for you to change?" she asked.

"It is." He paused, his throat working. "I must warn you; I need to take the rest of my clothes off."

Rosalie nodded, unable to form an answer. Lochlyn was already barefoot, as was she, since they'd gone straight from their bed to the balcony, and he'd left his shirt behind before they took off. That meant only a pair of trousers lay between her and him.

"Well," Rosalie said when he just stood there. "Get on with it."

"Yes, my love." He watched her as he unfastened his trousers, then her husband was standing before her completely, utterly bare. Rosalie was confronted with an undeniable truth.

Lochlyn Blackmoor was beautiful.

"Oh," Rosalie said. She took in his handsome form, and the pattern of scales that swirled in black and green down his legs in contrast to the ivory scales that coursed down the front of his torso and his inner thighs. Lochlyn made no effort to hide himself from her gaze, not even his cock, which was covered in pink human skin.

"You're quite well-proportioned," she began, then she blushed when he chuckled. She'd meant the proportion of scales to skin on his body—but she'd said it while staring at his manhood. Needing to hide her warm cheeks, she walked behind him. As she did, she felt his scales, verifying that even in this warrior form they were flat against his skin. Lochlyn held his wings close to his body as her fingertips trailed against his hips and lower back. "You are so lovely," she murmured.

Lochlyn laughed shortly, his wings vibrating with the sound. "I've never felt lovely."

"Well, you are." Rosalie dropped her hand. "Is this why Carys... why she left?"

"Yes." His wings drooped. "She saw my scales and called me a monster."

Rosalie came around to the front of him, and took his hands. "I'm so sorry she hurt you," Rosalie began, "but she was also wrong. Both your heart and your body are utterly beautiful."

"You truly are a gift," Lochlyn said as he bowed his head and kissed her. She slid her hands behind his neck and brushed against his wings. A moment later, his cock bumped into her belly.

"So that's what happens when I touch your wings," she said as she rubbed the smooth arches where his wings extended from his back. "What will happen if I kiss each of your scales, one after the other?"

Lochlyn rumbled deep in his chest, the sound raising every hair on Rosalie's body. "If you start that now, I'll forget why we came here."

"In that case, we'd better wait." Another soft, sweet kiss. "Please show me your dragon."

Lochlyn smiled, and said, "As you wish, beloved. Move back, please, so I don't hurt you."

Rosalie did as asked, pausing to look over her husband's attractive form as she did so. Lochlyn took a few steps back as well, then he rolled his shoulders and dropped onto all fours. Black sparks swirled around his body as they had on the balcony, this time so densely Rosalie couldn't see what was happening. She clenched her hands as the sparks moved faster, the cloud of them as big as a carriage...no, as big as a cottage. Then the lights dissipated, and Lochlyn roared so loudly that the mountain shook.

Her husband was gone, and in his place was the fiercest creature Rosalie had ever seen.

When the transformation seemed to be complete, Rosalie approached the dragon. Based on the scales Lochlyn wore underneath his human skin, she had expected him to be black, but he was green like pine boughs. His head was lizard-like, with a long serpentine neck that led to his wide, strong back, and dark, powerful wings. Golden horns curved back from his forehead, and both his teeth and talons came to wicked points. And, yes, he was big enough for her to ride him, seated between his wings.

"Now you're even more beautiful," Rosalie said as she glided her hand along his foreleg. His scales were more pronounced in dragon form, and she liked the feel of them. "Can you speak?"

He nudged her with his snout. "I'll take that as a no. Can you breathe fire, or does that only happen in storybooks?"

Lochlyn jerked his head toward the interior of the citadel, then he ambled inside. Rosalie followed, until they were in a room with a sunken area at one end and a hearth at the other. Lochlyn glanced at her over his shoulder, then he roared as a stream of living fire blasted from his mouth into the hearth, igniting the waiting logs.

"This is why you're always so warm," Rosalie deduced as she approached the hearth. "You have fire within you."

Lochlyn roared again, and Rosalie saw sparks out of the corner of her eye. A moment later he was in his human form as he stood behind her and wrapped his arms around her waist. "All dragons have fire in our hearts. It's why my kind tends to live in the mountains. The cold air doesn't bother us."

She turned and twined her arms around his neck. "I wasn't done admiring your dragon form."

The corner of his mouth curled up. "You prefer my dragon to me as a naked man?" he asked. She laughed, her face against his chest. Lochlyn kissed her hair, and he murmured, "When may I admire you?"

"Now, if you'd like." Rosalie loosened her bodice and pulled her arms free, then she let her dress fall to the floor. She closed her eyes, hoping Lochlyn found her body attractive or at least unoffensive, when he tilted her chin up.

"You're trembling," he said as he stroked her cheek. "Are you scared?"

Rosalie heard what he'd left unsaid; he worried she was frightened of him. "I'm not scared. Maybe a bit nervous," she admitted, then she looked up at him through her lashes. "Perhaps you should distract me?"

"An excellent idea, beloved." Lochlyn lifted her out of the mass of silk and lace, and he carried her to the sunken area of the room. As he laid her on the cushions, she realized it was a circular bed that was big enough for a dragon.

"Do you sleep here?" she asked, running her hands across the soft velvet cushions and knitted blankets.

"On occasion," he said. "When I'm in dragon form, and do a lot of flying, sometimes I don't have the energy to transform back right away."

"These transformations are tiring? Wait, is that why you eat so much?"

"That, and our cook is excellent." Lochlyn nuzzled her neck. "Rosalie, my rose petal. You're certain you want to be here with me, even now that you know everything?"

Rosalie pushed his dark hair back from his face so she could see his eyes. The pale blue hue hadn't changed when he transformed into a dragon, and he'd gazed at her with just as much love regardless of form. "When you said your kind mated for life, you meant dragon kind, didn't you?"

"Yes." He drew back and frowned. "The other night... I would have stopped if you'd asked me to, and I meant to tell you everything before we went too far. Rosalie, I would never trick you like that." He paused, adding, "It probably didn't seem that way."

"Lochlyn, I believe you," she said. "And I want to spend my life with you, my dragon."

Lochlyn's face brightened. "You do?"

"There is no place I'd rather be," she said as she curled a leg around his hips. "I'm yours, Lochlyn."

He dipped his head and kissed the curve where her neck met her shoulder. "Tell me what you like."

She laughed. "Why don't you show me what you like?"

Instead of replying, Lochlyn put himself between Rosalie's legs and paused with his hand atop her hip. He swept his gaze across her body from her thighs to her breasts. She was laid bare in more ways than one, but instead of feeling embarrassed, her husband's curiosity aroused her own.

"Have you ever seen a woman before?" she asked.

"I have," he replied as he stroked his hand up her side, eventually cupping her breast. "But I've never been so close to anyone I've loved this much." He leaned forward and kissed her belly, then he pressed his lips between her breasts. As he laid himself on top of her, he said, "You, ah, may know more about this than I do."

"I wouldn't call myself an expert." Rosalie reached down and grasped the hot, heavy length of him. "But I do know what I want."

Lochlyn nudged her thighs wider and rubbed himself against her entrance. His eyes locked with hers, and she nodded, then he pushed forward. Rosalie gasped as he filled her, threading her fingers into his soft, dark hair. He was a big man, but Rosalie hadn't expected to be so consumed by him. Lochlyn pushed until she didn't know where he ended and she began, then he rested his forehead against hers and sighed.

"Beloved," he murmured as he rained kisses upon her face. Rosalie had never felt so adored in all her life. "My sweet, sweet beloved."

"I want to call him Jonathan."

Lochlyn blinked himself awake, wondering if the past few hours had been a dream. He had done the most terrifying act of his life—he bared both his body and soul to Rosalie—and learned that his fears were unfounded. She accepted him as a dragon, fully and unconditionally.

Now he looked down at his wife, his beautiful, sweet rose petal. She was curled up against his side, languidly tracing the ivory scales on his belly. And, she had just named their son.

"Jonathan is a very good name," he said. "Does that name have meaning for you?"

"None at all," she replied. "That's why I think it will be a good name for the baby. A fresh, new name that's his alone."

"You wouldn't rather name him after your father, or one of your brothers?"

She laughed shortly. "Absolutely not. My father is an awful man, and my brothers do awful things to gain his favor. Why do you think I so readily agreed to marry you? There was no way living in Dragon Ridge could be worse than home."

"That's why you agreed to our marriage?" He shook his head. "And here I thought you loved me."

She playfully thumped his shoulder. "I didn't even know your name until the cleric said it. It's not like you knew anything about me either."

"Oh, but I did." Lochlyn moved Rosalie until she was sitting up and straddling his waist, ostensibly so he could meet her eyes. In reality, he couldn't stop raking his gaze across her form. "I was told many tales about how Lord Osman's youngest child was the most beautiful woman on earth."

"Youngest *daughter*," she amended, making no effort to cover herself. And why should she be shy after everything they'd shared? "I have several brothers younger than me."

"Apologies, beloved." He captured her hand, kissed the thin skin of her inner wrist, and felt her pulse jump at his touch. "Truth be told, I didn't pay attention to your brothers' birth order, but I did listen attentively to the stories of beautiful, feisty Rosalie. I was warned you'd carve out my heart and roast it with your glare," he added as she laughed.

"I'm neither of those things," she demurred, but Lochlyn shook his head.

"You are the most beautiful woman in the world, and the fire in your heart rivals my own," he insisted. "Add that to your sharp mind and endless compassion, and you're as perfect a woman who ever lived."

"And you are my perfect mate," she said. "Nevertheless, when I was at home, my mother was lauded as a great beauty, not me. And as for feisty, that was Caterina. I spent my days hiding in my room, wishing someone would take me away from the madness." She leaned forward and placed her hand against his cheek. "And then you did, my prince."

"I'm a duke. You really should have learned my title by now." They laughed, and Lochlyn noticed that the tips of her breasts were the same shade of pink as her lips. "Despite the events that led to our marriage, I fell in love with you the moment I saw you."

Rosalie stilled, then she claimed his lips as if she owned him. "My beloved," she murmured. "The Fates Themselves brought us together. We should honor them."

"How?" he asked, drunk on her kisses.

"Like this."

Rosalie raised herself up and fit his cock against her, and then she slid down onto him. Surprised and shocked and so incredibly in love with his wife, he grasped her hips and moved inside her, grinning as she threw her head back and laughed.

"My dragon," she said. "Show me how much you love me, my dragon."

Lochlyn flipped her onto her back and drove himself into her, pouring his heart and his soul into every movement. Rosalie gasped and cried out as she gripped his shoulders, and he slowed to a gentle rhythm.

"Lochlyn," she murmured as they moved together.

"Mmm?"

"I love you, too."

CHAPTER EIGHTEEN

THE ASH FIELD

"Did you sleep well, beloved?"

Rosalie opened her eyes, and saw Lochlyn smiling at her. They were still in bed at the Dragon's Den, and Rosalie couldn't think of any place she'd rather be... Then she remembered the castle they called home, and all the rooms within it.

Instead of answering his question, she laughed.

"What's so funny?" he asked.

"You have that huge bed at home," Rosalie began. "For that matter, I have a large, comfortable bed that we've slept in together. Yet we had to come all the way here to make love."

Lochlyn dipped his head and nuzzled her neck. "When we get home, we can visit both our beds," he suggested, kissing a path to her jaw. "There are many, many guest rooms, too."

"So much to explore." Rosalie imagined moving from room to room with Lochlyn, testing each bed in turn, as she stretched her neck for more kisses. He obliged. "I like that."

She felt Lochlyn smile against her skin. "Fates, I can't believe this is my life," he said as he caressed her shoulder.

"Our life," she amended. "As you've said many times, we now share everything."

"We do, my beautiful wife." He drew her against his chest and tucked her head beneath his chin. "As soon as we get back, I'll give you half of my ledgers. You can help me keep up with the Ridge's accounts."

"I'm quite good with numbers," she said, tracing tiny circles onto his skin. "We should put in an order with the seamstress, too."

"Why? For Jonathan?"

"No, for you. Now that we've consummated our marriage," she paused to kiss his throat, "you don't need to wear black any longer."

Lochlyn stilled, and Rosalie worried she'd made a grave error. "I assumed you wore black because of Carys," she said.

"She had nothing to do with it," Lochlyn said, then he sighed. "You want to know why I'm called the Black Duke."

Her heart broke at the pain in his voice. "You don't have to tell me, not if—"

"It's all right." He sat up and rubbed his eyes. "You should know where the name came from, and it will be easier if I show you. It's far, so we'll have to fly there."

"We're going somewhere?"

"Yes." His shoulders drooped. "An old battlefield in the Northern Reaches."

Rosalie embraced him, her cheek pressed against his back. "You think we should go now? What about the baby?"

"He's safe at home. Like as not, Madchen's already spoiling him." Lochlyn stood and retrieved Rosalie's dress from where they'd left it hours ago. "The winds up there are cold. Bring one of the blankets to wrap around yourself."

Rosalie put on her dress and pulled a blanket around her like a cloak. While she did that, Lochlyn shifted into his dragon form. Unafraid because under all those scales and spines he was still the man she loved, she approached the dragon and laid her hand on his leathery cheek.

"No matter what you show me, it won't change how I feel about you," she said, then she kissed the tip of his nose. "You're my dragon, and I'm not leaving you."

Lochlyn nuzzled her neck, then he went down on his belly and flattened his wings. Rosalie climbed onto his back, and she felt the warmth emanating from his skin. That was good, since he said the place they were heading to was cold. She grabbed two of his spines for handholds and said, "Ready."

Lochlyn stood, and Rosalie yelped as she slid to one side. He paused as she righted herself and adjusted her grip. "All right," she said, and then Lochlyn leaped into the sky.

The wind blew Rosalie's hair away from her face as she struggled to remain upright on Lochlyn's back. When they'd flown while he was in warrior form he held onto her, and made sure she was secure, but riding on his back was different. Nor was it like riding a horse; Lochlyn was too wide for her to steady herself with her legs, and the beat of his wings meant his muscles were constantly in motion beneath her. Finally, she hunkered down behind his neck, laid flat against his spine, and hoped it wouldn't rain.

Once she was as secure as she was going to get, Rosalie tried to focus on the beauty of the passing landscape, but she couldn't stop worrying. She hadn't meant to upset Lochlyn, especially not now when they were finally as close as she'd always wanted them to be. But what was done was done, and she did want to know why he was called the Black Duke. Even more, she wanted to know why he hated the title.

Lochlyn flew north into the heart of the mountains and landed in a sizable field. Rosalie imagined that it had once been beautiful, but no longer. Instead of wildflowers and tall grasses, the field was covered in a layer of black, sooty ash.

Her dragon went down on his belly, and Rosalie slid off his back. In doing so, she realized that the entire field wasn't burnt. Lochlyn had landed in the only circle of living plants.

"What is this place?" Rosalie crouched at the edge of the scorched ground and touched the blackened dirt. "I've never seen anything so thoroughly burnt," she said, cold dread forming in her stomach as she wondered what could have caused such destruction. "The soil has been rendered to charcoal."

"There was a war," Lochlyn said behind her, his voice rough. Rosalie turned and saw him again in his human form. She offered him the blanket, but he waved it away. "A clan in the north wanted our lands, our people. There's an old tale, a myth, really, about dragon scales granting the holder great things. Strength, health, even immortality." Lochlyn scoffed. "If only that were true. But the Northerners believed it, and they waged war against the Ridge. Against my family."

Rosalie approached him and set her hand on the scaly part of his forearm. "You went to war along with your family?"

"I didn't. Not at first." He focused on her, cupped the side of her face with his hand. "My brothers were born within five years of each other. They were quite a bit older than me. My eldest brother, Jerreth, had already reached his twenty-fifth year when I was born."

She imagined Lochlyn's brothers, all of them young men, being confronted with a new sibling. Being that she had several brothers who were much younger than her, Rosalie felt she understood their dynamic. "Your family must have been surprised to meet you, your mother most of all."

He smiled tightly. "She was. She was so good to us all..." Lochlyn cleared his throat. "In any event, this disparity in ages meant I was too young for war, while my father was too old. So, my brothers went and led the Ridge's soldiers."

"Were your brothers dragons, like you?"

"They were dragons. But not like me. Jerreth could shift to a warrior form, as could my father, but neither could attain a full dragon form. My middle brothers couldn't shift at all." He glanced at her. "I didn't stay home for long."

She nodded because Lochlyn was nothing if not a protector. "When did your father send you to join them?"

"He never sent me," Lochlyn replied. "We hadn't had word from the front in a week. My mother's nerves weren't good, and Father was so worried about her health that he didn't want to leave her side. Therefore, I defied my father, shifted into my dragon, and flew north. I landed here, where we're standing now."

Without looking, he raised his arm and pointed to his left. "That's where they were."

Rosalie looked to the side, saw nothing of import. "Who?"

"My brothers."

"Oh, is that where they led their campaign?"

"No." Rosalie watched as his jaw worked. Then, he continued. "That's where the Northerners displayed their bodies."

Rosalie gasped. "What happened next? Did you take command?"

"No. I roared." Lochlyn went to his knees and covered his face with his hands. "When I saw what happened to my brothers—they had Jerreth's wings pulled out on either side, as if he were a bat under glass—I couldn't think. I couldn't feel or speak or do anything but roar, and I drowned the field in dragon fire."

Rosalie swallowed, and she swept her gaze across the field. "Did anyone survive?" she asked, hoping that Lochlyn had led his soldiers home.

"No. By the time I arrived, my people were already dead, or captured and marched off to another site. My fire destroyed the rest." He dropped his hands to his sides and turned his face to the sky. "And this is why I am known as the Black Duke, he who is so evil he can render an entire army down to ash."

"You are not evil," Rosalie said as she knelt beside him. "You did what you had to do, for your people and your family. What happened to the Ridge's captured soldiers?"

"They were all returned to us," he murmured. "I told the Northern leaders I wanted every single man and boy returned unharmed, or I'd incinerate the rest of their kingdom."

"Then you saved people too." Rosalie tilted his head toward her. "How old were you when this happened?"

"Fourteen."

"Oh, beloved," Rosalie said, pulling him into her arms. Lochlyn held her so tightly she could hardly breathe, his face pressed against her neck as his tears flowed unchecked. "You were still a boy, and you had to act as a man. I'm so, so sorry."

"My mother didn't survive the loss of her older children," Lochlyn choked out. "My father passed soon after her, and it's been the servants and me ever since. Now you know why I had to negotiate marriages, instead of courting a woman like a normal man." He paused and stroked one of his hands down her back. "Even then, most wanted nothing to do with me."

"Then, for once, my father did something good when he drew up that contract with you." Rosalie drew back and wiped his cheek with her thumb. "Take me home. We don't ever need to come back here. And no one will call you that horrid name ever again. If they do, they'll have to deal with me."

"My fiery rose petal," he said, then he stood and drew Rosalie to her feet. "The Fates gave me the greatest gift when They put you in my path."

"A path we'll walk together, my dragon." She leaned up and kissed him, then she stepped back. Lochlyn rolled his shoulders and black sparks surrounded him as he shifted into his dragon form. Rosalie approached him, and kissed his nose.

"I love you in every form," she said as she stroked his cheek. "I want you to know that." Lochlyn growled deep in his chest, then his lizard-like tongue flicked over her lips. "Was that a kiss?"

He growled again, then he jerked his head toward his back. Rosalie climbed on top of him, and they flew back to Dragon Ridge. Once the castle was in sight, and Lochlyn's flight path made it clear he wasn't returning to the citadel for his clothes, Rosalie worried how they would get inside. Surely he wasn't going to walk through the front doors naked, or wrapped in a sooty blanket? Then the castle was directly below them, and Lochlyn landed on one of the glass roofs.

With one of his curved talons, Lochlyn unlatched the roof and opened it up, then he entered the castle. Somehow, Rosalie managed to hold on to him as he crawled down the wall, but only just. Once they reached the floor, and Rosalie slid off his back, she realized they were in his rooms.

"This is why your roof opens," she said, marveling at the simple yet effective engineering. She turned to ask Lochlyn about the mechanism, but he was lumbering toward the bed. *He said the transformations are tiring, and he's shifted form several times today.* Rosalie sat on the edge of the bed, and stroked Lochlyn's foreleg.

"Beloved," she murmured. His blue eyes flicked open. "I'm going to check on the baby. Rest for me." Rosalie waited for Lochlyn's eyes to close before she went to her rooms, where she found the baby nestled in Madchen's arms. Lochlyn was right, she was already spoiling him.

"You've returned," Madchen said as she stood, handing Jonathan over to Rosalie.

"Yes, just now," Rosalie replied. "How was he?"

"A perfect gentleman," Madchen replied. "He's just eaten, so he may sleep for a time." Madchen spied the layer of soot on the hem of Rosalie's dress. "He took you to the ash field?"

"He did." Rosalie regarded the housekeeper over the top of Jonahan's head, and realized that a barrier that stood between them was now dissolved. "I understand why you never divulged any of Lochlyn's secrets. Thank you, for your loyalty to him."

"Silas and I had seven sons when that war began," Madchen said. "Lochlyn rescued the four who'd gone off to fight. My loyalty is the least I can give him. And you also have that loyalty, my lady, from the moment you married him," she added.

Rosalie dipped her chin, acknowledging Madchen's heartfelt words. "You were here when Carys was?"

Madchen pursed her lips and looked away. "I was. She was not meant to be with the duke. Not in the way you are, my lady."

"I'm glad you think so," Rosalie began, but Madchen wasn't finished.

"Carys wasn't a bad person," she continued. "But she was... unsuited for life here on the Ridge. Our lord tried everything he could to make her happy, and in the end, she was only happy when she left." She glanced at Rosalie. "That was five years ago, and we'd begun to worry our Lochlyn would be the last Blackmoor."

Five years was such a long time to nurse a broken heart. "He must have been so lonely."

"He was, but he hid it well. At least, he thought he did." Madchen set her hand on Rosalie's, and continued, "Everything changed when he married you. When he came home to prepare the castle for your arrival, he was smiling and laughing like I hadn't seen him do in ages. In fact, he smiled more that day than he had since he was a boy."

Rosalie hugged Jonathan closer as she remembered her first day at Dragon Ridge; Lochlyn's wide smile when she finally arrived, the bouquet he dropped in order to catch her when she stumbled, and how he'd filled her rooms with flowers. At the time, the day had been overshadowed by her long and cold journey from Irontooth Keep, but she appreciated how Lochlyn had done his best to make her feel welcome. "If only I hadn't taken ill, who knows what would have happened."

"Who knows, indeed." Madchen clasped her hands in front of her. "Have you decided what we're to call the boy?"

"Jonathan," Rosalie replied. "Until we find Caterina, we're to refer to him as my and Lochlyn's child. In light of the king's letter and the bounty my father put on Caterina's head, we can't let anyone know she was here, or that she had a child. And as for the phoenix aspect..." Rosalie shuddered as she recalled how the Order treated its children, and she held the baby a bit tighter. "We don't want them learning about him either."

"Understood, my lady. What can I do for you now?"

"Lochlyn is resting, but I'm sure he'll want a bath soon," she replied. "And something to eat."

"There is plumbing in his washroom," Madchen replied. "He heats the water himself."

"Yes, I imagine he would," Rosalie murmured, recalling Lochlyn's warm skin courtesy of his dragon fire. "Can you have Cook put a meal together for him?"

"Of course," Madchen said. "I'll have it brought up to his sitting room. I've also taken the liberty of placing a cradle in his bedroom, and I had half of your clothes relocated to his wardrobe. Just in case," she added with a knowing smile.

"Thank you, Madchen," Rosalie said, then she embraced the older woman with the arm that wasn't cradling the baby. "I don't know what any of us would do without you."

"There, there," Madchen said as she patted Rosalie's back. "I appreciate your kind words, my lady. Now go, be with your husband."

Rosalie smiled and left the housekeeper. She took her time returning to Lochlyn's rooms. Along the way, she showed Jonathan around his home, including the large dragon sculpture in the atrium.

"That's our ancestor, the first Blackmoor," she whispered to the baby. Now that Rosalie had seen Lochlyn's dragon, she compared her husband's form to that of the sculpture. The dragon before her was larger, and its teeth were longer and came to a sharp point. On a whim, Rosalie pressed her finger to one of the fangs, hissing when she drew blood.

"I suppose that was foolish," Rosalie said to the baby. He remained asleep. "Let's see if Papa's awake," she said. She was halfway up the stairs before she realized what she'd said.

She'd referred to Lochlyn as Papa, which meant she was Mama.

Rosalie paused on the steps and kissed Jonathan's head, enjoying his sweet newborn scent. Her life had changed in so many ways since her father burst into her room and ordered her to marry Lochlyn, and she was happier now than she'd ever been. All she needed to do now was find her sister, and her life would be perfect.

"No matter what happens, Jonathan, Papa and I will always care for you," Rosalie said as she opened the door to Lochlyn's rooms. "We love you very, very much. Never forget that."

She approached Lochlyn's bed, where he slumbered in his dragon form. Rosalie laid down next to him and set the baby between them. Lochlyn cracked an eyelid, then he draped his wing across his wife and son. Soon enough, the family was asleep.

CHAPTER NINETEEN

FLOWER NAMES

The next few days after Jonathan's birth were a blur of naps and feedings, and the occasional bout of crying from adult and baby alike. Despite the madness that was life with a newborn, Rosalie had never been happier.

When Jonathan was two weeks old, Lochlyn asked Rosalie when she would like to visit the orphanage in the village. Rosalie was pleased that he'd remembered her idea and still wanted to make the trip.

"I don't know," she replied as she nestled closer to him. They were in the massive bed in Lochlyn's chamber, which had become Rosalie's and Jonathan's room as well. Originally, the little family planned to stay in Rosalie's rooms; it was closer to the laundry and kitchens, and, therefore, more convenient for the baby. After their sleep had been disturbed three times in one night—not by an infant, but by servants bustling in and out—Lochlyn finally declared that all three of them were relocating to his rooms in the tower. He drew up a schedule so the servants knew when to be attentive, and when to leave them alone. It was the best solution for everyone, since no one wanted to live with a cranky, sleep-deprived dragon.

On that day, Jonathan was in Rosalie's rooms being fussed over by Madchen and the rest of her staff. It had been Madchen's idea for her to take the baby for a few hours every day, to give Rosalie and Lochlyn time to themselves. Rosalie suspected that Madchen just wanted to enjoy having a baby in her arms, and she didn't begrudge the old housekeeper any of it.

"Is one day better than another?" Rosalie continued.

"Probably not, but we should go soon," he said. "My people know that I've wed, but very few have seen my beautiful bride. Now they can meet you and our son at the same time."

"Do your people know you're a dragon?" she asked as she traced the dark scales on his shoulder. "Or is that one of your many secrets?"

"I have no secrets from you, only things I've forgotten to mention. With regard to my lineage, everyone knows we're descended from dragons, but I'm the first full dragon shifter in my family in three generations. In fact, I know of no other dragons like me."

"Why is that, I wonder," Rosalie said. "Is it like what you mentioned about mortality breeding truer, regardless of the creature?"

"Exactly, beloved." Lochlyn kissed the soft spot behind her ear. "All Blackmoors carry the blood, but it's usually latent to a certain degree. My father and eldest brother could shift into warrior forms, but no one expected my dragon. The first time I shifted, my nursemaid fainted."

Rosalie giggled. "You must have been the most adorable tiny dragon, squawking and flapping around."

"I beg your pardon." Lochlyn propped himself up on his elbow and glowered. "I did not squawk! Or flap!"

"Oh, so you were born knowing how to fly and roar? I doubt that," Rosalie said, as Lochlyn growled deep in his chest. "Stop that. You know how those growls distract me, and we need to get ready to go to the orphanage. I'd like to go today if that's all right."

"Of course it is," Lochlyn murmured as he nuzzled her neck. "Even if there aren't any children we feel a connection with, we can let the headmistress know our intention of having a large family."

"And we should bring them a gift that everyone can use," Rosalie added. "We don't want any of the children we don't adopt to feel slighted."

Lochlyn's kisses traveled from her neck to her shoulder. "As you say, beloved."

A short time later, they went to Rosalie's chamber in order to collect the baby. As Madchen helped Rosalie with a sling that was designed to let her carry Jonathan against her breast, she showed Madchen the baby's left wrist.

"Madchen, I think he has a rash," Rosalie said as she pushed up Jonathan's sleeve. There was a reddish-brown mark on his inner wrist that resembled a flame. "At first, I worried it was a bruise, but now I'm not sure," she continued.

Madchen had a look at Jonathan's wrist and smiled. "Good eye, my lady, but this is no rash. It's just a birthmark."

Rosalie stroked the mark, then she kissed the baby's wrist. "Is it usual for these marks to appear so long after birth?"

"Oh, yes," she replied. "It takes time for a body to settle, and I'm sure Jonathan has many more surprises in store for us." She paused, then added, "It is interesting that his father was a phoenix, and now he has a flame-shaped mark."

"It is," Rosalie murmured. "Thank you, for your excellent care of him."

"Always a pleasure to spend time with our young lord," Madchen said.

With the baby secure in his sling, Rosalie joined Lochlyn in the atrium. "We're ready when you are, my love."

Lochlyn kissed the baby's head, then he lingered against Rosalie's lips. "When are you going to let me take him flying?"

"When it's warmer and he's older," she replied. She remembered well the frigid winds she dealt with while flying with her husband, and she worried they would freeze tiny Jonathan. "Are we taking the carriage to the village?"

"We are," he affirmed.

Rosalie sighed. She wasn't a fan of traveling by carriage, but it was better than walking down half of the mountain. Despite her impending carriage ride, Rosalie was dressed for walking, in brown trousers and boots, and a loose green blouse. The seamstress had been scandalized when Rosalie ordered trousers in her size, but Lochlyn thought they were quite becoming.

"You're certain you'd like to dress this way for your first foray among our people?" he asked. He was also wearing a new blue shirt that perfectly matched his eyes. The rest of his clothing was black, proving that change came slowly to dragons. "You do look lovely in them, but very few women in the village dress this way."

"Trousers are practical," Rosalie replied. "Whenever Cat and I went into the village back home, we wore them." Rosalie's throat tightened when she mentioned her sister, but she shrugged it off. Silas had assured her that the Ridge's spies were still gathering information, and she was confident she would see Caterina again. "Besides, I can wear a gown when we attend the midsummer celebration. Will that please you?" she asked, looking up at him through her lashes.

"Everything you do pleases me," Lochlyn said as he grasped her hip. "Ready, beloved?"

"Yes," she replied, eager to finally see the village. "Let's be off."

Thankfully, Jonathan slept through the bumpy ride; though Rosalie wished she could too, she kept her grumblings to herself. Soon enough, the carriage halted in the village square.

"A moment," Lochlyn said as he exited the carriage. Rosalie looked out one window, then slid across the seat to the other side, wondering where he'd gone.

Lochlyn reappeared in the doorway a few minutes later and offered Rosalie his hand.

"Where did you run off to?" Rosalie asked as he helped her out of the carriage.

"I checked over the square and ordered my guard to fan out across the area." Rosalie glanced around and saw no less than eight of Dragon Ridge's guards stationed around the square.

"Are eight men really necessary?" she asked. "I thought the village was peaceful."

"It is," he replied, retrieving a basket from the carriage; per Rosalie's suggestion, they were bringing gifts for all the children, and the basket was filled with toys and sweets for them to share. "However, I will not risk your safety, or Jonathan's. I waited all my life for you, beloved," he added as he caressed her cheek. "I refuse to let anything happen to either of you."

Rosalie ducked her head as her cheeks warmed. Being that she and Jonathan were standing beside a dragon, they were the safest people in Alessia. But Lochlyn was only overprotective because he loved them, and the least she could do was let herself be protected.

"I can't argue with that, now can I?" Rosalie said as her husband grinned. "Do you know the way to the orphanage?"

He did, and Lochlyn led her through the village's cobblestone streets that were too narrow to accommodate their carriage. Rosalie observed the many storefronts they passed and made note of the artist's shop. There was a lovely vine blooming in the castle's garden, and she wanted to paint it as soon as possible.

When they arrived at the orphanage, the headmistress was overjoyed to meet the new Lady Blackmoor, and to accept the basket of gifts.

"While we want for nothing thanks to our lord's generosity, the children will adore the gifts you've brought them," the headmistress said after Lochlyn presented her the basket. "We are most grateful."

"Think nothing of it," Lochlyn said, then the headmistress excused herself to bring the gifts to the storeroom.

"You're quite generous here?" Rosalie asked.

"I pay for all of the orphanage's expenses," he replied. "Clothing, food, tutors. Whatever the children need, I provide."

"That must be quite an expense," Rosalie said, but her dragon wasn't only her protector. He looked after all of his people just as carefully as he did her and the baby.

"It is, but they've already lost their families. It's the least I can do to ensure the children have as good a start to their lives as possible."

Rosalie kissed the bottom of Lochlyn's chin. "Just when I think I can't possibly love you any more, you go and do something amazing and wonderful. I can hardly stand it."

Lochlyn set his hand on the side of her neck and stroked her jaw with his thumb. "Keep not standing it. You have no idea what I'm capable of." He leaned close to her ear and murmured, "But I would love to show you."

Rosalie's face went hot, but before she could respond, the headmistress returned and clasped her hands over her heart. "My lord duke, it pleases me to see you so happily wed. And, my lady, may I see your son?"

"Of course," Rosalie said, and turned so the headmistress could see Jonathan's face. "I must warn you, he's so handsome you'll want to cover him in kisses."

"What a beautiful boy," the headmistress cooed. "My lady, you have given our lord the greatest of gifts. Now, your message said you'd like to find him a sibling?"

"That's right," Lochlyn replied. "We want to have a large family, and we're a bit impatient about it."

"Understood, my lord," the headmistress said. "Come with me, and we'll see what we can do."

Lochlyn followed the headmistress directly into the central dormitory, but Rosalie took her time. She wanted to learn more about the place her husband felt so strongly about. The rooms were clean and in good repair, and she believed that Lochlyn spared no expense for the children—if her dragon was guilty of anything, it was of a too-generous heart.

Eager to discover more about the orphanage, Rosalie stepped out into the courtyard. She saw several older children playing with a ball and sticks, but one girl was on the other side of the yard from the rest. She appeared to be a few years younger than the others and sat under a tree paging through a book. Rosalie smiled as she remembered her own youth; she'd had several brothers close to her in age, and she was forever trying to find a quiet spot to read.

Suddenly, the ball the others played with was thrown wide and crashed into the girl's book. Rosalie rushed toward her.

"Are you all right?" she asked. The girl, red-faced, nodded. Rosalie retrieved the ball and faced the other children.

"Whose is this?" Rosalie asked. A boy of around ten stepped forward.

"It was my fault, milady," the boy said. "Willy punted it toward me and I couldn't catch it in time. I'm sorry, Violet," he said to the girl.

"That's good of you to apologize," Rosalie said as she handed them the ball. "Now run and play. But be careful." The boys accepted the ball and ran toward the far side of the courtyard. Rosalie watched them for a moment, then she sat next to the girl.

"Your name is Violet?"

Violet nodded. "My mama named me after a flower."

"So did mine. I'm Rosalie."

"Roses are so pretty!"

"As are violets." Rosalie glanced at the book in Violet's lap; it was a heavy leather-bound tome of at least a hundred pages. She doubted Violet could understand the book, but she remembered when she was young, and she deliberately chose the longest books she could find too. "Do you like reading?"

"It's the only thing I like." Violet showed Rosalie her book. In doing so, she exposed her forearm, which bore a birthmark similar to Jonathan's. It was so similar she briefly wondered if Violet were related to Curran.

But Violet couldn't be related to Curran, Rosalie thought as she bit her lip. *Could she?*

"Violet, what happened to your arm?" Rosalie asked.

Violet looked down at her forearm and shrugged. "It's always been there," she replied, then she opened her book. "See, this story has a map." Rosalie murmured her appreciation, leaning closer to get a better look at Violet's birthmark. "Are you here to leave your baby?"

"No, not at all," Rosalie said as she adjusted Jonathan against her breast. "This is my son, Jonathan. My husband and I are looking for a sibling for him."

"Oh. Is your husband nice?"

"He is," Rosalie gazed thoughtfully at Violet. Even though she wasn't the baby Rosalie had in mind, Violet was smart and polite, and reminded Rosalie so much of herself when she was young. "Would you like to meet my husband?" When Violet nodded, Rosalie stood and offered her hand. "Let's go find him now. Don't forget your book." Rosalie started toward the entrance, but she saw the other children playing in front of the doorway. "Is there another way inside?"

"We can go to the front," Violet said as she led the way. They slipped through a gap in the fence and found themselves in the alleyway. When Rosalie stepped onto the main street, she almost collided with the mason who'd visited Dragon Ridge a few weeks prior.

"Pardon me, Lady Blackmoor," Zephyn began, then he spied the bundle at Rosalie's breast. "I didn't know you had a child."

"He's but a newborn," Rosalie replied as she took a step back and reached for Violet. "Meet our lord's heir, Jonathan Blackmoor."

"Well met, my young lord," Zephyn said as he bowed to the baby. "I must say, Lady Blackmoor, you have a strong constitution. When we met two weeks ago, you gave no indications of a recent birth."

Rosalie sucked in her breath, unsure if the mason were complimenting her or insinuating that Jonathan had been born from another woman. Which, of course, he had, but there was no way the mason could know about Caterina. Before Rosalie could form a response, Lochlyn strode out of the orphanage's front door.

"There you are." Lochlyn frowned when he saw her anxious expression. "What's wrong?"

"Nothing," she replied, a bit too quickly. "The mason was just saying hello."

Lochlyn's eyes narrowed, but he didn't question Rosalie. He turned to the other man and said, "Zephyn, I wasn't expecting to see you today. How goes work on the bridge?"

"Splendidly, my lord," he replied. "I was just complimenting Lady Black-moor on having such a wonderful boy." The mason took a step toward Rosalie with his hand outstretched. Lochlyn growled and put his body between the mason and Rosalie.

"Don't approach my wife," Lochlyn warned. "Ever."

"Apologies, my lord," the mason said, the blood draining from his face. "I meant no disrespect."

"If you'll excuse us," Lochlyn said as he placed his hand on Rosalie's back and guided her indoors. Rosalie looked over her shoulder, beckoning Violet to follow them.

"Making all sorts of friends?" Lochlyn asked when he noticed Violet trailing behind them.

"She has the same birthmark as Jonathan," Rosalie whispered.

"Jonathan has a birthmark?" he asked. Rosalie showed him the baby's wrist. Lochlyn frowned, then he drew Rosalie close and kissed her hair. "We'll talk at home," he whispered.

Rosalie nodded. "Why did you growl at the mason?"

Lochlyn's face darkened. "My dragon saw him as a threat. I'm not sure why, but I trust my instincts."

Rosalie trusted Lochlyn as well, but she didn't want to dwell on their inter-action with the mason. Instead, she said, "Before I saw the mason, I was in the courtyard, where I met Violet. She asked if you were nice."

Lochlyn turned and bowed to Violet. "Lovely to meet you, Violet. As to whether or not I'm nice, I do my best, but my lady wife is by far the more amenable of us two."

Violet giggled. "You're funny."

Lochlyn ducked his head. "I suppose I am. Rosalie, the headmistress has someone she would like us to meet."

"Does she?" Grabbing Violet's hand as naturally as if she'd known her for years, Rosalie followed Lochlyn deeper into the building. They found the headmistress bundling up a baby who was twice the size of Jonathan.

"There you are, my lady," the headmistress said, then she indicated the baby. "We've been calling this bruiser Maximus because he's so big. He's been here for two months, and he has the brightest eyes and happiest laugh." Headmistress supported his back as she helped Maximus sit up on the table. Rosalie, already quite taken with the boy, stroked his hand.

"Hello, Maximus," she said, glancing at her husband, who was beaming at them. "You two have gotten on well?"

"I am prepared to make a strong case for bringing Max to Dragon Ridge," he replied, then there was a commotion at the door. The headmistress set Maximus in his cradle, and then she went to find out what was happening.

"I suppose it will be good for Jonathan to have a brother," Rosalie said. "Did I tell you that Violet likes to read?"

"Oh?" Lochlyn arched a dark brow. "Violet, what kind of books do you like?"

"Ones with maps," she replied.

"Much like my Rosalie," Lochlyn said. Violet opened her book and showed him the map that had so thoroughly intrigued her, then she launched into a detailed description of the story's plot. While Lochlyn and Violet got to know each other, Rosalie approached the other cradle in the room. In it was an infant wrapped in a gray blanket. When the headmistress returned to them, she spoke to Rosalie first.

"What was all that about?" Rosalie asked.

"Just a delivery," Headmistress replied. "I see you've met our newest resident. Her mother perished in childbed, and her family has no way to care for her."

"The poor thing. What of her father?" Rosalie asked.

"Her father has unfortunately passed as well," Headmistress replied. "If you're both agreed on adopting Maximus, this child will be our youngest."

"We can take her, too," Rosalie began, her heart going out to the girl, then she glanced at Lochlyn. "If you agree, of course."

Lochlyn stood beside the cradle. "She's beautiful, like you. She'll fit right in."

"Of course she will," Headmistress said as she scooped up the infant. "She's only been here a few days, and this blanket is all she came with. It will be good for her to go to a family."

"I suppose that's our answer," Lochlyn said. "Beloved, we have our family."

"We do," Rosalie murmured, but she didn't want to leave Violet behind. Rosalie crouched down in front of her, and asked, "Would you like to come live with us at Dragon Ridge? We have a library."

"You do?" Violet asked, her eyes going wide.

"We do," Rosalie said. "Lochlyn, how many volumes are there?"

He set his hand on Rosalie's shoulder and squeezed. "About ten thousand, give or take."

"Ten thousand," Violet squeaked, and then she looked to the headmistress. "May I go with them? Please?"

"Of course she's coming with us," Rosalie said, and Lochlyn nodded.

"We have plenty of room. And books," he added.

"As wonderful as this is, I will miss you, Violet," the headmistress said, then she passed the infant girl into Lochlyn's arms. "But you will have a good life with Lord and Lady Blackmoor. I'll just gather your things, my sweet girl."

The headmistress stroked Violet's hair, then she went to gather Violet's possessions. Rosalie approached Lochlyn and the infant girl cradled in his hands.

"Look at how well she rests with you," Rosalie murmured. "She's your baby, no doubt about it."

"Our baby," Lochlyn said, then he focused on Violet. "Well, Violet, it seems that you have a brand-new sister. What would you like to call her?"

"I can name her?" Violet asked as she approached Lochlyn. He knelt down so Violet could see the newborn's face. "Since we already have flower names, she should have one, too. Let's call her Lily."

"Lily," Lochlyn repeated. "What a beautiful name." He adjusted Lily's blanket, then he stood and whispered to Rosalie, "Beloved. There is ash on her blanket."

Rosalie touched the ash. She never thought one type of ash would be different from another, but the substance on Lily's blanket was identical to the slippery gray drifts she'd dug through to find Jonathan. On a hunch, Rosalie went to Max's cradle and pushed up his sleeve. He had a flame-shaped birthmark just below his elbow.

"Lochlyn," Rosalie said. He approached the cradle, frowning when he saw the boy's birthmark. When the headmistress returned with Violet's things, he faced her.

"Do you know what happened to this girl's parents?" Lochlyn asked.

"Apparently there was a fire," Headmistress replied. "I was told that was how the child's father perished." She looked between Lochlyn and Rosalie, and she asked, "Is something wrong, my lord?"

"No, no," he replied. "We were merely curious. Thank you for collecting Violet's things so quickly. Is there anything else you need from us?"

"Not at all, my lord," Headmistress replied. "And thank you for coming by today. I know the children will have the best life with you and Lady Blackmoor. We should all wish for so much."

"You adopted three babies?" Madchen demanded, her hands on her hips.

Lochlyn and Rosalie, along with all four of their children, had just returned from the village. Madchen met them in the atrium, eager to meet the new child. To say she hadn't been expecting to meet three new people was an understatement.

"Have you any idea how hard it will be to care for four babies at once?" Madchen continued.

"I'm not a baby," Violet said. "I'm almost seven!"

"Apologies, young lady," Madchen said, then she demanded of the adults, "Exactly who is going to care for these three babies and one six-year-old?"

"Lochlyn and I will," Rosalie said, unaffected by Madchen's ire. "At home, I often cared for my younger brothers, and the other children in the Keep."

"But, three." Madchen shook her head, then she gestured toward the infants. "At least tell me their names."

"This is Maximus," Rosalie began, indicating the baby in her arms. Since Max was so big, Rosalie carried him while Lochlyn managed the other two. "You've already met Violet. And our little girl is Lily."

"Lily?" Madchen repeated, as she turned toward Lochlyn. "Much like your mother."

"My mother's name was Lilianna," Lochlyn explained to Rosalie. "And it was Violet that named her."

"Well, perhaps that name is a sign," Madchen said. "However, we may need to bring in a nursemaid or two to help look after everyone."

"I can help too," Violet said, ready to stand by her new parents who gave her access to a library. "I like helping, and Max is a very good boy. Lily's the only one that cries, but she's tiny. Headmistress says that all tiny babies cry."

"Violet, you are the only one here with any sense," Madchen said. "Would you like to go to the kitchens with me, and inform Cook about our new residents?"

Violet gasped. "Will there be cakes in the kitchen?"

Lochlyn laughed. "Violet, where Madchen is concerned, there are always cakes."

Madchen narrowed her eyes at Lochlyn. "Behave, young man, or there won't be any cakes for you. Come along, Violet," Madchen said as she took Max from Rosalie. Violet happily skipped behind Madchen.

"Those two became fast friends," Rosalie murmured as she took Jonathan from Lochlyn. Lily had already made it quite plain that she only wanted to be nestled against Lochlyn's dragon-warm chest. "And Madchen has claimed Max as well."

"She's already claimed Jonathan, and she'll have Lily soon enough," Lochlyn said. "All the children of the Ridge belong to Madchen, whether she's met them or not."

Rosalie adjusted Jonathan against her breast and glimpsed the birthmark on his wrist. "What do you want to tell me about these birthmarks?"

Lochlyn's face darkened. "Let's get some milk for the children, and then we can talk in Silas's study."

After they obtained two bottles of milk, Lochlyn led Rosalie upstairs to Silas's office. It was one of the most secure rooms in the castle, second only to Lochlyn's own study. Being that the steward compiled the most sensitive information they received, his office was nigh on impregnable.

Rosalie had reservations about entering Silas's room without him present.

"You're sure he won't mind us coming in here?" she asked as Lochlyn opened the door.

"I am, and we'll only be here for a moment. Ah!" He located the box he'd been searching for and set it on the desk, opening it one handed. "Ever since we returned from Irontooth Keep, Silas has been compiling information about phoenixes. Being that Caterina ran off with a phoenix knight, it seemed prudent at the time."

"Agreed," Rosalie said. "Has Silas learned a great deal about them?"

"Oh, yes. One thing he learned was that all phoenixes who are able to fully shift are marked by flame." He set a sheet of parchment on the desk between them. On it was a sketch of a man's back, with flame-shaped markings drawn along his spine.

"You're thinking that the marks on the children denote them as phoenixes?" Rosalie asked, and Lochlyn nodded.

"It would make sense," he replied. "We know Curran could shift, and most who carry the blood are in some way marked by their creature." He pushed up his sleeve and exposed his scales.

"I don't remember Curran having any markings," Rosalie murmured. "Then again, I only ever saw his face." She held Jonathan a bit closer. "Let's say all four of our children are phoenixes. Why are they here in Dragon Ridge? And why did Curran tell Cat to come here if she needed help?"

"That, I don't know." Lochlyn replaced the parchment in the box, then he led Rosalie out to the corridor. "But I do mean to find out."

CHAPTER TWENTY

LINEAGE

D espite Madchen's misgivings, the Blackmoor family quickly settled into a routine. Violet helped whenever she could, though her assistance usually involved reorganizing Silas's library and finishing leftover sweets. As for the infants, they laughed more than they cried, which Lochlyn took as a good omen. The Fates had smiled upon him the day he met Rosalie, no doubt about it. Now, two months on from Jonathan's birth, Lochlyn couldn't imagine being happier.

Lochlyn stepped into his study, but he left the door open. He'd been doing that more often of late, as a way of inviting Rosalie to share in all aspects of his life. Of course, wherever Rosalie went, Violet was close behind, but he didn't mind. In fact, after being alone for more than half of his life, he enjoyed having his wife and children with him while he worked.

Sitting on the center of his desk was a sheaf of letters. It had been a rainy spring, and the road to the village had washed out during a particularly intense storm. That meant messengers were delayed while the repairs were being completed, so he had more correspondence than usual.

"What to read first?" he muttered. Sitting on the top of the package was a letter from Rosalie's father. Lochlyn set that one aside, so he could open it when his wife was present. He continued sorting through the letters until he found a package that originated from Serpens, the realm's capital city.

A soft knock distracted him. He turned around and saw Rosalie standing in the doorway with Lily in her arms.

"Too busy for us?" she asked.

"Never," he replied as he set down the package and went to kiss her. "How has she been?" he asked, with a nod toward Lily.

"No changes," Rosalie replied. Lily was a weak and sickly child who didn't like eating, which Madchen attributed to the trauma surrounding her birth, and, perhaps an undernourished mother. Jonathan's birth had also been quite traumatic, but luckily Caterina had been well cared for. Therefore, Jonathan was a good eater, as was Max.

"But she did smile at me when she woke up and drank three whole sips of milk before she went on this latest hunger strike," Rosalie added.

"I thought her smiles were only for me," Lochlyn said in mock outrage. He stroked Lily's tiny hand. "And so much milk! At this rate she'll eat us out of house and home."

Rosalie smiled, but Lochlyn noticed the shadows under her eyes. Even though the children were well-behaved, caring for three infants was just as exhausting as Madchen had said it would be. "Let me take her," Lochlyn said as he claimed the baby. "Where are the other three?"

"Max and Jonathan are with Madchen and her staff in the nursery," she replied as she sat on the edge of the desk. "Violet disappeared into the library after lunch, but as soon as she knows Lily's here with you, I'm sure she'll be along."

"That's fine. I love all my girls." Lochlyn caressed his wife's cheek. Never, not in his wildest dreams, had he ever thought he would find a partner who accepted him wholly and unconditionally, much less have a family. Now, he had Rosalie and their children, and each day was better than the one that came before it. "There's a letter from your father."

"Fates, what could he want?" Rosalie murmured. "Did you open it?"

"I was waiting for you to do the honors," Lochlyn replied. Rosalie sighed, then she cracked open the seal and flattened the parchment against the desk.

"First of all, this letter is addressed to you. I'm not even mentioned," Rosalie began. "Apparently the king has written to Father about Caterina. Both the king and Father are, and I quote, 'most anxious to locate our missing princess'." She paused. "I hope we find her before they do."

"We will, beloved," Lochlyn assured her. "Our spies are searching for her as we speak."

Rosalie reached across the desk and squeezed his forearm. Then, she returned her attention to the letter. "Father goes on, we must find her and punish Curran, blah, blah, blah... Oh, he does mention me. He asks if you've gotten me with child yet."

"We can work on that later," Lochlyn said. Rosalie offered him a coy smile and continued reading. "How long is this letter?" Lochlyn asked when she'd been silent for a time.

"My father loves the sound of his own voice and sharing his supposed brilliance with the world. His letters are just as long and boring as his speeches." She brought the parchment closer to her face, her brows pinched. "He wants us to foster Devlin."

"Really?" Lochlyn asked, surprised. Most lords wanted their children to remain as far from Dragon Ridge as possible. "How old is Devlin?"

"He'll be seventeen next month," Rosalie replied.

"That's a bit old for fostering," Lochlyn said. "What do you think? Would you like your brother to come here, or should we decline?"

"Devlin is the best of my brothers," Rosalie said. "It's always been my hope that he wouldn't take after Father. Out of all our siblings, Cat and I can't be the only decent ones." Rosalie read a bit further. "This is odd. He says that if we're not interested in taking Devlin, he'll just send him to the Order of the Sun instead." Rosalie put down the parchment and faced Lochlyn. "I thought they only took full shifters?"

"That's what I've always been told," Lochlyn replied. "But Devlin's your full-blooded brother, correct? You don't have phoenix blood."

"No, I don't," Rosalie murmured. "That means two things. My father is up to something, *and* he's using my brother to do it." She pulled out a fresh sheet of parchment and began writing.

"Responding to him right away?" Lochlyn asked.

"Yes. I think we should make arrangements for Devlin to come here as soon as practical, if for no other reason than to get him away from whatever my father has gotten involved in." She met his eyes. "If you agree, of course."

"You know I do," Lochlyn replied. "Perhaps he can be here by midsummer and take part in the celebration."

"Perhaps," she murmured as her pen scratched against the parchment.

Lochlyn watched her for a moment, before recalling another piece of correspondence waiting to be opened. "When you're done with your reply, there's an interesting package from Serpens."

"From the capital?" Rosalie set her half-written reply aside and looked through the rest of the mail. "It's from the temple! Do you have any idea what it could be?"

"I have an idea," he said, smiling as Rosalie examined the leather envelope. "Go ahead. Open it."

Rosalie opened the envelope and withdrew a scroll secured with two jeweled end caps. "This looks like one of the lineage scrolls the noble families keep," she said.

"That's exactly what it is." Lochlyn stood beside his wife and nodded toward the scroll. "I believe you'll like what it says. Unroll it."

She did, and she covered her mouth with her hand when she saw her own name listed next to Lochlyn's. Rosalie Greenwood Blackmoor. "What does this mean?" she asked, her voice hardly more than a whisper.

"I had you added to our official lineage," he replied. "This way, no matter what happens or how the king schemes, you and our children will always be Blackmoors. Although, I do need to have the children added." Lily made a soft sound against his chest, which Lochlyn took as the baby's approval.

"Oh, Lochlyn," Rosalie said as she leaned against his shoulder. "Did you do this because the king still wants you married to Caterina?"

"Olivar had nothing to do with this. Remember when we had our first fight, and you challenged me to make an effort?" He paused to caress her hair. "This is my response. Instead of yet another hollow declaration of love, I made our union official in every way."

"Your declarations were never hollow," Rosalie said. "But I never expected this. Thank you, Lochlyn. I can't imagine a better partner than you."

Lochlyn kissed her forehead. "Nor I you, my beloved."

A short time later, Lily drifted off to sleep, and Rosalie went to put her in her cradle. Lochlyn remained in his study, sorting through the rest of his mail. Most of it had to do with the Ridge's financial interests, but one letter near the bottom was from his spymaster. He'd ingratiated himself with an elder from the Order of the Sun, and one night when they were deep in their cups, the spy asked the shifter why phoenixes held Dragon Ridge in such high regard.

In short, the phoenix knights considered Lochlyn their savior.

It all went back to that awful day when Lochlyn, in his dragon form, decimated the Northern army with his dragon fire. What Lochlyn hadn't known was that the Northerners had conscripted an entire company of the Order's knights. Many, if not all of the phoenixes, had perished long before Lochlyn had arrived, but Lochlyn's fire had resurrected each and every one them. If it hadn't been for Lochlyn's intervention, those fallen phoenixes would have lain lifeless in the field until someone found their remains and set renewal fires, or their bodies simply rotted away and rendered them truly dead. Lochlyn had effectively saved an entire generation of phoenix knights, and over half of the Order.

The Order's Master was an ancient phoenix called Arthus Flameborn—and one of the knights Lochlyn had saved that day was his only living son. He was called Curran.

Lochlyn flopped back into his chair, thoroughly shocked by what he'd read. Now he understood why so many phoenix fledglings had ended up in the Ridge's orphanage. The Order saw him as a safe haven, and that extended to his village. And Curran had sent Caterina to Dragon Ridge, hoping that the man who'd resurrected him would keep his lover and child safe.

"I must tell Rosalie at once," Lochlyn muttered, and he went in search of his wife. He found her in the atrium, speaking to a messenger. The man bowed and departed. Then, Rosalie turned around and saw Lochlyn.

"My dragon," she said as she slid her arms around his waist. When he gathered her close instead of replying, she asked, "What happened?"

"I've just read something interesting," he began and told Rosalie everything he'd learned.

"Does the letter say how many phoenixes you saved?" Rosalie asked.

"Not specifically, but the Northerners hired a full company. That's usually a hundred soldiers." Lochlyn tightened his arms around Rosalie and rested his forehead against her hair. "All this time, I have thought of that day as one where I rained death upon that field. I never knew I saved people too."

"And if you hadn't saved Curran, he wouldn't have run off with Cat, and we wouldn't have married," Rosalie said.

"Without that day, I wouldn't have you, or any of our children," Lochlyn murmured. "I lost my brothers, but I gained the rest of my life."

Rosalie flattened her hand over his heart. "I'm so sorry I never got to meet them."

"Me too." He kissed her hair. "My mother always said that we need to trust in Fate, because even the greatest tragedy can hold the seeds of future happiness."

"Your mother was wise," Rosalie said. "She must have been quite beautiful too, to have such a handsome son."

Lochlyn laughed softly but stilled when he realized how little Rosalie knew of his lineage. "There are portraits of her. My father and brothers too. I had them put in storage, but we can have them rehung."

Rosalie set her hand on his cheek. "Only if seeing them will bring you more happiness than sorrow. I can wait to see them until you're ready."

He nodded, wondering yet again what he'd done to deserve such a perfect mate. "You're very patient with me."

"That's because I love you."

"And you are my much-loved wife." He stroked her hair behind her ear, smiling because he would never get tired of hearing her tell him she loved him. "I saw you speaking with the messenger."

"I sent him off with my reply to Irontooth Keep," she replied. "I told my father that we would gladly foster Devlin for the foreseeable future. I hope this goes well."

"As do I, beloved."

CHAPTER TWENTY-ONE

SIGNS AND TRUTHS

T
wo weeks after Rosalie sent the message to Irontooth Keep confirming that they would gladly foster Devlin was the village's midsummer festival. For the occasion, and because she promised Lochlyn she'd wear a gown the next time she ventured among their people, Rosalie had a new dress made in forget-me-not blue. After her final fitting with the seamstress, she slipped into Lochlyn's study to surprise him while he worked.

"Are you busy?" she asked.

"Not at all." Lochlyn looked up from his ledgers, his jaw dropping. "Fates," he murmured.

"Do you like my dress?" Rosalie asked as she turned from side to side, letting the skirts twirl around her ankles. Much like her last blue dress, it had a full skirt with a fitted bodice and sleeves. The seamstress had even salvaged the pearl trim from the original dress, and she'd used it to decorate Rosalie's neckline.

"I remember how much you liked the blue dress I wore to our first dinner together," she continued, "but it was beyond saving. Our seamstress has made an excellent replacement, hasn't she?"

"You are the most beautiful woman that's ever lived, no matter what you wear," Lochlyn said as he rose to embrace her. "Are you excited for the mid-summer celebration?"

"That, and Devlin's due to arrive later today, so he can go to the village with us." She walked her fingers up Lochlyn's chest and stroked the bare skin beneath his throat. "I hope he gets on well with everyone here."

"I'm sure he will." Lochlyn kissed her hair. "Do you want to watch for his arrival?"

"We can't see very far down the main road," she began, but Lochlyn shook his head.

"We don't have to watch from the front balcony. The northern tower has an observatory at its peak." When Rosalie raised her brows, he continued, "I wasn't keeping it from you. We just haven't had a reason to go up there. Until now."

"You have a point," she allowed. "All right, my love, I would like to see this observatory."

"As you wish." Lochlyn led her from his study down to the atrium, then across the room to the northern tower. When they reached the base of the tower's spiral staircase, Rosalie tilted her head back and looked up.

And up.

"How tall is this tower?" she asked, her feet already aching at the prospect of climbing to the peak. "There must be a thousand steps."

"Only about three hundred," Lochlyn replied, and then he pulled his shirt up and over his head. "And what makes you think we'll be walking?"

Rosalie laughed as sparks flew. Wings burst from Lochlyn's shoulders and talons extended from his fingers as he assumed his warrior form. When the transformation was complete, he gathered Rosalie against his chest.

"Ready to fly?" he asked.

"Always," she replied as she linked her hands behind his neck. Lochlyn extended his wings, and they slowly ascended to the observatory.

"This is much better than walking up three hundred steps," Rosalie said as they passed the second-floor landing. Instead of replying, Lochlyn tilted up her chin and kissed her. It was soft and sweet, and if Rosalie hadn't already been head over heels in love with her husband, that kiss would have pushed her over the edge.

"Are you watching where we're going?" she asked when they parted.

"I know the way." Lochlyn glided into the topmost room and landed on the cool wood floor. Rosalie stepped back as he shed his warrior form, looking around the observatory.

The observatory didn't have a glass roof like the library, or like her and Lochlyn's bedchamber did. Instead, the entire space was ringed with tall windows, and four brass telescopes sat at regular intervals. Chairs upholstered in rich purple velvet were placed next to each telescope for the observer's comfort, along with small writing desks. In the center of the room was another chair and a full-sized desk, and a larger telescope built right into the ceiling above that central research station.

"This is amazing," she said as she ran her hand across the central chair's backrest. "Why was this room built? Was it to watch for dragons coming and going?"

"That, and to watch the stars." Lochlyn gestured toward the cabinets pushed up against the far side of the room. The long, shallow drawers told Rosalie they were for maps. She must remember to tell Violet. "My great-grandfather was something of an astronomer. He was forever charting celestial bodies."

"What a fascinating hobby." Rosalie approached the windows and walked around the perimeter until she found the road that led to the castle. She went to the closest telescope and asked, "Do I just look through the eyepiece?"

"Yes. There are several lenses you can adjust, so the image is clear." Lochlyn reached around her shoulders and showed her how to make the adjustments. When he was done, Rosalie bent over the eyepiece. "Is everything in focus?" he asked, after she fine-tuned the controls.

"Yes. Thank you." As Rosalie searched the road, Lochlyn's hands searched her body. "Are you petting me?"

"I like your dress," he said, his hands on her waist as his lips were against her neck. "You smell amazing."

"I used that lavender soap you like," she began, then Lochlyn's hands were on her bodice. "Don't you dare rip my dress! I waited weeks for it to be finished!"

"Never," he said as he stroked her skin just above her dress's neckline. "When you wore that silk dress to dinner, with that low bodice edged in pearls, my heart nearly stopped. I wanted to snatch you out of your seat and carry you off to bed."

"If only you had, I might have avoided that vile soup," she said. Lochlyn tugged down her bodice and cupped both of her breasts. "What are you doing?"

"Loving my wife." One of his hands moved behind her, then she felt his cock pressing against her back. "Perhaps my wife wishes to love me as well?"

"Here?" she asked, her pulse quickening.

"Here." Lochlyn reached in front of her, turning the chair around, so the seat was facing her.

"Put your knees on the chair," he said as he helped her into position. That done, he lifted her skirts and grasped her hips. "Yes?"

"Yes," she said, then he slid inside her. This wasn't the first time he'd suggested they make love in an unusual location, and she'd never said no to him. As he moved in a gentle rhythm, murmuring endearments in her ear, she couldn't imagine ever saying no to such pleasure.

She couldn't imagine living without him.

Afterward, Lochlyn flew them down to the ground floor, and they returned to their chamber. Rosalie let Lochlyn help her out of her dress, and they took a bath together.

"I do enjoy how you keep the water warm," she said as he leaned against his dragon-warm chest. "Very convenient. And thank you for not tearing my dress," she added.

"You're welcome for both," he replied. "And I will only tear your clothes off if you specifically request it," he added, nuzzling her neck.

"I'll remember that," Rosalie said. Then, she felt something odd on Lochlyn's arm. "I can feel your scales."

"Can you?" Lochlyn held up his arm. Instead of lying beneath his skin as they usually did, each scale was in stark relief.

"Is it because of the bath?" Rosalie asked.

"I don't think so," he replied. "This has never happened before."

"Why is it happening now?" Rosalie demanded as panic squeezed her heart. "Is something wrong? How do you feel?"

"I feel fine." He got out of the tub and looked down at his legs. Those scales were also standing up, all of them glinting like emeralds thanks to the water. "What does my back look like?" he asked as he turned around. Rosalie got out of the water and stood behind him. She ran her hands over his skin.

"The scales are pronounced wherever I touch them, but here," she stroked a line down his spine, "and here," she glided her fingers across his shoulder blades, "they're up in a line. Almost like a cat when it's frightened and its fur stands up on end." She went around to the front of him. "You're certain you feel fine? You're not sick, or tired? You would tell me if anything was wrong?"

"Beloved," he said, cupping her face with his hands. "I promise you, I feel the same as ever. Perhaps a bit better after our time in the observatory."

Rosalie blushed, but she refused to let the memory of their lovemaking distract her. "This must be happening for a reason. How can we find out why your scales are changing?"

"Let's get dressed and go to my study," Lochlyn suggested. "I've got several of my father's diaries. Perhaps he or another family member also dealt with this and wrote about it."

"Very well," Rosalie said. A short time later, they were hunting through the study's drawers and bookshelves. Lochlyn had all of his father's writings organized by date instead of subject, which meant the diaries were filed along with ledgers and correspondence from the same time period. Rosalie soon learned that Gorlas Blackmoor had been a prolific writer, and he had saved everything.

"Here's one of his diaries," Lochlyn announced as he held the leather-bound book aloft. He opened it and read the first page. "This passage is about his sister's marriage."

"You have an aunt," Rosalie said. "What's she like?"

"I've only met her once, and that was when I was very young," he replied. "I remember her being wise, and kind. She was my mother's closest childhood friend."

"That's lovely. Could she shift?"

"I'm not sure," he said. He read a bit further. "There's mention of her wings, so she could at least attain a warrior form." He turned the page and was confronted with a miniature portrait of his aunt. "This is her. Elin Blackmoor Farseer."

"Farseer," Rosalie repeated. "What sort of a family did she marry into?"

"She married a gryphon prince from beyond the southern sea," he replied. "It's why the miniatures were painted. The land is far, and my father understood he might never see his sister again. But she loved her husband dearly, and she was willing to follow him to the ends of the earth."

"I'm lucky I only had to go to the mountains." She regarded Elin's portrait, noted her dark hair and bright blue eyes. "You look like her. Does she resemble your father?"

"Oh, yes," he replied. "My mother also had dark hair, but her eyes were brown."

"Must be why you're so handsome," she began; just then Silas knocked on the doorframe behind them.

"My lady," Silas began, then he spied Lochlyn's forearms. He'd rolled up his sleeves for ease in searching through the bookshelves, and his rigid scales were on full display. "Congratulations. You both must be very happy."

Rosalie blinked, then she glanced at Lochlyn. He shrugged. "Why are you congratulating us?" he asked the steward.

"Your scales," Silas replied. "Gorlas's scales only stood up like that whenever Lilianna was with child. Something about the dragon protecting his young."

When Rosalie and Lochlyn only stared at him, he asked, "Did you not know that?"

"No," Lochlyn murmured as he stroked a hand over his forearm. "I didn't." He faced Rosalie. "A baby."

"A baby," she repeated. "You're certain a baby is the only reason his scales are reacting this way?" she asked Silas.

"It's the only reason I've ever heard of," Silas replied. "There are a few books on dragon anatomy in the library. I'll have them sent to your room." He looked between the couple and added, "I came to tell you that Lady Blackmoor's brother has arrived. I'll have Madchen keep him occupied for a time." With that, Silas left the study and closed the door behind him.

Rosalie turned to her husband. Her hands were trembling, so she balled them into fists. "A baby," she said again, then she remembered the horrific circumstances of Jonathan's birth. "Are dragons born in fire?" she demanded.

"I wasn't," Lochlyn replied. "Neither were my brothers. Madchen was present for all of our births. She can tell you exactly what happened."

Rosalie nodded, and she took a shaking breath. "I've seen plenty of births. As long as there's no fire..." Her voice trailed off. She saw Lochlyn staring at her, his brows halfway up his head. "Do you believe Silas? That your scales standing up are a way of protecting me and our baby?"

"I've never heard of such a thing, but yes. Yes, it feels right." His throat worked. "Beloved, I thought you would be happy."

"I am, but I was so worried you were sick and that I might lose you, and I had no idea I could be with child, and now my brother is here," she rattled off. Lochlyn wrapped his arms around her, comforting her as only he could. Immediately, her tension melted away. She took another shaky breath. She let herself be happy for herself and her husband.

And their baby.

"You're certain you're happy?" he murmured against her hair.

"Yes," she replied. "I'm very happy for the baby, and I'm so relieved you're not sick. I don't know what I'd do if anything happened to you."

He tilted up her chin. "I will always be here for you. Dragons are the strongest of the Otherworldly creatures. There are very few ways we can be harmed."

"Oh, thank the Fates." Rosalie snuggled into his arms. "Are you strong enough to withstand Madchen's fury when we tell her there will soon be a fifth child in the castle?"

"Madchen will be joyous," he said, scooping Rosalie into his arms and settling them on the window seat. He stroked her hair behind her ear and murmured, "A baby."

"You won't be the last Blackmoor," Rosalie said. "We'll have our baby dragon by next spring."

"I already have heirs," Lochlyn said, referencing their adopted children. "But it will be good to have another dragon in the house." He spread his hand across Rosalie's belly. "Beloved. We're having a child. How do you feel?"

"Honestly? I don't feel any differently. It must be very new." She set her hand atop Lochlyn's forearm. "You knew before I did," she said as she stroked his scales. "Is that because it's your duty to keep us safe?"

"By fire and claw, beloved." Lochlyn kissed her cheek. "You're both the safest people in the realm."

A short time later, Rosalie and Lochlyn went downstairs to welcome Devlin to Dragon Ridge. They found him in the kitchen, surrounded by Madchen, Violet, and enough food to feed the entire staff. When Devlin saw his sister, he jumped up to greet her.

"Rosie," he said as he embraced her. Rosalie heard Lochlyn growl behind her, and she hoped he wouldn't lash out at anyone, least of all her brother. "This castle is amazing!"

"It is," she agreed as she squeezed him back. "Has Madchen been taking good care of you? And I see you've met Violet."

"Madchen is a gift from the Fates," Devlin declared. "Even Father's expensive cooks never made food this good."

"I don't disagree," Rosalie said as Madchen smiled contentedly. "You remember Lochlyn?" she asked as she drew her husband forward.

"My lord," Devlin said as he began to bow, but Lochlyn halted him with a hand on his shoulder.

"Here at the Ridge, we don't bow to family," Lochlyn said. "Was your journey good?"

"It was a journey," Devlin replied with a grin. "Madchen tells me you have four children now? How is that possible?"

"It's a long story," Rosalie began, then Violet jumped up from the table and grabbed Devlin's hand.

"I'll show you the babies," Violet declared as she dragged Devlin behind her.

"I suppose we should follow them," Rosalie said as she leaned against her husband. "Madchen, are you sure you don't mind staying here with the children while we go to the village?"

"I am too old for the midsummer festivities," Madchen replied as she stood and began clearing the table. "And you, my lady, are in a most delicate condition. Take care not to overexert yourself."

Lochlyn wrapped his arm around his wife's shoulders. "I'll look after her, Madchen."

"See that you do," Madchen said. "I'll have an herbal footbath prepared for when you return."

"Thank you," Rosalie said, after which the housekeeper shooed them out of the kitchen. "I suppose Silas told her about the baby?" she asked as they walked toward the nursery.

"Most likely," Lochlyn replied. "He's far too intelligent to attempt keeping anything from her, and she's far too crafty to not know if he's hiding something. Secrets wouldn't do between the two of them."

"Perhaps that's the hallmark of a good marriage," Rosalie said. "No secrets."

Lochlyn kissed her hair. "Perhaps."

When they reached the nursery, which were Rosalie's old rooms repurposed, they found Devlin staring at the row of cradles shaking his head. "You're filling the place up with babies, just like things were at home," he said when he saw his sister.

"Things will be a far sight better here," Rosalie declared. "I still can't believe some of the things I witnessed under Father's roof."

"You and me both," Devlin agreed.

"Papa," Violet said as she tugged Lochlyn's sleeve. "Can I ride on your shoulders?"

"Yes." Lochlyn knelt down so Violet could climb onto his back. "We'll be back after we make our rounds," he said as he took her toward the windows.

"Good that he likes children," Devlin said. "You seem happy with him, Rosie."

"I am," she replied. "I never thought this would be my life, but it suits me."

"You always were a caretaker," he said, and then he jerked his chin toward the cradles. "Which one is Cat's baby?"

"What?" Rosalie demanded, as her pulse raced and cold sweat bloomed across her back. "How could any of these babies belong to Cat?"

"Melly says Cat and Curran ran off because he got her with child," Devlin replied. "Claims she found one of those herbal syrups that change color if the woman's in a family way hidden in Cat's room."

"Well, we all knew about her and Curran," Rosalie said, instead of answering Devlin's question. "I'd venture that Father knew as well. I wouldn't be surprised if he'd planned all along for Cat to take up with Curran in order to get a grandchild who could shift."

"Actually, his plan was for you to get into a tangle with the knight," Devlin said.

Rosalie blinked. "What?"

"Father wanted his golden child married into the dragon clan," Devlin explained. "But you know how he's always got schemes to back up his schemes, and he really wanted a shifter in the family. He figured you had a good chance of having a phoenix child, and that your blood would attract Curran. Turned out that one only had eyes for Cat."

"My blood?" Rosalie repeated. "Devlin, there's nothing special about my blood."

"Yes, there is," Devlin insisted. "Our mother was a phoenix."

Rosalie gasped so loudly Lochlyn heard her all the way from the far side of the room. He set Violet on her feet and began walking toward her. "She... How do you know this?" Rosalie asked.

"Everyone knows," Devlin replied. "It's why we have scars on our necks. Mama burned off our birthmarks to keep Father from finding out. After she burned me, he sent her away."

Rosalie took a step back, her head spinning as she touched the slick skin on the back of her neck. The scar that was so old she couldn't remember getting it, that was somehow identical to the scar on her brother's neck. "No, no," she murmured, then Lochlyn was in front of her.

"What's wrong?" he demanded. When Rosalie didn't answer, he rounded on Devlin.

"Why is Rosalie upset?" Lochlyn demanded as his eyes flashed red, then black. "What did you say to her?"

"Man, your eyes," Devlin said, backing away.

"It's his dragon fire," Rosalie explained, turning to Lochlyn.

"Don't be angry with Devlin." She pressed her hand to her breast, feeling her heart hammering against her ribcage. "He only told me the truth."

"The truth about what?" Lochlyn asked.

"We're phoenixes." Rosalie looked up at her husband. "Our mother was a phoenix. My scar, she burned off my mark." She looked at the cradles. "We're all phoenixes."

Lochlyn pulled her into his arms, then he fixed Devlin in his gaze. "How were you privy to this information while Rosalie wasn't?"

"I, ah." Devlin rubbed the back of his neck. "I heard it from some of the ladies Mama worked with."

"You went to her brothel?" Rosalie demanded.

"It's not like she was the one working," Devlin said. "When I turned sixteen, some of our older brothers brought me. Called it an initiation."

Rosalie turned into Lochlyn's chest. "Please, don't give me a single detail about this initiation."

"I wasn't planning to," Devlin snapped. "But afterward we were talking, and once the ladies found out I was Aurielle's son, they told me all sorts of things about her."

"And this is why Osman wanted to send you to the Order of the Sun," Lochlyn concluded. "Do you want to train as a knight?"

"Not really," Devlin said. "I would have gone though, if only to get away from Irontooth Keep. Every day there is a battle for survival. I was so busy trying to stay out of everyone's way, I never really got to be myself."

Rosalie sighed. "I remember that feeling all too well. I don't think I realized how miserable I was at home, not until I left."

Lochlyn growled, which shocked Devlin.

"You really are a dragon," he said, awestruck.

"I am," Lochlyn said as he pushed up his sleeve and exposed his scales. "And dragons defend their own. Devlin, you may stay here for as long as you need. Dragon Ridge can become your permanent home if you'd like. But even if you move on, know this: you will always have a home here, and you never need to deal with the depravities of Irontooth Keep ever again."

Devlin's shoulders sagged in relief. "I'm so glad to hear you say that. And I can't really go home again anyway. There are seven brothers ahead of me, and one of them will inherit the Keep and turn the rest of us out. Even though I grew up there, the Keep was never and will never be my home."

Rosalie nodded. "Perhaps we were both meant to be here with the dragons, after all."

CHAPTER TWENTY-TWO

SCALES AND SPINES

As soon as Violet had Devlin distracted with her books and maps, and Rosalie had assured him that Devlin could be trusted around the babies, Lochlyn drew his wife into the bedroom at the rear of the chamber. He softly closed the door and paused a moment before he faced her.

"Are you angry with me?" she asked, her voice trembling. Lochlyn spun around. Rosalie's arms were wrapped around her stomach, her eyes wide and scared. Fates, the last thing he wanted was for her to be frightened of him or anything.

"No, never," he said as he gathered her against him. "Why would I be angry with you?"

"Because you thought I was human," she sobbed into his chest. "Because now I might go up in flames like Cat did, or be captured by the Order, and then our children won't have a mother—"

"Hush, hush," he murmured against her hair. "I've got you."

"Lochlyn." She fisted her hand in his shirt. "I'm so scared."

"Beloved. I'm not going to let anything happen to you." He couldn't, not after finally knowing what it was like to love unconditionally and be loved in return. "And it's too early for us to worry. Your blood might be dormant, just like my middle brothers."

"Were all of your brothers marked?" she asked.

"Yes." He found the slick patch of skin on the back of her neck, stroked it with his thumb. It was the only mark on Rosalie's body, save for a handful of freckles that danced across her cheeks. "We all have—had—scales. Have you ever felt like you needed to shift?"

She scoffed. "I have no idea what that would feel like." She looked up at her husband. "I thought you chose when to shift, but you're compelled to do it?"

"Yes. It's a feeling in the blood."

"I know about creature's blood," she began, but he shook his head.

"Not the hereditary aspect. I mean, I feel it in my actual veins." He pressed his face against Rosalie's golden hair, and he tried to put into words something that was as natural to him as breathing. "When I choose to shift, my blood flows faster. More intensely. It surges in my veins until, finally, I change form and all of the pent up...I don't know, dragon-ness?...is released. And if I don't shift for a time, the dragon-ness builds up in my blood until my muscles are sore and my bones ache."

"Then it's not optional," Rosalie said. "You need to change, just like you need to sleep and eat." She leaned back and met his gaze. "I've felt my bones ache, but I've never once felt my blood surge. Devlin must not have, either, if he only learned about our mother's true nature when he was sixteen."

"Then, my guess is that you're both latent," Lochlyn said. "My middle brothers never felt the blood surge either." He caressed Rosalie's cheek. "When you're ready, we should ask Devlin what else he learned about your mother, though I suspect she was hiding both of you from the Order. I can think of no other reason why she would intentionally burn both of her children."

"I got this scar so long ago that it never mattered to me," she murmured as she touched the mark on the back of her neck. "I remember, barely, when Devlin was burned as a baby. By the time I was old enough to realize how odd it was for us to have identical burn scars on our necks, Mama was gone." She found Lochlyn's hand, tangling her fingers with his. "There's something else."

He kissed her forehead. "Tell me."

"According to Devlin, Father hired Curran hoping he would fall for me." She shuddered, continuing, "Father knows I'm a phoenix. He's known all along."

Lochlyn felt his dragon fire rising in his breast. "I have many opinions about your father. None of them are good."

"I'm sure we feel the same way." She linked her arms behind Lochlyn's neck. "Devlin immediately asked me which baby was Cat's. Both Father and the king want to find her, and if they learn about Jonathan, they'll want him too. Are any of us truly safe here?"

"Yes," he replied. "A thousand times, yes. The Ridge is strong, and I won't cower before your father or the king. If need be, I'll reach out to the Order for added protection without revealing that you and Devlin have phoenix blood. They do owe me a very large debt," he added.

"I know you're strong," she began, tracing the gold chain around his neck. "You told me that there are very few ways a dragon can be hurt. What will hurt you?" When Lochlyn tensed, she added, "I need to know, so I can protect you."

He smiled at his sweet, delicate wife who would nevertheless destroy anyone who dared threaten their family. "I can suffer all the usual injuries—broken bones, stab wounds, and the like—but I'll heal from most anything. The magic we tap into when we shift brings us to a healthy version of whatever form we're moving into."

"Then, an injured man could become a whole dragon?"

"Exactly, beloved. Add to our magic our scales and spines, and we're quite indestructible. The only definitive way to kill a dragon is to cut off his head, steal his scales, or break his heart." He stroked his thumb across her forehead. "The last one is the most painful. I could never go on without you."

"You'll never have to. Where you go, I go." She stood on her toes and kissed his chin. "You pretend to be a big scary man, but underneath all the roars and dragon fire is a large, loving heart who will do anything for his family."

"Don't you ever forget it," he said, and then he kissed her. "And my scales and dragon fire will shield you, and all our children." He spread his hand across her midsection. "Since we have a baby coming, I'm especially dangerous."

"Are you?" Rosalie laughed as if she weren't pressed up against the most terrifying man in Alessia. "Then, I suppose I feel especially protected."

Lochlyn tightened his arms around her. "How are you feeling? We don't have to go down to the village if it will be too much for you."

"We absolutely need to go," Rosalie said. "Our people are excited to see us. We shouldn't disappoint them. Besides, it will be good for Devlin to have some fun in the village, too."

"As you say, beloved. But if I think you're getting tired, we leave with no argument."

"And what if I do argue?"

"I'll toss you over my shoulder and fly you home."

She looked up at him through her lashes. "Do you promise?"

CHAPTER
TWENTY-THREE

MIDSUMMER EVE

An hour later, Rosalie, Lochlyn, and Devlin were in the carriage as it rumbled toward the village square. Rosalie again wore her new blue dress, which Lochlyn declared to be his favorite item in her entire wardrobe. As for Lochlyn, he was wearing his usual black pants and coat, but his shirt was crimson. Devlin was still wearing what he'd traveled in. Rosalie hoped he'd brought at least one change of clothes with him to the Ridge.

As Rosalie suffered the bumps and jolts inherent to a carriage ride with a minimal grumbling, she considered all that she'd learned earlier about her mother, her own nature, and her coming baby. Devlin's revelations and all the uncertainties that came with them aside, she was happy. She and Lochlyn were having a baby—their fifth child!—which was a dream Rosalie had never thought would be fulfilled. If her life had gone as planned and Cat hadn't run away with Curran, Rosalie would be sequestered in a convent by now, and she wouldn't have the life she so cherished.

Although, her only confirmation that this baby was coming was Lochlyn's raised scales. She didn't doubt her husband's instincts, or Silas's information; nevertheless, she needed another way to confirm what was happening deep inside her womb. Of course, she could just wait for her courses to stop or her belly to grow... but Rosalie had never been patient.

"Lochlyn," she murmured as she stroked the scales on his forearm. "How do you know?"

He didn't ask for clarification. "Your scent," he replied. "My dragon noticed it immediately when we flew up to the observatory, then things...progressed."

"You can fly?" Devlin asked as Rosalie's face warmed at the memory of their time in the observatory. "That's amazing!"

"Um, yes," Lochlyn said, then he faced his wife. "I've been thinking about that time. I noticed your scent, and my scales reacted soon afterward."

"You can fly and Rosie smells," Devlin said, looking out the window. "We have an odd family."

"Devlin," Rosalie said. His mention of family reminded her of something he'd said earlier. "When you met the children, you asked me which one was Cat's. What possessed you to ask such a question?"

"One of Father's men went to the Keep and claimed Cat was hiding in Dragon Ridge," Devlin replied. "He didn't see her, but he heard people talking about her."

"Who told Osman this?" Lochlyn demanded.

"Zephyn," Devlin replied. "He's a mason. You remember his brother, Borneas? He's the one who drove you up to the Ridge, Rosie."

Rosalie fell back against the seat cushions. Borneas had indeed driven the carriage that brought her to Dragon Ridge. He'd also stolen a chest of maps from Lochlyn and was never seen again. The mason, Zephyn, was not only Borneas's brother, but when he saw her in the village, he had been far too interested in her and Jonathan.

"Lochlyn," she began, but he took her hand.

"I will handle it," he growled.

"Perhaps you should throw Zephyn off his precious bridge," she suggested as Devlin blanched.

"Perhaps I will. But such retribution can happen tomorrow." Lochlyn said as the carriage lurched to a halt. "Tonight, my bride, we celebrate."

"I am excited," Rosalie admitted. "I suppose after tonight I can leave my Greenwood surname behind permanently."

Lochlyn got out of the carriage, and he helped Rosalie step out. "Whatever you wish, beloved."

"That's another thing I learned," Devlin said as he bounded out of the carriage like an acrobat. "Mama's surname wasn't really Greenwood. It was Flameborn."

"Oh," Rosalie murmured. "I wonder why she changed it."

Lochlyn stepped in front of Devlin. "You're certain the name you heard was Flameborn?"

"Definitely," he replied. "All the ladies said the name suited Mama. On account of her red hair."

Lochlyn frowned, then he handed Devlin a few coins. "Enjoy yourself, and don't do anything that will embarrass your sister," he said to the younger man. "Meet us at the carriage at ten bells."

"Until then," Devlin said, and then he disappeared into the crowd. Lochlyn took Rosalie's hand and indicated the far side of the square. Several other couples waited on a raised platform while the village magistrate addressed the crowd. Across from the couples was a small band playing a lively tune, and several people were singing along to them.

"We're supposed to wait with the other couples," Lochlyn said as he led Rosalie across the square. "The village magistrate announces everyone's names and wedding dates to the crowd."

"It looks like we'll be last," Rosalie murmured. There were a few couples standing in front of them. While they waited, she looked around the square. Garlands of flowers and ribbons were draped overhead, and many people were dancing in the center of the area. Rosalie spied a few vendors hawking food and drinks, as well as a fortune teller off to one side. As interesting as all of that was, what she really wanted to know was why Lochlyn had such an intense reaction to learning her mother's true surname.

"Where else have you heard the name Flameborn?" she asked. When Lochlyn didn't answer readily, she said, "I saw how you questioned Devlin."

He ran a hand over his dark hair. "The Grand Master of the Order of the Sun is called Arthus Flameborn."

"Oh," Rosalie said, her mind racing. "Do we think my mother was related to him?"

"I've no proof, but I have a strong suspicion." The attendant greeted them, and Lochlyn gave her their names and wedding date. "I will find answers for you, beloved."

"I know you will." Rosalie had complete faith in her husband. She knew he would do anything to protect her and their family. Speaking of which... "Earlier, you said you could smell me?"

Lochlyn smiled and pulled her closer. "My dragon has always been able to scent you. It gives me clues about your mood."

"My scent changes? How? And what do I smell like?"

"Your scent is more intoxicating than the most exotic flowers," he replied. "During our first night together, I thought it was your perfume, but it's your natural scent."

"And this scent arouses you?"

"More than you can imagine," he replied. "But sometimes, such as if you're sad, your scent becomes heavier, and it makes me want to comfort you. When you're angry, your scent becomes acrid, and I struggle to make amends." He put his mouth close to her ear, murmuring, "And when you are aroused, my sweet rosebud, I struggle to keep my hands off you."

"Good thing I like having your hands on me," she said as Lochlyn's warm breath and intimate words sent shivers across her skin.

Lochlyn smiled at her, then he put his arm around her shoulders as they watched the magistrate introduce the other newly married couples. When it was their turn, the entire square stopped what they were doing and watched the duke and his bride ascend to the center of the stage.

"Your people are interested in us," Rosalie said, dozens of pairs of eyes observing them.

"They are," Lochlyn murmured. "None of my brothers married. We are the first Blackmoor union since my parents were wed."

They took their place on the stage, and the magistrate spread his arms wide. "Friends, we now celebrate the marriage of our most gracious lord, Duke Lochlyn Blackmoor, to his bride, the Duchess Rosalie Greenwood Blackmoor," he announced, his voice booming across the square. The crowd cheered, and flower crowns were placed on Lochlyn and Rosalie's heads. "May the Fates bless your union with a child within your first year!"

The cheers grew louder. Lochlyn led Rosalie down the steps and to the center of the square. The musicians began to play again, and many in the crowd paired off to dance.

"Dance with me, beloved?" Lochlyn asked.

"Yes," she replied as he swept her into his arms. "Since we already have four children, it seems we truly are blessed."

"We are," he replied. "In many ways, we are." He grasped one of her hands while his other hand rested on her lower back. "Since we now know more about your true nature, this increases the odds of us having a dragon shifter."

"Does it?" she asked. "I would think having two parents with dragon blood would be the best way."

"Some creatures are dominant over others," he said. "But any creature's blood will enhance the stronger blood."

"And dragons are strongest of all," Rosalie murmured. "Was your mother a shifter?"

"Yes. She was a selkie."

Rosalie laughed. "Who would have thought a dragon and a selkie would pair off so well? I would think fire and water would be opposites."

"Despite their opposing natures, they were happy together," Lochlyn said. "Just as happy as we are, my beloved."

Lochlyn led Rosalie through two lively dances, then the music slowed for the third. As their pace relaxed, and Lochlyn drew her closer, Rosalie straightened his flower crown.

"Why don't dukes wear crowns?" she wondered as she arranged the white blossoms against his dark hair. "They suit you."

"We have a crown in the vaults. My ancestors wore it." He caressed her hair. "I can look for a matching tiara for you if you'd like. Diamonds would look lovely upon your brow."

"I prefer flowers," she began, and then she saw one of the Ridge's guards out of the corner of her eye. Wondering why he was scowling at such a happy celebration, she craned her neck for a better look. That was when she noticed the guard's tabard... and the green basilisk emblazoned across it.

"Lochlyn." Her tone made him immediately stop moving. "Is he one of the king's soldiers?"

Lochlyn followed her gaze. "Yes."

"Why is he here?"

"He has no reason to be." He took her hand. "So, let's ask him why he's come. Stay close to me, beloved."

Rosalie nodded; not that she had any intention of straying from her husband's side when there were strange men about. She and Lochlyn approached the soldier. "Are you here to celebrate midsummer with us?" Lochlyn asked the man.

"We're here to summon you and your wife to the king's court in Serpens," the soldier replied, handing over a sealed parchment. "Immediately."

Lochlyn rumbled deep in his chest, then he broke the seal on the parchment. He angled the letter so Rosalie could read it with him.

Lord Blackmoor,

Please bring yourself and your lady to my court in Serpens at once. I have a matter to discuss with you that I believe you will find most interesting. Due to the delicate nature of these discussions, I prefer to speak face-to-face.

May the Fates guide your journey,

Olivar the Magnificent

Lochlyn crumpled the parchment in his hand. "Do you know what this is about?" he demanded of the soldier.

"Our orders are to bring you and your wife to Serpens," the soldier replied, moving to grab Rosalie's arm. Lochlyn roared as he pulled Rosalie away from the man.

"Touch my wife and I will relieve you of your hand," Lochlyn growled. "Understand?"

The soldier, white-faced, nodded. "We have a carriage waiting," he began.

"That won't be necessary," Lochlyn said. "Lady Blackmoor and I will make our own way to Serpens."

"Our orders—"

"Have changed," Lochlyn declared. "Now, my wife and I will continue our celebration. If you and your men wish to take part, you're more than welcome. Good night."

With that, Lochlyn turned on his heel and led Rosalie back into the square. He signaled for the musicians to resume playing, then he drew Rosalie closer. "It seems we'll be making a journey," he said.

"Is this wise?" she asked. "You threatened to take that man's hand off. If the king tries to touch me, will you threaten him too?"

"Yes," Lochlyn replied without hesitation. "My duty is to protect you against all threats, Olivar included."

Rosalie shuddered. "How far is Serpens? Have you been there before?"

"I've been to court many times," Lochlyn replied. "I will send my guard ahead, and you and I will fly there. My family has an estate in Serpens. We can stay there instead of at the king's palace."

"You don't," Rosalie began, then she glanced at the other revelers surrounding them. Lochlyn always said his people were loyal to him, but she didn't want to test that loyalty by speaking ill of the king. "Is there somewhere we can talk?"

"Come with me." Lochlyn led her away from the brightly lit square and toward an alley. Along the way, he removed his coat and draped it across her shoulders, then he pulled off his shirt and tucked it into his belt.

"We're flying?" Rosalie asked.

"Just to the rooftop," Lochlyn replied, before rolling his shoulders and shifting to warrior form. With Rosalie in his arms, he flew to the top of the highest building in the village.

"This is the guildhall," Lochlyn explained when they alighted on the roof. "There's nothing directly below the roof but rafters, and none of the other roofs are close enough for anyone to overhear us. As long as we're quiet, we can speak freely here."

Rosalie swallowed and looked toward the celebration in the square. A few moments ago, she was happily dancing with Lochlyn with the rest of the villagers, but now she was filled with dread. "You don't like the king, do you?"

"I don't," he replied. "He's a weak man, and he puts others down as a way to boost his own ego. Olivar has had his share of setbacks, but sometimes I wonder if the Fates are merely giving him his due."

"Caterina never liked him either," Rosalie said. "Nor did her mother. Is it true that he can't properly shift?"

"Olivar has been trapped in a half form for many years," Lochlyn replied. "I wouldn't call it a warrior form, since he has none of the abilities associated with a basilisk save for his venom. He's a serpent from the waist down, and that's the only change."

Rosalie nodded, intrigued by this bit of information. Olivar's many proclamations and decrees portrayed him as a deadly warrior, though no accounts placed him on any battlefields. Lochlyn's description, coupled with what Caterina had told her about her uncle, made more sense than the king's propaganda. "Then it's his half form that makes him a weak king?"

"You're exactly right. Thanks to his condition, he cannot procreate and has no heirs. He's terrified a relation will come forward with a claim to the throne."

"Interesting," Rosalie began, then an image of a man with a serpent's tail from the waist down flashed across her mind. "If he has that tail and is bereft of his manhood, how does he piss?"

Lochlyn threw back his head and laughed. "I have no idea how that works," he said, "and I'm not privy to the state of Olivar's manhood, thank the Fates for that."

Rosalie smiled, but she was still concerned. "I just don't understand why he wants us to go to court. First, he wanted you married to his cousin, then Caterina, then he tells you to find Cat and do away with me..." Her breath caught. "What if he's summoning us to dissolve our marriage?"

"He cannot do that," Lochlyn said, draping his arms across her shoulders. "I had you added to our family lineage in the temple. No one can dissolve our union except you or I. Olivar has no say in the matter."

"Then he's a weak king in more ways than one," Rosalie murmured. "At any other time, I would love to see Serpens, but I don't like being told where to go based on a madman's whim."

"Nor do I, my rosebud. But if we refuse, we risk his anger. And I'd rather not go to war against Serpens."

"But you would?"

"If I had a good reason, and my people backed me, I would decimate Olivar." He kissed Rosalie's hair. "But I would never raise a hand to the king without first securing your agreement, beloved."

Rosalie leaned against his shoulder. "Let's hope it doesn't come to that."

CHAPTER TWENTY-FOUR

PREPARATIONS

The next morning, Lochlyn told Madchen and Silas that he and Rosalie would be traveling to Serpens within the next few days. Neither the housekeeper nor the steward was pleased about this development.

"Rosalie is in no condition for such a journey," Madchen declared. "A woman with child needs a calm environment, not to cross half the kingdom rattling around in the back of a carriage."

"I'm afraid there's nothing to be done," Lochlyn said. The three of them were speaking in Silas's study while Rosalie and Devlin were having breakfast with the children. "Olivar himself summoned us. If we don't comply, it will be treason. Rosalie and I will be flying to Serpens instead of riding in the carriage."

"How many of ours do you want me to send ahead to The Talon?" Silas asked, referencing the Blackmoors' secondary estate in Serpens. "The regular staff is always present in the house of course."

"Led by the always capable Phillipa," Madchen added; to which Silas rolled his eyes.

Lochlyn wiped a hand down his face. "Fates, I've no idea how many men to take. How many of our soldiers would we need to hold off the king?"

"Is an attack a possibility?" Silas asked.

"An attack is always possible. It's my job to be prepared." Lochlyn laid the crumpled summons down on the desk. "I wish I knew what he was playing at."

"There's no mention of Caterina," Madchen said as she read over the summons. "Perhaps he's given up on finding her."

"Not likely," Silas said as he shook his head. "Olivar isn't known for giving up. Even when that mad alchemist convinced him that dragon scales would cure his shifting, and he failed miserably, he just executed the man and hired a new alchemist to replace him." When Lochlyn grimaced, Silas added, "I shouldn't have spoken of that event in such a callous way. Apologies, my lord."

"What? No, you were right to make the point. No apologies are needed." Lochlyn rubbed his chin. "I'm worried about bringing Rosalie to court. Olivar can be dangerous when crossed, and I don't want her getting hurt."

While Madchen comforted Lochlyn, Silas went to the cabinet in the rear of the room. It had been spelled by Lochlyn's grandfather in decades past, and only Silas could open the doors. As Lochlyn watched the steward retrieve a stack of paperwork, he wished his grandfather had lived long enough to teach him a few of those eminently useful spells.

"According to my notes, we currently have five spies in Serpens," Silas announced. "I can send a message today and they'll start gathering intelligence and mapping alternate routes out of the city."

"I don't need an alternate route," Lochlyn grumbled. "If Olivar tries anything, I'll fly out with Rosalie."

"In full view of the entire city?" Madchen asked.

"Why not?" Lochlyn countered. "The entire kingdom knows I'm descended from the dragons of old. It will be good for them to see my true form. Perhaps they'll be frightened enough to leave Dragon Ridge be, so Rosalie and I can to raise our children in peace. Fates know my parents never got the chance."

"But I really want to see the capital," Devlin whined. Again.

"You only got here yesterday," Rosalie said. "Don't you want to get to know the Ridge? It's very nice here, and the people are welcoming."

"That celebration last night was amazing," Devlin said. "But I bet there's lots of fun celebrations in Serpens."

"I bet there's a lot of danger in Serpens too, certainly more than we deal with here," Rosalie retorted.

Devlin shrugged. "It can't be worse than what we grew up with. Remember when Alaric slit Edmund's throat?"

"Yes," Rosalie said, shuddering as she recalled the time her two eldest brothers got in a fight over a scullery maid. Edmund had barely survived, and he couldn't speak for almost a year. As for the maid, she fled the Keep and was never heard from again. "Honestly, Devlin, that's all the more reason for you to stay here. It's bad enough I'll be worrying about Lochlyn's safety. If I'm worrying about you, too, I'll surely go mad."

"Well, when you put it that way," Devlin said, and Rosalie breathed a sigh of relief. "But I do want to see the capital."

"Me too," Violet said. "We can all go!"

"We'll ask Papa when we can plan a trip for all of us," Rosalie began, but she was distracted as Lily let out a soft cry. Rosalie lifted her tiniest child out of her cradle and patted her back.

"Ready for breakfast, my flower?" she asked the baby. The boys had already eaten and were having their morning nap. "Or were you just telling us your opinion on visiting the capital?"

"See that," Devlin said. "Lily knows what's good. She also wants to go have a look 'round the place."

Rosalie smiled at Devlin, then Lochlyn entered the room. No matter how many times Rosalie watched her husband stride into a room, tall and strong with his piercing blue gaze, the sight never failed to take her breath away.

"Beloved," Lochlyn said as he bent to kiss Rosalie and stroke Lily's downy head. "Good morning, Devlin, and my shy Violet," he added as he picked up his eldest and sat with her on his lap.

"Good morning to you," Rosalie said. "Did you and Silas decide when we will be leaving?"

"Preparations for our journey are nearly complete," Lochlyn replied as he reached for a roll. "We've a dozen men leaving today. They'll transport our luggage. We can fly out tomorrow shortly after dawn and spend the day at The Talon before reporting to court."

"You can really fly all the way to Serpens?" Devlin asked. "How do you keep from getting lost?"

"The same way you would," Lochlyn replied. "I follow the road. It's quite easy to see from above."

Devlin shook his head. "I would love to fly like that."

"Perhaps you'll meet a shifter who wouldn't mind taking you up," Rosalie said as she gave Lily her bottle.

"You know where I'm more likely to meet a shifter? In Serpens," Devlin said. "Father says they all go to the palace to try and impress the king."

"Father is not the authority on shifters or Serpens," Rosalie said.

"It's true that there are more shifters in Serpens, but that's only because it's a large city," Lochlyn said. "Wherever you have more people, you naturally have more shifters as well. However, our kind has gotten rarer over the past hundred years or so. No one's certain why, but my father thought it was due to shifters marrying humans and diluting the blood."

"Interesting," Devlin said. "So, why'd you marry Rosie? You thought she was all human, didn't you? Seems to me you should have held out for a shifter lass."

Violet looked up at Lochlyn. "Didn't you marry Mama because you love her?"

"You're absolutely correct, Violet," Lochlyn said, smiling at Rosalie. "I loved her the first moment I saw her, and I love her more every day. Her ancestry didn't matter to me, not one bit."

"That's a good answer," Rosalie said, and they laughed. Despite her outward happiness, Rosalie was dreading their trip to Serpens. Her instincts told her that nothing good would come of meeting with the king.

CHAPTER TWENTY-FIVE

FLIGHT TO SERPENS

The next morning, Rosalie and Lochlyn said goodbye to their family, and they prepared to fly to Serpens. After they'd said their farewells, promising Violet they would bring back some new books, they walked behind the castle to the stables. Lochlyn needed to disrobe to shift into his dragon form, and he preferred doing so without an audience.

"I'm going to miss them so much," Rosalie said as she cast a final glance over her shoulder. "They'll be all right without us, won't they?"

"They will," Lochlyn reassured her. "Madchen has cared for scores of children, and ours are well-behaved. Except for that Devlin," he added, with a grin.

"He wouldn't dare disobey Madchen," Rosalie said. "Even though he's only been here a few days, I think he'll be happy with us. He's already more comfortable than he ever was at home."

"You're wrong."

Rosalie stopped walking. "Wrong? About what?"

"You referred to Irontooth Keep as home," Lochlyn replied as he set his hands on her shoulders. "The Ridge is your home. Now and forever."

"I meant our prior home," Rosalie said, linking her hands behind Lochlyn's neck. "I know we promised Violet a trip, but after we return, I want to stay here for a long, long time."

"May the Fates make it so," Lochlyn murmured as he bent to kiss her. "Hopefully, we'll handle whatever Olivar wants to discuss quickly and we'll be back in less than a week."

"Agreed, my husband." Rosalie threaded her fingers through the dark curls at the nape of his neck. She loved stroking his soft hair almost as much as she enjoyed stroking his scales. "Now, take your clothes off."

"As you wish, beloved." Lochlyn released her and shed his clothes. Rosalie stored them in a satchel she'd brought along. She slung the bag across her torso and fastened her cloak, then she watched as Lochlyn shifted into his dragon form.

"You are the loveliest shade of green," she said as she kissed his scaly nose. He nuzzled her neck, then went flat on his belly so Rosalie could climb onto his back. As she did, she remembered the first time she'd ridden him, and how, many times, she'd almost fallen off during that initial flight. Luckily for her, they've flown together a few more times since then, and she was better at holding on.

"I'm ready," Rosalie said as she grasped two of his spines. Lochlyn glanced over his shoulder and at their home, then he leaped into the sky. He flew past the front balcony twice, so both Violet and Devlin could see him with his wings spread in flight.

"You are such a proud dragon," Rosalie said around her laughter. Her vain husband rumbled deep in his chest, then he aligned himself above the mountain road and flew toward Serpens. Instead of sitting up, Rosalie lay close to his back, both to avoid the biting winds and to enjoy his natural warmth. As she did, she watched the mountain peaks speed past. That view, and the steady motion of Lochlyn's wings, lulled her to sleep.

"Rosalie!"

She blinked herself awake as Lochlyn's face came into focus above her. His brows were pinched together, his eyes wide and terrified.

"What's wrong," she began, before feeling a rough stone floor beneath her instead of their bed and seeing open sky overhead. After a moment, she realized they must be on The Talon's roof. "Oh, have we arrived?"

"Yes, just now," he said as he caressed her hair. "When I landed and you didn't slide off my back, I thought something had happened to you." He rested his forehead against hers. "Fates, I was so worried."

"I must have fallen asleep," she said. "You're a very comfortable dragon."

"Don't scare me like that again." Lochlyn helped her sit up, and then he opened the satchel that was still slung across her body and retrieved his clothes. As soon as he was dressed, he picked up Rosalie and carried her toward a door on the far side of the roof.

"And you're carrying me, because?"

"Because I like holding you, and after that fright you gave me, I'm not ready to let you go," he replied.

"I was just sleeping," she said, but that was her only protest. Rosalie enjoyed being in Lochlyn's arms, and if he wanted to carry her around for a bit, she didn't have a problem with it. "There aren't any glass roofs here?" she asked, looking over the tiled roof.

"No. My father meant to have one built, as did his father before him, but as you can see, they never got around to it." Lochlyn entered the house through an open archway and walked down a wide staircase. "My ancestors once divided their time between here and the Ridge, but that ended a few generations ago."

"I wonder why," Rosalie murmured. At the bottom of the stairs was a large circular room with white marble walls and floors. The whole of it was ringed with intricately carved columns. Between the columns sat pedestals that held vases of colorful flowers. The center of the ceiling had an oculus, and everything was bathed in bright light.

"This room is beautiful," Rosalie said as Lochlyn set her on her feet. "Do you always keep so many fresh flowers here?"

"I sent instructions to have the house filled with flowers for you," he said, kissing her knuckles. "The Talon hasn't hosted a Lady Blackmoor for some time. We needed to make the place worthy of you."

"I'm sure it's always been worthy," she said as she investigated the nearest vase. It was filled with orange lilies, the scent heady. "Where is everyone?"

"Downstairs, most likely." Lochlyn held out his hand. "Let's find them and get settled into our rooms. I aim to have one more night of peace before we attend court tomorrow."

"You think the king's court won't be peaceful?" Rosalie asked as they descended to the ground floor.

"Olivar and his court, are unpredictable," Lochlyn replied. "We need to be vigilant." They entered yet another large room. This one had a dark wood floor, and the walls were painted with bright frescoes. A single vase of white lilies sat on a central table. Next to the table was a woman wearing a long-sleeved white dress. Her hair was the color of thunderclouds and piled haphazardly on top of her head. Her hair color, along with her darkly tanned skin and twinkling black eyes, seemed familiar to Rosalie.

"My lord, I trust your journey was pleasant?" the woman asked, then she bowed to Rosalie. "And Lady Blackmoor, I am so pleased to finally meet you."

"Our journey was quite good," Lochlyn replied, and then he turned to his wife. "Rosalie, this is Phillipa. She's the caretaker here."

"Oh, like a city version of Silas," Rosalie said, and Phillipa laughed.

"My little brother wishes he could handle things as well as I do," Phillipa said. "Come, I will show you to your suite. Would you like dinner at the usual time?"

"That would be perfect. Thank you, Phillipa." Lochlyn draped his arm around Rosalie's shoulders, and they followed Phillipa to their rooms. They were large and airy, with the balcony doors thrown open and sunlight bathing the interior with golden light.

"Of course, my lord, please let me know if you need anything," Phillipa said. "I will fetch you when dinner is ready." With that, Phillipa closed the door. Intrigued, Rosalie investigated their temporary accommodations.

"It's so beautiful here," Rosalie said as she approached the balcony. The estate was surrounded by a high stone wall, and beyond that she could see the terracotta roofs of the other dwellings. "Why don't you come here more often?"

"Serpens is lovely, but the Ridge is home." Lochlyn stood behind Rosalie and wrapped his arms around her. "Besides, while Serpens is interesting, the faster pace of city life easily wears on me."

"You? Worn out? I doubt that." He just flew them all the way from Dragon Ridge, and he hasn't yawned even once. "I didn't know Silas had a sister."

"Ah. Silas's family has worked with mine for generations. My father claimed the association went all the way back to the Great Migration, but there's no proof of that." He kissed the side of her neck. "Father was known for embellishing things from time to time."

"Something you'd never do," Rosalie said, making Lochlyn laugh against her hair. "Still. It's a wonderful story."

"It is." Lochlyn tightened his arms around her. "No matter what happens tomorrow, I will protect you."

"I know," Rosalie said. "I'm not afraid of the king." *But I am wary.*

CHAPTER TWENTY-SIX

THE KNIGHT

Their evening at The Talon was peaceful, just as Lochlyn had intended. The next morning was, as well, but he and Rosalie were due in the king's palace by noon. Lochlyn ground his teeth as he brushed off his coat and buttoned his vest. It irritated him that Olivar had dragged him and Rosalie all the way to Serpens to... what, exactly? The summons hadn't deigned to give him a hint as to what this important discussion would be about. For all Lochlyn knew, the king wanted to discuss what color to repaint the palace corridors.

"Rosalie," Lochlyn called over his shoulder. "The carriage will be here soon."

"I'm ready."

Lochlyn turned around and lost his breath. His wife was wearing a green silk gown edged in purple velvet. It had a fitted bodice with a full skirt and sleeves, and a golden belt circled her hips. Her hair was pinned up at her nape, and she'd tucked some white and pink lilies behind her ear. The only jewelry she wore was her gold pendant, which depicted the Blackmoor crest.

She was so beautiful he nearly forgot to speak.

"My beauty." Lochlyn bowed as Rosalie giggled. "No blue dress today?"

"That dress is only for you," she said, taking his hands. "Not for this foolish king. I thought you liked green; it's the same color as your dragon."

Lochlyn thought of himself as the color of stately pine trees, not sparkling emeralds. "I'm not purple," he said as he stroked the velvet ribbon on her shoulder.

"No, you aren't." She stood on her toes and kissed him. Lochlyn had half a mind to fabricate an emergency so they could instead go to the palace tomorrow, and he could take Rosalie back to bed now. But he wanted to get this over with, and to bring Rosalie home as soon as possible.

"Ready to meet the king?" Lochlyn asked.

"As I'll ever be."

Lochlyn offered her his arm. She accepted it, and they left their rooms for their waiting carriage.

"We can't walk to the palace?" Rosalie asked as they took their seats on the upholstered bench. "I can see it from here."

"We could, but nobility doesn't walk within the city," Lochlyn replied. "Anywhere we travel beyond our own estate is done via carriage."

"What if you wanted to visit the market?" she pressed. "To look at the vendors, or perhaps to pick up a small meal of flatbreads and honey?"

"That simply isn't done," he replied. "If we wanted such a thing, we would send someone to obtain it for us."

"Hmmph," Rosalie said, turning toward the window. "That explains why your ancestors stopped coming here. Can't have any fun with all these foolish rules."

"Would that it were the reason." When Rosalie glanced at him, he continued, "A few generations ago, dragons began disappearing. At first, plague was thought to be the culprit but then scores of bodies were found. The missing dragons had been skinned. Every last one of them."

"That's awful," Rosalie said. "So, your grandfather brought everyone home to protect them?"

"Exactly." Lochlyn slid closer to his wife, and he pointed toward the palace through the carriage window. It was surrounded by a tall circular wall, and the main tower was topped with a dozen white pillars.

"See those pillars?" he asked. "Times past, when dragons were still the king's guardians, my people had flown out from the top of the palace."

"That must have been a sight," Rosalie said. "Have basilisks always ruled Alessia?"

"No," Lochlyn replied, but then, the driver announced they had arrived. "History lessons will have to wait. Beloved, welcome to the palace."

Lochlyn exited the carriage, and then he helped Rosalie step down onto the ground. The carriage had brought them all the way to the palace steps, and he watched as Rosalie tilted her head back to see the entire façade. The exterior was beautifully constructed with white and gray marble, and elegant in its simplicity. That all changed once they were inside, and they were surrounded with an abundance of gilded and jeweled accents.

"I thought the king was running out of money," Rosalie whispered as they passed a gold candelabra twice Lochlyn's height. "Can't he just melt down a few candlesticks?"

"One would think," Lochlyn whispered back. They reached the entry to the main hall, and he gave the footman their names.

"Lord and Lady Blackmoor of Dragon Ridge," the footman announced. Everyone in the hall turned toward them and watched as they descended the carpeted stairs.

Lochlyn kept his hand on Rosalie's lower back as he guided her into the king's hall. The walls and floor were made of pale peach stone, and thick crimson carpets edged in gold kept the sound at a bearable level. Above them, the ceiling soared three stories high, and the top third of the walls were stained-glass panels depicting the Great Migration from the Otherworld. The bright midday sun illuminated the panels, and rays of rainbow-colored light danced across the walls.

"This place is beautiful," Rosalie breathed as she regarded the panels. "Truly breathtaking."

"It certainly is," Lochlyn agreed. He had been to the grand court many times, and he was used to the gaudy excesses Olivar surrounded himself with. He'd worried that the blatant displays of wealth would overwhelm Rosalie, but while she appreciated the artistry, she was at ease among the gilded furniture and crystal-encrusted windows. Then again, she had grown up with a man who valued gold above all else.

"It's almost like being back at home," Rosalie murmured, surveying the garish hall. She studied a tapestry that depicted a rampaging basilisk wearing a golden crown. "I knew Father idolized the king, but I never realized how much he imitated him."

Lochlyn grunted, which was all he was willing to say about Rosalie's father. He turned toward the dais, and saw the empty throne flanked by two phoenix knights. "I wonder when our king will join us."

"If he wants to speak with us privately, won't he call us into a side chamber?" Rosalie asked.

"Olivar likes to handle his affairs in front of an audience. Everything with him is a performance; the theme always about his strength and power," he replied as he jerked his chin toward the dais. "He's even got knights guarding an empty throne."

Rosalie followed his gaze, suddenly clutching Lochlyn's forearm. "That's Curran," she said, nodding toward the knight standing at the throne's left.

Lochlyn sucked in a breath as he considered the implications of Curran's presence. The king had lied to him when he claimed he wasn't aware of Curran's whereabouts, and Rosalie's father probably had too. He wondered if they'd also lied about Caterina.

And, Fates save them, what if they knew about Jonathan?

"Let's get his attention," Lochlyn said. He and Rosalie walked toward the dais. When Curran spotted Rosalie, he said something to the knight standing beside him, then he exited the hall. They followed him and found Curran waiting in the darkened corridor.

For a moment, the three of them watched each other. "The child. He's safe," Rosalie said, breaking their silence.

"Thank the Fates," Curran said as his shoulders sagged in relief. "He?"

Rosalie nodded. "And my sister?"

"She's here," Curran replied.

"What?" Rosalie demanded. "For how long? Is she all right?"

"Caterina's been here ever since the birth. I haven't seen her in weeks, but she's as well as can be expected." Curran faced Lochlyn. "I owe you everything. I can't thank you enough for all you've done for Cat and our child."

"You may thank us by explaining why Caterina is here, and why you are attending the king," Lochlyn replied.

"I'm not attending him," Curran replied. "My post here is part of my punishment for abandoning my assignment at Irontooth."

Lochlyn nodded. "Is Caterina also being punished?"

"Olivar's using Cat as bait," Curran replied. "The plan is to trade Cat's life for yours."

"That's awful," Rosalie said as Lochlyn finally understood the king's plan.

"He wants my scales," Lochlyn said. "Over the years, many have claimed that dragon scales could help the king shift back to human form, but they're all wrong. Dragon scales can't cure anything, not even a toothache. All those legends are false."

"False they may be, but Olivar's desperate," Curran said.

"But why is he desperate now?" Lochlyn demanded. "He's been trapped in this half form for almost two decades."

"From what I understand, in the beginning Olivar had accepted his new body," Curran replied. "That all changed around fifteen years ago when he employed an alchemist who claimed he could use dragon scales to create a cure and give him his legs back."

"Fifteen years was a long time ago," Rosalie said. "Why is he still chasing something that hasn't happened?"

"Olivar tried negotiating with Gorlas," Curran continued, referencing Lochlyn's father. "He wanted your father to turn over a criminal who carried the blood so they could harvest his scales. Gorlas, who, unlike the king, was a man of honor, wasn't willing to sacrifice a dragon to the king's alchemist. That enraged Olivar, and he manipulated the Northern Reaches into a war against Dragon Ridge."

Lochlyn's body went hot, then cold. The war in the Northern Reaches had torn his family apart, and if Olivar had orchestrated that conflict... "How certain are you of this?" he demanded.

"I was there when Olivar went to the Grand Master to hire us," Curran replied. "I was part of the company that died on the battlefield, and then I was reborn in your dragon fire." Curran bowed his head, and he added, "As I said, I owe you everything."

"You want to clear your debt? Help us save Caterina." Lochlyn glanced at Rosalie, continuing, "I understand that you were only following orders during the war. I don't fault you or any other phoenix for what happened then. But if Olivar *is* responsible for that war and, therefore, the death of my brothers, I will hold him accountable. When that happens, you and Caterina need to be far from here."

"Agreed," Curran said, "but I'd rather help you fight." He glanced at Rosalie, and he added, "We need to send Cat and Rosie away for their own safety."

"Where Lochlyn goes, I go," Rosalie declared. "And there's something else you should know. My mother's name was Aurielle Flameborn."

"You're Aurielle's daughter?" Curran asked as he took a step back. "My father would be shocked to learn that, and nothing shocks the old bird."

"Why is that?" Lochlyn asked.

"Aurielle was my sister." Curran looked into the hall. "I need to return before I'm missed," he said, walking away from them.

Lochlyn clamped his hand onto Curran's arm. "Not yet," he said.

"Take your hand off me," Curran seethed.

"If you want to return to the hall quickly, then answer my questions quickly," Lochlyn said. "We both know I'm stronger than you. Don't make me prove it."

Curran's nostrils flared, but he nodded. "Fine. Ask."

"Why are you here?" Lochlyn demanded. "What is Olivar planning now? And why did Caterina turn up at Dragon Ridge heavy with child and all alone?"

Curran rubbed the back of his neck. "After we fled Irontooth Keep, Cat and I were living together. We found a quiet village, and I was working as a blacksmith. One day, I went to get supplies. I took a chance and shifted." He glanced at Lochlyn, then he continued, "You know how it is when you haven't shifted for a time."

Lochlyn nodded. "Go on."

"The Order must have been searching the area, because that was when they found me," Curran continued. "They bound me in lead chains and forced me back into human form, and they imprisoned me in the Sun Temple."

"But you never told them where Cat was," Rosalie said.

"No. I never did. At that point, the only way I could keep her safe was by claiming I didn't know what happened to her. But they didn't believe me, because somehow they knew I'd gotten her with child."

"Melly," Rosalie hissed.

"Aye. Melly's the one that caught us." Curran didn't face them when he continued, "When the birth was close, and Cat was calling for me through our bond, I was instructed to retrieve her and our baby, and to bring both of them back to the temple." He paused, his throat working. "Cat has maintained that the baby did not survive."

"To keep your Order from searching for him," Rosalie said.

Lochlyn loosened his grip on Curran's arm, his heart going out to the man who believed he'd lost his child all these months. "Why bring Caterina to Serpens? Why not escape and start your lives over?"

"Because no matter where I go, they will find me," Curran said. "No matter where we hide, eventually I will need to shift, and when I do, our location will be revealed. The names and parents of every living phoenix are recorded in the Sun Temple. If sightings came in about a rogue firebird, they would hunt me down and capture Cat regardless. At least, with her here, I can watch over her to a degree."

"The temple does not have a record of every living phoenix," Rosalie said. "There's me, for one, and my brother. We also know of several others outside the Order's purview."

"That's impossible," Curran said, shaking his head. "The Order—"

"Is an awful organization that needs to end," Rosalie said. "I've heard enough about them. Let me guess, now that you've delivered Caterina into the king's hands, he's hatched this new plan to obtain my husband's scales?"

"This isn't the king's plan," Curran replied. "It's your father's."

Rosalie's jaw set as her eyes narrowed, and Lochlyn was certain she had fire within her just as he did. "Where is my sister now?" she demanded.

Curran's face darkened. "She's being held in the king's chambers," he ground out.

"Why are you allowing that to happen?" Lochlyn demanded.

Curran held up his arms, revealing two metal cuffs around his wrists. "I'm bound in lead. Until these are off me, I can't shift.—not that I wouldn't cut my hands off for Cat. But for now, she's safe, and I'm of more use to her whole."

"How can we remove these?" Rosalie asked.

"They're welded on," Curran replied. "I know Olivar can't touch her, but..." He straightened and met Lochlyn's gaze. "I have no right to ask you for anything, not after everything you've already done for me."

"We will get those cuffs off you, and we will help you save Caterina," Lochlyn declared. "No one should be held captive, and no child should be separated from their parents." In the hall, the crier announced the king's imminent arrival. Curran glanced into the hall and frowned.

"Go," Lochlyn said. "We'll find you later."

Curran nodded, and then he returned to the hall. As soon as he was out of sight, Lochlyn pulled Rosalie into his arms.

"She's alive," he whispered against her hair. "How does it feel to know?"

"I can hardly believe it," she murmured against his chest. "But I *can* believe my father's involved. He's heartless, and he will do anything to impress the king."

"We'll deal with Osman after Caterina is safe," Lochlyn promised. "I will make sure he never harms you or your sister again."

"I'm not sure that's possible," Rosalie murmured. "What did Curran mean about sensing Cat through their bond?"

"Shifters can feel their mates, even when separated by some distance," Lochlyn replied. "I've always sensed you to a degree, but I assumed our bond was weak because you're human." He glided his fingers across the scar on his wife's neck. "But now we know differently."

"What if my blood's not dormant?" she asked. "What if it's bound, like how Curran's bound with those cuffs?"

Lochlyn rested his cheek against Rosalie's head. He'd never heard of a shifter's blood being bound, but he'd never heard of a mother burning off her children's marks either. "We can go to the Sun Temple. I'll petition for an audience with Master Flameborn himself, and we won't leave until we get answers." He tightened his arms around his wife. "As much as I want answers for you, first we must focus on Caterina."

"Our advantage is that Olivar doesn't know we are aware of his plan," Rosalie said. "Even so, we aren't the least bit safe here, are we?"

"Do you doubt I will protect you?"

"No. My faith in you is never ending." Rosalie stood on her toes and kissed him. Then, she drew back and straightened his coat. "Let's go have a look at this king and figure out a plan to get my sister back."

CHAPTER TWENTY-SEVEN

IF THINGS TAKE A TURN...

A rm in arm, Rosalie and Lochlyn reentered the hall. She felt a bit out of place, being that she had never been to the royal court before, and her knowledge of official functions was limited to what she'd witnessed at Irontooth Keep and what she'd read in Danae's letters to Caterina. The first thing Rosalie noticed was that, while the king was a madman, his hall was clean and orderly. The servants were helpful yet unobtrusive, and everyone in attendance spoke in hushed tones. Rosalie wondered if they were being polite, or simply afraid of breaking protocol and risking Olivar's wrath.

If Olivar was willing to hold Caterina, his own niece, captive and trade her life for Lochlyn's scales...

"How would someone take your scales?" she whispered. When Lochlyn raised an eyebrow, she added, "I need to know."

"Normally, they could only be taken if I was skinned while in dragon form," he murmured. "However, now my scales are above my skin."

"Oh," Rosalie gasped as she covered her mouth with her hand. Lochlyn's raised scales meant they could be taken while he was in human and warrior form too. "We must flee!"

"We don't have to go," Lochlyn said. "It's known that a dragon's scales rest beneath his skin while in human form. No one will expect anything otherwise, and I don't plan on taking off my clothes around Olivar."

Rosalie nodded, relieved. She looked toward the throne and noted that Curran was no longer at his post. "Do you know where his chamber is?"

"I believe it's on the top floor of the central tower," Lochlyn replied. "There's a rooftop garden. He only invites his favored guests to view it." Lochlyn moved to say more but held his tongue when another man approached them.

"Ah, Lord Blackmoor," the man said as he stopped in front of Lochlyn. He was tall and slender, with pale brown hair and eyes. "I haven't seen you at court in ages. How fares the Ridge?"

"As well as ever," Lochlyn replied. "Have you been in Serpens for some time?"

"I arrived this morning," he replied, then he glanced at Rosalie.

"Allow me to introduce my wife," Lochlyn said, his hand on the small of Rosalie's back. "Beloved, this is Lord Cervus. Cervus, meet my wife, Rosalie."

"A pleasure, my lady," Cervus said as he bowed. "How you convinced such a beauty to join you in those chilly mountains is a mystery, Blackmoor."

"I quite enjoy life in the mountains," Rosalie said. "Are you from a warmer region?"

"My kind keeps to the lowland plains," Cervus replied. Then, he noticed movement near the throne. "I believe our king is about to join us."

A horn sounded and everyone turned toward the dais. Rosalie watched as eight men, all of them bare to their waists with muscles bulging, carried in a gilded palanquin upon which reclined the king. When they reached the throne, the palanquin was lowered. Two men lifted Olivar off the platform and sat him in the golden chair. Rosalie, who had always been curious, leaned to the side to get a better view of the monarch.

Olivar the Magnificent was indeed a serpent from the waist down, as evidenced by the wide green tail that curled beneath his velvet robe. As for his human half, his skin was pale and appeared damp, his face was wide and flat with watery eyes and a wispy beard. The king's hair was long and brown, and while a golden crown restrained a portion of it, the rest fell in lank clumps around his shoulders. Rosalie glanced at his hands, and saw his fingers were topped with claws that were smaller versions of Lochlyn's talons.

The man seated on the throne did not match the powerful basilisk depicted in the tapestries and paintings scattered throughout the palace.

"Have you met our king before, my lady?" Cervus asked.

"I have not," she replied. "And I am honored to be in his presence."

Cervus dipped his chin toward her. "An excellent response. I'll meet up with you later, Blackmoor," he said to Lochlyn, before moving off to greet other folk.

Rosalie watched Cervus walk away, then she whispered to her husband, "There's something more happening here. More than what Curran told us."

Lochlyn angled himself to shield Rosalie from the king's sight. "How so?"

"Twelve years ago, the Northerners went to war to get dragon scales," she began. "They failed, as did the phoenixes. Curran used to tell stories back at Irontooth, and I recall him saying that the king is the biggest employer of phoenixes in Alessia. Now he and Cat are here, and the king seems to have a renewed interest in obtaining dragon scales."

Lochlyn's jaw went rigid. "You're right. Something must have changed."

More people entered the hall. At the front was a small man swathed in bright red and purple scarves and a green silk shirt and trousers. He also had several golden chains wound around his neck and waist. The colorful man took his place next to the throne, and he surveyed the room as if he were the monarch instead of Olivar.

"Who is that?" Rosalie asked. "For that matter, do you know anyone here aside from Cervus?"

"That man is Zosimos. He's the king's current alchemist, and I'm familiar with most in attendance." Lochlyn set his hand on Rosalie's shoulder, and she covered it with hers. "Why?"

"Just wondering who's on our side."

"We are on our side," Lochlyn said. "If things take a turn, I can have you out of here in the blink of an eye."

A horn sounded at the main entrance to the hall. Everyone turned toward the arched doorway and watched as a wizened old woman made her way down the center aisle. Her hair, jet black and shot with gray, hung down her back in a thick braid beneath a black veil, and her plain black dress was stark compared to Zosimos's riot of color. When she reached the dais, the alchemist helped her up the steps, then she sat on a stool next to the king.

"Is that the king's mother?" Rosalie asked.

"A seer," Lochlyn replied. "She's been employed by the de Serpens for generations. Some say she's the daughter of Fate Herself."

Rosalie turned back to the dais and scrutinized the seer. Had she gone to the convent as planned, she would have been surrounded by such women for the rest of her life, or at least until she left the community. While Rosalie had never wanted to take the third veil and become a full priestess, she had always been in awe of those who wielded such power.

"Her predictions are the main reason the king's family has remained in power for so long," Lochlyn continued. "They are guided by the Fates Themselves."

"Do many noble families employ a seer?"

"I'm sure many would like to, but it's not possible," Lochlyn replied. "The seers must return to the temple every night at sundown when the doors are sealed. Even the king's seer refuses to remain in the palace after dark."

Rosalie nodded, impressed by the amount of power held by the seers. To do as one wished even while in the king's palace was a rare form of freedom. She remembered how Caterina had repeatedly refused marriages and suitors because she wanted to retain as much of her autonomy as possible.

What do these seers think of Olivar keeping my sister trapped in his rooms like a pet? Instead of giving voice to her treasonous thoughts, Rosalie let her gaze travel around the hall. Even though the king was present, and the room was teeming with nobles, no announcements had been made, and Olivar was merely watching the crowd.

"Why is nothing happening?" she whispered to Lochlyn.

"I'm not sure." He squeezed her shoulder. "Be strong, beloved. Once we return to The Talon, we will be able to speak freely."

Rosalie leaned against her husband, all the while wondering how he managed such composure. If Curran's information was correct—and really, neither she nor Lochlyn had any reason to doubt him—the king was responsible for his brothers' deaths. She remembered that his parents had also passed soon after that war's conclusion, and she shuddered.

"I'm sorry you found out this way," she said. "About the war, I mean."

"As am I, beloved," he said, his voice rough but steady. "But it's always better to know the truth, even if that truth is painful." He glanced toward the dais. "Something is happening."

She followed his gaze and saw the seer swaying back and forth on her stool. Suddenly her eyes snapped open, and she whispered something to the king. Olivar scanned the room until his gaze landed on Lochlyn.

"Lord Blackmoor," Olivar called. "Please, attend us."

Rosalie took Lochlyn's proffered arm, and they approached the king. Once they reached the base of the dais, Lochlyn bowed while Rosalie went into a deep curtsey; she may be the daughter of a pirate, but she knew how to behave around royalty.

"I see you received my summons," Olivar said when they rose.

"Yes, Your Majesty," Lochlyn replied. "Thank you for your generous invitation."

"We'll see how generous it is." The tip of Olivar's tail flicked back and forth as he looked over Rosalie. "I assume this is the woman you wedded instead of my niece?"

"Yes, sire," Lochlyn replied. "Allow me to introduce my beloved wife, Rosalie."

Rosalie curtsied again. When she rose, she smiled at the king. "I am so pleased to meet you, Your Majesty."

"Yes, I imagine you are." The king faced Lochlyn. "Have you given up searching for my niece?"

"I have not," Lochlyn replied. Then, the seer stood.

"Things are changing as we speak," the seer intoned. "Lochlyn Blackmoor is no longer the sole living dragon shifter in Alessia."

The hall went deathly quiet as the king's gaze returned to Rosalie. "Could it be?" he murmured. "Is the whore's daughter carrying a dragon? Why, if I seize you and your child, I'll no longer need to deal with the Blackmoors' reticence to help their king."

"I don't know what you're talking about," Rosalie said, her gaze darting between the king and the seer. "Your seer is mad."

"As is your alchemist," Lochlyn snapped. "Scales cannot cure you! All taking mine will do is kill me."

"Untrue," Zosimos said. "I only need a few of your scales, then I will treat them with basilisk venom in order to reverse the king's shift. You will not die, and our ruler will be whole again. Do you not want to serve your king in his hour of need?"

"No." Lochlyn made a cutting motion with his hand. "I will not agree to anything that will harm my family or put my people in danger."

"Treason," Zosimos bellowed as he pointed at Lochlyn.

The seer bowed her head. "I warned you he would refuse."

"No matter." Olivar gestured toward his guards. "This isn't the first time a dragon has defied me and suffered the consequences. Take the woman and do away with Blackmoor."

"No!" Rosalie screamed as the guards advanced, then Lochlyn roared louder than any lion. The ground shook and black fire obscured Rosalie's vision as Lochlyn's dragon appeared.

The assorted nobles and courtiers, who'd been watching the Blackmoors' exchange with the king, screamed and trampled each other as they fled the hall.

Lochlyn ignored the chaos behind him and leveled his massive head with the king's.

"Take his scales now," Zosimos ordered. A soldier advanced with his sword drawn. Lochlyn batted him away without breaking the king's gaze.

"Take the woman instead," Zosimos yelled. A second soldier approached Rosalie, but Lochlyn grabbed her with his clawed foot. The soldier made contact with her arm, then he screamed and snatched his hand away, his clothing singed.

"Resume human form, Blackmoor," Olivar bellowed. "I command it!"

Lochlyn roared in the king's face, toppling his throne and sending the monarch and the alchemist tumbling backward off the dais. Rosalie clutched Lochlyn's long serpentine fingers, then she saw the seer standing calm among the chaos.

"How can I unbind my blood?" Rosalie demanded.

"Your mother told you how," the seer replied.

Another soldier rushed at Rosalie with his sword out. She screamed. Lochlyn yelped and flew straight up toward the ceiling. When they reached the top of the hall and the long expanse of priceless stained glass, Lochlyn spun around midair and shattered the windows with his tail. As he flew out of the palace amid shards of colored glass, Rosalie's mind replayed what the seer had said.

Your mother told you how.

It was a short flight from the palace to The Talon. Lochlyn gently set Rosalie onto the roof, then he collapsed behind her.

"Lochlyn!" Rosalie cried, as the dragon fell to the floor. She scrambled toward him as his eyes drooped closed. "Beloved, what's wrong?"

He grunted, rolling onto his side, thus exposing a slash that ran the length of his belly and stained his ivory scales bright red. A sword bearing a basilisk on the hilt lay on the roof beneath him.

"Did you fly with a sword in you," she marveled, then she noticed his labored breathing.

"Lochlyn," she said as she pulled his massive head onto her lap. "You need to shift. Shifting will heal you."

Her dragon remained silent and his breathing slowed.

"Lochlyn, you must shift!"

Nothing. No movement, not even a breath.

"Lochlyn Blackmoor, you are not allowed to die," she said. "You told me you will always take care of me, and you can't do that if you're dead! I am your wife, and I am ordering you to shift this instant!"

The dragon remained still. Rosalie bent over his head and wailed, her heart shattering into a thousand tiny pieces. No matter that she hadn't been with Lochlyn for a full year, he'd become the center of her world.

She had only just met him, and, already, she had no idea how she would live without him.

The weight on her lap lessened. With her eyes still closed, Rosalie stroked Lochlyn's ridged brow... and didn't feel any ridges. Nor did she feel scales or horns, but she did sink her fingers into his soft, wavy hair. Hardly believing what she felt, she opened her eyes and saw Lochlyn sprawled out on the roof in his human form.

"Beloved," she murmured as she stroked his hair. "I thought I'd lost you."

"Never," he rasped then he grabbed his side. He had a long purple mark on his torso where the sword had pierced him in dragon form. "Though Olivar did his best to make that happen."

"I thought shifting healed you."

"Normally, it does. But the blade was poisoned." Lochlyn pushed himself upright. "Olivar's guards are known for their tainted blades. It's an insidious solution, and it takes a few shifts to be fully nullified."

Rosalie watched as her normally strong husband trembled and struggled to breathe. "You can't shift now. You're exhausted."

"Be that as it may, we can't stay here," he said. "After that spectacle in the throne room, Olivar's men will already be on their way here."

"Can you ride?" she asked as she helped him stand.

"We'll soon know," he said. "Beloved, what you said while I was still in dragon form. I was nearly gone, but you pulled my soul back into my body."

"You heard me, like how Curran hears Cat," Rosalie said. "A mate bond."

"More than the bond," he replied as he stroked her cheek. "You saved me."

"And I'll save you again if I need to," she said, trying and failing to quell the trembling in her voice. "I need you, Lochlyn."

"I need you too." He kissed her hair. "Let's get to the stable and find a way out of the city."

"Actually, I think we should stay," Rosalie said. "I want to talk to the seer."

Lochlyn frowned. "Is that wise?"

"Probably not, but she mentioned my mother," Rosalie replied. "If the seer knows something about my mother, I need to talk to her."

"Very well," Lochlyn said, moving toward the doorway. "But our escape has just gotten much more complicated."

CHAPTER TWENTY-EIGHT

SANCTUARY

Lochlyn crept toward the edge of the building and surveyed the market square from his place at the mouth of the alley. He couldn't see any of the king's soldiers, but that didn't mean they weren't out there, blending into the crowd and watching for him and Rosalie to make an appearance. Add to that uncertainty the hot, throbbing pain in his side, and he was starting to doubt if he could protect his wife and unborn child.

"We're safe, for the moment," he murmured.

Rosalie found his hand and squeezed. After she'd helped him down from the roof, and Rosalie had shed her formal gown, they'd put on discreet traveling gear topped with rough brown cloaks. Once that was done, Lochlyn ordered his people to disperse with instructions to meet up at Cervus's estate in two days' time while he and Rosalie made their way toward the Temple of the Fates. All the while, Lochlyn struggled not to pass out from the pain.

"You need to shift," Rosalie said when he groaned.

"Not here." He didn't add that the pain in his side was so great he wasn't sure he could shift, and he was fairly certain he knew why: poison. Olivar, ever the cheater, was known for using poisoned weapons. Some even said that poison was what led to Olivar's current physical predicament.

The last thing Lochlyn needed was to end up trapped in a half form like Olivar. Then he truly would be useless.

Olivar... Lochlyn clenched his fist as he suppressed a growl. Not only did he finally have confirmation that Olivar had orchestrated the war that destroyed his family, the weakling had tried to take Rosalie from him as well. To avenge his family and protect his beloved, Lochlyn vowed to destroy the monarch and anyone who assisted him.

Even if Lochlyn never shifted again, his determination to end the mad king would keep him going until the deed was done.

"Shift soon, then," Rosalie insisted. "I don't like seeing you in pain."

"I don't like being in it," he said as he continued his visual sweep of the market. Their current plan was simple: shortly before sundown, he and Rosalie would enter the Temple of the Fates and beg the priestesses for sanctuary. Assuming their request was granted, Rosalie could speak with the seer about her mother. Then, at sundown the temple doors would be sealed, and they would be safe for the night. As for what would happen at sunrise, that was anyone's guess.

They'd already managed to cross the city without being apprehended. Now, the only thing that stood between them and the temple was the market square. Lochlyn glanced toward the sky and saw that they had some time before sunset. He didn't want to risk setting foot in the market until the last possible moment, lest one of the king's men decided to follow them inside the temple. Waiting in the alley would have to do.

And there was something he had yet to discuss with his wife.

"Beloved," he began, taking her hand. "When I grabbed you in the throne room and the guard lunged for you, you burned him."

She nodded, but she kept her eyes downcast. "I did," she murmured. "At first, I thought I was remembering things incorrectly, but when I took off my dress and I checked the sleeve, it burned from the inside out." She rubbed her arm. "If I've been a phoenix for my entire life, why did my fire only manifest now? I've been in danger before."

He growled at the thought of his beloved in danger, then clutched his side as the vibration made his wound ache. "The difference is that you weren't with child before. We shifters are protective and possessive, but the addition of children heightens our abilities."

"Like your scales." Rosalie stroked the raised scales on his arm that had only become pronounced after her womb quickened. "I've been thinking about my mother."

"So have I."

Rosalie looked up at him. "You have?"

"I remember you told me she had a fever, that she became hot to the touch. I wonder if she suppressed her urge to shift for so long, she succumbed and her fire took her."

"That can happen?" Rosalie asked, her green eyes wide.

Lochlyn gathered her against him. "Yes. One of the surest ways to destroy a shifter is to make them resist the blood surge until their body gives out. If your mother was suppressing the urge to keep those around her—like your father—from knowing her true nature, she would have progressively weakened."

"Oh." She slid her arms around his waist, avoiding his wound. It pained Lochlyn to speak of Rosalie's mother's death, thus causing his beloved distress, but they needed to understand her true nature. "It makes sense. Everything my mother did was to keep Devlin and me safe. And I don't think she burned us, so much as she bound us."

"You mentioned that at the palace." Lochlyn had never heard of a shifter's abilities being permanently bound, but he'd rarely worked with magic. "How so?"

"The song she used to sing. *Little one is bound, little one is bound, turn round and round and the little one is found.*" Her voice caught, pausing before she continued. "That rhyme makes no sense. But what if it was really a set of instructions?"

"She sang that to both you and Devlin?" Lochlyn asked, and Rosalie nodded. "Then we can potentially unbind both of you." He rested his forehead against her hair, enjoying her sweet, intoxicating scent. "We'll be able to fly together, beloved, two creatures of fire soaring over the land."

"That would be amazing," she said, then she leaned around his body and checked the sky. "The sun's close to setting."

He untangled himself from his wife and turned toward the market. "The temple is directly across the market. It's made of white and green marble, and it has three columns at the top of the steps." He held her face close to his, and added, "If we become separated, don't wait for me. Run to the temple and beg sanctuary. I will make my own way to you."

"I'm not leaving you," she said. "If I have to, I'll carry you."

"Think of our dragon," Lochlyn said as he lightly touched her belly. "He's our priority."

Rosalie nodded, but he knew his beloved well. If he so much as stumbled, she would turn back, and remain by his side until either help arrived, or they were captured. That meant he'd better not stumble.

Hand in hand, Lochlyn led Rosalie out of the alley. Even though it was close to dark, the market still bustled with activity, with hawkers selling everything from silk ribbons to wagon wheels, and food stalls offering grilled meats and cool drinks. At any other time, he would be enjoying the market dressed as a commoner instead of as a noble. He would leisurely make the rounds with Rosalie, buying her trinkets and sweets until it was time to return home. Now, he only wanted to cross the square as quickly as possible.

They were halfway across the square when Rosalie pulled him to a halt. When he glanced at her, she pointed toward a table filled with hair combs. "Aren't these lovely?" she asked.

"The green one matches your eyes," he said as he scanned the area behind them. Lochlyn saw nothing of import, but Rosalie wouldn't have stopped for no reason. "Would you like one?"

"Maybe you can buy me one tomorrow," she said, then she took his hands and walked backward as she drew him away from the booth. "Something to eat?"

"If you like." Lochlyn's eyes darted about; again, he found nothing. That meant whatever Rosalie was avoiding was behind him. "What would you—"

A hand clamped down on Lochlyn's shoulder as a second man moved behind Rosalie and pulled back her hood. Lochlyn roared as he shifted to warrior form, and drove his talons into the hand on his shoulder as he snatched Rosalie from the guard's grasp. He pulled her close to him as he readied to fly—

And realized his wings hadn't manifested.

"I can't fly," he said, panicked.

"Then we run," Rosalie said as she shed her cloak and grabbed his hand. A soldier stepped into their path. Rosalie evaded him while Lochlyn raked his talons across the guard's chest, slicing through his tabard and shattering the chain mail beneath.

"There it is," Rosalie yelled. Lochlyn faced forward and saw the temple steps. The last slanting rays of sunlight illuminated the entrance. In mere moments, the temple would be sealed.

"Go," Lochlyn yelled. Then, Rosalie stumbled. Using his last ounce of strength, he grabbed her waist and hauled her up the steps. Once they were inside the temple, he fell to his knees and collapsed on the floor.

"Sanctuary," Rosalie shrieked as Lochlyn's world went dark. "I beg sanctuary! My husband is hurt, and I need help!"

CHAPTER TWENTY-NINE

RECOVERY

R osalie swallowed the lump in her throat and addressed the Mother Priestess. "And I'm to spread the salve across the wound whenever I change his bandages?"

"Yes, but don't use too much," the priestess replied. "We're using a weaker poison to combat the poison that's already inside him. Add too much, and he'll be overwhelmed."

"Is it safe for me to work with such a substance?" she asked. "I'm with child."

"Use the spoon to apply it," the priestess instructed. "When you remove the soiled bandages, don't throw them in the fire. Set them aside, and we'll dispose of them. After you tend him, wash your hands thoroughly with lye soap." When Rosalie's lower lip trembled, the priestess's eyes softened.

"My lady, your husband is a dragon," she said. "They are the strongest of creatures. Even without our care, he will recover."

"Thank you for saying that, and for everything you've done for us," Rosalie said. After Lochlyn collapsed on the temple floor, and Rosalie screamed her throat raw begging for help, six priestesses had appeared and carried Lochlyn to the room they now occupied. While Rosalie watched, the priestesses washed his wound, determined the type of poison in his body, and created the salve that would purge his blood and make him well again.

It struck her that, if she hadn't been told to marry Lochlyn, attending to those who stumbled into the temple pleading for help would have been her life.

"Not so long ago, I had planned on joining the convent in the lowlands," she told the priestess. "My intent was to take the first veil and teach children."

"Oh?" the priestess asked as she refolded the bandages. "What made you change your mind?"

"Lochlyn did." Rosalie stroked his hand. His skin had regained its characteristic warmth, though he remained pale. Even his scales had taken on a bluish cast. "It was an arranged marriage. I wasn't even the one who was supposed to marry him, but so many things happened so fast. Before I knew it, we were standing next to each other at the altar. Now, I don't know if I could go on without him."

"Of course you would go on," the priestess said, "but you won't have to. While I've never taken the third veil, I can say that for Fate to alter your path so completely, it must have been with good reason. You and your dragon still have far to go on your shared journey." She gathered up her supplies, and added, "Although, I'm also certain you would have made an excellent priestess."

Rosalie bowed her head. "Thank you, Mother. I appreciate everything you've done for us."

"No thanks are needed," she replied. "Lady Fate sent you to us, which makes you our charges. Your sanctuary here is sound until you both decide you can move on." The priestess glanced between the two, and she added, "I'll give you two some time alone, but do ring us if you need anything."

With that, the Mother Priestess departed. Rosalie sat on the edge of the bed and stroked Lochlyn's fingers. His talons remained present, as did his pronounced scales, but when he last shifted, his wings never manifested. She didn't know if that meant he hadn't fully attained his warrior form, or if the poison had somehow damaged his wings. All she could do was sit with him, monitor his wound, and pray.

It didn't matter to her whether or not Lochlyn could become a dragon. Rosalie fell in love with him long before she knew he was a dragon, and she would love him just as much if he remained a human man for the rest of his life. However, shifting mattered to Lochlyn. He loved everything that came with being a dragon, from flying to breathing fire, and she worried he wouldn't be able to cope without those traits. Much how she wasn't sure how she would cope if her suspicions were true, and she unbound her phoenix abilities.

What if her fire consumed her?

Rosalie sighed. She couldn't answer any of her lingering questions until Lochlyn recovered. He was her priority, along with their baby dragon, and she would do whatever was necessary to keep the both of them safe. Since Lochlyn's wound was seen to, she got in bed with him and curled up against his unhurt side. After she said a quick prayer to the Fates, she let sleep claim her.

Rosalie blinked herself awake, then she heard it again. A quiet groan and labored breathing. She pushed herself up on her elbow and drew the blankets back from Lochlyn's wound.

"Beloved," she murmured as she checked the bandages. "How do you feel?"

"Like I've been stripped naked by a gaggle of nuns so they could spread this caustic grease on me," he grumbled. Rosalie smiled; if he was grumpy, that meant he was feeling better.

"The salve's purpose is to counteract the poison," she explained. "The priestesses said it would take a few days to fully cleanse your blood. Then, you just need to heal."

"Is that all?" He caressed her cheek with his palm, careful to keep his talons away from her skin. "What are you doing here? You once told me when I was ill you would leave me alone in my sickbed for weeks."

"I'll do that next time." She laid her head on his shoulder and slid her arm across his midsection. "Over the past few days, you've saved me at least twice. Now, let me save you."

"As you wish, beloved." He kissed her forehead. "Have you spoken to the seer?"

"I haven't even asked about her. Ever since we got here, I haven't left your side."

"Even though I'm still recovering, we came here to get answers for you," he said. "Promise me you'll seek her out."

"I will, especially now that you've awakened." She rolled onto her back and stared at the ceiling. "I wish Curran were here."

"As a guard?"

"No. Well, yes, but also so I could ask him about shifting."

Lochlyn faced her. "You do know that I'm a shifter."

"Yes, but he grew up around shifters." When Lochlyn only arched a brow, she continued, "All right, you did as well. Since you're feeling well enough to answer a few questions, let me make my first inquiry. Are all shifters the same? As in, do different types of creatures experience shifting the same way?"

"Yes and no," he replied. "The most obvious difference is in how we shift, and our abilities after we attain our other forms. But we all feel compelled shift, and to use those abilities whatever they may be. It's not something we can ignore."

"You said your mother was a selkie. Did she have a warrior form?"

"She did, but it was quite different from mine. Her warrior form manifested as a sealskin cloak, and it helped her blend in with her surroundings."

"That's amazing," Rosalie murmured. "I wish I had grown up like you, around magic and creatures."

"It seems you did." Lochlyn touched the scar on the back of her neck. "As soon as I'm able to get out of this bed, we'll find your answers. Then, we'll rescue Caterina and leave this city behind."

"Will Olivar follow us to the Ridge?"

A low growl deep in her husband's chest. "I'm sure he'll try."

Over the next two days, Lochlyn slept fitfully as his body fought the poison in his blood. During the few times he was awake, he told Rosalie everything she needed to know about taking care of Dragon Ridge. He explained their finances, which of their lands were the most lucrative, and which could be left fallow if necessary, as well as which drawer in his study held the keys to the castle vault. Finally, Lochlyn told her where his aunt's information was kept, and how to notify her family in the gryphon lands in the event of his demise.

"I'm not notifying her about anything of the sort," Rosalie said; she'd listened attentively to the information about the Ridge, but she wouldn't hear anything about Lochlyn's potential death. "The only thing I'll be writing to Elin about will be news of our children."

"Beloved," Lochlyn said as he caressed her hair. "I'm only trying to be practical."

She hid her face against his shoulder. While she appreciated that Lochlyn was only trying to look out for her, she hated the thought of a future without him in it. "I know. Perhaps we can talk about something else for a bit."

"As you wish, my love." They were sitting up against the headboard, which Rosalie took as a good sign for his recovery. Earlier he'd gotten out of bed and walked around the room, though he'd tired quickly. Still present were his talons, which a visitor of theirs thought was quite interesting.

"It was good of Cervus to come by," Rosalie said. Cervus arrived at the temple that morning. After Rosalie convinced the priestesses he was a friend, he spoke with Lochlyn alone for a short time. "Although, if he knows we're here, Olivar must as well."

"Cervus probably learned of our location from Olivar himself. I'm sure the king's guards were forced to give a full report as to how a mortally wounded man and his brilliant and stubborn wife evaded them."

"You think I'm brilliant?" Rosalie asked. Her stubbornness had never been in question.

A kiss that held more passion than a wounded man should be capable of. "You know I do."

"Then, I have a question." She slid her arm around his waist, careful to avoid the salve spread across his abdomen. They'd removed the bandages earlier so his skin could breathe, and she didn't want to risk touching too much of the substance. "Will a shifter automatically recognize if another person is a shifter?"

"It's possible, but not in every instance. Some creatures are quite subtle." He eyed her. "You want to know if Cervus is a shifter."

"You two seem especially close," she said. "I was wondering if that closeness grew from your shared abilities."

"You're partially right, my love." Lochlyn moved so he was facing her, and he cursed under his breath when the motion strained his wound. "Cervus is a stag shifter. He's also my spymaster."

"And he pokes about right under the king's nose? Amazing. Or is Olivar's entourage really that incompetent?" Before Lochlyn could reply, Rosalie drew another conclusion. "Cervus is the one who worked his way into the Order of the Sun?"

"He is," Lochlyn replied. "He's become good friends with some of the elders. I don't know if he's on such good terms with the Grand Master himself, however."

"The Grand Master is my grandfather," Rosalie murmured. "And Curran is my uncle. Who else am I related to in this city?"

"It's good to be related to powerful people," Lochlyn said. "From what I've gathered, Arthus has had many children over the years, but Curran is his only living son. Not only are you Arthus's grandchild, so is Jonathan. Hopefully, that means the phoenixes will no longer so readily serve Olivar."

"Based on what Curran told us at Irontooth Keep, the Order isn't beholden to the king," Rosalie said. "The king hires them for one assignment at a time, and there's been a few instances where he couldn't pay his debts."

"That doesn't surprise me. Many of Olivar's supporters have abandoned him over his lack of an heir. They assume the de Serpens line will end with him, and they're waiting to back whoever rises to power after Olivar." Lochlyn worked his fingers between hers, his talons clicking as he did so. "Did the priestesses tell you what sort of poison was on the sword?"

She nodded, the memory making her slightly nauseous. "They said it was basilisk venom."

"Not just basilisk venom. Cervus told me that Olivar's own venom coats his guards' swords." Lochlyn studied his shiny black talons. "That's why I think I'm trapped halfway to warrior form. Whatever's impaired Olivar's shifting has now infected me."

"Then we will counteract this infection any way we can," Rosalie declared. "Do you know if Olivar was fed poison, or if an illness caused his issues?"

"A few stories claim he was poisoned, but most say he was cursed," Lochlyn replied. "The stories vary as to why he was cursed, but most agree that a woman was at the center of it all." He grimaced, continuing, "There is also the fact that the longer Olivar remains in that half form, the more his mind and body deteriorate. When I first attained my title and he summoned me to court, he was much more lucid." Lochlyn scoffed. "At the time, he framed the invitation as him welcoming me to his inner circle. Now we know he was merely taking the measure of his newest opponent."

"I'd like to chop off his slimy tail for all he's done to you," Rosalie muttered.

"Beloved. Serpents aren't slimy."

"No, they're not. And your scales are silky and smooth, and I hope to spend my life feeling them," she added as she caressed his forearm. "However, the king is decidedly damp, and it's repulsive."

Lochlyn suppressed a laugh, his first laugh in days, and Rosalie's heart somersaulted in her breast. "That repulsive dampness is his venom. He can't shift and expel it, so it seeps out of his skin. Many think the constant layer of venom on his body is what's driving him mad."

"It would drive *me* mad," Rosalie muttered. "Something else we need to figure out is how my father is involved. I don't recall him being close to the king, but he hid much from his children."

"And he hid your mother's identity from the Order and the king," Lochlyn said. "When Cervus was here, I'd tasked him with sending someone to Irontooth Keep. Their mission is to speak to Borneas, Zephyn, and Osman, if possible."

"Fates save him if he ends up alone with my father," Rosalie said. "Father is old, but his black heart keeps his reflexes sharp and his aim true. I don't want anyone else getting hurt. Unless it's Olivar," she added.

"Agreed, my love," Lochlyn said. "I've no good will left for our king. Perhaps he'll be removed one way or another soon enough, and someone else will replace him."

"But who?" Rosalie asked. "He doesn't have an heir. Except—"

"Caterina," Lochlyn finished. "And Jonathan."

CHAPTER THIRTY

FATE SPEAKS

When the noon bell rang, Lochlyn declared that he hated his bed, and that he didn't want to look at it for another moment. Rosalie helped him dress, and soon they were walking in the temple's central garden.

"It's so beautiful here," Rosalie said as she paused to admire a honeysuckle vine. Lochlyn admired how the sunlight glinted off her golden hair. "I wonder if the priestesses will let me take a few cuttings for our garden at home. Although many of these lovelies won't survive where we live."

"Regretting your decision to live in the mountains?"

"The only thing I regret is not meeting you sooner," she replied as she leaned up and kissed the bottom of his chin. When she turned back to the flowering vines, she stiffened. Lochlyn followed her gaze and saw an armed man standing near the edge of the garden. He didn't recall the temple employing any guards, then he noticed the basilisk symbol emblazoned across the man's chest.

"Why are they here?" Rosalie asked as she nodded toward the guard.

"To watch us, I assume," Lochlyn replied, putting his hand on her elbow and leading her away from the guard. He didn't think Olivar's soldiers would attempt anything while they remained in the temple, but he refused to risk Rosalie's safety. "Olivar may be mad, but the entire city knows our location. But it's a good thing, since it gives our own people time to escape and fortify our home."

"What good is a fortified home if we can't get to it?" She glanced side long at her husband. "Or do you have a plan for that, too?"

"From the beginning, my plan has been to fly out of here with you on my back," he replied. "Then we would collect Caterina and go home."

"As simple as that," she murmured. "What about Curran?"

"He can fly on his own. We just need to get those cuffs off him." Lochlyn cast a final glance toward the king's soldier, then he drew Rosalie toward the stone temple in the center of the garden. It was the shrine to Lady Fate, the eldest of the three sisters who wove the threads of time into the map that guided Alessia's people on their paths. "Have you visited the shrine yet?"

"I haven't," she replied. "I wanted us to go together."

Lochlyn brought her hand to his mouth and kissed her knuckles. He hadn't been inside a shrine in many years, but he needed to pay his respects to Lady Fate, and to thank her for putting Rosalie in his path.

He led his beloved to the sanctuary, which was a circular building with a domed roof clad in gold. After they removed their shoes, they walked down the cold marble steps and to the grotto. The tiled walls gave way to rough brown stone, and aquamarine streams flowed on either side of the raised path. In the heart of the grotto, set atop a boulder in the pool, was the statue of a woman.

"Oh," Rosalie gasped as she moved closer to Lochlyn. "Is that Her?"

"Yes," he replied, draping his arm around Rosalie's shoulders. "Lady Fate Herself."

Rosalie leaned against Lochlyn's unhurt side, and they contemplated the gray stone effigy. Lady Fate was tall and regal, and She wore a white silk dress topped with a heavy purple mantle. Her hair was pinned up at Her neck and, save for the silver clasp on her mantle, the statue wore no finery.

Really, no gold or gems could enhance her appearance. She was all, and everything.

"She's barefoot, like we are," Rosalie whispered.

"So, she may walk her path unfettered," Lochlyn whispered back. "Like you did, when we were married."

"I'll never forget how cold my feet were that morning. But when I saw you, I forgot all about the chill."

Lochlyn drew her close, but before he could speak, he heard someone enter the temple behind them. A moment later, the king's seer entered the grotto and stood next to them.

"My lady," he greeted with a bow of his head. "Well met."

"Dragon," the seer said. Then, she asked Rosalie, "Have you also forgotten why you're here?"

"I haven't," Rosalie replied. "But I needed to make sure my husband was recovering from his injuries before I sought you out. Was that wrong?"

The seer closed her eyes. "No," she replied after a moment. "It is good that you love your husband so, although it is an aberration."

"In what way?" Lochlyn demanded as Rosalie whispered for him to be respectful.

"No one foretold your union," the seer replied. "And no one, not even I, saw your dragon child, who will grow to be more than a dragon." The seer's eyes snapped open. "You both bear the hand of Lady Fate Herself."

"I question if it were fate, or love," Lochlyn said. "I loved Rosalie the moment I saw her. Did Lady Fate pave the way for me to meet my wife, or was something else in play?"

"That, I cannot say," the seer replied. "But our lady had spoken to me about your parents," she added with a pointed glance at Rosalie.

"A-Are you at liberty to share what you've been told?" Rosalie asked.

"Your mother was a legend in the Order," the seer intoned. "No knight was faster than her, or more deadly with a sword and her flame. Yet, she wanted more than what a warrior's life could give her. So, she ran away."

"How did she end up at the brothel?" Rosalie asked.

"She went there because it was the one place she knew her father wouldn't look. The Grand Master's greatest weakness is his pride. In his eyes, no daughter of his would ever lower herself to serve others in such a manner."

"But he set up those breeding programs," Rosalie protested. "How is that any different?"

"The Grand Master is too prideful to see anyone's view but his own." The seer turned toward the statue of Lady Fate and bowed her head. "You should know, child, that the Lady Herself finds no shame in the sort of work your mother did."

"She doesn't?" Rosalie murmured. Once, during a vulnerable moment, she'd told Lochlyn of all the names and the curses Osman had regularly yelled at her mother, and then at Rosalie herself. As if Lochlyn needed another reason to hate the man. "Then, why did my father treat her so poorly?"

Next to her, Lochlyn scoffed. "Have some respect in the temple," Rosalie whispered, harsher than before.

"The dragon sees the truth of your father," the seer said, "for all that he expresses his views so roughly. As for the Irontooth, he enjoyed keeping a phoenix as a pet, but when you were born, Aurielle didn't want you beholden to any man, be he your father or the Grand Master himself. And, so, she bound you, and then she bound your brother, and then she was cast out of her home."

Rosalie nodded as a tear coursed down her cheek. "She was cast out. Father did do that."

Lochlyn drew his wife against his chest and kissed her hair. "Can Rosalie and her brother be unbound?"

"They have the same weaknesses as all phoenixes do and, therefore, can overcome those weaknesses." The seer faced them. "Things between the Irontooth and the king were set in motion long ago, and against our advice. If you seek

Fate's council, hear it now. Return to Dragon Ridge and be with your children. Danger will come for you soon enough, but your safest place is at home."

"But my sister," Rosalie said. "Olivar's keeping her captive in his rooms."

The seer's face darkened. "The king wishes to use her claim to the throne to further himself. She will not long survive his presence." She glanced at Lochlyn's midsection, and she added, "The venom. It will drive her to madness."

"We will retrieve Caterina and bring her to safety at the Ridge," Lochlyn declared. "May I ask you a direct question?"

"You may ask anything," the seer replied, "but Fate only speaks when She wishes to."

"Understood," Lochlyn murmured. "Will I be able to shift again?"

The seer closed her eyes. "Yes. You will be able to shift when you need to, but not when you want to."

Lochlyn bowed his head. "Thank you."

"I must leave you now," the seer said. "Lady Fate blesses you both."

Rosalie watched as the seer moved deeper into the grotto and disappeared behind the statue. After she was gone, Rosalie said, "Now you know you'll shift again, my dragon."

"But not when I want to," Lochlyn murmured. "We need to concentrate on unbinding you, beloved."

"She didn't tell us how to do that," Rosalie said. "You're right, though. We also need to figure out how to rescue Cat. The thought of her trapped with that madman makes my skin crawl."

"What doesn't make sense is how Olivar is keeping Curran from her," Lochlyn murmured. "If you were being held in the palace, I would pull the building apart brick by brick if I had to, regardless of any lead cuffs. From what you've told me, Curran is as devoted to Caterina as I am to you."

"He is," Rosalie replied. "And he's so close to her, yet he cannot rescue her. Something must be keeping him out of the king's chamber. Something very strong."

"I have an idea," he began, then he turned toward the statue. "My Lady, I thank you for your help today, but I must confess I am more thankful for my

Rosalie. I don't know if I can ever truly express how grateful I am that she is my wife."

"And I am grateful for you, my husband," Rosalie murmured. Then she, too, addressed the statue. "My Lady, my appreciation for you is never ending. Thank you."

They bowed to the statue, then they climbed the steps out of the grotto and emerged in the garden. "I feel so calm," Rosalie said. "Our situation is still dire, but now I'm confident we will overcome it."

"As am I, beloved," Lochlyn replied. "Care to hear more about my idea?"

"Of course."

He leaned close to her ear, saying, "Let's visit the temple archive."

CHAPTER THIRTY-ONE

THE ARCHIVE

As Lochlyn watched his wife pore over the books and scrolls the archivist brought her, his heart swelled in his breast. Rosalie was in her element, with the research energizing her as much as a night's rest would, perhaps more so.

"I worry you love these tomes more than me," Lochlyn teased.

"Never," she replied with a smile. "But being in a new library with an entirely new collection of books is always exciting." She looked over her shoulder at the stacks, which outsiders were expressly forbidden from approaching. "If only I had free rein to roam the aisles here like I do at home."

"The archivist loves books as much as you do," Lochlyn said as he moved a sheet of parchment to the side. While Rosalie learned about phoenix lore, he studied maps of the city, and a set of palace blueprints the archivist had produced from one of their older collections. Since Lochlyn probably wouldn't be able to fly into the palace, he was hoping he could find a tunnel that let out inside the walls. "You really would have made an excellent priestess," he added.

She glanced up at him through her lashes. "Lucky for you, I prefer being your wife."

Lochlyn smiled because she was right. Having Rosalie in his life meant he was the luckiest man who ever lived. Now, if only he could heal from this poisoned stab wound, he could rescue Rosalie's sister, bring them both to Dragon Ridge, and get on with his blessed life.

"Have you found any tunnels?" Rosalie asked, making Lochlyn wonder yet again if she could read his mind.

"I haven't," he replied, then he cursed under his breath as his talons tore a corner of the floor plan he was reading. The archivist had already cautioned him to be careful with the irreplaceable parchments. He set a book on top of the tear to hide the damage, and he continued, "The palace is a well-built and well-fortified structure. Even the sewers are secured with iron gates at both ends."

"Then, perhaps the answer lies in the interior floor plan," Rosalie suggested. "Is there anything unusual about the rooms? The layout, perhaps?"

"Not especially. But now that you mention it." Lochlyn shuffled through the blueprints and found one that depicted the palace's topmost floor.

"This is the king's apartment," he said, pushing the map toward Rosalie. "Do you see how it's outlined in a different color than the rest of the walls?"

"That's because it's constructed from a different material." She glanced at Lochlyn, and she smiled. "Violet and I do love our maps."

"My girls," Lochlyn said, a pang in his heart as he thought of their four children waiting at home. Although, if things go to plan, Jonathan would soon be reunited with his parents. "I don't know why, but something's telling me that this unknown material is significant."

"It's not unknown," Rosalie said as she searched through the parchments for the master diagram. "Every map has a key, and the key explains everything. Here we are."

She came around to his side of the table and set the sheet of parchment with the key on it next to the map Lochlyn was studying. "Most of the walls are made of stone, but these walls…" Her voice trailed off as she traced the layout of the king's chamber, then she touched the corresponding color on the key. "These walls are lined with lead." She turned to Lochlyn and asked, "Why would anyone bother to line a room with lead?"

The archivist, who'd been watching them toss maps and books about with interest, cleared her throat. "If you wouldn't mind my input, the lead is most likely there to keep something out," she said.

"We welcome your opinion," Rosalie said, and the archivist's shoulders relaxed. "But what can one repel with lead?"

"While I do not know the exact answer," the archivist began, "I do know that certain creatures can be bound with lead. Phoenixes, for instance. If the lead were enchanted after it was installed, it could—in theory—keep a phoenix out of the area."

Rosalie sat heavily in the chair next to Lochlyn's. He set his hand on hers, and he asked, "The term you used was bound? As in, lead could force a phoenix to its human form, and then keep them from shifting?"

"Oh, yes," she replied, her head bobbing. "I've heard from those associated with the Sun Temple that chaining phoenixes with lead is a favored punishment. Brutal, but effective." She looked pointedly at the book on creature anatomy that lay on the table unopened. "Chapter twelve discusses the properties of lead in exquisite detail."

"I will be sure to read it," Rosalie said. The archivist bowed and went to attend to someone who'd just entered the reading room. Rosalie looked down at the map and shook her head.

"That's why Curran can't get to her," she murmured. "The lead is keeping him out."

"And he did mention how, when the Order found him, he was bound in lead chains, and he's currently in lead cuffs that are keeping him in his human form." Lochlyn set his hand on Rosalie's neck and traced the circular scar over her spine. "Beloved, would your mother have used lead to bind your abilities? As in, did she put lead in your body, and hide it with a scar?"

"I've no idea," she murmured. "How can we find out?"

"I can only think of one way, but it will be painful."

Rosalie nodded, and then she stood and stacked up the books and maps. "All right. Let's go to our room and try it."

CHAPTER THIRTY-TWO

Unbound

R osalie assumed they would go straight from the temple archive to their room. Instead, they stopped by the kitchens, where Lochlyn requested a platter of bread and meat, pickled vegetables, and a jar of olive oil.

"And, please, do send a bill for everything we've consumed—food and otherwise—to The Talon," Lochlyn said as the staff assembled the requested items. "My treasurer will pay it immediately."

"We need no compensation," the priestess, who oversaw the kitchens, replied. "All we require is to serve Lady Fate however we can. She put you in our path. Therefore, we will feed and house you until your needs can be met elsewhere."

"Then, consider the payment a donation to your temple." When the priestess remained unmoved, Lochlyn added, "I appreciate all of Lady Fate's gifts, this wonderful food included. Is it wrong for me to offer something in return?"

"I suppose not," the priestess said. "We will bring this food to your rooms, and we will send a bill to your estate. Thank you, Lord Blackmoor, for your generosity."

"Of course," he said, watching as three novices left the kitchens with covered platters. "And, thank you, Mother Priestess."

Once they were inside their rooms, Rosalie began removing lids from the platters. "Why did you order so much food?" she asked. "We'll never finish all of this."

"I requested these dishes mostly because this is the first time I've felt hunger in days," Lochlyn replied, to which Rosalie sighed in relief. His lack of an appetite had led the priestesses to speculate if his stomach had been pierced by the poisoned sword. Granted, his shift from dragon to man should have healed the wound, but as they knew, the poison lingered on.

"Hearing you say you're hungry is the best news I've heard all day," she said, her voice catching at the end. He hadn't eaten anything at all for the first two days after he was stabbed, and on the third he only took some watered broth to placate her. "I feared you'd... you'd..."

"What?" he asked as he gathered her against his chest. "Be the first dragon to starve to death since the dawn of time?"

"It's not funny," she said, halfheartedly thumping his chest. "I can't raise this baby dragon without you."

"Rosalie, you can do anything you set your mind to," Lochlyn murmured against her hair. "Every day, I'm in awe of you."

Rosalie nodded, her throat too tight to speak. She knew she was capable of raising all of their children on her own, but she didn't want to. What she wanted was a long life with Lochlyn by her side.

"Since you're so hungry," Rosalie said as she surreptitiously wiped her cheek, "you'd better eat before the food gets cold."

He kissed her hair. "As you say, beloved." A second kiss, and then he released her. "There's mutton," he said as he looked over the food. "I wasn't expecting anything like that."

Rosalie smiled, watching as Lochlyn filled his plate with bread, assorted vegetables, and enough grilled meat to feed three men. While Lochlyn ate everything within reach, she nibbled on some bread and a few olives.

"Aren't you hungry?" Lochlyn asked when he paused to grab more mutton. "Are you feeling well?"

"I am," she replied, leaving off how the smell of the grilled meat was turning her stomach. "I ate well this morning. Why did you ask for a flagon of oil?"

"Ah." Lochlyn wiped his mouth, then he grabbed the oil and stood behind Rosalie. "Do you have a way to put up your hair?"

She wound her hair into a knot perched on top of her head. "Is that sufficient?"

"Perfect." He kissed the back of her neck. Then, he began rubbing the skin above her spine with three oiled fingers.

"Have you ever had a massage?" he asked.

"Of course, I have."

"Then you know that when your skin is oiled, the bones beneath are quite easy to feel. Sometimes, everything unseen is put into sharp relief." The pressure of his fingers intensified and threatened to lull Rosalie to sleep.

Round and round, the little one is found

"I found it."

Rosalie blinked. "Found what? My spine?"

"The lead. At least, I think it's lead." He pressed close to the base of her skull. Rosalie felt a pinprick of pressure, but no pain. "There's a ball here where it shouldn't be. My theory is that when you were an infant, your mother put lead under your skin and cauterized the wound to seal the metal inside your body. She bound your abilities, so no one could use them against you."

She swallowed. Hard. "Can you get it out?"

Lochlyn moved in front of her and knelt. "I can," he said, setting his talons on her lap. "But it will hurt, and you will bleed."

"I've been hurt before, and I've bled many times," she murmured as she stroked his shining black claws. "I can bear it again, especially if it means finally becoming what I was born to be."

He rose up on his knees and kissed her. "I adore you, my brave one."

"You're the brave one." Instead of courage, Rosalie's stomach roiled at the thought of Lochlyn cutting open her neck, but she could see no alternative. "Please do it now, before I change my mind."

"As you wish." Lochlyn moved behind her and set one of his hands on her shoulders. A moment later, she felt the tip of his talon pressing against the skin just below her skull.

"That's it?" she asked.

"Yes." The pressure intensified against her neck while his firm hand held her in place. "Ready?"

She put her hand on his. "Ready."

The pain was sudden, and intense. For a moment, Rosalie thought she would faint. Then, it passed as quickly as it came, and all that was left was a warm stickiness on her back.

"Balls," Lochlyn muttered as he grabbed a napkin and pressed it against Rosalie's neck. "I cut too deeply. Are you all right?"

"I'm fine," she said, and she meant it. In fact, Rosalie felt better than she had in years. "Actually, I feel wonderful. It's as if I were exhausted and just had the best nap."

"The bleeding's slowed," Lochlyn announced, relieved. "No wonder your mother cauterized the wound."

"Do we need to do that now?" She twisted around and saw his bloody hands. "Did you find anything?"

"Yes." Lochlyn moved around to the front of her and showed her a tiny lead charm resting in the center of his palm. "I thought it was a ball, but it's a charm shaped like a dragon."

Rosalie gasped and picked up the tiny lead dragon. "Perhaps Mama knew I only had to wait for my dragon, and all would be revealed."

"Perhaps." He caressed her cheek and tilted her head up to face him. "How do you feel?"

"Amazing. Truly, truly, amazing." She stood and kissed his chin. "I've never felt better. How do I fly?"

Lochlyn laughed. "We should start small, then work up to leaping out of windows."

"Is that how you learned?" she asked, images of a tiny Lochlyn running after his older brothers playing in her mind's eye. "Or did Jerreth toss you off the balcony?"

A devilish glint shone in his eye. "Perhaps he did. Do you feel the blood surge?"

Rosalie closed her eyes and considered what was happening inside her body. "I feel like I'm moving very fast, even though I'm standing still." Her eyes snapped open. "Should I be attempting any of this, what with the baby?"

Lochlyn frowned. "I've never heard of a female shifter not being able to attain her other forms while she was with child, but I'm no midwife."

"And there is a midwife in the temple," Rosalie finished. "Let's go to her now and ask."

Lochlyn agreed and, after they'd cleaned up his hands and the blood from Rosalie's neck, they sought the temple's midwife. She was alone in her alcove and was quite interested in Rosalie's condition.

"And how far along are you?" the midwife asked. When Rosalie didn't answer, she prompted, "How long have you been married?"

"Five months," Lochlyn replied, which stunned Rosalie. She mentally counted the weeks and months, and, yes, Lochlyn was correct.

"It feels like it's been forever and an instant at the same time," Rosalie murmured. "But my main concern is that I'm a shifter, but I didn't know until recently. If I try to shift, will I harm my baby?"

"How did you not know you're a shifter?" the midwife asked. Lochlyn held out the dragon charm he'd cut out of Rosalie's neck.

"Oh, you were bound," the midwife said as she reached toward the charm. "May I?"

Lochlyn glanced at Rosalie, who nodded. "Yes. Of course. Have you seen a charm like that before?"

"I certainly have," the midwife replied. "A little more than two decades ago, a lovely woman came here begging for help. She was a shifter, and she was pursued by many. She feared her actions would be held against her child, so she wished to bind their abilities to keep them safe. We helped her, and we gave her an assortment of charms suitable for many different forms. Although, I don't remember one of them being a dragon," she added as she scrutinized the charm.

"Was she a phoenix?" Rosalie asked.

"No. She was a fox. Although, she had been sent here by another woman who was also a shifter, and who was also expecting a child," the midwife replied. "As for her name and creature, that I do not know."

"Then, many shifters have sought to bind their children," Lochlyn murmured. "I wonder why."

"Safety, of course," the midwife replied. "It's all well and good if you're born into a wealthy family, but the poorer shifters tend to be scooped up by pirates and slavers and sold off to the highest bidder. By binding their children, the parents can pretend that the blood isn't strong with them and give their babies a better chance."

Lochlyn's brows pinched, then he glanced at Rosalie. "I never considered that," he murmured. "I was born into privilege, and to a family that loved me. What becomes of shifter children without wealth or resources?"

"They end up in an orphanage," Rosalie said, referencing their three adopted children. She faced the midwife, and continued, "We found three phoenix children in Dragon Ridge's orphanage."

The midwife nodded. "I'm not surprised to hear that. Occasionally, if the blood is latent in the parent but appears strong in the child, people find their options to be limited, and, at times, not very good." The midwife held her hand out toward Rosalie. "Your wrist, please."

Rosalie obeyed, and the midwife hunched over her wrist as she traced the pale veins. "Your veins are weak. Did you bleed recently?"

"Yes, when Lochlyn cut the charm out of my neck," Rosalie replied. "That's all."

The midwife grunted, then she turned her hand over. "Meat bothers you?"

"Not really. Just the smell."

"I won't order mutton again," Lochlyn began, but Rosalie hushed him.

"Eat what you like," she said. "Bread will do me just fine."

"It most certainly will not," the midwife said. "You are growing a dragon in your womb, young lady. Therefore, you must eat like a dragon. Hearty broth will do for now, but whenever your husband has meat, take at least a bite or two of his portion. By the time your belly shows, you should be having meat with every meal."

Rosalie nodded, though her stomach wasn't pleased by the suggestion. "Yes, priestess. If I use my phoenix abilities, will it harm the baby?"

"Most definitely not," she replied, to Rosalie's relief. "If anything, I'd say the baby dragon will enjoy feeling his mother's flames. Your kind prefers the heat, do you not?" she asked Lochlyn.

"I wouldn't say we prefer heat, so much as we are drawn to fire," he replied. "The oil lamps used in the temple are fine and elegant, but give me a roaring blaze any day."

"There you have it," the midwife said as she turned Rosalie's palm upright and set the lead charm upon it. "And, no, in all my years of helping mothers and babies, never once has a mother shifted and harmed her child, no matter how far along she was. You're meant to change form, as is your child. Lady Fate will watch over you both, of this I am certain."

"That's wonderful," Rosalie said. "If I may ask a final question, we need to enter a room lined with lead. Since lead can bind a phoenix, how can we counteract that?"

The midwife shrugged. "Why don't you just enter the room in your human form?"

"What if the lead is enchanted?" Rosalie pressed.

"Ah. You want to enter the king's rooms." The midwife eyed Rosalie, who neither confirmed nor denied what she'd said. "The enchantment on Olivar's room is specific. It's also very old." She leaned closer and continued, "You see, Olivar's grandfather had a row with a powerful man, then lived in fear he'd be murdered in his sleep. Therefore, the enchantment is to keep out men with murderous intent."

"You're certain of this?" Lochlyn asked. "Is it the intent the magic is attuned to?"

"Evidently so," the midwife replied. "Therefore, all you have to do is not intend to kill the king, and you'll be fine."

"Huh." Rosalie considered what the midwife had told her. She had no idea magic could be so specific, but it made sense why Curran couldn't get to Caterina. Curran would definitely kill Olivar if he harmed Caterina in any way. "Thank you. For everything."

"You're quite welcome," the midwife said. "I would ask a boon in return."

"Anything," Lochlyn said. "If it's within my power to grant it, I will."

"Your orphanage, the one where you found the abandoned phoenixes," the midwife began. "If I encounter shifter parents unable to care for their children, may I send them to you?"

"Of course," Lochlyn replied. "Send them to Dragon Ridge and we will care for them as best we can. All shifters are welcome there."

The midwife bowed her head. "The Fates chose you well, Lochlyn Black-moor. See to it that you make Them proud."

CHAPTER THIRTY-THREE

HEALING FIRE

A fter the midwife had finished her examination of Rosalie, and she had assured her that her phoenix abilities wouldn't harm her baby, she and Lochlyn returned to their room. Cervus had promised to return before sundown with whatever information he'd gathered, though Rosalie doubted he'd have anything of import to report after only a few hours of reconnaissance. When she shared her opinion with Lochlyn, he shrugged.

"He may, or he may not," Lochlyn said. He was standing in front of the window that faced the palace, his hands clasped behind his back. "Either way, it's good to keep abreast of the situation."

"How can he move so freely, and right underneath Olivar's nose too?" Rosalie murmured as she turned a page. The archivist had allowed her to bring the text on creature anatomy back to her room, and she was studying the chapter on phoenixes. "Although, when we met at the palace, he didn't act like a spy."

"The best spies never do." Lochlyn left the window and sat next to Rosalie. "Have you learned anything interesting?"

"So many things," she replied, before returning to an earlier section. "I was reading about the mate bond creatures share." She looked up at her husband. "Fates, *I'm* a creature."

"You are, but you're human too," Lochlyn said. "The true creatures are confined to the Otherworld."

"I'd love to learn more about the Otherworld, and the first creatures. However," she continued when Lochlyn began explaining the Great Migration, "I found something interesting about the mate bonds. We can't harm each other."

"That's true," he said. "At least, in theory it is. My dragon fire shouldn't hurt you no matter how hot I burn, though I confess I'm too nervous to actually try it."

"And my phoenix fire can't burn you, but..." She turned the book so Lochlyn could read it, and she pointed to a certain passage. "It can *heal* you."

She watched Lochlyn's eyes dart from side to side as he read the passage. "It says a phoenix can burn away certain types of injuries and illnesses." He set his hand on his side, above where he'd been stabbed. "Beloved, do you think you can affect the poison?"

"I can try," she began, then she looked at her hands. "But how do I make fire?"

"You've already done it," Lochlyn said as he took her hands. "When we were escaping the throne room and one of the guards tried to capture you, you burned him. Do you remember doing it?"

"I do, though I didn't realize what was happening at the time." She closed her eyes and recalled those few terrifying moments. "You'd just shifted, and you grabbed me. I was trying to move around and hold onto your leg, but the guard put his hand on me, and I..."

"You screamed," Lochlyn finished. "I remember, because I turned and lost sight of a man on my right."

"And then you were stabbed." She opened her eyes and put her hand against Lochlyn's cheek. "I'm glad you protected me, but next time eliminate the guards first."

He kissed her palm. "An excellent plan, beloved. When the guard touched you, how did you feel?"

"Scared. And... and angry. I was so angry that these fools were trying to take you away from me, and that they'd use our baby..." Rosalie clenched her fist, remembering how she'd wanted to use all of her strength and push the guard far away from her.

Flames licked up between her knuckles, and she gasped.

"I did it," she said, and then she opened her hand and the flames extinguished. "They've gone!"

"But you can bring them back," Lochlyn said. "Latch on to that anger, and they'll return."

Rosalie looked at her flameless palm and frowned. "I don't want to make myself angry all the time."

"In time, you won't need anger to tap into your fire. Our abilities are tied to our emotions. The stronger we feel, the easier it is to bring out our abilities, and to shift."

"The stronger I feel." Rosalie looked at her hands, then she pulled Lochlyn's shirt up and pressed her palm over his wound.

"I feel rather strongly about you," she said as she rubbed her hand across the stab wound he'd gotten while protecting her. "And, I would very much like you to be well."

"As you say, beloved," Lochlyn said as he claimed her lips. Rosalie melted into the kiss as the smallest of flames danced between their skin, but she pulled back when she smelled smoke.

"Oh! Your shirt!" She withdrew her hand from underneath the charred garment and waved away the smoke. "Are you hurt?"

"No. It wasn't even hot." Lochlyn pulled his shirt over his head, then he looked down at his abdomen. All traces of the wound were gone. "Rosalie, you healed me."

"Thank the Fates," she murmured as she glided her fingertips across his skin. "Is the poison completely gone? Can you shift?"

He closed his eyes, then shook his head. "I feel much better, so I assume your fire dealt with all of the poison. My dragon didn't come when I called, but it's all right." He looked at his hands, which once again had ten human fingers. "My talons have retreated, which will make almost every task easier."

"Then I pushed away your last bit of dragon-ness," Rosalie murmured as she bowed her head.

"You didn't push anything away," he said, pulling his wife tight against his chest and kissing the side of her neck. "All you did was help me. The seer said I will be able to shift again, eventually. I suppose this is Lady Fate's way of teaching me patience."

Rosalie laughed softly as she traced the edges of the ivory scales on his chest. "I fear we can both use those lessons."

Cervus arrived a short time later. Along with information, he brought a trunk of Rosalie and Lochlyn's belongings from The Talon.

"This is wonderful," Rosalie said as she pulled out her favorite pair of trousers. "I appreciate the clothing the priestesses shared with us, but I'm sick of looking like a novice."

"I don't know," Cervus said. "Lochlyn makes a rather convincing priest. Must be the ever-present scowl."

Lochlyn did indeed scowl at Cervus, which made Rosalie laugh and Lochlyn scowl even harder. "If you're done amusing my wife," Lochlyn said, while trying to suppress a smile, "I assume you have news for me."

"That I do." Cervus sat at the small table across from Lochlyn and withdrew several scraps of paper from his breast pocket. "What would you like to hear first? The basic news, or the fairly important yet awful news?"

"Awful first," Rosalie said as she rummaged through the trunk. "Best get it over with."

"Lady Blackmoor is as wise as she is beautiful," Cervus declared. "Olivar has declared, against the advice of literally everyone around him, that if you two haven't left the temple by sundown today, he's going to storm the gates and have you apprehended."

"That's outrageous," Lochlyn said while Rosalie cried, "Blasphemy!"

"Agreed," Cervus said. "The idea is stupidity itself, and Olivar was having a hard time gathering support. I left court before any of the details were finalized."

"What did you hear about these plans?" Lochlyn asked.

"Olivar wants to hire the full Order of the Sun for this mad offensive, but Arthus refuses to raise a sword against the temple," Cervus replied. "Rightly so, I might add."

"The Grand Master is honorable then?" Rosalie asked, trying and failing to appear disinterested.

"Oh, yes. He lives by a strict code, and while some of his decisions are questionable, he never strays from his ethics." Cervus tilted his head to the side as he watched Rosalie for a moment. "You do have his eyes."

Rosalie stopped moving. She turned to Lochlyn. He shook his head slightly, then he asked Cervus, "You're familiar with the Grand Master's eyes?"

"They're a particular shade of green that's common in the Flameborn line," Cervus replied. "His daughter's eyes were the same color."

"What an interesting fact," Rosalie said in a rush. "Since the Grand Master is refusing to assist the king in breaching the temple walls, are Lochlyn and I safe here for another night?"

"Unsure," Cervus replied. "An all-out assault against the temple is unlikely, but we cannot rule out the odd fellow thinking he can infiltrate the sanctum, capture you, and demand a reward. It would be best if you left quickly and quietly."

"Understood," Lochlyn said. "What news do you have from Irontooth Keep?"

"Zephyn and Borneas are both there." When Cervus saw Rosalie's brow pinch, he added, "I employ falcons as messengers. They can cover amazing distances in only a few hours."

Rosalie nodded. "And my father? Was he floating in his wine cup as usual?"

"Osman's here, in Serpens." Cervus unfolded a scrap of parchment and glanced at the writing. "He's here to sign a marriage contract between the king and his daughters."

Rosalie threw her hands up in the air. "If my father thinks he's giving Cat to that foul—"

"Wait," Lochlyn said, as he put his hand on her forearm. "You said daughters? This contract involves Caterina and Rosalie?"

"Yes." Cervus frowned, refusing to meet their eyes as he continued, "Olivar wants to wed Caterina to reinforce his claim to the throne. He's convinced she will give him an heir, his own condition notwithstanding. And he wants to take Rosalie as a concubine in order to claim the dragon child as his own."

"He'll be disappointed because he won't get either of us." Rosalie picked up Lochlyn's sword. "I'm going to chop off Olivar's slimy tail and shove it down his throat."

"Beloved," Lochlyn said just as Cervus burst into laughter. "Cervus, you're not helping."

"I think we should follow Lady Blackmoor's suggestion," Cervus said as he got himself under control. "Although, should Olivar expire without an heir, I believe Princess Caterina is next in line for the throne."

Rosalie put the sword down and sat on Lochlyn's knee. "How is that possible? After her mother died, Olivar wrote to Cat explaining how far down the line of succession she is."

"Things have changed. Olivar has been systematically removing those with royal blood, either by marrying them off to foreign lands or by more permanent means. When Caterina was all that remained, he and Osman hatched their plan to marry her into the dragon clan. As you know, that did not work out in their favor."

"The seer said no one foresaw Lochlyn and I being together," Rosalie murmured. "Perhaps Lady Fate has had enough of Olivar's madness."

"I know I've certainly had my fill," Lochlyn said. "Beloved, if you're in agreement, we'll leave the temple tonight."

"You know I am."

Lochlyn kissed her knuckles. "Cervus, Rosalie and I need a way inside the palace."

"Is that wise?" Cervus asked.

"Probably not," Lochlyn admitted. "But we must rescue Caterina—"

"And Curran," Rosalie added.

"And Curran," Lochlyn repeated. "Only then will we retreat to Dragon Ridge. We can regroup there."

"I can get you inside," Cervus said. "One question, though. This Curran you want to rescue, do you mean the phoenix knight?"

Lochlyn nodded. "Yes, that's him."

"My information is that he's being punished for refusing to complete his last assignment," Cervus said as he shuffled through a few more papers. "I'm sure you both know more about that situation than I do."

Lochlyn drew Rosalie's hair behind her shoulder, the gentle caress making her shiver. After she healed Lochlyn, she'd used her phoenix fire to cauterize the wound on the back of her neck. While the wound was gone, her skin remained especially sensitive. "We're familiar with the incident," Lochlyn said.

"What you don't know is that his punishment was ordered by the king, not the Grand Master," Cervus continued. "It's another point of contention between the king and the Order. Also, neither Arthus nor Olivar believe that Princess Caterina's child was stillborn, as both she and Curran claimed it was."

Rosalie dug her fingernails into her palms, willing herself to be calm. "And what are they planning to do about that?"

"The king wants Curran removed from Serpens, but Arthus wants Caterina reunited with him so they can have another child. The Order does love a fertile woman, and Arthus has no living grandchildren." Cervus paused, his head tilted to the side as he regarded Rosalie. "None he knows of, that is."

"Does that mean if we liberate Curran, we will be doing the Grand Master a favor?" Lochlyn asked as he squeezed Rosalie's hand.

"Yes, I believe so." Cervus shuffled through his scraps of parchment once more, then he rose and cast them into the hearth. As he watched his carefully collected notes reduce to ash, he added, "And a return favor from a man like that is valuable indeed."

"Then it's settled," Lochlyn declared. "We'll get Caterina and Curran, retreat to Dragon Ridge, and once everyone is safe, we'll call in this favor with the Grand Master. I've no doubt we'll need it."

CHAPTER THIRTY-FOUR

The Hayloft

Shortly after Cervus left, Lochlyn and Rosalie quietly slipped out of the temple. They left through the kitchen entrance, their brown hoods drawn low over their faces, darting through the city's alleyways; at the end of the third alley was an inn called The Stag's Head.

"Of course, Cervus would send us here," Lochlyn murmured. "The stables are around back."

They crept around the inn, went across the courtyard, and entered the stable. As Cervus had promised, it was empty save for the horses.

"Do you think he actually paid the owner to keep everyone out of the stable?" Rosalie asked as they walked past stalls of sleepy horses.

"With Cervus, anything is possible." Lochlyn hoisted himself onto the loft, and then he went to the window on the far side. "I can't see a single person near the inn or in the adjoining yard. I wonder if he cleared the entire area?"

"Wouldn't that be a great expense?" Rosalie asked as she climbed the ladder to the loft. A moment later she was standing next to him. She slid her arms around him underneath his cloak. "Perhaps he's related to the owners," she suggested, pointing at the sign depicting a stag's antlers.

"Perhaps." Lochlyn kissed her hair. "How do you feel?"

"Fantastic," she replied without hesitation. "And I can tell you're much improved."

"Oh? How so?"

"You're warm again." Rosalie hugged him, her cheek resting over his heart. "When you were poisoned, your skin was cooler. Not cold, but like a regular man's. Now you're dragon-warm, and I love it."

Lochlyn wrapped his arms around her, reveling in her soft lavender scent. "You've always craved warmth," he murmured, remembering the first time she'd remarked on his unusually warm body after he held her in their home's atrium. "Fire, too. Our candle and lamp oil budget has doubled over the past few months."

"I need light to read by! And paint!"

"And I don't begrudge you a single drop of wax," he said, meaning it. If he needed to, he would convert the courtyard into an apiary so there would always be plenty of beeswax on hand to make all the candles she desired. "But I am wondering if the phoenix in you craves fire."

"I never thought of it that way. Then again, I never knew I was a phoenix." She held out her hand and watched a few flames dance on her palm. "You were right about emotion being the key to my abilities. Whenever I feel especially loved by you, my fire comes to the surface."

"In that case, Serpens will be cinders by morning," Lochlyn said. Rosalie laughed and snapped her palm closed to extinguish the flames. "We could always burn the palace down."

"While I do think that would teach Olivar a lesson, too many innocents would be hurt." She tightened her arms around Lochlyn's waist. "The king seems to be alone in his madness."

"Agreed." He kissed her hair. Then, he drew back and surveyed the loft. "We're going to be here until just before sunrise. Might as well make ourselves comfortable."

"We can rest on the bales," Rosalie said as she moved away from the window and took a seat. "Is this the first time you've been in a hayloft, Lord Blackmoor?" she asked, gazing at him through her lashes.

"Of course not," he said as he sat beside her. "I had to learn how to care for a horse before I was allowed to ride one."

"In between lessons, did you sneak up to the loft with pretty girls?" she teased.

"I never got the chance," he replied. "Becoming the duke at fourteen left no time for that. By the time I was interested in such things, word had spread of the Black Duke, and most women wanted nothing to do with me."

Rosalie moved closer to him and laid her head on his shoulder. "I'm sorry, for bringing that up."

"It's all right." He gathered her close and thanked the Fates yet again for his sweet rose petal. "You only wanted to know how I grew up. I enjoy hearing similar stories about you. Perhaps I'll ask Devlin to share a few once we're home."

"Don't you dare," Rosalie said. Then she stood to remove her cloak. "Want me to hang up your cloak too?" she asked as she tossed hers over the rafter. As she did, Lochlyn took in her form silhouetted in the window's light.

"What's wrong?" she asked as she looked down at herself. "Is there something on me?"

"Nothing's wrong," he replied. "I was imagining you with a belly."

"I suppose I'll have one soon enough." She approached Lochlyn and put his hands on her midsection. "When Cat was with child, the midwife said a phoenix's heat makes the baby grow faster. It won't be long before I have that belly you're so interested in. A little while after that, we'll be able to feel him moving around."

"Him?" Lochlyn's heart swelled at the idea of another son, though he would love a daughter just as much. "You think so?"

"I really don't know," she said, combing his hair back with her fingers. "Boy or girl, our baby will grow up knowing nothing but love."

Lochlyn caught her hand and kissed her inner wrist. "All of our children will grow up that way. Safe, loved, and happy." Rosalie smiled, but it didn't reach her eyes. "What's wrong?"

"I miss our babies," she said as she continued stroking his hair. "And Violet."

"Who is not a baby," Lochlyn added, making Rosalie laugh softly.

"No, she is not." She gave his hair a final ruffle, then sat beside him. "Although, I do enjoy having you all to myself."

"We didn't have much time together before we filled our home with children, did we?" he asked as he wrapped his arm around her shoulders. "But soon, we will be home, and you will have me by your side day and night until the end of time. Will that please you?"

"Very much." She burrowed deeper into his arms. "I can't wait to be home with you."

"Nor can I, beloved." He kissed her hair, all the while ignoring the nagging feeling that he might not be able to protect her without his dragon fire. "Soon."

Cervus came for them in the dark hour before dawn. Along with breakfast, he brought them a map of the palace, a ring of keys, and three sets of servants' clothing.

"As you can see, there's only one way in or out of Olivar's rooms," Cervus said. They were reviewing the palace's floor plan by candlelight, while Rosalie delicately nibbled some bread and Lochlyn devoured a joint of mutton. "Rosalie, I brought you two of the chambermaid's dresses."

"Why two?" she asked.

"Based on what I know of other women he's kept, your sister might need the second," Cervus replied as Rosalie muttered her favorite threat of chopping off Olivar's tail. "While you collect the princess, Lochlyn will find Curran. You might need the keys to leave the king's chamber unawares," Cervus added, nodding toward the key ring. "Sometimes the women are locked in with him."

"Rosalie and I won't be together once we're inside?" Lochlyn shook his head. "I don't like that."

"It can't be helped," Cervus said. "Olivar doesn't allow men in his private rooms, and the area where Curran is most likely to be in is off limits to women. They don't want to risk another potential unrecorded phoenix."

Rosalie bristled but remained silent. She wasn't sure if Cervus was merely stating facts, or fishing for information about Jonathan. He was a spymaster, after all. "Assuming I collect Caterina with no interference, then what?"

"We will meet in the scullery behind the main kitchens; from there we will make our escape," Cervus replied as he indicated the room on the floor plan. "I have several of my people in place throughout the palace and ready to cause distractions as needed, but I'm hoping we'll be able to move through the building unnoticed. Olivar is hosting some of his benefactors today, so there will be more activity than usual."

"Benefactors?" Lochlyn repeated. "Are his coffers so low he's soliciting handouts?"

"His coffers have been low for some time," Cervus replied. "Olivar's all but begging for money at this point, and he's got no qualms about where he gets it."

"And my father's here," Rosalie murmured. "What sort of favors is Olivar giving out in exchange for gold?"

Cervus shrugged. "Anything within his power to grant, I assume. He's grown quite desperate over the years."

"What is he spending all of his money on?" Lochlyn asked. "He can't have wasted the entire treasury on his alchemist, and their foolish quest for dragon scales."

"Dragon scales were only the beginning," Cervus replied. "The aftermath of the war in the Northern Reaches nearly bankrupted Alessia. Since the kingdom as a whole wasn't at war, most landowners refused to pay their taxes for years, and that further drained the treasury. In fact, that series of events was what led Olivar to rely so heavily on his seer and this new alchemist."

"What happened to the original alchemist?" Rosalie asked.

"After Olivar was unable to secure a dragon's body, and he remained trapped in his half form, he had the man executed for treason," Cervus replied. "Many of his advisers cautioned him against such a harsh punishment, but as usual, he ignored them. After the alchemist's death, he began removing those with a claim to the throne in earnest. The only person safe from his wrath and paranoia was the seer. Even Olivar knows better than to insult Fate's messenger."

"Did anything happen to the temple last night?" Rosalie asked since Olivar had planned to break the sacred bond of sanctuary to capture her and Lochlyn.

"Arthus refused to let anyone move against the temple. For once, Olivar listened to him." Cervus rubbed his forehead. "But he did send men to wait for the temple doors to open, and to report on your movements once they gained entry. It's good you got out when you did."

Lochlyn grunted. "It will be good when we're back at Dragon Ridge. When do the servants enter the palace for the day?"

"Just after sunrise. That's when the night shift is sent home and the day workers come in to replace them," Cervus replied. "As soon as you're both ready, we'll get moving."

CHAPTER THIRTY-FIVE

MORE COMPLICATIONS

When the sun peeked over the horizon, Lochlyn and Rosalie were waiting in the palace courtyard with the rest of the day's servants. The exterior walls of the palace were white marble, and the rising sun painted them in blazing oranges and yellows.

"At any other time, I'd think this sight was beautiful," Rosalie whispered as she watched the sunlight reflecting off the fountain and tossing rainbows around the courtyard walls. "Now, I wish I'd never seen any of this."

"Soon, beloved, we'll be away from all of it," Lochlyn said as he squeezed her shoulder. While he had no problem reassuring his wife, he was having a hard time reassuring himself. "What do you think the children are doing right now?"

"Violet is reading," she began. "Jonathan is still asleep, but I'm sure Max is already on his second breakfast. As for Lily..." Rosalie moved closer to Lochlyn's chest. "I worry about our little one. She must miss you so much."

"She craves warmth, much like you do," Lochlyn murmured. "She'll be pleased when you show her your fire."

"She will be," Rosalie agreed. Finally, the doors were dragged open. She and Lochlyn stood to the side as the tired overnight servants exited the palace, then a footman announced for the replacements to queue up.

"Be safe, beloved," Lochlyn said as he caressed Rosalie's cheek with his knuckles.

"You too, my love," she whispered. Rosalie joined the other women wearing the silky white robes and matching veils that denoted them as the king's chambermaids. Lochlyn watched her for a moment, then he joined the rest of the men wearing the dark blue shirts and pants and brown cloaks of the heavy laborers. He followed the group into a stone-lined room behind the main kitchen where a man in a green satin robe issued orders. Lochlyn waited near the wall until the man said he needed firewood hauled to the Order of the Sun's section of the palace.

"I can do that," Lochlyn said as he stepped forward.

"Very well." The man made a notation on his ledger and motioned for two boys to bring forward a sack of wood. "You're new. Do you know the way?"

"Yes, sir." Cervus had insisted that Lochlyn memorize the palace's floor plan. "I do."

"Take this key," the footman said as he handed Lochlyn the object. "There's a lock on the room. It's made of lead, and because it's a soft metal, it sticks, but you'll be able to pull it apart."

"Many thanks," Lochlyn said as he pocketed the key. He then shouldered the heavy sack and moved toward the Order's quadrant. He kept his head down as he walked even though it was unlikely for anyone to recognize him. He rarely attended court, and no one would expect to see the infamous Lord Blackmoor dressed as a servant hauling wood. Then he turned a corner and came face-to-face with the alchemist.

"Ah, good," Zosimos said. "I've been waiting for more wood. Follow me."

Lochlyn almost protested that the wood was meant for a different purpose, until he remembered that a servant wouldn't argue with someone so close to the king. He was there to follow orders, not question them. He silently followed the alchemist through the palace and up a flight of stairs, until they reached a heavy iron door. Instead of a key, Zosimos made a few gestures over the lock and the door swung open.

"This is my laboratory," Zosimos said as he swept his arm toward the interior of the room. Lochlyn glanced around the room. He saw a long table covered with vials, and beakers filled with cloudy brown and yellow liquids. He didn't know what the liquids were, but the room stank like a midden heap.

"Don't mind the smell," Zosimos said when Lochlyn coughed and covered his mouth. "I'm just preparing some of the king's venom. I render it down to a paste, and we spread it onto the guard's weapons."

Lochlyn nodded, and asked, "Where shall I put the wood?"

"Next to the hearth." Zosimos watched as Lochlyn unloaded the wood. "Are you needed elsewhere, or can I assign you a new task?"

"How may I serve you, my lord?" Lochlyn asked, keeping his back to the alchemist as he stacked wood.

"I've a very important experiment going and I need new ingredients," Zosimos said. "You see, the king's benefactor was able to procure a few more dried dragon skins."

Lochlyn dropped a large piece of tinder. "Something the matter?" Zosimos asked.

"No, my lord," Lochlyn ground out. "Apologies for my error."

"Good. As I was saying, I've been soaking the skins, much like one would soak a slab of dried meat to make stew. My intent is to harvest the scales once everything is plumped up, so to speak."

Having finished with the wood, Lochlyn stood and faced the man. "Would you like me to fetch you fresh water?"

"No, I don't think more water will help," Zosimos replied. "You see, this dragon was skinned quite a long time ago, and the scales just aren't rehydrating as they should. What I need is for you to shift to your dragon form, Lord Blackmoor, and let me take a few of yours."

Lochlyn pushed back his hood. "That will not be happening."

"Then I'll force you to shift," Zosimos began, drawing his dagger. Lochlyn rushed forward and grabbed the man's wrist with one hand and his neck with the other.

"Drop it," Lochlyn ordered as he squeezed the alchemist's wrist. Lochlyn heard the man's bones crunch, and the dagger clattered to the floor. "I truly don't understand why you, a man of science, have held on to this myth for so long. Dragon scales cannot do anything but protect a dragon. What will Olivar say when he realizes you've been lying to him all these years?"

Zosimos's arms flailed, and Lochlyn loosened his grip so he could speak. "Let me live, and I'll tell you where I got the dried skins."

"Why should I care?"

"Because they came from a pirate in the Northern Reaches," Zosimos wheezed as his eyes bulged. "He made his fortune hunting and skinning dragons."

"Is this murderer still alive?" Lochlyn demanded.

"He's your wife's father, Osman Irontooth."

Lochlyn faltered and almost let go of the alchemist. Instead, he choked him until he passed out, then he dropped the man on the floor.

"This has just gotten more complicated," Lochlyn muttered.

CHAPTER THIRTY-SIX

SISTERS

Rosalie stood in the courtyard with the rest of the king's maids, waiting for the footmen to grant them entry. She watched as Lochlyn's group entered the palace before them and move toward the kitchens. Her husband towered above the rest of the men, and on display were his broad shoulders that were sculpted by years of flying in his warrior form. As he strode into the palace, proud and tall, Rosalie realized no one with a set of working eyes would mistake him for a servant. Fates, she hoped he would at least hunch over a bit.

At last, the footmen waved them into the palace. There were six maids, including Rosalie, each of them wearing white veils and white silk dresses that were more like nightgowns than a practical garment to clean in. In addition to being made of a slippery fabric, the dresses were quite thin, and Rosalie could see the outlines of the other maids' bodies when they stood in the sunlight. That wasn't the case for Rosalie, however, since she was wearing two dresses. She couldn't figure out how to carry the second garment Cervus had given her without attracting attention, so she just put them both on.

As they climbed the stairs in single file, Rosalie was grateful for the veils they were made to wear since she could surreptitiously learn about her surroundings. She did wonder why Olivar didn't want to see his maids' faces, but the king was madman. A better question was why he thought he could get away with forcing Caterina into a sham marriage. Her sister excelled at destroying plans, and, with Rosalie's help, they would destroy this one as well.

The group reached the top of the stairs and stood on the landing as they waited for additional instructions. Rosalie stayed in the middle of the group, using the other women as shields in case anyone present recognized her from when Lochlyn destroyed the throne room. Then, a senior maid began issuing orders, and Rosalie almost fainted.

The woman speaking was the maid from Irontooth Keep, Melly.

"Now, girls, there's no time for dillydallying," Melly's shrill voice declared. "The king is currently at his morning meal, so we only have a short time to straighten his rooms. We'll begin with the bedchamber and move outward."

Melly clapped her hands, and the maids filed into the rooms. Rosalie deliberately didn't look at Melly as she wondered how her sister's maid had ended up in Serpens. Then again, Cervus had mentioned that her father was here, and he'd likely brought Melly along as a gift for Olivar. Being that her father saw others as pawns and possessions, he thought nothing of giving anyone away.

It was what he had done to her.

Rosalie entered the bedchamber, helping another maid strip the sheets from the king's bed. As they tossed the linens into a pile in the center of the floor, Rosalie's gaze darted around the room. She saw a smaller room behind the king's bed and moved closer to the partition to find out what was inside. Then she gasped.

Caterina was sitting on the window seat.

Her sister was wearing a long green dress, easily as thin as the maids' costumes, and her blonde hair was loose against her back. She was staring at the sky, and Rosalie wondered what she was thinking about. Her son she'd born three months ago that she never got to hold? Or perhaps the man she loved who was imprisoned only a few floors away from her? Rosalie couldn't imagine being so close to Lochlyn without being able to see him or touch him. She hoped this isolation hadn't driven Caterina mad.

Heart in her throat, Rosalie tiptoed across the room. When she reached her sister, she put her hand on her shoulder.

"Yes?" Caterina asked, her annoyance plain. Then she looked up, and Rosalie pushed back her veil.

"Fates," Caterina gasped as she stood and pulled Rosalie into her arms. "How are you here? Rosie, it's not safe!"

"We're here to get you and Curran out of the palace," Rosalie said as she held her sister so tightly she could hardly breathe. "Soon, we'll all be back at Dragon Ridge."

"How do you keep saving me?" Caterina asked. "I'm older. I'm supposed to save you."

"You protected me my entire life. It's time for me to return the favor." Rosalie drew back and said, "We named him Jonathan."

Caterina's face crumpled, and she hugged Rosalie again. "Jonathan," she murmured as her tears flowed freely. "Jonathan is a good name. He's a good boy? Healthy?"

"Happy and strong, and he yells almost as loud as you do." One of the maids dropped something in the main chamber, startling the sisters.

"Let's get you out of here so you two can have a proper reunion," Rosalie said. "I've got a maid's costume for you."

Caterina bit her lip. "I don't know if me wearing different clothes will be enough for us to escape. Melly's here."

"I saw her. But Lochlyn is here too, and he has people throughout the palace." Rosalie pulled off one of her dresses and handed it to Caterina. "Put that on, and let's get moving."

"You wore two dresses at once?" Caterina asked. "Wasn't that uncomfortable?"

Rosalie regarded her sister. "Really? That's what you're concerned with right now?"

"Fair point." Caterina turned around and shed the thin shift she was wearing, it's then that Rosalie saw the red marks scored across her back.

"Cat," Rosalie murmured as she reached toward the scratches. "What did Olivar do to you?"

"Not as much as he wanted," Caterina muttered. She slipped the maid's costume over her head and fastened the belt. "He's constantly oozing venom—"

"That is disgusting."

"You have no idea." Caterina suppressed a shudder, then she picked up the veil and pinned it to her hair. "Regardless, the man has...ideas. He gets into the bath to rinse off as much venom as possible, and then he wants to touch everyone within reach." Caterina extended her arm, revealing more scratches. "His tiny claws make their presence known."

"Filthy man," Rosalie muttered. "Did he... Cat, I thought he was a serpent from the waist down."

"He is, mostly. He retained his manhood, but it isn't good for much." Caterina grimaced. Rosalie recognized that expression as Cat pretending everything was fine when, in reality, it was awful. "Don't worry, Rosie. Curran is the last man I was with, and I don't plan on being with anyone else."

"Thank the Fates for that." Rosalie pulled out the keys Cervus had given her. "Please tell me you know of a second exit? We're to meet in the scullery."

"And Curran will be there?" Caterina asked.

"Yes," Rosalie replied. "Have you seen him at all since you've been here?"

Instead of replying, Caterina grasped Rosalie's hand, the one holding the keys, and pushed it down. She shook her head and looked toward the king's bedchamber. Rosalie peeked over her shoulder, and her heart fell.

Melly was staring at them.

CHAPTER THIRTY-SEVEN

ANCESTORS

Instead of following the plan and locating Curran, Lochlyn was ransacking the alchemist's lab.

Zosimos had claimed he had a stash of dried dragon skins, procured from none other than Osman Irontooth. His beloved Rosalie's father. The man who'd crafted the contract that caused him and his wife to meet.

The man who—if the alchemist's claims were true—Lochlyn was honor bound to kill.

Dragons weren't always the rarest creatures in the kingdom. In ages past, they numbered in the thousands. They acted as guardians, and, from the time of the Great Migration, the weaker clans looked to the dragons for protection. In time, they administered matters of the law, oversaw the building of cities and roads, and regulated banking and other trades. Even though they weren't kings, dragons effectively ruled Alessia.

All of that changed during Lochlyn's grandfather's time when dragons began disappearing. At first, only a few elders went missing, which could have been attributed to their age. The creatures were long lived, but not immortal. Then, dragons of all ages disappeared by the dozens, and no one knew what was happening. Due to their natural strength and intelligence, dragons had no natural predators, and any illness they contracted could be healed by shifting. Then, the first skinned dragon corpse was discovered and the unthinkable became reality.

Humans had learned how to kill dragons, and they were murdering them for their scales.

The Blackmoor clan retreated to Dragon Ridge, the most fortified stronghold in the land, and they sent out the call for other families to join them. But the call went out too late; one by one, the other clans fell to whoever was hunting them. By the time Lochlyn's father was born, there were only a dozen dragons left in Alessia. Within a few decades, Lochlyn was the last living dragon.

But I won't be the last, he thought as he went through the alchemist's notes. *Rosalie is carrying the next dragon. Neither my line nor my kind will end with me.*

He cursed under his breath. He had to tell Rosalie what he'd learned, and while she saw Osman for the despicable man he was, he was still her father. It wouldn't be an easy conversation to have with her, and he had no idea how she would react. Then again, Osman had treated Rosalie the worst of all his children. Rosalie might mourn Osman's death, but Lochlyn doubted she would miss him.

Lochlyn swore again. He'd searched through heaps of notes and ledgers and found nothing, and he couldn't afford to waste any more time in this cursed laboratory. He had just decided to wake Zosimos and demand more information about the skins, when he spied a cabinet in the back of the laboratory that was chained shut.

Dragon skins were a valuable, if morally black commodity, and something that dear would likely be held under lock and key. Lochlyn approached the cabinet and scrutinized the iron padlock. He didn't have the time or patience to search for a key, so he drew his sword from where it was hidden under his cloak and struck the lock with the hilt. Thanks to him being dragon-strong even in human form, the lock faltered. Two more blows and the metal broke apart. Lochlyn flung the lock and chains aside and opened the cabinet doors.

The interior held dozens of dried skins stacked one on top of the other, the iridescent scales beautiful even in death.

Lochlyn fell to his knees, mourning those he never knew, but who were nevertheless his kin. His people, his kind, and even though he didn't know their names, or which clans they belonged to, he needed to honor them. And he could do that best by destroying the skins and ensuring that Olivar and his alchemist couldn't desecrate them further.

His human breath was hot enough to melt wax, but it couldn't ignite the skins. Lochlyn went to the alchemist's hearth and used a brass shovel to scoop up some hot coals, then he dropped them onto the skins. They caught slowly, so he added more coal. Soon enough, they were smoldering away. Lochlyn said a prayer to the Fates as he watched his ancestors' skins burn, then he grabbed the alchemist's notes and flung them into the fire, destroying his work and hopefully keeping future dragons safe from such mad schemes. The blaze intensified, with flames leaping toward the ceiling.

Lochlyn bowed, saying a final farewell to the dragons, then he left the laboratory. As for Zosimos, who remained unconscious on the floor, Lochlyn showed him exactly as much care as the alchemist had shown his ancestors, ignoring him as he passed. Whether or not the man survived the fire was now up to the Fates.

CHAPTER THIRTY-EIGHT

A KEYRING AND A CANDLESTICK

"Do you think she recognizes us?" Rosalie whispered as she turned away from Melly's confused stare.

"She's well aware that I'm here," Caterina said, not bothering to lower her voice. "This whole mess is her fault. She found Curran and me in bed, and then she ran to tell Father."

"Father's here," Rosalie said. Based on Caterina's shocked face, she hadn't been aware of his presence in Serpens. "He's drawing up another contract to give both of us to Olivar."

"Where did you hear this?" Caterina demanded.

"Lochlyn's spymaster told us this morning, right before we came here." Rosalie leaned closer, asking, "You haven't seen Father?"

Caterina shook her head. "The only people I've seen are the maids, and Olivar's stinking form. But I can feel Curran," she added as the corner of her mouth curled into a smile. "It's not the same as being with him, but at least I know he's safe." She regarded her sister. "Can you feel Lochlyn?"

"Not really, but I was only unbound yesterday," Rosalie began.

"What do you mean unbound?" Caterina demanded.

"I'm a phoenix. It's why my mother burned me," Rosalie replied, then she heard Melly speaking to the other maids. "Why hasn't Melly come in here?"

"I don't know, but we need to move." Caterina held out her hand. "Give me those keys."

Rosalie handed them over, and Caterina sorted through them. "These are copies of the steward's keys," Caterina murmured. "Where did you get these?"

"Yes, girls," Melly said as she stepped around the partition. "Where did you get such a thing? Our king won't be pleased to hear you stole something."

"Then we won't tell him," Rosalie announced. "Cat and I will be leaving now!"

"I can't let that happen," Melly said. "I don't know why you're here, Rosalie, but you need to stay in this room until the king returns."

"I'm here to get my sister away from this madness," Rosalie said as Melly lunged toward Caterina. Rosalie thrust herself in front of her Caterina as flames leaped from her hand and singed Melly's sleeve.

"Fates, what just happened?" Caterina demanded.

"You're a fire bitch like your mother," Melly accused as she held her injured arm against her breast. "I remember when Aurielle burned you to hide the mark you'd been born with. I kept her secret, and what did it get me? A beating from Osman, that's what."

"Come with us, and you'll never see Osman again," Caterina offered. "I forgive you for everything you've done to me over the years. Melly, you must know what a monster he is!"

"He's one of the few that's not a monster!" Melly squeaked. "The rest of the lords go around with filthy creature blood in their veins, hardly more than rutting animals—"

Rosalie grabbed a nearby candlestick and brought it down on Melly's head.

"My husband is *not* a rutting animal," Rosalie declared as the maid crumpled to the floor. Caterina crouched down and checked Melly's breathing.

"Still alive," Caterina said as she straightened. "Her head will probably hurt for days though."

"Good," Rosalie said. "Let's go."

"Wait." Caterina put her hand on Rosalie's arm, nodding toward the other maids who were watching them from the main chamber. "They don't want to be here either."

Rosalie frowned. They didn't have time to rescue five additional women, but what kind of person would she be if she left them behind to face Olivar's wrath? Or worse, wash his tail?

She entered the king's bedchamber, pulling back her veil. "Hello," she began. The other women watched her intently. They'd all heard her and Caterina yelling. And, now, there's Melly lying on the floor. Rosalie could hardly imagine what was going through their minds.

She cleared her throat, and began again.

"Hello," she repeated. "My name is Rosalie—I'm Lady Blackmoor of Dragon Ridge—and I came here to rescue my sister. She tells me that none of you want to remain in the king's service, not that I blame you. If you want to leave with us, I can promise you sanctuary at Dragon Ridge. That is, assuming we make it out of the palace, and out the city. Escaping won't be easy, but it's got to be better than washing the king's filthy body day in and day out."

"That speech was awful," Caterina muttered.

"Feel free to add your thoughts," Rosalie snapped when one of the maids stepped forward.

"You're right," the maid began. "We don't want to be here. The king is awful, and..." Rosalie couldn't see most of her face, thanks to the veil, but she caught the way the maid's eyes squeezed shut. "I think we'd all like to escape with you, my lady."

"Call me Rosalie," she said as she pulled her veil down over her face. "What's the best route to the scullery?"

CHAPTER THIRTY-NINE

ESCAPE

Lochlyn crept through the servants' passageways, venturing deeper into the castle. He hadn't encountered another person since he exited the alchemist's tower. That was good, at first. Soon after he slipped into the secondary corridors used by the palace staff, he realized he had no idea where he was going.

Cervus could have let me keep the map. Instead, he'd burned it—which was how Cervus dealt with most of his gathered intelligence. Once the information was committed to memory, the evidence was destroyed. An efficient habit for a spymaster, but Lochlyn hadn't memorized the entire floor plan.

Letting me hold on to one map wouldn't have derailed this operation. Lochlyn kept his mutterings to himself, not that anyone was around to hear him, and kept moving toward what he hoped was the eastern quadrant of the palace.

The Order's section of the palace faced the rising sun, which made the area easy enough to find. If only he could pass by a window and confirm he was heading in the right direction.

Eventually the corridor sloped downward and bisected into two distinct lanes. One was constructed of the same gray stone walls and floor of the corridor he was currently standing in, but the other was made of pale sandstone, and a sun was carved over the transom. Lochlyn chose the sun-marked corridor, following it for what felt like an hour. When he emerged, it was in a vast underground chamber. Torches burned in brackets against the walls, and steps led to a darkened area deeper in the palace. Lochlyn stood in the entry for a moment, letting his eyes adjust to the flickering torchlight, then a man wearing the insignia of a phoenix knight approached him.

"Oi," the man called. "Why are you here?"

"I'm to attend the prisoner," Lochlyn replied.

"Why's that?"

Lochlyn shrugged. "I've no idea. I only go where I'm sent."

The knight frowned but didn't argue. "Take the left corridor," the knight said as he pointed toward the entrances, "then take the second left after that. You'll see him soon enough."

"Many thanks, sir knight." Lochlyn offered the knight a shallow bow. He then entered the left corridor as instructed. He took the second left and emerged into a small room with a barred door on the opposite side. Standing guard in front of the door was Curran.

The knight didn't look any different than he had a few days ago back in the throne room. He was still wearing his red tabard emblazoned with a phoenix, as well as his usual chain mail and boots. He was even armed, which Lochlyn thought odd for a man being punished. Then, Lochlyn considered the barred door behind him, and he realized that when he'd asked the other man where the prisoner was, he hadn't been directed to Curran.

There was another prisoner hidden in the Order's depths.

"What are you doing here?" Curran demanded when Lochlyn stepped out of the shadows. "After what you did in the throne room, Olivar's men will kill you on sight."

"They can try," Lochlyn said. "We came to free you and Caterina. Who's in the cell?"

Curran's face darkened. "No one's sure, but he claims to be Olivar's brother."

"Fates," Lochlyn murmured; if Olivar had a brother, then the Serpens line wouldn't end with the madman currently ruling it. It also meant that, if Olivar was removed from power, there wouldn't be a mad scramble for the throne. "Should we free him?"

"You just learned of this man's existence, and you want to free him?" Curran shook his head. "What if he's lying? And you don't even know what he's done to earn that cell."

"What if he's not lying?" Lochlyn countered, then he shook his head. "We don't have time for a debate. I set the alchemist's laboratory on fire—"

"You what?"

"Keep your voice down," Lochlyn hissed. "He had a hoard of dragon skins. I couldn't let him abuse my ancestors, so I burned them."

Curran nodded. "I understand, but a fire will only make Olivar lock down the palace even tighter."

"I have a way out." Lochlyn produced the key he'd been given earlier. "Now, do you want to be reunited with Caterina, or should I leave you here?"

"You already know my answer," Curran replied. "Though I don't know how we'll breach the king's chamber."

"Rosalie's already there," Lochlyn said. "Give me your hands. I have a key."

"These are welded together," Curran said, as he extended his hands toward Lochlyn. "They can't be removed without a smith's tools, and I'm all but useless with them on."

Lochlyn took one of Curran's wrists, examining the cuff. It was a smooth circle of metal, with no seams or any other apparent weaknesses. "You were awake when they were welded shut?" Lochlyn asked, noticing the badly healed burns underneath the cuff.

"I was," Curran replied. "The pain was so intense I shifted one half of my body, then they wrapped me in lead chains. When I reverted to my human form, they welded on the other one."

Lochlyn nodded, then he remembered what the man in the scullery had told him; lead is a soft metal and Lochlyn could pull it apart. Since he had no better options, Lochlyn grasped either side of the cuff and tore it in half.

It helped that Lochlyn was dragon-strong.

"Lead is a soft metal," he recited. He grabbed Curran's other wrist and tore off that cuff as well. "Let's get out of here," he began, then he brandished the key he'd been given when he arrived.

"Do you know what this opens?" Lochlyn asked, since it obviously wasn't for Curran's cuffs.

"It looks like the key to a cell," Curran said, then he took the key. With it, he unlocked and unbarred the cell behind him.

"I thought you didn't want to take the prisoner with us," Lochlyn said.

"I don't. But if the fire spreads down here, I don't want him to burn to death either," Curran replied. "Now he has a chance."

Lochlyn nodded. "Fair enough."

They walked down the corridor that would bring them to the palace. When they reached the corridor that led to the other sentry, Curran extended his arm.

"Walk behind me," Curran said. "Act like a servant, and we may be able to get out without having to fight any of my brothers."

Lochlyn adjusted his stride so he was two paces behind Curran. "Did any of them speak up for you when you were cuffed?"

"No, but that's not how things work here," Curran replied. "My father's word is law, but even he needs to answer to the king."

"Would your father have chosen a different punishment?"

Curran scoffed. "Who knows. But my father wanted Caterina put in a harem, whereas the king only wanted her in his chambers. As awful as Olivar is, I couldn't let her stay with the Order to be bred like a heifer. Accepting the king's punishment was the best I could do for her." Curran glanced over his shoulder. "They made me choose the punishment. I sent Caterina to that madman."

"Fates," Lochlyn murmured. "But I agree, it seems like the lesser evil."

"I only hope Cat doesn't hate me for it," Curran said. "Rosie's brother, Devlin. He's also my sister's child?"

"That's correct."

"Amazing. We never knew—"

"Oi," called the knight who'd questioned Lochlyn earlier. "Where are you taking him?"

"To the king," Lochlyn replied, then he remembered he was supposed to be a servant. "My lord."

The knight crossed his arms over his chest. "This is highly irregular."

"When are things ever regular in Serpens?" Curran asked. "Isn't that why we're always taking assignments away from the palace? Anyway, the king awaits."

Curran walked past the knight as if the matter were resolved. Lochlyn followed, but he had to halt when the knight stepped in front of him.

"I don't know you," the knight said as he peered at Lochlyn's face. "But you're no servant."

"Fates, Eochaim, what do you think he is if not a servant?" Curran demanded. "Come on. We're keeping the king waiting."

"The king doesn't want to see you," Eochaim said to Curran. "He wants you gutted. The only thing keeping you alive is your surname." Eochaim stepped closer to Lochlyn. "Which means you weren't sent by the king."

"I wasn't," Lochlyn admitted, then he grabbed Eochaim by the throat. "But that's my business, not yours."

Eochaim clawed at Lochlyn's hand, but to no avail. Lochlyn raised him higher until his feet were no longer touching the floor.

"Are you friendly with this man?" Lochlyn asked Curran. "Or should we dispose of him?"

"Eochaim's a good knight," Curran replied. "But I don't want him following us."

"What if he gets caught in the fire?"

Curran pointed toward the opposite side of the room. "If the fire spreads down here, a guard will sweep the area for knights. Eochaim will make it out."

"Very well." Lochlyn tightened his grip. Eochaim struggled to breathe, then he passed unconscious. Lochlyn set him against the wall and hoped he would remain asleep until they were clear of the palace. "Are there any other sentries between here and the scullery?"

"Probably," Curran replied. "All the more reason to get moving."

Rosalie reached the bottom of the stairs and held up her arm so the rest would wait behind her. It had taken them hours to creep down from the king's private rooms while avoiding everyone else in the palace, and Rosalie worried how Lochlyn would react if they didn't arrive in the scullery soon. Their only saving grace was the keyring Cervus had given them. They'd locked Melly in the king's room from the outside, which meant she was trapped until either the king returned, or the night shift reported for duty.

Now, they were finally on the ground floor of the palace, and Rosalie could all but taste freedom. In front of the staircase, she and the other maids waited in what was a small open area. Along the opposite wall were the entrances to three hallways. "Which corridor is the best way to the scullery?" she asked her sister.

Caterina shrugged. "How should I know? I've been confined to Olivar's rooms since I got here."

"The best way is through that gallery," Seren said, pointing to the right. Of the five chambermaids they'd decided to rescue, only Seren had spoken to her or Caterina. Rosalie didn't know if the other four were shy, or spoke a different language, or were born mute—and she honestly didn't care. As long as they stayed quiet, it would be easier to get everyone out alive.

"What's in the gallery?" Rosalie asked. "Are there people we'll need to deal with?"

"It's not a place where people linger," Seren replied. "It's a hall dedicated to Olivar's accomplishments."

"So, it's a short hallway?" Caterina asked.

"If only it were," Seren replied. "It's long and winding, like a serpent's tail. But it lets out into the courtyard, and then we only need to cross that yard to get to the kitchens."

"All right." Rosalie grabbed two handfuls of her skirts. "No one's about, so we go now, quietly, single file. If anyone questions us, Melly sent us on a task for the king."

Without waiting for anyone's agreement, Rosalie hurried across the room and entered the gallery. It was, indeed, winding; with curved walls painted dark red to offset the many white plaster sculptures on display. Curious despite it all, Rosalie paused to examine one of the sculptures. It depicted a basilisk in warrior form, his bare arms and chest heavily muscled, and his long tail coiled around three armed men.

"Is this supposed to be Olivar, or one of his ancestors?" Rosalie asked. The weak, pale monarch she'd met did not resemble the man depicted.

"I believe that's what Olivar wants people to think he looks like," Caterina replied. "He more closely resembles a lump of mashed vegetables."

Behind them, Seren and the other maids tittered. "Fates, we'll have to hire a mind mage to scrape those images out of your memories," Rosalie said as she crept down the winding gallery. "How did you manage to not vomit on him?"

"Actually, nausea is quite common around the king," Caterina replied. "The stench from his venom makes people sick to their stomachs. It's why there were always so many maids in his rooms, so we could step away when we felt ill."

"I spoke to his seer," Rosalie said. "She said his venom would eventually drive you mad."

"Yes," Caterina said. "I believe that. Rosie!"

Caterina grabbed Rosalie's arm and dragged her behind a screen. Seren and the rest similarly hid themselves just as five soldiers ran past them. "They didn't even notice us," Caterina murmured. "Something must be happening."

"I hope Lochlyn's all right," Rosalie said. "When we were here a few days ago, things got out of hand."

Seren stood and dusted off her dress. "You mean when a dragon attacked the king in broad daylight?"

"Um. Yes. And he didn't attack anyone," Rosalie muttered. "Olivar tried separating me from Lochlyn. My husband was only protecting me."

"Your husband is the dragon?" Seren asked. When Rosalie said he was, Seren continued, "How was that not an attack? He destroyed the entire throne room. Not that I'm defending the king in this matter," she added.

Rosalie nodded, though she wasn't seeking the woman's approval. She only wanted her husband to survive this rescue mission. "We should keep moving."

"Lochlyn is a full shifter?" Caterina asked as they resumed walking down the gallery. "When did you find out?"

"The day after Jonathan was born." She glanced at her sister. "Lochlyn was afraid I wouldn't want him once I knew."

Caterina scoffed. "The man is a fool because anyone could see how much you adored him. And it was plain how he felt about you as well," she added. "Is he good with Jonathan?"

"He is." Rosalie smiled as she remembered Lochlyn with the baby in his arms, soothing him and making up silly rhymes to make him smile. "He treats him like his own son. We've also adopted some children."

"Fates, Rosie, how many children do you need?"

"We'll have one less now, since you'll soon be reunited with Jonathan." Rosalie pursed her lips, adding, "They all came from the village's orphanage, and they're all phoenixes."

"Oh." Caterina swallowed. "That's quite interesting."

They reached the end of the gallery, where an arched doorway led to the courtyard. It wasn't the same yard Rosalie had waited in that morning, but a vast formal garden complete with fountains and trimmed hedgerows. If it were any other time or place, Rosalie would have liked to spend the day in such a place. Now, she only wanted to cross it as quickly as possible.

"Seren," Rosalie whispered. "Which way?"

"There." Seren pointed toward an arch diagonally across from where they were standing. "That's the way to the kitchens."

"All right." Rosalie stepped into the courtyard, just then a dozen soldiers burst into the area. They didn't spare the women a glance, running into a third entry marked with a sun.

Heart in her throat, Rosalie turned to Seren. "Where does that archway lead?"

"It goes to the Order of the Sun's quarter of the palace," Seren replied. "There must be something happening with the knights."

Caterina gasped. "Curran!"

CHAPTER FORTY

THE GRAND MASTER

Lochlyn heard noises coming from up ahead and paused in the corridor. "Curran!" he hissed when he heard the distinctive clang of chain mail and weapons. "Soldier's approaching!"

With nowhere to go, he and Curran raised their swords. When the soldiers came into view, they motioned for them to move.

"Stand aside!" the lead man barked. Lochlyn and Curran flattened themselves against the walls as the soldiers ran past them.

"What's happening?" Curran yelled after them. But the soldiers didn't respond, and they were soon out of view.

"They're heading toward the Order," Curran said. "Eochaim must have raised the alarm."

"Come on," Lochlyn said as he headed toward the kitchens. "We need to put distance between us and them."

Curran glanced over his shoulder. "What if it's the prisoner I was guarding?"

"Feel free to go back and have a look," Lochlyn said. "I'm getting my wife, and then we're leaving this place."

"You'll only get dragged back," Curran said. "That's what the Order does. They get their claws in you. No matter what you do, or how far you run, they drag you back to the nest. Every so often we get a small taste of freedom, but it's always a lie."

"Is that why your sister ran?" Lochlyn asked.

"It is." Curran glanced at Lochlyn. "When she left, I ran with her."

"I didn't know that."

"I imagine you didn't," Curran replied. "It was quite the scandal when both of the Grand Master's children left at the same time, so it was kept quiet."

"Did you have the same reasons for leaving?"

"Yes. Aurielle and I wanted to live our lives on our own terms, not the Order's," Curran replied. "We slipped away while our father was on an expedition. We traveled together for about a year, then we split up so we'd be harder to track. I never knew what happened to her."

Lochlyn was surprised to hear that. "You've never noticed Rosalie's eyes?" he asked. "We've been told they're a shade of green common in your family."

Curran scoffed. "While I was at Irontooth, I didn't spend much time looking at Rosie. I didn't even realize her eyes were green until you mentioned it just now."

"Then she doesn't look like her mother?"

"Not really. Aurielle was tall and built like a warrior, and she had flaming red hair. Although now that I think about it, Rosie acts like my sister," he added. "Righteous and fiery, and too stubborn to know when to quit."

Lochlyn smiled; that was an excellent description of his rose petal. He jerked his chin toward the arched doorway up ahead. "What's through there?"

"That's the formal courtyard," Curran replied. "We just need to get past that yard, and the kitchens will be on the other side." Curran paused, then he asked, "Caterina will be there?"

"She and Rosalie should already be waiting for us," Lochlyn replied, mindful of the time he'd wasted while searching the alchemist's laboratory. "If they haven't made it to the scullery, I'll find my man on-site, and we'll make a plan to locate them. I'm not leaving here without Rosalie."

"I'm not leaving without Caterina either," Curran said. "Let's get our women."

Lochlyn couldn't agree more. He stepped out into the courtyard, glad to feel the sun on his face after spending so much time in the bowels of the palace, and took a deep breath as he scanned the area. On the opposite side of the yard, he spied a group of women wearing the silky white dresses of the chambermaids, then he spotted Rosalie's golden hair. Next to her was Caterina, though Lochlyn had no idea who the other five women were.

"Curran." He indicated the group of women. "See her?"

Curran spun around, his gaze instantly landing on Caterina. "My princess," he murmured. But before he could take a step toward her, two companies of soldiers rushed into the courtyard from opposite sides. Lochlyn bellowed Rosalie's name as they were cut off from one another.

"Seize the shifter!" yelled one of the soldiers.

"No!" yelled another. "We're needed in the dungeons!"

"There's a fire in the tower," a third bellowed. "The alchemist said it was the dragon!"

"Blackmoor," Curran growled. "We need to shift."

"Actually, I can't shift," Lochlyn said, raising his sword. "But I can fight."

"No!" Caterina screamed as she lunged toward Curran, who was squaring off against two opponents.

"Stop." Rosalie grabbed her sister's arm. "We need to stay here. If we run into the fight, we'll only make it worse."

Caterina nodded, but her gaze never left Curran. "We need to get out of here before the Grand Master arrives. He'll do whatever is necessary to keep Curran here, and no one can overpower Arthus." Caterina paused, then she added, "Perhaps Lochlyn could."

"I can," Rosalie said. "Not physically. But I know something that might stop him."

"Can you also stop that?" Caterina demanded as she watched the melee in the courtyard. Some of the soldiers had run deeper into the palace, but others had recognized Lochlyn and Curran and were trying to capture them. As Rosalie wondered how she could help her husband so they could make their escape, she remembered the keys Cervus had given her.

"Give me the keyring," Rosalie said. "We can lock all the doors leading into the courtyard, so no more soldiers come at them."

"But which key is which?" Caterina asked, handing over the ring. "We can't waste time testing them all."

"There's a skeleton key," Seren said. "It should fit all the doors on the first floor." Rosalie handed her the ring, and Seren selected an ornate bronze key. "Wish me luck," Seren said, before darting across the courtyard to the northern entrance.

"Follow her!" Rosalie yelled. The rest of their group sprinted around hedgerows and sword wielding men. When they reached the door, two of the maids slammed it shut, then they wedged their shoulders against the wood while Seren tried to turn the lock.

"It's not working," Seren cried. "The key's wrong!"

"Try another one," Caterina said, but the door had already been flung wide open. Seren was pushed aside as more soldiers poured into the courtyard. Rosalie grabbed her sister's arm and dragged her away lest she be trampled.

"Everyone, get behind me," Rosalie yelled. Lochlyn paused when he heard Rosalie's voice and was almost impaled by a palace soldier. As Seren and the rest scrambled to safety, Caterina snatched the keyring from where it had fallen and faced her sister.

"We need to go," Caterina muttered. "You're right. Us being here is a liability to Curran and Lochlyn."

"I know," Rosalie said, unable to tear her gaze from Lochlyn's back. "But I can't leave him."

"What do you mean, you can't shift?" Curran demanded as he parried a blow.

"When I escaped the throne room, I got stabbed," Lochlyn replied, bringing his sword's hilt down on a man's helmet and rendering him unconscious. Even though he was trapped in his human form, he remained dragon-strong. "The blade was poisoned."

"Fates," Curran hissed, then he pointed across the courtyard. "Where are they going?"

Lochlyn spun around and saw Rosalie and the rest of the women bracing the door shut. "They're helping us," he said, but the door was breached, and a new group of soldiers shoved them aside. Rosalie screamed, and Lochlyn faltered, parrying a blow at the last moment.

"Why are there so many soldiers?" Lochlyn demanded as he evaded another strike. "Are you really so dangerous?"

"If they were coming for me, the knights would be here instead of the palace soldiers," Curran replied. "This must be about the prisoner. Or the fire you set."

Balls. Lochlyn scanned the perimeter of the courtyard, and saw a solid stone wall punctuated by three doors in addition to the one behind him. He wasn't concerned with two of the doors, but their escape lay behind the western archway.

"Get to the women, then get to the kitchens," Lochlyn yelled, and then he ran full tilt at the soldiers. As the soldiers scattered before him, the door to the kitchens opened and Cervus stepped into the courtyard.

"Rosalie," Lochlyn yelled as he approached her. He grabbed her hand. "Run, now!"

"Follow us!" Rosalie yelled over her shoulder to the other maids, and then they were sprinting toward the kitchens.

A fireball exploded above them. Lochlyn thought it was Curran's doing, but the knight halted.

"He's here," Curran said as he pulled Caterina against him. "My father."

Lochlyn put his body between Rosalie and the phoenix as he watched Arthus Flameborn descend to the courtyard in a column of flames. The Grand Master of the Order of the Sun wore armor that didn't melt, neither did his sword belt ignite. Lochlyn wondered if they were magically treated, or if the Grand Master could control the heat of his flames. Then, Arthus landed, and the ensuing shockwave gave Lochlyn his answer.

The Grand Master wasn't just powerful. He was a *power.*

"What is the meaning of this?" Arthus boomed. "Curran, why have you left your post?"

"Why do you think?" Curran shot back. "Caterina didn't deserve to be trapped with the king, nor does she deserve a life in those harems of yours. I had the opportunity to save her, and I took it!"

Arthus frowned, then he faced Lochlyn. "Dragon."

"Grand Master," Lochlyn replied. "I understand your Order owes me a debt."

"That is true," Arthus admitted. "You may leave, but my son remains."

"We're all leaving," Rosalie said as she stepped in front of Lochlyn. "Me, my husband, my sister, and your son. As well as the others who stand with us. We're all leaving, and you won't stop us."

Arthus scoffed. "Child, to whom do you think you're speaking?"

"I believe I'm speaking to my grandfather." Rosalie stepped toward the Grand Master, though she kept hold of Lochlyn's hand. "My mother was Aurielle Flameborn."

The Grand Master's eyes widened as his nostrils flared. "You lie!"

"I don't," Rosalie replied. "I'm told I have her eyes."

Arthus took a step toward Rosalie, but Lochlyn growled as he pulled her back. "Do not get your flames close to my wife," he warned.

"If you're Aurielle's child, you belong here with me," Arthus said. "Not hiding in the mountains with a dragon."

"If you separate me from Lochlyn I'll slit my throat," Rosalie declared. "Then you'll lose not only your grandchild, but your great-grandchild, too." Rosalie set her hand on her belly, her meaning clear. Arthus looked at her hand and he nodded.

"I would know you," Arthus said.

"I'd like that, but at another time," Rosalie said. Shouts wafted toward them from the interior of the palace.

"Arthus, what's happening in the palace?" Lochlyn demanded.

"You dare say my name?" Arthus retorted.

"Father," Curran implored. "Tell us."

Arthus opened his mouth, just then a basilisk crashed through the palace walls and into the courtyard. The creature was twice as large as Olivar, with glittering black scales and round yellow eyes.

"Who loosed the prisoner?" Arthus demanded as he lobbed a fireball at the basilisk.

"Now," Lochlyn hissed as he pulled Rosalie toward the kitchens. The rest followed. Once they were inside the kitchens, Cervus closed and locked the door.

"Who are these people?" Cervus asked as he stared at Seren and the maids.

"Olivar's attendants," Rosalie replied. "We're giving them sanctuary at Dragon Ridge."

"Of course you are," Cervus muttered, then he withdrew a horn and sounded it. "Follow me. My people will meet us in the yard."

"What people?" Rosalie asked him, then she glanced at her husband. "Are you all right? You weren't hurt, were you?"

"I should be asking you that," Lochlyn said as he pulled her along. He spared a glance for the other maids running behind them. He didn't mind granting the other women sanctuary, but they needed to keep up. "You were quite brave back there."

"Desperate is more like it," Rosalie muttered. "I wasn't really going to slit my throat. I'd never do that to you."

"I know," Lochlyn said, though he left off how her words had made his heart plummet to his feet. They emerged into the yard where he and Rosalie had waited with the other servants that morning. Lochlyn spied the man in the green robe who'd given him the assignment of carrying firewood, as well as the key that freed the imprisoned basilisk.

"You're with Cervus?" Lochlyn asked.

"Until my dying breath," the man replied, then he shoved Lochlyn aside as antlers erupted from his forehead. Soldiers had followed them through the kitchens. The stag shifter impaled one on his antlers and flung him aside.

"Everyone, shift!" Cervus ordered. Seven stags and five enormous falcons shifted in the courtyard. "Ride or fly, everyone choose now." Cervus approached Lochlyn and knelt.

"My lord, my back is big enough for you and your bride," he said, morphing into a stag larger and broader than two warhorses. Lochlyn helped Rosalie onto Cervus's back, then he mounted up behind her.

"We'll keep watch from above," Curran said as flames crept across his skin. Caterina, unaffected by her lover's fire, wrapped her arms around his neck as he flew straight up in a fiery streak.

"Go," Lochlyn ordered, and Cervus leaped over the courtyard wall. Cervus had just touched the ground on the other side when the rogue basilisk grabbed his hind leg and dragged him to a halt. Lochlyn and Rosalie were thrown from his back, with Rosalie tumbling out of Lochlyn's reach.

"Beloved!" he called, the basilisk looming above them. Venom dripped from its fangs, and Lochlyn had to roll away from the noxious secretions.

"Rosalie!" Lochlyn saw her push herself up on her elbow. The basilisk leaped toward her. Heart in his throat, Lochlyn flung his body on top of hers as the basilisk roared.

CHAPTER FORTY-ONE

PHOENIX, RISEN

R osalie was stunned.

They'd just escaped the palace walls. She could taste freedom. And, then, she was no longer on the stag's back.

She was flying through the air alone.

Striking the ground.

Tumbling over and over until she worried she'd be sick.

Dazed, she pushed herself up on her elbow and pressed her hand to her belly.

A basilisk roared as he stalked toward her.

"Olivar?" she mumbled. But there was no way the creature in front of her could be the weak king she'd met. This basilisk was strong, and enormous. It was easily as large as Lochlyn's dragon, with obsidian scales glittering on its undulating body, and its yellow eyes—

She turned away, mindful that a basilisk could mesmerize its prey. "Lochlyn?"

"I'm here." Her husband pulled her into his arms, tucking her face beneath his chin. "Don't look at him. I'll protect you."

"But you—"

"My scales can withstand his venom, and a basilisk's gaze can't affect dragons," he murmured. "I imagine it's why Olivar and his ancestors hunted us down. He couldn't compel us to go along with his whims."

"You were hunted?"

"We were." He turned his face toward the sky. "I'm going to signal Curran. He's strong enough to carry you and Caterina."

"But what about you?"

He didn't look at her when he replied. "I will remain here, and give you time to escape."

"No!" Rosalie put her hand on Lochlyn's cheek. "We stay together."

"Beloved," Lochlyn began, but he was interrupted by the stags' screaming as venom burned through their hide. When Lochlyn turned toward the noise, Rosalie took advantage of his distraction and ran toward the basilisk.

"Stop," she ordered. The basilisk looked up from its prey, and it growled.

"You will let us leave," Rosalie continued, trying to avoid compulsion by staring at the creature's feet instead of its eyes. "Do whatever you like in the palace, but we," she gestured to encompass every man, woman, and shifter in her party, "are leaving."

The basilisk slithered toward her. Venom dripped from its mouth and scorched the ground, the stone pavers sizzling and steaming. "How will you stop me, girl?"

"I'm not a girl." She squeezed her eyes shut and held out her hands. "I'm a phoenix."

"What you are is next to die," the basilisk said, lunging toward her.

Screams rent the air—the basilisk's screams.

Rosalie's eyes snapped open, and she saw the basilisk through a wall of fire. *Her* fire. The creature writhed on the ground, howling as her flames wrapped around his body. Feeling that he'd had enough, she snapped her hands closed and the flames extinguished.

"Fool," the basilisk yelled as he launched himself at Rosalie. She ducked as Lochlyn roared, then he buried his sword in the creature's chest.

"No one hurts my wife," he said. He watched the creature fall to the ground, then he took off his shirt and wrapped it around Rosalie. Thanks to her fire, her clothes had been rendered to ash.

"Bring everyone to The Talon," he said to Cervus. "After we tend to our wounds, we're leaving this city behind."

CHAPTER
FORTY-TWO

HOME

I t didn't take long for the group to cross the city thanks to the stags and falcons that carried them. Phillipa, who had returned to The Talon that morning along with the rest of the staff, immediately began ordering hot food and fresh clothes to be brought out for everyone. While the others were seen to, Lochlyn and Rosalie slipped away to their rooms.

After they'd washed up and dressed, Rosalie remarked on how lucky they were that no one was pursuing them. Lochlyn's response surprised her.

"I set the alchemist's rooms on fire," he told her, describing the stacks of dried dragon skins he'd found in the laboratory. "That, coupled with the basilisk's escape, means that those in the palace were too busy to pursue us."

"Where did that bastard get dragon skins?" Rosalie muttered.

"Beloved." Lochlyn took her hands. "I was told that the skins were obtained from your father. I don't know if it's true, but Zosimos said that Osman made his fortune in the Northern Reaches by hunting and skinning dragons."

"Oh! I... oh." She looked at their feet, unable to meet her husband's eyes. "I really don't know how Father made his fortune. I do know that he was a pirate, like his father and grandfather before him, and that he sailed in the Northern Seas. I'm so, so sorry, Lochlyn."

"Why are you sorry?" When she didn't answer, she felt Lochlyn's hand on her chin tilting her face up. "Whatever he did happened long before you were born. I don't hold his actions against you."

"Oh, thank the Fates," Rosalie said as she fell against his chest and embraced him. "What are you going to do about Father, and the skins?"

"For now? Nothing. His influence can't reach you at the Ridge, and I know exactly where every dragon in Alessia is. That means he can't hurt us anymore." He stroked Rosalie's hair and kissed the top of her head. "More importantly, I won't be the last dragon."

"You won't." Rosalie kissed his throat. "Let's find the rest."

Hand in hand, they went downstairs. Thanks to The Talon's extensive store-rooms, everyone had gotten a new set of clothes. Seren and the other chambermaids were dressed like regular citizens instead of women confined to the king's rooms. Even Curran and Caterina had gotten new clothes, since theirs had burned up as Curran flew above them.

"If I keep using my fire, I'm going to go through a lot of clothes," Rosalie said.

"Good thing I like you naked," Lochlyn said. Rosalie playfully swatted his chest as Cervus walked up to them.

"We're ready to depart, my lord and lady," he advised. "I have a team of wagons waiting out back. Each wagon is covered, and we can fit six in the back of each. It will be slow going, but we should reach the Ridge by morning. Noon at the latest."

"Thank you," Lochlyn said. "We'll be ready soon."

Cervus nodded and left to oversee their final preparations. Rosalie looped her arm with Lochlyn's; together they approached Curran and Caterina where they were waiting on the far side of the room. Curran had his arm around Caterina's shoulders, and she was leaning against his chest.

"It seems we'll be traveling by wagon," Rosalie told them. "Will you fly on ahead?"

"If it's all the same to you, we'll be taking the wagons too," Curran replied. "Whether it's day or night, I'm too easily spotted. My father doesn't know where we're headed, and I'd like to keep him in the dark for as long as possible."

"Will we be leaving soon?" Caterina asked. "I can't wait to see Jonathan."

"Everything's ready," Lochlyn said. "Follow us."

They went out to the stables and observed the mad chaos that was The Talon's staff packing up everything of import. Due to Lochlyn's involvement in the events at the palace, he didn't want to leave any of his staff behind in the city where they could become the object of Olivar's wrath. Rosalie hoped they could find everyone new positions in the castle. Then again, she was certain that Madchen and Silas would take care of everything.

"Beloved," Lochlyn whispered as he gently shook Rosalie's shoulder. "We're home."

She blinked herself awake just as the wagon was lurching to a halt. She smiled at her husband. "Thank the Fates. Is Cat awake?"

He gestured toward the opposite side of the wagon where Caterina was asleep in Curran's arms. Rosalie didn't want to disturb their rest, but there was someone they needed to meet.

"Cat," Rosalie said. "Cat, we're here."

Caterina's eyes snapped open. "We're at Dragon Ridge? Where is he?"

"Let's find him," Rosalie said, then the sisters clambered out of the wagon. They found Silas waiting at the top of the steps, watching the wagons circle the courtyard.

"Lady Blackmoor," he greeted, then he spied Caterina. "Princess! Lovely to see you again. Who are all these people?" he asked as The Talon's staff and the rescued maids began stepping out of the wagons. "Why is my sister here?"

"Lochlyn will explain," Rosalie called over her shoulder as she and Caterina ran inside the castle. They sped across the atrium and toward the nursery as the rest of the staff gaped at them. Rosalie waved, but she didn't slow her pace.

When they reached the eastern tower, Caterina pushed open the nursery doors, her gaze landing on the three cradles. Instinct telling her which child was hers, Caterina approached the central cradle and picked up her son for the first time.

"Mama's here," she murmured as she held the baby against her breast. "Jonathan, I missed you so much. I'm so sorry I was gone for so long, but I'm here. Mama's here."

Rosalie picked up Lily, then she went to Max's cradle and stroked his hand. "As you can see, Jonathan was never lonely."

"Thank you so much for taking care of him," Caterina said, her voice catching at the end. "I was so worried I'd never see him again, but I knew he was safe with you."

Curran burst into the room soon after. "Where is he?"

Caterina spun around, her smile brighter than the sun. "Here."

Curran crossed the room in two long strides, and he embraced Caterina and their son. Wanting to give them some privacy, Rosalie carried Lily toward the door where Lochlyn stood with Violet in his arms.

"Mama," Violet called. "I missed you!"

"I missed you too," Rosalie said. "We brought books back from The Talon. They're being unloaded out front."

Lochlyn set Violet on her feet, and she ran to the front of the castle, eager to look over the new books. As Lochlyn went to get Max from his cradle, Devlin entered the nursery.

"What's all the commotion?" Devlin asked, then he spied the couple across the room. "Cat! And is that Curran?"

"In the flesh," Rosalie replied. "You may have already guessed this, but Jonathan is their son."

"I knew it!" Devlin said. "Other than bringing back our sister, what else happened in Serpens?"

"Lochlyn set the palace on fire," Rosalie said. "He freed a dangerous prisoner too."

"Rosalie unbound her phoenix abilities, and nearly burned a basilisk to death," Lochlyn added as he joined them.

"Lochlyn roared in the king's face and destroyed the throne room!"

Devlin shook his head. "And you two told *me* to behave. Now that you've gone and made us enemies of the royal house, what are we going to do?"

Rosalie looked up at her husband. Lochlyn kissed her forehead and said, "Let's worry about that tomorrow. Today, we need to get settled in."

CHAPTER FORTY-THREE

Tomorrow, and Tomorrow

I t took more than a day for everyone to get settled in, but it happened.

Despite Rosalie's concerns, Madchen eventually found positions for everyone from The Talon who wished to remain in the castle. Cervus and his spies relocated to a nearby manor house, planning new ways to gather intelligence and stay one step ahead of their enemies. As for Seren and the other chambermaids, two began an apprenticeship with the seamstress, while the rest decided to open a tavern in the village. Lochlyn, of course, funded the entire project.

"It will be good to have a new tavern in the Ridge," Lochlyn said one evening, while he and Rosalie lounged in their rooms with their children. Lochlyn had opened the glass ceiling, and a gentle breeze wafted through the chamber. "Seren told me that her family has run taverns and pubs for generations. I'm interested to see what they offer."

"You're interested in having a new place to eat mutton," Rosalie said. Lochlyn didn't dispute it. "It was good of you to help them get started."

"After what they endured in the palace, it's the least I could do." Lochlyn picked up Violet from where she'd fallen asleep with her book, and he gently laid her on her bed. "Has Caterina spoken of her time there yet?"

"She hasn't," Rosalie replied. "Cat usually ignores what she doesn't want to deal with, so she may never tell us what happened with Olivar. In fact, since we've been here, she's only wanted to talk about Jonathan."

"I hope that means she's doing well," Lochlyn said as he walked by the cradles to check on Max and Lily. "I also wonder how long we'll have before Olivar comes crashing down on us."

"Arthus will probably be here first," Rosalie said, standing beside Lochlyn and lacing her fingers with his. "Curran claims he's rather possessive of all phoenixes, especially his family. And he wanted Cat put in a harem!"

"Arthus can visit, but only if you want him to, and only if he behaves," Lochlyn said, making Rosalie giggle. "What's so funny?"

"You just said the Grand Master of the Order of the Sun needs to behave," she replied. "If you said that to his face, he would turn purple!"

"Perhaps he would." Lochlyn wrapped his arms around Rosalie, gazing into her eyes. "Even though I can't shift, I can still protect you. You and the rest of our family are as safe as they've ever been."

"I know," Rosalie said. "And you will shift again. The seer said as much. But until then, you can help me learn to control my fire."

Lochlyn smiled, and Rosalie's heart did a somersault in her breast. "I can't wait."

"Tomorrow we can work on flying!"

"That, we should wait for—but not for long." He stroked Rosalie's hair behind her ear and gazed at the woman he loved. She was a creature of fire, just as he was, and his perfect mate.

I hope you enjoyed Rosalie and Lochlyn's story as much as I loved writing it. Please leave a review on the platform of your choice —those reviews really make a difference!

Rosalie and Lochlyn, and Caterina and Curran will return in Dragon Descending. Keep scrolling for a sneak peek, and grab a copy here: https://books 2read.com/FireandClaw-PhoenixRising

Happy reading!

DRAGON DESCENDING

CHAPTER ONE: A NEW MISSION

L ochlyn Blackmoor hated waiting.

Yet, it was all he'd done for months. Waited for blowback from Serpens about their daring rescue of Caterina and Curran. Or news of the rampaging basilisk he and Curran had freed from the palace dungeons. For the Grand Master to appear in the courtyard demanding to see his family.

Waited to be able to shift again.

Nothing happened.

Lochlyn set his hands on the balcony's railing, and watched the early morning activity in the castle's courtyard. While he appreciated the calm days and nights they'd enjoyed at Dragon Ridge, retribution was inevitable. He'd insulted the king, committed several acts of treason, and set the palace on fire. King Olivar wasn't a forgiving man; he was more likely to take Lochlyn's head and mount it on his wall.

Still. Nothing.

Perhaps Olivar was taking his time so Lochlyn would slowly descend into madness.

A laugh floated toward him, a bright sound that Lochlyn would know anywhere. He turned toward the gardens, and saw his Rosalie walking with her sister, Caterina. They both carried baskets of flowers, but behind Rosalie's basket was her rounded belly, and inside her belly was their child.

Their child's birth was something else Lochlyn was waiting on, and for that he was most impatient of all.

He and Rosalie already had three adopted children, and he loved them and his nephew, Jonathan, dearly. Somehow, he found yet another measure of love in his heart for this child he'd yet to meet, a babe who would be a dragon, like him.

As the strongest of the Otherworldly creatures, Lochlyn's own blood meant the child would take after him, but they wouldn't know if the child would be able to shift until he was around a year old. While Lochlyn could attain both dragon and warrior forms, his eldest brother could only shift to warrior, and his middle brothers couldn't shift at all.

Whether the child could shift or not didn't matter to Lochlyn. Either way, he couldn't wait to meet their baby. Before Rosalie fell pregnant, Lochlyn had been the last living dragon in Alessia. Now both his kind and his name would live on, thanks to his beautiful wife.

"Lochlyn," Rosalie called from the courtyard, waving to get his attention as if he hadn't already been entranced by her every move. "There were some daisies in bloom, and the birds spared us some blackberries."

"And elderberries," Caterina added, as she held up her basket. "Madchen can make more of her famous wine."

Lochlyn laughed softly; there were enough casks of Madchen's elderberry wine in the castle's cellar to get half of Alessia drunk. "Are you two coming in for lunch?"

Rosalie opened her mouth to reply, but whatever she said was drowned out by the thunder of a dozen hooves. Lochlyn looked toward the gate, and saw three gigantic stags enter the courtyard. The central and largest stag approached Rosalie and bowed.

"Hello, Cervus," Rosalie said, as the stag's antlers scraped the ground near her feet. "And you really don't need to be so dramatic. Will you join us for lunch?"

Cervus raised his head, and after he glanced at the balcony, he and his two companions went toward the stables, which had a changing area for shifters. Lochlyn watched them depart, then he returned his gaze to his wife. His leisurely afternoon with Rosalie would have to wait. As Lochlyn's spymaster, Cervus had been in Serpens for the past three weeks, gathering information. For him to personally return to Dragon Ridge instead of sending one of his messengers, he must have learned something especially dire.

Lochlyn met Rosalie at the door. "Beloved," he greeted, as he spread his arms wide. "I missed you."

"We were only in the garden for an hour or so," Rosalie said, then she stood on her toes and kissed the bottom of his chin. "But I missed you, too. You should have come with us."

"Next time," he promised, as he stroked her golden hair behind her ear.

"Where's Curran?" Caterina asked.

"Last I saw he was teaching Jonathan how to fly," Lochlyn replied.

"He better not," Caterina grumbled, then she handed Rosalie her basket, grabbed two handfuls of her skirts, and marched toward the nursery. Rosalie leaned against Lochlyn's arm as they watched her go.

"You only said that so she would leave," Rosalie accused.

"Beloved, you wound me," Lochlyn said, as he clutched his hands over his heart. "But if Cervus is here it's because he learned something important. I thought it best to not upset Caterina unless it was absolutely necessary."

"She's been better, lately," Rosalie said, and Lochlyn admitted that was true. Caterina hadn't woken up the entire house with her screams in at least a week, and, counting today, she'd left Curran alone with their son twice. "We just need to be patient with her."

"And we will be." Lochlyn understood well that pain was individual, and every person needed to deal with it in their own way. "Let's go to the dining room. I'm sure Cervus and his men will be hungry."

Lochlyn claimed the baskets of flowers and berries from Rosalie's hands, and escorted her to the dining room. When they reached the room, lunch was just being laid out. They took their seats, and Lochlyn began filling Rosalie's plate, though she eyed the platter of grilled meat warily.

"Remember, you need to eat meat for the baby," Lochlyn said, as Rosalie wrinkled her nose. "The midwife at the temple said you need to eat like a dragon."

"I'll just have a bite of yours," she said, then she proceeded to devour an entire joint of mutton. She'd just started on her second when Cervus joined them.

"My lord and lady," Cervus said, as he bowed. "May I join you?"

"Of course," Lochlyn replied. "Hungry?"

"Famished," Cervus replied. "We ran straight through from Serpens."

"You must be exhausted, as well," Rosalie said. "Where are your men?"

"In the kitchens, with Madchen," Cervus replied. "I thought it best we speak alone."

"Understood," Lochlyn murmured, then he gestured toward the platters of food. "Please, eat. We can talk once you've had your fill."

"If it's all the same to you, I'll talk while eating," Cervus said, as he filled his wineglass. "Running is thirsty work."

"I imagine it is." Lochlyn observed as Cervus drained and refilled his wineglass, and as a servant delivered a plate to him. Once that was done, Lochlyn signaled for the staff to depart. "Were you able to gain entry to the palace?"

"I could not personally enter," Cervus replied. "The palace is locked down tighter than any dungeon, but the fire you set in the alchemist's lab burned through the tower's roof."

Lochlyn frowned; he'd set the fire because the king's alchemist, Zosimos, had a horde of dragon skins he was experimenting on. A persistent rumor led Zosimos to believe that dragon scales could cure the king, who'd been trapped in a half form for decades. That rumor was false, and Lochlyn burned the skins to keep the alchemist from further desecrating his ancestors.

Zosimos also claimed that the skins had been procured by Rosalie's father, Osman Irontooth. Osman's punishment was something else Lochlyn was waiting on, and he meant to deliver it himself.

"After we memorized the guards' schedules," Cervus continued, snapping Lochlyn free from his memories, "we were able to get a few falcons inside through the hole in the roof."

"Did the alchemist survive the fire?" Lochlyn asked.

"Sadly, Zosimos emerged from the blaze unscathed," Cervus said. "However, the chambermaid you struck across the head, my lady, is no longer with us."

"Melly?" Rosalie asked. "I didn't kill her, did I?"

"No, she recovered quite well from the blow," Cervus replied. "Osman ordered her execution for allowing his daughters to be abducted."

"That is not what happened," Rosalie snapped. Lochlyn set his hand on her forearm, felt the heat of her fire even through her sleeve.

"I understand, my lady, and I have never questioned your account of the events," Cervus said calmly. "But your father was desperate to save face in front of the king, and he has manipulated the facts. Being that there were no witnesses to corroborate Melly's version of what happened, and how much our king loves a scapegoat, the woman's fate was sealed."

Rosalie's shoulders sagged. "Melly was little more than a spy for Father. She's the one who alerted him to my sister's affair with Curran, and she betrayed both of us many times. I... I suppose she got what was coming to her."

Lochlyn squeezed her arm. "She walked her path," he said; even though Melly had hurt both Rosalie and Caterina, his wife would mourn her. Her sweet, gentle heart was one of the things Lochlyn loved most about her. "Was anyone else punished?"

"Punished? Yes. Executed? No." Cervus paused to wipe his mouth. "By and large, you and Curran Flameborn are being labeled as the villains of the incident, although the Grand Master is attempting to absolve his son."

"Is Arthus implying that I infiltrated the palace for any reason other than to free Caterina and Curran?" Lochlyn asked.

"He claims he doesn't understand your motivations, which is close enough to the truth for him," Cervus replied. "He's more concerned with clearing Curran's name than with your reputation. However, there is the matter of the rogue basilisk."

Lochlyn pursed his lips as he glanced at Rosalie. When he'd found Curran in the palace dungeons, the knight had been guarding an unmarked cell door. No one knew exactly who the prisoner was, but he was rumored to be the king's brother. The captive turned out to be a very large, very angry basilisk.

"Curran is the one who unlocked the cell," Lochlyn said. "In case the fire spread to the dungeon, he didn't want him to burn to death trapped in his cell."

"How noble of him," Cervus deadpanned. "We still don't have confirmation of the basilisk's identity."

"Isn't he dead?" Rosalie asked. "I burned him, then Lochlyn impaled him."

"Yes, but then he shifted," Cervus said. "That shift did more than heal him. Since no one knows what he looks like in his human form, he merely got up and disappeared into the city."

"Then we have him to contend with, as well," Lochlyn said. "Has he been sighted since then in his basilisk form?"

"Yes, but that's still not our most pressing issue." Cervus pushed his plate back, and drank more wine. "The king's seer has been marked for death."

"The king can't do that," Rosalie said. "She answers to no one but Lady Fate!"

"True, but Olivar believes she betrayed him," Cervus said. "Our king is of the opinion that the seer lied about you carrying a dragon child, and that she orchestrated the incident in the throne room."

"That's nonsense," Rosalie muttered.

"Where is the seer now?" Lochlyn asked.

"She's retreated to the temple, and hasn't been seen in weeks," Cervus replied. "Olivar has threatened to burn the temple down to flush her out, but the priestesses are unmoved."

Lochlyn glanced at his wife, and asked, "What has the Grand Master said about the seer's fate?"

"Arthus vowed to protect the temple and everyone in it until his dying breath." Cervus rubbed his forehead. "I fear Arthus is the only person keeping the palace from descending into total chaos, but as we know, Olivar is a petty and vindictive man. If he musters enough support, and his soldiers end up pitted against the knights from the Order of the Sun, Serpens may fall."

"Perhaps Serpens needs to fall," Rosalie said. "Perhaps what Alessia needs is to move on from these weak, bitter men like the king and my father and establish a new capital elsewhere ."

"You're not wrong, beloved," Lochlyn said. "But we cannot let the seer suffer over our actions."

"Yes," Rosalie agreed, her green eyes sparkling. "We will rescue her and prove that the king is nothing but bluster!"

"You want to pull off another rescue?" Cervus asked, then he shook his head. "I'm all for staying on Lady Fate's good side, but that's a suicide mission. Every soldier in Serpens has been instructed to kill you on sight. For now, the seer's better off staying in the temple, and you're better off staying here."

"I—" Lochlyn shut his mouth, and looked away before he declared he could fly to the temple in dragon form under cover of night, collect the seer, and be gone before anyone knew he was there. Because he couldn't shift, and he did not know when he would get that ability back.

But the seer had told him that he would shift again. You will shift again, not when you want to but when you need to. Those few words had given him hope, and for that reason alone Lochlyn had to try to save her.

"We'll make a plan," Lochlyn said at last.

"What about Curran?" Rosalie asked. "He's not as strong or as stealthy as you are, but he flies very fast. Perhaps we could send him to retrieve her."

Lochlyn shook his head. "His fire would burn her. No, there must be another way."

"I knew you were going to say that," Cervus said. "What of the basilisk on the loose?"

"Let's worry about him after the seer's safe."

Dragon Descending will be available everywhere September 1, 2026. Preorder here: https://books2read.com/FireandClaw-PhoenixRising

Gorlas Blackmoor —— Liliana Seaward Blackmoor

Aurielle Greenwood —— Osman Irontooth

Ferreth Blackmoor

Garron Blackmoor

Alexander Blackmoor

Lochlyn Blackmoor —— Rosalie Greenwood Blackmoor
Devlin Greenwood

Violet Blackmoor

Maximus Blackmoor

Lily Blackmoor

Danae de Serpens

Curran Flameborn ————— Caterina de Serpens

Jonathan de Serpens Flameborn

ALSO BY JENNIFER ALLIS PROVOST

Fire and Claw, an epic romantasy

The Phoenix and the Cat

The Dragon and the Selkie

Phoenix Rising

Dragon Descending

Basilisk Burning

The Chronicles of Parthalan, a six volume epic fantasy (and one short story collection)

Heir to the Sun

The Virgin Queen

Rise of the Deva'shi

Pieces of Parthalan: Six All-New Stories From The Land of Parthalan

Golem

Elfsong

Sunfall

The Copper Legacy, a four book urban fantasy:

Copper Girl

Copper Ravens

Copper Veins

Copper Princess

A duology based in the Copper world:

Redemption

Salvation

Poison Garden, an urban fantasy filled with seers, witches, and one

seriously hot detective:

Belladonna

Oleander

Bleeding Hearts

Thornapple

Wolfsbane

Mistletoe

Mandrake

Holly and Ivy

Gallowglass, an urban fantasy set in

Scotland and New York:

Gallowglass

Walker

Homecoming

The Shades of Elphame

Winter's Queen, an urban fantasy set in

Scotland and Elphame:

Touch of Frost

Giant's Daughter

Elphame's Queen

Merrowkin, an urban fantasy set in Ireland

above and below

A Sea of Secrets and Salvation

Merrowkin

Death's Door

Manannán's Pearl

Changes, a contemporary romance:

Changing Teams

Changing Scenes

Changing Fate

Changing Dates

ABOUT THE AUTHOR

Jennifer Allis Provost is a native New Englander who lives in a sprawling colonial along with her beautiful and precocious twins, a dog that thinks she's a kangaroo, a parrot, a junkyard cat, and a wonderful husband who never forgets to buy ice cream. As a child, she read anything and everything she could get her hands on, including a set of encyclopedias, but fantasy was always her favorite. She spends her days drinking vast amounts of coffee, arguing with her computer, and avoiding any and all domestic behavior.

Find Jenn on the web here: http://authorjenniferallisprovost.com/

For up to the minute sale notifications, follow her on Bookbub here: https://www.bookbub.com/profile/jennifer-allis-provost
   For exclusive content, follow her on Patreon: https://www.patreon.com/jenniferallisprovost/
   Friend her on Facebook: http://www.facebook.com/jennallis
   Follow her on Instagram: @jenniferaprovost
   Happy reading!

324